Blame It on Paris

Blame It on Paris

LAURA FLORAND

A Tom Doherty Associates Book ☀ New York

BLAME IT ON PARIS

A Forge Book
Published by Tom Doherty Associates, LLC
175 Fifth Avenue
New York, NY 10010

www.tor.com

Forge® is a registered trademark of Tom Doherty Associates, LLC.

Library of Congress Cataloging-in-Publication Data

Florand, Laura.
  Blame it on Paris / Laura Florand.—1st ed.
    p. cm.
  "A Tom Doherty Associates book."
  ISBN-13: 978-0-765-31508-3
  ISBN-10: 0-765-31508-4
  1. Paris (France)—Fiction. 2. Man-woman relationships—Fiction. I. Title.
PS3606.L585B57 2006
813'.6—dc22   2006003298

First Edition: October 2006

Printed in the United States of America

TO SÉBASTIEN

And here I have lamely related to you the uneventful chronicle of two foolish children in a flat who most unwisely sacrificed for each other the greatest treasures of their house.

— O. HENRY

AND TO OUR FAMILIES

Of all who give and receive gifts, such as they are wisest. Everywhere they are wisest. They are the magi.

— O. HENRY

One

Eleven o'clock on a Friday night. The seamy, sex-obsessed center of Paris. I balanced over a Turkish toilet in a tiny bistro, one stiletto heel propped against the wall to make some kind of writing table out of my knee, trying desperately not to touch anything around me as I wrote an invitation to my dorm's next student party. And I used to imagine a life of foreign adventure as so romantic.

Okay, so it's not that this wasn't romantic, in its way; but heretofore, tottering over a reeking hole in the floor of a two-foot-square room had not been part of my vision of romance. Before I moved to Paris as a graduate student, it had not even been part of my vision of possible ends to the digestive process. In my hometown, in Georgia, women didn't have a digestive process; we only used the ladies' room to freshen up. Highly refined women used the "little girls' room," but that was why I had fled the country. The mind could only take so much before it cracked.

How, with this upbringing, had I sunk to writing an invitation to a strange man while trying to avoid falling into *merde*? Two possible explanations offered themselves: either I was desperate, or it was all somebody else's fault. I couldn't possibly be desperate, so I figured I should blame it on Paris.

Paris and I, well, we just weren't hitting it off. Maybe she'd been oversold, or my attitude had been affected by my first month, during which I cried myself to sleep every night over a necessary breakup the move to Paris had facilitated.

"Maybe I'm just not meant for a big city full of French," I told my sister Anna on the phone.

"You have to like Paris," she said. "Everybody loves Paris. You have a moral responsibility to love Paris. What is wrong with you?" It's amazing how many conversations I have where that question comes up.

"It's got an awful lot of French people in it. A disconcerting amount, really. I read about that in Mark Twain, but you don't really appreciate the impact until you're here. Do you know I scare people?"

My sister choked. At five-foot-three, I rarely evoke terror until people get to know me better. "Well, you scare *me,*" she said, proving my point. "But I'm kind of surprised you're having this effect at first sight. What do you do? Wear white tennis shoes?"

Okay, I just want to point out here that my sister thinks white Keds are stylish. Any comments from her to a woman who had just bought a pair of black stiletto boots were way out of line. True, I'd only bought black stiletto boots because I couldn't find any other kind of boots in Paris, but at least I owned some. "I smile."

She burst out laughing.

"I'm not kidding! Today an older woman actually jumped back and put up her umbrella to ward me off. I was just being friendly." Not being raised in a barn, I tended to nod and smile at anyone whose path I crossed. This provoked surprisingly panicked reactions in Parisians, as if they thought I was insane.

On the other end of the line came lots of choking sounds, as if my sister were coughing up a hairball. This is possible. She has lots of long curly blond hair, and when we were little one of our brother's friends mistook her for a poodle. Really. I wouldn't mention it, but she was mocking my pain. "Sorry," she said, finally spitting out the fur. "I really shouldn't talk to you while I'm eating. Any other woes you want to tell me about today besides terrifying old ladies?"

I pulled the phone far enough away from my ear to glare at it, my phone card clicked down to its last unit, and we lost the connection. I stepped out of the phone booth, past a waiting fellow student who gave me an intolerant look for talking so long, and looked around at the Cité U, my home sweet home. The Cité Universitaire is a giant collection of student dorms on the south side of Paris, across from the Parc Montsouris, the only park in all of Paris that rambles instead of following classical geometry. Evening was settling in, and students traipsed to and from their various houses and the main building, where our student status qualified us to eat very bad food for very little money. I had a credit card and planned to win the lottery in a few years to pay it off, so I didn't take advantage of this privilege nearly as much as I should have.

Aside from the food, I loved the Cité Universitaire, with its vast parklike grounds and its thirty-seven different houses sponsored by thirty-seven different countries. I liked to walk past the fields of students playing soccer, the students chatting each other up, the men pretending they were students to try to hit on young women, and study the houses each country had built. We had everything from a sedate neo-Gothic to something that strongly resembled a bomb shelter. As the architecture suggested, the place hosted a lot of oddball cultures: French, Moroccan, Danish, Canadian. There were even some Americans who, taken out of their element, are about the strangest creatures on the globe. I tried to hang out with them at first, but when they caught me speaking French with the natives, they considered me a snob and a traitor to class, country, and above all, language, and pelted me with the half-eaten pastries they always had in one hand. Okay, I made that up about being pelted with pastries. Still, no Europeans ever nibbled on delicious pastries in the Métro. How come I was the only American who noticed, realized eating in public was considered barbaric here, and *stopped doing it*? I'm rarely considered a paragon of perception and sensitivity to others, so come on, how hard could it be?

Anyway, rumors of roaches surrounded the Fondation des États-Unis, so I ended up living in the Maison du Canada. There, students also tended to hang out in large groups dissing the French, but at least we did it in French, so those obnoxious Frenchmen could understand us. The Canadian house made me pay extra rent to live there, though, which was downright rude. Did they have any idea how much of my tax money went to pay for their nuclear shield or to subsidize businesses that destroyed their ozone layer?

I hadn't figured out how to make calls from my room yet, mostly because it involved putting down a hard cash deposit, and I had spent my last bit of cash at a really nice chocolate shop that didn't take credit cards. My sister could call in, though, and a week or so later she caught me, huddled under my rough, orange, dorm-issue blanket, clutching my teddy bear for warmth. The dorm hadn't turned the radiators on yet; for some reason they thought it didn't get cold enough until November. "Where have you been?" she said. "Did some old lady stab you with an umbrella? I was starting to worry."

"No! I've been trying to enjoy this stupid city. Do you know I've got an art history professor card that lets me go into the Louvre *anytime I want*? For free! Three-hour lines of tourists circling around the Pyramide, and I just wave my card at a guard in the Cardinal Richelieu gallery and waltz right in. It's like having my own secret entrance to the Bat Cave, only better because there is cooler stuff inside."

"But you're not an art history professor," Anna pointed out. "You don't know anything about art."

"I wish you wouldn't get caught up in the details. Valérie gave it to me. She's at the study abroad program where I work. I can get into the Musée d'Orsay and all the other public museums that way, too."

"I wish I were in Paris," Anna said. "I would *love* to be able to do that. And I wouldn't spend all my time whining about it like you."

"Yes, you would, too. It's freezing here, it hasn't stopped raining for the past three weeks, and guys keep coming up to me talking about my breasts."

A pause. We had both grown up in the same small, polite Southern town. "Eww," she said. "I thought Frenchmen were romantic."

"Yeah, well, welcome to the non-Disney version. They also seem to think I'm a blonde."

My sister snorted. Possessed of long, wavy *chestnut* hair, I had given her a hard time with the blond jokes while we were growing up. "So is the Louvre open late at night? Because I've been calling at, like, ten there." Ten is late in Georgia.

"No, let's see, last night I went to see Molière with a friend, and then two nights ago, we went to see a play by Marivaux." A fellow graduate student was doing her dissertation on Marivaux, and I loved his dialogue and his hilarious send-ups of early eighteenth-century society. "Friday night I went out to a restaurant and then dancing with some new students I met here. Oh, and Tuesday, my program had tickets to the opera."

"Wow," she said. "It's too bad you hate Paris. Otherwise, you might be able to have fun there."

"I do hate it! It's cold, it's gray, and people are hateful. They've got no call to be that rude, really they don't. But I've got a contract to stay here for a year, so I can't waste it, can I? I've got to try and enjoy it."

"Yes," she said, "you do. Every time I turn on the radio these days, there's some Lucy Jordan woman singing about how her life has been wasted because she never rode through Paris with the top down and the wind blowing in her hair. You are in Paris right now! You'll look back on this moment when you're fifty and gloat because you haven't wasted your life!"

Well, I'd look back on living in Tahiti and Spain and gloat at not having wasted my life. Paris I wasn't so sure about. "You *can't* joyride through Paris with the top down. It's too cold, it's usually raining, and you wouldn't have the wind running through your hair, you'd be stuck in a traffic jam with dozens of angry drivers honking all around you."

"You're violating the myth of Paris with a little bit too much reality for me," Anna said. "Do you want me to come visit you in the spring or not?"

I sighed. It's not like I wasn't trying. As a graduate student, I should have been spending my time in classrooms and the library, but I was afraid to let my sister down. I had a moral obligation to love Paris and to enjoy every minute of it, and I couldn't do that in a classroom or in a library. So I went to the theater and saw Marivaux acted in the centuries-old Hôtel de la Monnaie that could have been the real setting for his comedy of manners. Period-dressed actors greeted us at the door as if we were house-guests along with the characters in the play, and a period-dressed chamber orchestra played Lully as we climbed the wide stone steps to the room in which the play would take place. The next night, I heard Corneille declaimed in grandiose *alexandrins* in a tiny stale theater with an audience of a dozen and one actor who smelled so bad we knew whenever he was waiting in the wings. I got off work afternoons and said, "Hey, I haven't seen Monet's Rouen cathedrals in *days*," and strolled into the Musée d'Orsay, installed myself in a chair, and just stared for an hour at those extraordinary paintings and all the heads that kept blocking my view of them. Before, I had only ever seen Monet on greeting cards and as a poster on my dentist's bathroom wall. Bless Valérie for my art historian card. I lived in fear that one day some security guard would look at the card, squint at me suspiciously, and ask some trick question. "What's the point of such-and-such in the Pompidou?" he would ask. I'd try to stammer out something logical, which would be a dead giveaway, and the jig would be up. I wouldn't be imprisoned, but when Parisians sniff at you the humiliation scars you for life.

Still, I braved it, waltzing past security guards with increasingly aloof confidence and grinning giddily every time it worked. Emboldened, and showing great discipline in my determination to enjoy Paris, I set out to explore every chocolate shop in the city.

"Wow," my sister said, "you're so gutsy."

"Well, I *am*. Do you know how many chocolate shops there are in this city? It's the chocolate capital of the world!"

"Just shut up already. Although I did figure out what's wrong with that city. It's the Eiffel Tower. I was reading a feng shui book."

"Bless you."

"No, it's—don't you keep up with U.S. fads? It's about the way the space you're living in is arranged and how that affects you. The author said having that great rusty arrow pointing up above the city bleeds all its hope out of it."

"It's got a great big lighthouse beacon beaming from the top of it, too," I said. "It circles over the whole city. The government said the beacon was to symbolize how Paris was the center of the world and everyone should come to it, or something like that. But lighthouses really are supposed to *warn people away* from dangerous rocks." How like the Parisian government to warn people away with their attempts at hospitality.

She was growing on me, though, the Eiffel Tower. I didn't want to admit it, but at night when the lights came on, that daytime rusty metal look changed to a warm copper glow. There was something so glamorous and romantic about her, there above the city.

Sensing weakness, my colleague and only Parisian friend Valérie convinced me to give Ladurée a try. This took some doing because every time she mentioned Ladurée's legendary macaroons, I got unpleasant visions of coconut. When I finally ducked through the velvet curtains on rue Royale into this nineteenth-century *salon de thé*, I discovered instead *macarons*, concoctions made of lightly crusty air and luscious ganache. As I sat on a park bench eating a chocolate one that could have been served in heaven, a couple passed by, and the older man grinned at me, the first unsalacious grin I had ever received from a strange Parisian: "They're the best in the world, aren't they?"

I hated to confirm a Parisian in any conviction of superiority, but I had to give him that one. Okay, I said to myself. A city that can produce *macarons* like that has to be survivable. Keep at it, girl.

Still, when I went home for Christmas, I thought I had died and gone, if not to heaven—which might be a little sophisticated for me—at least back where I belonged. I drove down that long country road, where a farmer still had a tractor upended in a ditch from an accident twenty years ago, and when I saw the sign, PIGS 4 SALE, I about had tears in my eyes.

Our house is set on a hill removed from all civilization, and the access to it vaguely resembles a roller coaster. I drove up that bumpy driveway and saw my dad standing outside in shirtsleeves with a television sitting on a pillow in the clearest spot in that wooded yard. He held a remote in one hand, and every once in a while, he would gaze thoughtfully at the sky and adjust a small satellite dish. "Finally," I said, "I'm back where people act normal."

"If you need a hair dryer, you can borrow your dad's," my mom said, after she'd finished hugging me, our collie had finished jumping all over me, and our black half chow chow stray had finished gazing at me with dark, reproachful steadiness. "He bought one to dry out his ear."

Well, maybe a little on the eccentric side of normal. But at least this place wasn't *strange*. It was mine. The dried leaves underfoot.

The light of sunset shimmering off the dark river water. The fuzz of moss on bark or the flake of lichen.

"Swimmer's ear," my dad explained. "A hair dryer is a perfectly logical thing to use."

"We bought all the ingredients for your fruitcakes," my mom said, her eyes gleaming in anticipation. So I sank my hands deep into slick batter, brightly colored fruit, and the sharp slivers of almonds and cooked Christmas food with my family until the tables overflowed. I hung out in a squirrel-eaten hammock, barefooted and in shirtsleeves, and watched a giant mosquito-catcher float through the soft day, tossing in the breeze, glimmering in the sunlight against the backdrop of green grass.

I didn't want to come back to Paris. I didn't even start crying on the plane, I just sank into my seat in despair. Well, and nausea, since I get sick on planes, but the two feelings combined very well to reflect my attitude toward Paris. I had to do it, though, and it wasn't just because of my contract. I was the world adventurer, and I couldn't bail on a year in Paris just because it wasn't going in the skippy-dippy way all my other travels had gone.

A couple of days after I got back, I had a strange experience. No, the sun didn't come out or anything; I'd been told that didn't happen until May. I got off work just at six. It was already dark, with the early, depressing winters of this northern city. I stopped at a *tabac* to buy a stamp, and the owner yelled at me and pounded his fist on the counter because I forgot and tried to put the money directly into his hand instead of sliding it to him on the counter as Parisians did. I sighed, wishing I had the guts to tell him he was an asshole. But I didn't, and I humbly took my stamp, then continued to the Métro. On the long descent of the sloping street, the Eiffel Tower was clearly visible across the city. She really was growing on me, the Eiffel Tower. She had a certain Auntie Mame style. I was thinking this as I descended the street, and a guy in pink grunted at me like a pig and tried to bite me. I dodged him and continued on without breaking pace, by now

17

used to this kind of thing; and a couple of seconds later, the Eiffel Tower started sparkling. She went up like a bottle of champagne, in white lights like a horde of escaping Tinkerbells. She just fizzed and danced and sparkled her little heart out, there above the gray, winter city.

Two

I was hard at work the next day when the e-mail came in, from a friend I hadn't seen since last summer. Her baby sister was coming to Paris and needed someone to look out for her for a few days. "Sure," I typed back, little knowing that the request was a crossroads and I'd chosen the turn that would eventually have me locked in a small room spattered with feces. Paris sends too many mixed messages. The promise I'd imagined in that magical moment with the fizzing Eiffel Tower hadn't included Turkish toilets in it at all.

The phone rang before I could go ask Valérie for help with the baby sister issue. "Where am I?"

I just loved it when phone conversations started like this. It happened a lot more than anyone who hadn't worked in study abroad could suppose. "I couldn't begin to guess. Why don't you tell me?"

"I don't know. I'd like to know."

A light clicked on as I recognized the voice and remembered the student earlier that day asking me to show him on a map how to get to Charles V, one of the various branches of the University of Paris. "Did you find Charles V?"

"No, I can't."

When the gods wished to punish study abroad workers, they gave students cell phones. If only this student had forgotten to recharge his battery, he might have had to look at a map or talk to a passerby. "Well, where are you?"

"I'm exactly where you told me to go," he said indignantly.

I have previously found that if people are *exactly* where I told them to go, they don't call in for further directions. "Perhaps we could be more specific. What street are you on?"

"*Exactly* the one you told me to get on!" He was getting annoyed now.

"And which one would that be?"

"I don't know."

I rested my chin on my hand and contemplated my culture's youth bemusedly. "Are you on a cell phone right now or not?"

"Well . . . yes."

"Then why don't you try walking until you see a street sign, and I will look at my map of Paris and tell you where to go from there, okay?" He should have been able to look at a map himself, of course, but I wasn't going to go into that difficult concept at this juncture. With a little less patience this time, I got him to figure out what street he was on and guided him from there, and he managed to complete his day without once having to speak to a non-American.

I reread the e-mail from my friend, digested its implications, and went to find Valérie. I needed a reasonably priced restaurant, and Valérie was the source.

"Valérie," I said. Her curly red head was immersed in student applications, her round face set in a baffled glower, and she didn't immediately look up. The offices of my university's study abroad program in Paris' fifth arrondissement were in a building several centuries older than my country. Across from Valérie's window, currently lined with the potted sprouts our director dreamed of turning into lime trees, half a dozen construction workers stripped, pounded, and plastered an equally old apartment building, a restoration job that had started long before I arrived. Valérie had chosen her office for the regular morale boost: the workers never failed to flirt with any woman who leaned out the window.

Five minutes' walk to the west of our offices was the Luxembourg Garden, by which all of us passed every day as we came out of our subway stop and headed to work. Filled with statues and fountains and grass you couldn't touch, the Luxembourg Garden had a strict, classical beauty. I loved to stroll through it and watch the people: a woman in a baggy red coat, alone, pushing herself across in her wheelchair; a couple in their thirties, him crouching and angling to try to get just the right picture of her with the fountain; teenage girls carrying tennis rackets, one with a wrap around her knee. My first week in Paris, I tried to read there in the afternoon after work, feeling elegant and intellectual and strongly Audrey Hepburnish. But then dust off the gravel walkways blew up under my contacts, making me cry, and a man tried to sit in the same tiny chair I was in, promising to make it better. This city was out to get me.

Eight minutes' walk to the east of our offices, on the cobblestoned medieval rue Mouffetard, an Italian-trained gelato maker sold ice creams shaped like flowers. I had discovered him soon after my move to Paris by going upstream against blissful faces until I found their source. His sorbets induced pure rapture. But just before I started thinking Paris wasn't so bad after all, the temperature dropped, the rains set in, and I discovered a sign on his shop that said, "Closed until March."

"Valérie," I tried again to get the attention of my colleague, who was scowling at a student photo. Her vivid hair straggled around her face as if she had recently dragged her hands through it. Rounded, in direct rebellion against Parisian toothpick norms, high-energy Valérie was almost always in a good mood, except when dealing with rudeness or incompetence.

"They're *des têtes à claques*," she growled. This had come to be a reassuring expression, as it indicated that, at heart, our cultures might have a point in common. Not every English speaker could have found an equivalent in his language to *des têtes à claques*; but coming from the South, I knew it simply meant they had "heads to be smacked upside of." Valérie used the phrase about five times a day in reference to the bane and joy of her life, American study abroad students. "The list is very clear. I need four photos, a copy of the passport, and this form. So they send one photo, or no photo, or no passport, or sometimes even no form. And then you can be sure if they don't get their student visas or if their student IDs aren't ready fast enough, they'll complain to their parents, and their parents will call and yell at us. *Des têtes à claques.*"

"No kidding," I said, fresh from my phone conversation. "Listen, I need your advice. A friend's little sister has decided to backpack through Europe on her own without any guidebook, and without knowing anything at all about the places she's going, so this friend is calling all her friends everywhere to see if we can meet her at train stations and show her around." By the brooding, baffled look Valérie gave me, she was clearly wondering if helplessness was genetic or in the American water, and in either case, how the hell had we managed to build McDonald's all over the world. "I'm the friend in Paris. Do you know of a good restaurant I could take her to on our student budgets?" My graduate assistant stipend fell woefully short of Paris' cost of living.

Valérie's eyes brightened, and she sat back from her desk. Here, finally, was a *real* task, something worth her time. "I know of a really nice little place called Le Relais du Vin near Châtelet. . . ."

Valérie has impeccable taste in restaurants, but sometimes she can be a tad oblivious to location. Le Relais du Vin was nestled in the heart of Paris, Les Halles. The original heart of Paris—that giant, unhygienic, life-filled market that used to be Les Halles— was destroyed in 1963, the single most appalling city-planning decision Prime Minister Pompidou would make in his tenure of architectural horrors. Since 1135, Les Halles had been the biggest market in Paris, and perhaps even in Europe, the market that supplied all other markets, filled with energy at all hours of the day and night. 1135. 828 years. The government replaced it with a glass and aluminum mall, the Forum des Halles, so now you can stroll among a bland collection of chain stores full of cheap clothes in the spot Zola called the stomach of Paris and that Napoléon III called the people's Louvre.

Les Halles is the nexus of most of Paris' Métro and RER lines, and people cram up and down escalators onto other lines or into the three underground levels of the Forum des Halles. The racial and social tension vibrates against your skin as you walk through the area until the fine hair on your arms stands straight up from the charge. This tension streams in along the RER lines from the suburbs, where Paris exiles its housing projects, and compacts into dense, hard energy at Les Halles. It hovers on the steps outside the Forum, where most of the drug trades seem to take place, judging by the odors and the police busts, or prowls the surrounding cobblestones.

"Fuck your race!" one man screamed at another as my friend's little sister and I crossed the street in front of the Forum. "Fuck your whole race!"

I smiled weakly at the little sister I was supposed to be keeping safe. She didn't speak French, but when two men start screaming at each other in the middle of a dark street, it's so rarely a good sign.

Across from Le Relais du Vin, the neon words SEX SHOP blazed red. Up and down the street, rivals in the sex sales business competed using their own sledgehammer-subtle titillation, neon glistening on rain-wet cobblestones. "Ssss, ssss, miss, miss," men called, coming out from their crêpe stands or their straps-and-leather clothes shops or, not tied down by any job, simply strolling along behind us.

We were actually doing better this evening than the last time I had walked across Les Halles, in broad daylight. Two men had fallen into step behind me as I headed from the Métro down to rue de Rivoli, which has at least a hundred shoe shops but somehow never a shoe without four-inch heels. "Oh, girl, you've got to stop walking like that. My dick's gonna bust if you keep walking like that. It's rising, it's coming up, it's gonna bust. I told you to stop. . . ."

Ah, Paris. City of Love.

In the midst of this sordid world, Le Relais du Vin took up the space of a handkerchief. From the street, we could barely make out the faded gold name swirling above the door and could see only a crowded bar through the glass front window. I hesitated, but the hissing men moved closer at that first sign of weakness, so we plunged in. An American restaurateur couldn't have fit five people comfortably in this spot, but the man behind the bar, with the balding pate and the wild gray hair, had managed to orchestrate seating for a cheerful twenty. We slipped past a Prévert poem painted above the dumbwaiter as we fit our way between the bar and two round bar tables. The mural on the Relais's wall appeared not to have been touched in twenty years. The trompe l'oeil painting gave the impression that we were looking out from our own homey apartment over the rooftops of the old Halles, in the days when it was an ancient, famous marketplace.

The waiter greeted us with that French courtesy, not smiling, but not *not* smiling either: calm, reserved, and competent. I couldn't help noticing he was drop-dead gorgeous as he pulled a table out far enough that my hiney barely even grazed the edges of our neighbors' plates when I squeezed into a corner. (They smiled, flicked a piece of lettuce off my tush, and said that was quite all right.) *Very* nicely formed biceps eased the table back to lock me in and let my friend's sister, Tory, sit down. I saw black hair, a five o'clock shadow, and a long, lean, well-muscled body all in a flash. Wow, I just had time to think, and then the menus were on our table, and he was gone to bring somebody a bottle of wine.

Tory, a cute and slender brunette, fit right in with this crowd, except for the daypack she had insisted on bringing with her and the worried look on her face. The worried look was either due to the cramped seating and aged decor or to the fact that her seat left her back to the waiter. Then again, it might have been the SEX SHOP sign we could still see flashing through the window. "I hope this is okay," I said. "Valérie has great taste in restaurants usually. Anyway, even if the food is bad, that waiter is really cute."

"One to ten?" Tory asked promptly.

"Over," I said, looking at him again. "This guy is seriously gorgeous. Look at him. Look at the way he moves." He was negotiating the tight quarters and multiple demands with a sexy economy of motion, and never once did he even brush against a table, let alone knock something over.

"He's French, though," Tory pointed out.

"Well, I'm only *looking*. I'm not stupid. Of course I wouldn't actually try to date him."

"Because the French cheat," Tory said. "Everybody knows it."

"And they're male chauvinists," I agreed firmly. "Everybody knows that, too. Plus, he's probably gay. Plus, who would want to get involved with someone who lives in this stupid city? Look at the way he opened that bottle of wine. Isn't that beautiful?" He moved with such no-nonsense smoothness, as if it was the most natural thing in the world to be that sophisticated, that graceful. A Polynesian-style armband of a tattoo peeked out from under the short sleeve of his pressed black shirt as he pulled the cork from the wine, hard muscle flexing just a bit to hold the bottle steady as he did so.

"He probably *is* gay," Tory agreed with pseudo-regret. She was only spending three days here, so what did she care? "If he's that cute and he's got a sense of style."

"Well, he's Parisian. He could be well dressed and straight. The thing is—"

24

The object of our conversation stopped by our table. My tongue froze, and a flush climbed up my cheeks. He looked down at us with courteous attention. *"Vous avez choisi?"* Have you decided?

"I—I've got a question about the menu." Never say I can't think fast when I need to.

"Yes?"

I put my finger on a menu item at random and lowered my voice. He leaned closer automatically to hear me. "The *boudin,* what is that?"

He smiled. It was just a little smile, but it warmed those dark brown eyes like a fondue flame warms chocolate. "It's delicious," he said enthusiastically. "You'll love it, I promise. It's intestine filled with blood, pork fat, and onions."

I blinked.

"It's really good," he promised, smiling at me with those warm chocolate eyes.

"I'll take one of those, then." Was I insane? "And, um, the *bavette.* What's that?"

"It's a type of steak. Very good, too. I recommend the blue sauce."

Thank God. "And the *bavette* for my main course."

"Saignant, à point?"

Okay, it was maybe pushing it to pretend not to know the words for "rare" and "medium rare," but he had a faint scent of vanilla that was just luscious with him standing so close to me. *"Saignant* is . . . ?"

"The meat's red all the way through. It's the best way to eat meat."

A faint hesitation must have shown in my eyes.

"But if you prefer," he said consolingly, *"à point* is cooked just a little past that and is quite good, too." For sissies, I caught the subconscious thought. He didn't seem to mind that I might be a sissy, though, or even hold it against me that I had an American accent.

25

"*Saignant,*" I threw caution to the winds.

"Very good. And I'll save you the last chocolate mousse for dessert," he whispered. "If you're sure that's what you want."

Wow. Not only was he cute, he was my hero. "Is that what you recommend?"

His smile widened, glints of lust for chocolate mousse dancing in his eyes. "It's the best. Didier always saves one for me."

I was hoping Didier was the chef, but then again he might be his boyfriend. Or both might be true. Oh, well, if the waiter was gay, I had the benefit of being in safe territory. "I'll trust you, then," I said, which was a big lie, because he was way too cute and French to be trusted. I really only trusted him on the subject of chocolate mousse, and I was in a Paris restaurant, how wrong could I go with that?

Lacking French, Tory just pointed wordlessly to a salad and a steak while I hid a smirk. Hey, it wasn't *my* fault she had chosen to travel in France without speaking enough of the language to act like an idiot.

He left, face serious again, moving efficiently about the confined space, and I realized he wasn't flirting with me; he was just doing his job. Fine, I wasn't flirting with him either; I was just trying to order a meal.

"What did you order?" Tory asked.

"Intestine stuffed with blood."

She choked on her water and began to laugh.

"Blood sausage," I realized. "I bet he was trying to describe blood sausage. Oh, my God, I had that once in Spain." I still remembered the stink of it and the thick taste on my tongue.

Tory couldn't stop laughing. People at the other tables grinned, which showed something about the ambience. There were restaurants in Paris where people would have glanced at us sidelong and sniffed at the loud table.

"Well, he recommended it," I said pitiably. "What was I supposed to do?"

26

"I don't know," she said, shaking her head, seeming to find me hilarious. "Ask for another recommendation?"

"Critic."

"Now you have to eat it," she said. "You couldn't insult his recommendation by not eating it."

"I know." I bared my teeth at her. "But did you see how gorgeous he is?" His five o'clock shadow graced a chiseled masculine face. Right now, as he moved around the place, focused on his job, that face looked stern. But sometimes, someone at another table or at the bar would throw a remark his way that I couldn't catch, and his face would split into laughter.

"When he brings things to the table beside us, I could accidentally brush his tush," Tory murmured, sotto voce. "He's that close."

I frowned at her.

"He's got a great butt," she said. "Definitely over a ten, I've got to agree with you."

"Aren't you too young to be sexually harassing people? How old are you, anyway?"

She started laughing again.

The gorgeous waiter arrived back with my *boudin* on its bed of salad. "You're in luck. There was only one left, but I got Didier to save it for you. It's really good." The scary thing was, I could tell he thought he'd done me a favor.

"Thank you!" I beamed at him. I didn't look down right away. I kept my eye on his tush for as long as I could, postponing the moment. Finally, when he disappeared up the spaghetti-thin stairs into the kitchen, I dropped my gaze to what awaited me. Blood sausage. And he had so nicely described how it was made: blood, pork fat, and onions, all held together by some intestine.

Tory was making choking, snortling sounds as if suppressing interior explosions, but I ignored her. People do that all the time around me.

"Shut up," I said, and sliced into the *boudin*. The sooner I got this over with the better. Other than a fire starting in the kitchen above and the cute waiter rushing down to save me before all others, there was no way out of this but through it. When I lived in Tahiti, people always used to serve me raw fish as the local delicacy. I had learned to eat it with an enthusiastic smile on my face, and I drew on those skills now.

Blood sausage is worse than raw fish.

Fortunately, in France, no waiter would dream of being so uncouth as to interrupt someone eating to ask how things were, so I didn't have to fake a smile too often. He didn't come back to the table until a few minutes after I was done and had fled to the toilet to vomit. I fled right back out again, stomach settled by the fear of vomiting in a place like that. "That toilet is awful," I whispered to Tory. "Avoid it, if you can."

"Was everything all right?" The waiter returned, reaching for our plates. He smiled when he saw how empty mine was, almost reward enough. "It's good, isn't it?" he met my eyes with his warm chocolate ones.

"Delicious," I said, hypnotized.

He nodded and disappeared with the plates and dirtied flatware.

Tory was having a hard time keeping a straight face. "My sister told me you were pretty shy and standoffish with guys."

"I prefer to think of myself as selective," I said indignantly. Besides, who didn't have a pathological fear of dating these days? There was so much to lose: freedom, solitude, independence. There was so little to gain: the occasional burp in one's ear, extra dishes to wash, and dead deer on the walls. And there were so many good romance books out there whenever an evening felt lonely.

"So are you going to ask him out?"

I stiffened, appalled. "Are you crazy? He is way out of my league. No way I'm humiliating myself like that. Plus, we already talked about this. He's French. Everyone knows the French are chain-smoking, manic-depressive, faithless, male-chauvinistic snobs. Forget it."

That was awfully good chocolate mousse, though. It had a flavor—rich, dark, creamy—about like the sound of his voice. I got out of there before I could do anything stupider than leave him way too big of a tip. The tip was embarrassingly obvious when I thought about it, but that was okay. I didn't realize how embarrasing until after I'd left, and by that time I had made a very intelligent resolution: I wasn't going to come back.

Three

You're right, he's cute," my friend Adela agreed as soon as she saw him, when baby sister Tory was long gone on a train down to Madrid and probably still snickering. I just hope somebody fed her blood sausage while she was in Spain, that's all I can say. I had had the best intentions about not going back to Le Relais, but a few nights later it was my turn to pick the restaurant, and Paris has such limited choice in restaurants I could only think of one.

I was *not* flirting with the waiter, as I had to keep telling unperceptive people. I am not given to pursuing stunningly gorgeous men who could date supermodels. I'm just not that into hurting myself. However, now that I had discovered Le Relais, I did think it was a great place to eat, with great food, a great view, and even a convenient location, if you carried assault rifles and could get enough similarly armed people to go with you. The assault rifles were absurdly hard to obtain in France, but living in the Cité Universitaire, at least I had plenty of friends.

Some of them were crazy, though. Adela was a case in point. "So ask him out," Adela suggested for the tenth time. She was starting to sound like a broken record with that idea, but then, I'd heard insane people could be obsessive. On this occasion, we were standing outside the fastidiously elegant displays of Fauchon at the place de la Madeleine. Little *tartes* stretched out in the window before us, pristinely perfect: glazed with orange or powdered with sifted white sugar around an imposing F stencil that revealed the cake beneath. Over our heads, the trademark Fauchon pink canopy sheltered us from the fine drizzle of the dark evening. Behind us, the Acropolis-style Église de la Madeleine dominated the *place* with its Corinthian columns. Cars circled around it in a pattern of red and white lights and blinking yellow turn signals, the lights glistening off the damp pavement. Napoléon had originally commissioned Madeleine as a Temple to His Glory (Napoléon's, not God's); the structure had been consecrated to God instead after his exile but had remained ambiguous in appearance ever since.

Adela was one of the Spanish students living in the Maison du Canada. The Canadian house and the Collège d'Espagne had a system of exchange to fulfill Cité U requirements that 30 percent of any house's students be from some country other than the host one. Adela had frizzy dark hair, brown eyes, and dominant eyebrows. She had only moved from Seville to Paris to study European law a few months ago, and she had already gotten into yelling matches with every single one of her professors. She also had a weird flaw, which I blamed on her culture: she actually thought that if you saw somebody cute, you should attempt a relationship. "Just ask him out," she repeated, staring at the exquisite Fauchon tarts. "It's not that hard."

"Adela, are you nuts? You've seen him! He's gorgeous! People like me don't date people like him. We watch them from a distance."

Adela gave me an incredulous look and refocused on a chocolate-glazed tart with a gold F in the center of it.

"You can get hurt going out with cute guys, Adela. You know that."

Adela pressed her nose against the elegant window, trying to peer deeper into the store.

"Besides," I said. I was basically engaging in a monologue with no audience at this point, I could tell. So I might as well express myself. "Men are just heavy. Sure, they look cute, but then they *land* on you like a two-ton anchor, and your bright little ship that could sail to any horizon gets battle-chained to a good school district and a job with benefits. And then you're stuffing your three kids into an SUV and taking trips to *Disneyland.*"

Adela pulled her face back from the window, leaving a large smudge on its glistening surface, and stared at me.

"I'm not *kidding,*" I protested. "It happened to all my school friends. And you can't tell me the French don't have their equivalent, only with small, environmentally sound diesels and an annual beach vacation rental in Normandy."

"You people really drive SUVs? It's not just in the movies? Well, what should I expect from people who won't sign the Kyoto Treaty." Adela pushed through the door to Fauchon's *confiserie/patisserie* section, past the massive security guard clad in Armani. I slanted a second glance over his elegant suit. Surely that wasn't really Armani. What did I know from Armani, anyway?

I felt a qualm. Adela knew of Fauchon's existence only because she had eaten up all the chocolate-covered almonds I had bought here. I hadn't really thought the almonds were worth a dollar apiece, but I had wanted the little pink tin they came in, emblazoned as it was with "Fauchon" and a black-and-white photo of Fauchon in the 1920s. Fauchon was the most famous and most expensive place to buy food in Paris. Now that Adela had convinced me to show her where the store was so she could have her own tin, I wasn't sure how well she and it would mix. This was not a place for arrogant and aggressive impoverished students. It was a place for meek students who didn't mind being treated like bugs that had crawled out from under a rock. "I'm wearing jeans," I hissed at her. We were talking in Spanish, all the better not to be understood by supercilious guards, clerks, and the multimillionaires shopping around us. "I don't have the self-confidence to shop at Fauchon's in jeans."

I'd developed a uniform for Paris shopping: black boots, black pants, a long black coat, black leather gloves, and a red scarf, all carried with a self-assured stride. The ideal accessory for this look was a shopping bag emblazoned with Fauchon or Ladurée or something similar, but this could get expensive. If the bag's edges grew battered from repeat use, sales girls got that disdainful pinch to the corners of their mouths again; then I had to buy something else at a luxury store and start over. Jeans and tennis shoes, even black ones, were fatal for shopping around the place de la Madeleine or on the rue Faubourg St. Honoré, needless to say.

Adela rolled her eyes and batted a hand at me, rather as she might at an annoying fly, and kept going. Pink tins with black-and-white photos, exactly like the tin Adela had emptied on her last visit to my dorm room, climbed up a wall to our left. We wove through customers in furs, passing display cases of chocolates, *marrons glacés* or candied chestnuts, *paté de fruits,* cakes, and small *tartes.* Some pink tins had upturned lids, with a handful of different types of candies in each, demonstrating what was inside the tins in that row. "Look!" Adela exclaimed, delighted. "They have samples!" She helped herself to a blue wrapped candy, which proved to contain a stick of brown sugar.

"Adela. Those aren't samples." I glanced around. The exquisite and enormous security guard was watching us.

"Of course, they are," she made the fly-swatting motion again. "But we're getting off the subject. How many more times are you going to make me go back to that restaurant before you ask this guy out?"

"It's not like you've had to eat there that often!" I protested. "*You*'ve only been there with me three times! And seriously, Adela, those aren't samples." The security guard was crossing the room.

Her lips twitched. "I've only been there three times? How many times have you been there with other people?" She picked up a dragée and popped it into her mouth.

"That's beside the point. The food is good; the waiter is cute. When you go to a movie, do you try to date the actor?" I asked, confident of a clincher.

"I would if I met him," said Adela, who was, after all, Spanish. "You know, these chocolate ones you got before are the best." The security guard stopped behind her and stood there, hands crossed behind his back. Oblivious, she took the whole handful of chocolate almonds from the lid, popped a couple more in her mouth, and paused. Her eyes began to gleam. "What we need is to devise a stratagem."

"No!" Good Lord, what was she trying to do, ruin my life with a beautiful romance? Besides, never let a woman who eats displays while shopping devise stratagems for you. "I mean, maybe you're right after all. We should try a different restaurant tonight."

I might not have gotten off that easily, but Adela turned at that moment and bumped nose first into the security guard's chest. She looked a long way up. He looked back down at her as if she were a beggar who had crawled—rags, stench, and all—in off the street. Brown eyes stared back at him incredulously for a moment, and then her eyebrows slammed together like two tectonic plates.

"If you are hungry," he said, "may I suggest one of the Restos du Coeur?" One of the soup kitchens. Oh, dear. This was not going to end well.

Adela sniffed. "Could you box me up some of those chocolates?" she said to him as if he were her servant, flicking her hand airily at chocolates that sold for around the price of gold. "And some of those *marrons glacés*. Nice packages, please. They're for gifts."

"*Vous pouvez commander là, madame,*" he opened one straight hand to indicate a girl behind the counter.

Adela swept to the counter and repeated her order. The security guard walked behind her, and Adela threw him a dismissive glance over her shoulder. "I'll teach them to treat me like that," she hissed to me in Spanish. "They're supposed to be so elegant, but look at them. I'm not someone they can treat like that. *And that, too,*" she told the cool, disdainful woman behind the counter, indicating several of the tins. "They'll see I'm exactly the kind of person who spends a fortune in this store," she continued to me in Spanish. "They'll see."

You'd almost think the security guard had been trained in this method of getting customers to overspend, because the supercilious look on his face never faltered, and every time Adela glanced back and saw it she bought something else. He stayed beside us as her purchases got bigger and bigger, and when she finally had her sacks in hand, he escorted us back out into the rain.

"Damn," she said, somewhere on the Métro ride home, staring at her black and white bags full of outrageously priced sweets. "I'm going to have to call my father for rent money this month. But I taught them, didn't I? Don't you think I taught them?"

"Definitely." I was never going back to Fauchon again. Not even disguised in a black coat, black pants, a red scarf, and one of their shopping bags. "By the way, can I have some of those bags, Adela? You don't need all of them, do you?"

"You're right, he is cute," Valérie agreed. I'd switched restaurant-visiting partners for a while to take the heat off. Adela was getting far too impatient, as if she expected some kind of action. Adela in action made me nervous. "I thought you were talking about the other one."

"That's right, another waiter was here instead one night." I had gone to great pains to convince new people to go to Le Relais du Vin with me, to avoid wearing out Valérie's and Adela's tolerances, and when we got there, the right person hadn't even been waiting tables. The other guy was cute enough, but . . . it just wasn't the same.

Valérie's lips twitched. "You mean you've been back here with other people?"

I jumped. "Oh . . . just once."

She speared me with a look that said she didn't believe me for a second. "So ask him out."

"Here we go again," I sighed. "What *is* it with you Europeans and the urge to ask out guys you're attracted to?" I smiled at the waiter as he passed our table, but he was focused somewhere else and didn't even notice. "See," I told Valérie accusingly. "It's not like I'm getting that much encouragement. He could ask *me* out if he really wanted." Which he didn't, because I just wasn't in his league. He probably was nice to me only because I gave outrageously big tips.

"He is cute," Valérie repeated at work to Giulia, who was *au courant* of the story. Due to my utter disinterest in dating this waiter, I couldn't help talking about him to every person who gave me half a chance. The director rolled her eyes and left the room to care for her plants—avocados this month—but Valérie and our other colleague Giulia grinned at each other. Giulia, a thin, antique blond woman with an obsession for shoes, was half Italian, half New Yorker and therefore had many weird ideas. She shook her head in despair at my emotional incompetence. "I wouldn't even hesitate. That's what you *do* if you're interested in someone. You ask him out. What century do you live in? Do you think it's the male role to ask you out or something?"

She and Valérie exchanged glances. Behind Giulia's head, metal shelves climbed to the ceiling, filled with the fat stiff binders favored for organization here. The only folders in the office were floppy colored paper things that sank ignominiously to the bottom of any hanging file folder, making it impossible to flip through them and spot what you were looking for. I had tried to convince Valérie and the director to order normal manila file folders, so I could use them in my two-drawer filing cabinet, but Valérie had looked appalled and handed me a binder. The fax machine beeped on the other side of the glass window of Giulia's office, and a student in chunky tennis shoes ducked in to fill her water bottle at the office water cooler. Neither distracted Valérie and Giulia.

"You'll never make it here," Valérie scoffed, using exactly the same tone in which she normally spoke of the more helpless of our American exchange students. She'd be calling me a *tête à claques* any minute. "You're competing with *French*women, after all." Her emphasis made it clear I was out of my league. "If a Frenchwoman sees someone she's interested in, she's not afraid to let him know. I would have asked him out the first evening!" She paused and glanced at me slyly. "You know, each day you hesitate, you increase the risk that someone else is going to grab him before you do."

Giulia shrugged. "That's the way it's done, Laura."

"A, someone's already grabbed him. You don't think someone that cute is running around loose, do you? And B, what if I don't want to go out with him?" I ventured timidly. "What if I just want to have a nice little crush on him and never do anything about it?"

Valérie stared at me in open-eyed wonder and then exchanged disgusted looks with Giulia. "Well, I guess if you want to be a coward, no one can stop you."

I stalked back to my office cum reception desk and stared out the window. My side of our offices looked down on a tiny *place,* or plaza, in the roughly triangular junction of three streets. The *place* made a charming refuge of trees and a fountain, lined with classic green Parisian benches. About halfway through my year there, I had noticed in our library an enormous yellow book on the history of Parisian streets and looked up our area. The same little *place* where people sat reading at lunch during nice weather was named after a method of torture. On this very site, deserters and thieves used to have their hands tied behind their backs and weights attached to their feet before being lifted high and dropped repeatedly to just above the ground, until their bodies were just an unholy mess. In 1687, Louis XIV's government moved the site for this *estrapade* punishment elsewhere, and for the next century deserters got shot to death on this *place* instead.

When you thought about it, the view from my office was a message. Things of beauty could have a lot of complications behind them, not all of them pleasant. I went to explain this message to Valérie and Giulia, and they rolled their eyes at me and went back to work.

"So," Adela said when I got home from work that day. I had followed the dancing promise of the Eiffel Tower down to the Métro, into whose depths I had descended for a packed and smelly ride home with some man standing behind me singing odes to my butt. "It's a good thing you know this cute guy."

"What?" We were sitting on the cheap, burnt orange blanket that covered my bed. Some students bought decent comforters to replace the dorm's linens, but I was thrifty. I only believed in the most essential of expenses, like chocolates from the various luxury chocolate houses whose beautiful boxes and tins currently decorated the two long shelves that circled the tiny room. My pink Fauchon one was still there, although Adela gave it a dirty look. My orange teddy bear sat at one end of the bed and studied us. He was French, brought back from a trip for me when I was a toddler, and very Gallic—that is, obsessed with food, feisty, and argumentative—probably because he had grown up in America surrounded by my stereotypes. Programs and theater flyers littered the long board of a desk, amid stacks of books. I was studying for the prelims I would have to take soon after I got back to the States in order to continue my Ph.D. studies. There were some four hundred works of French literature to memorize, along with the principal theoretical analyses of the same, so I'd been reading nothing but French classics for a couple of years now in preparation. I wanted to do my dissertation on the cultural renaissance in French-speaking, tropical, smiling Tahiti, but my department wouldn't let me do that until I'd survived the capital of France and passed my prelims. Above my bed was an enormous map of seventeenth-century Paris, torn in one corner thanks to that yellow tacky stuff that's supposed to hold things up. Cheap white toile veiled a window looking down at the picnic tables in the dorm's courtyard, a major center of gossip.

Adela peered through it. "You're so lucky," she sighed enviously, not for the first time. "I can barely even see the courtyard from my window. Now look at that! Why didn't you tell me Marina and Jack were sitting at the same table?" She turned back from the window and opened my mini-refrigerator to discover the narrow, long mint-green box of eight small *macarons* I had just brought back from Ladurée that afternoon. I sighed. That girl sure could sniff things out. She took a bite of a chocolate one, which made me feel as if her teeth were sinking directly into my heart, and switched back to her original subject. "Because we're going to need a cute guy around here."

"*What?*" I decided she must be talking about some other guy, one who wasn't tall, dark, and gorgeous and who might even recognize me if he saw me again. I knew a few cute guys, honest. I mean, ones that knew me back and with whom I'd actually exchanged names.

"You know that blond witch, Candy?" Adela was stuffing my *macarons* down her throat at an alarming speed, favoring the chocolate and pistachio flavors. I grabbed one for myself. There are two kinds of friends: those who admit their addiction to chocolate openly and therefore buy chocolate from time to time themselves, and those who claim others are chocoholics while eating all of the other's stash. Adela was the latter. And if you tried to hoard your chocolates under your bed because you knew she might pop in, she found some totally logical excuse to look under your bed and then went and told everyone in the dorm you were selfish and didn't share. I don't know how she managed this. One minute she'd be sitting on my bed chatting to me about the most recent fight with her professors, and the next she'd be under the bed hauling things out, and I'd be the one smiling weakly and feeling guilty. "She smiled when she passed me in the hall."

"Damn her," I said. "I hate it when people smile at me." Maybe *that* was why people ducked in terror when I smiled at them in the street. It was a deadly insult in Europe.

"And you know why," Adela said bitterly.

"Because she's a witch," I remembered. Candy, with her perfectly straight blond hair and blue eyes, lived in the same hall as Adela and had featured in her conversations before. "And she sleeps around. So she smiles at people. It's really nasty of her."

"Because he *told her!*" She gripped a *macaron* in a hot little fist, unnerving me. It was bad enough she was eating them; she'd better not start crushing them to crumbs.

"He did? When?" Who was he? What did he tell her about? Did I dare reveal my ignorance?

"Probably right after it happened!" Poison was clearly eating at her wounds. "He kissed me and then ran to brag about it to all the girls in the hall to say how easy I am! And what a player he is!"

I blinked a few seconds. "Adela, we aren't still talking about the guy you kissed when you both were drunk at the last party two months ago, are we?"

She stared at me. "Of course we are! How many people do you think I've kissed? I'm not like that Candy. Oh, he thinks he's so cute. To kiss me and never even call me the next day. Well, I'm not one of his girls, that he can jilt when he wants to, and he's going to learn it."

"Yeah, but—Adela. You were both drunk, and you only kissed. He might not even remember it or think anything about it." Adela stared at me with pure venom in her eyes, and I backed down. "The scumbag." Well, I still needed her to go with me to a certain restaurant occasionally.

"So *what we're going to do,*" Adela said firmly, to keep me on track, "is this. Our next dorm party is coming up. We all have two invitations we can give out. You haven't given one of yours out yet, have you?" she checked sharply for insubordination.

"No." Pretty much everyone I knew already lived there, except Valérie and Giulia, who wouldn't want to come.

"So you have two. I have two. And I can get more. Not everyone uses theirs, there are people in this dorm who spend their time studying." She said this on a note of incredulity. The only time Adela studied was when she wanted to get out of doing something, and then she didn't really study; she called me on the phone and told me how so-and-so's light was still on across the dorm courtyard but he wasn't answering his phone when she called him, what did I think that meant? "So what we're going to do is: I'm going to invite Eva and Pilar and all my prettiest friends."

"Check," I said, wondering where we were going with this. Was it a scheme to show the jilting heartthrob that we were all lesbians and so Adela couldn't care less about that kiss? Wow, my friends never talked me into doing this kind of stuff back home.

"And *they* will use the extra invitations I come up with to invite all their cutest guy friends. And there we will be, all these beautiful girls and all these beautiful guys. And that will show *him.*"

"Right," I said. The scary thing was, she explained this with such conviction that it almost made sense. It's the same way she kept ending up with my chocolates, which is not that easy to do.

"And the person who knows the cutest guy here is you."

"What? Who?"

40

"The guy at the restaurant!" Adela exclaimed, out of all patience. "The one you keep dragging me back to see every week!"

I cleared my throat. "I think 'know' might be considerably exaggerated in this context." I wouldn't say the waiter actually broke into a smile, but his eyes crinkled up and warmed when I walked into the restaurant, and he seemed to enjoy helping me choose things on the menu. This brazen flirtation was as far as I'd got.

"Laura," Adela said, and my heart quailed, and I almost dove under my bed myself to haul out my Christian Constant chocolates. It was that tone of voice. "I have been patient with you. But that patience is at an end. You have been going to that restaurant for three months, and if you do not ask him out the next time we go there"—her eyebrows formed menacing, curly crags—"I *will never eat with you in that restaurant again.*"

Four

Adela was one of the few friends still willing to go to Le Relais du Vin with me, and I knew I wouldn't find the gumption to go there alone. "Okay," I said. I remembered Valérie and Giulia dismissing me with disgusted glances. I had lived in four different countries, I spoke several languages, and I had eaten blood sausage. I had to be capable of seizing romance, right?

"I'll try." That sounded kind of wimpy for someone who had eaten blood sausage. Adela narrowed her eyes at me.

"I'll do it! I'll do it! You've got to come with me to the restaurant, though."

I needn't have worried. Adela had no intention of leaving this event unwitnessed. A few hours later—2:00 A.M., to be exact—she called and woke me out of a sound sleep. When she had first started doing this, early in our acquaintance, I would leap in cold panic out of my bed, sure of some emergency in the family. Now I buried my head under my pillow until the tenth ring, when I finally despaired and answered the phone.

"Guess who else is going to come?"

"You . . . invited someone else? To the party, you mean."

"No, no, to the dinner when you're going to ask this guy out!"

I paused. "It wasn't actually meant to be a public spectacle."

"Oh, it's only Eva and Pilar!" She named her two most beautiful friends. "Nobody else could come."

"Nobody else." I blinked awake. "How many people did you invite, exactly?"

"Not very many. Natalie, Stéphanie, and Kamila were busy, and I haven't been able to get in touch with Marina."

I digested the implications of this. First of all, considering the way gossip flew around these dorms, inviting Natalie, Stéphanie, Kam, Marina, Eva, and Pilar meant at least three hundred people now knew of my embarrassing plan to ask out a complete stranger. Second, Eva was after a man herself, and Pilar was drop-dead gorgeous. I would have strangled Adela, but I was pretty sure if police came looking for a motive, every finger in the dorm would point at me.

Therefore, the next Friday night, I stood in front of the small mirror over my dorm-room sink and looked desperately at my reflection. Both Eva and Pilar were sitting in my room, and both were prettier than I was. Eva had a fairly typical Parisian look and so might lose out to me in terms of exoticism, but Pilar was half Thai, half Spanish, with a flood of black hair that fell down to her knees.

"You know, he's probably gay," I said, not for the first time. I would far rather he be gay than fall for Pilar. I would far rather he be gay than try to go out with him, too. I was still having trouble coming to terms with my intentions.

42

"Could be," Adela said. "Ah . . . are you seriously thinking of wearing that blue sweater?"

"What?" I said, immediately paranoid. "I thought it matched my eyes."

"Maybe something a little more . . . conservative."

"Black," Eva clarified, for the slow-witted such as myself. "You want black."

I frowned doubtfully. "My father always said black rejected people, and that if I wanted to make people like me, I should wear blue."

All three European women stared at me as if I had fallen off the moon.

"And heels," Pilar said, while Eva pulled out a black spandex top that wouldn't have qualified for legal in the U.S. "You do have shoes with heels, don't you?"

I had thought I was wearing shoes with heels, but two inches apparently did not qualify. As item by item my own idea of what was attractive was dismissed, I grew increasingly insecure; but nobody noticed because I had been insecure ever since they met me. "Or he's got a girlfriend. There's no way someone that cute doesn't have a girlfriend," I added.

"True," Adela said. "Here." She had unearthed the four-inch stiletto boots I had bought in desperation after being unable to find any Parisian winter shoes with shorter heels. The stilettos made me feel like such a man-hunter I had been reluctant to wear them in the actual situation: that is, a hunt for a man. I was hunting a man. God, where was my dignity?

"Or he'll be an absolute jerk and only interested in one thing and that for about an hour," I said.

"What do you think about the skirt, Eva?" Adela asked, ignoring me as they flicked through my closet. "Do we want to go for classy or sexy?"

"Both, of course," Eva said, and a few minutes later gave me a crumpled, puzzled look when she realized I didn't have anything in my wardrobe that did both classy and sexy at the same time. This was not a situation in which a French or Spanish woman my age would have found herself.

"Besides, I'm lousy at relationships," I said. "Really. The longest one I've ever had was six months." I had started dating a dark-haired, exotic foreigner far too cute for me, someone I met in a dance club and knew was an impossible choice for a stop-traveling-and-commit-yourself kind of relationship. Not that I noticed any parallels here. I hoped not, because that time I had gotten myself into a real mess with an emotionally messed-up guy. Paris had been my escape.

All three women gave me puzzled looks this time. "Well, that works out all right, then, since you're only here for two more months. Besides, if he's gay, you don't really have to worry about it, do you? Um . . . Laura? Maybe you should take the feathers out of your hair."

I clutched at the little blue dangling things, my last item of color. "What! They're cutting-edge fashion." The feather fad that year in Paris promised to be the only time in my life I would get to wear feathers in public without social ruin, and I had seized on the opportunity enthusiastically.

"You never know what can turn someone off," Eva said diplomatically, twitching them away and passing them to Adela. I thought that if wearing feathers was likely to turn him off, maybe we should get it out of the way immediately. He might be cute but feather fads only came once a lifetime.

But it was too late. We were on our way to the restaurant.

The instant we got there, Eva's eyes lit up like a wolf's at the smell of blood, and I knew I was doomed. If I didn't ask him out now, Eva would, and that was just too galling to allow.

I'll skip over the giddy, giggling details of a three-course dinner among four women when one of them is planning to ask their waiter out at the end of it. It all went by in a blur for me anyway. I was too stressed. By the time we got the bill, I was a basket case, but Eva kept looking at me with an anticipatory gleam, just dying for me to bail.

You're a sex goddess, I whispered to myself. *Any man would love to go out with you.* It's much easier to believe my sex goddess pep talk when I'm actually better-looking than the guy in question. Butterflies swarming in my stomach, I pulled out the printed party invitation.

"Tsk, tsk, tsk," Adela's voice penetrated my wound-up conscious, chiding the others. "We don't want to give *too* big a tip. We don't want to seem like we're trying to buy him."

I looked up. "Well, we don't want to leave a small one. We don't want to seem rude. And it's not his fault if he doesn't like me."

Adela gave me an incredulous look. "Yes, it is. That invitation should *be* his tip. He should be willing to sacrifice a whole week of tips for that invitation."

"Well, let's not go overboard," Eva said. I never did like Eva much. She'd probably stolen my feathers just so I wouldn't look distinguished. "Maybe medium."

They all could agree on that. "But what's medium?" Pilar asked. "And, Laura, you have to actually write something on the invitation for it to work."

I hunched, fiddling with the pen. "I don't want him to see me write it."

Three pairs of bemused eyes turned on me. "Why not?"

"I just don't."

"He won't actually know what you're writing until after we leave," Pilar pointed out kindly.

"It doesn't matter! It's just too embarrassing!"

Adela buried a laugh behind her hand. "Well, there's always the bathroom."

45

And thus I found myself at eleven o'clock on a Friday night, in the seamy center of Paris, in a tiny room whose prior occupants had all had poor aim. There was no turning back now. Tottering above that Turkish hole in the ground, I put pen to pre-printed party announcement and scribbled *Voulez-vous venir à une fête demain?* (Do you want to come to a party tomorrow?), then tried to sign my name and number without touching anything. Romance was never like this in Harlequins. Of course, Paris was never like this in the movies either. Blame it on Paris.

Back at the table, I tucked the invitation under the tip, dumped a few extra coins in apology for my effrontery, and left the restaurant at a brisk pace, making what could even be considered a mad dash toward the Métro escalators as soon as I was out of sight. Eva, Adela, and Pilar lingered outside the restaurant window and then ran after me, giggling still. "He picked it up!"

My heart jumped in pure terror.

"Well, did he *smile* or anything?" I asked, despite myself.

"I don't know, I couldn't tell," Eva said.

"I think he laughed," Adela said.

"Oh, God."

"In a *nice* way," Pilar insisted. "Like he was pleased."

"Of course he was pleased," I groaned. "What guy wouldn't be pleased to have women leaving him invitations on tables?" I collapsed into my seat on our RER train, my hands shaking with nerves. Pilar petted my back consolingly, and the other two laughed and talked excitedly, all keyed up over their adventure. My hands didn't stop shaking until the end of the twenty-minute ride. And right at the end of it, a thought occurred to me. Good Lord, what if he actually called? Did that mean I would have to go through even *more* traumatic experiences, like talking to him?

But maybe he wouldn't call. That would be good, because my heart could only stand so much.

Five

Like any reasonable woman, I stayed out of my room from 7:00 A.M. to 2:00 A.M. the next two days. Since I didn't have an answering machine, I could thus protect myself from knowing whether he had blown me off or not. Granted, if he did try to call me, this plan would prove self-defeating, but only in one sense. In another, it would allow me to retreat back into my unfettered life, the life in which I had only two more months of adventuring in Paris to do and could then move on to a country that didn't give me lung cancer.

England, I kept thinking. I'd never been to England and had just applied to Cambridge's summer program.

I did go on a special shopping trip to buy skin-clinging black leather pants and a black nylon top that dipped down to my navel, just in case this French waiter came to the party without calling. Not that I wanted him to call or come or anything, but if he did, I wanted him to realize I was a leather-wearing sex goddess and not a shy and desperate woman with a ridiculous crush. I only succeeded in having to spend a night protecting my tail from drunken fellow students in the big, dark, smoky main hall filled with amateur strobe lights, plastic cups stained with Adela's very own sangria, and a mass of people in various stages of inebriety. He never showed.

"Sorry," I said to Adela.

"Sorry about what?" she asked, busy flirting with some new person. "Did something happen? Oh, hey, where's that guy you asked out?"

By Monday after work, my guard was down, and when I walked into my room to find the phone ringing, I thoughtlessly picked it up.

The half laughing, half embarrassed male voice over the phone sparked no recognition. *"Bonjour, Laura?"*

"Oui, c'est moi."

"C'est Sébastien, Sébastien Florand."

I stared blankly at the phone. He laughed again, more embarrassed. "You left me an invitation. I've been trying to call you all weekend!"

I giggled, which was supposed to pass for sophisticated conversation, and sat down on the bed. My legs had collapsed under the weight of excruciating embarrassment. "For the party Saturday, right." He had called? Was he crazy? Was he desperate? He looked way too cute to be desperate. Why would he call *me*?

"I couldn't make it," he said. "I had to be at a friend's birthday party out in the country. But I've been trying to call you."

"Yes, I—haven't been here very much." I am a very popular person even if I am so desperate as to leave invitations for strange men. And don't you forget it. I wondered if there was a way I could work my leather pants Saturday night into the conversation. Subtly, you know, as in, "Eat your heart out."

"Really," he said. "I did. My friends can vouch for me. They had to keep loaning me their cell phones."

I had two thoughts. First, I was going to meet his friends? Whoa. Just a few days ago, he had been a comfortably distant crush, an actor on the film screen of Paris. And now he wanted me to meet French people? What had I started here?

Second, he had so wanted to call me that he had kept borrowing cell phones from his friends, publicly admitting he was trying to get in touch with a girl who wasn't answering? Aww.

Third, what *was* wrong with him anyway?

Fourth, could I wear the leather pants again for the first date, or would that be too obvious? Was I getting a little obsessed with leather pants?

Okay, I had more than two thoughts. It must be nice to be a man and only able to think of one thing at a time.

"So would you like to meet for a drink sometime this week?" he asked. "Say Wednesday?"

Wednesday was the day after tomorrow. I began hyperventilating. "Sure. I get off at six."

"Yes, me, too. But I start at Le Relais at 7:30. Can we meet at the fountain at Châtelet? That will give us an hour."

"Okay," I said. An *hour*. How was I going to seem witty and attractive for a whole hour? Even with a menu on hand, I could only keep the conversation with him going about five minutes. And believe me, I can usually talk about food for a long time. "Umm, where else do you work?" I asked, practicing my conversational skills.

"*Sciences et Vie*," he said. Wasn't that a major scientific magazine? I remembered seeing it in the kiosks, something like our *Scientific American* or maybe *Discover*. "I do their illustrations."

"And then you go work nights in a restaurant?"

He laughed. "Well, I work for *Sciences et Vie* as part of a co-operative learning program, so it doesn't pay much. I got tired of eating pasta, and my best friend's father owns Le Relais, so I started working there, too. I finish up my graphic arts degree this summer. Only a few months more and I'll be able to quit at the restaurant." He sounded deeply relieved, which, when I thought about it, made sense. He was a student, working nearly full-time at this magazine, and waiting tables nights. He must work from eight in the morning to one in the morning with almost no break most days of the week. And then study?

49

Okay, so whatever other flaws he might turn out to have, he clearly wasn't lazy. Maybe he was calling me back because he didn't have time to go hunt down a girlfriend; he had to take whoever fell into his lap.

A lot of girls must fall into his lap at that restaurant. Maybe he was a notches-on-his-belt kind of guy. Maybe he just figured I was easy pickings.

Why had I done this? What was the matter with me? And even on the very remote chance he turned out to be worth something, I finished up my contract here in just a little over six weeks. So what was the point? Other than the fact that he was really cute.

"So I'll see you Wednesday, then," I said.

It took me a few minutes to recover, after I hung up. I ran out of the room, ran straight into Adela, grabbed her hands, and started dancing around the hall singing, "He called, he called, he called!" I should probably not mention that. For lack of emotional courage, I generally try to maintain a cynical persona, which is not reinforced by this type of behavior. Besides, given that I had stayed out of my room the whole weekend to make sure he couldn't reach me, normal people might find me inconsistent.

"Wow," Adela said. "He *called?* It actually worked?"

I froze. "What do you mean, 'It actually worked'? You never thought it would work?"

"Well, I mean, I thought it would let us change restaurants, yes, but . . . and then, I mean, it *could* have worked."

At work, Valérie and Giulia stared at me as if I had just shown up in a beret. "You actually DID it? You asked out some man you didn't even know? I've never known anyone to do something like that before!"

I counted to ten. "You told me French women did that kind of thing all the time. You told me you wouldn't hesitate a second. You told me I was a wimp, you—"

"Are you kidding? I've never seen anyone do anything like that in my life. We just made all that up to encourage you! We didn't think you would actually fall for it!"

I folded my arms. "Why is it that all my friends have a vicarious taste for adventure for which I'm always the damned patsy?"

Valérie grinned at me. "Well, it worked, didn't it?"

By Tuesday night before the big meeting, I had vacillated back to terror, or rather, vacillated back to letting terror have the upper hand. "I'm not going," I said as Adela went through my wardrobe again, trying to figure out what I could wear for a first date. "He's French. You know I can't stand Frenchmen. They're arrogant, faithless, gloomy, and live in Paris. I hate this city."

"You know, he was French before you asked him out, too," Adela said. "I just mention it."

"I *left him an invitation on one of his tables.* How am I supposed to look him in the face after that? Besides, I don't have enough black clothes for a long-term relationship!"

"You're right about the black. But if you don't go after all this, I'll murder you. Try this on!"

Thanks to Adela, I found myself in stiletto boots at work the next day, something I would not normally have worn to work in the U.S. Here, a high-heeled TV show hostess only the day before had demonstrated how to fit a ten-minute step exercise program into my daily routine. "After ten minutes," the show's hostess promised, panting, "I can promise you that you will have had a *serious* workout." Well, that explained why I couldn't find a good spin class in this city. Taken in context, French skinniness was even more annoying than it had been from the other side of the Atlantic. "*Mais attention* to your feet!" She tapped the four-inch heel of her boot; and just when I thought she was going to tell her viewers that this was insane footwear for exercise, she clarified her point: "*Always* exercise in heels. How else can you get yourself in shape for the workday? After all, you're hardly going to leave the house in flat shoes."

Balanced on my own stilettos in Giulia's office and slicked out in black again, I folded my arms across my chest and clenched my fists. "I'm not going," I told Valérie and Giulia.

"Yes, you are, too, going," Giulia said.

"If you don't go, you'll never be able to hold your head up around here again," Valérie said. "What's so hard? You get on the bus; you go meet him; you like him, or you don't like him. Americans!"

I didn't, at the time, seize on that bus reference, but I should have. Valérie knew I usually took the RER train or walked from Luxembourg, where we worked, to Châtelet, where I had agreed to meet Sébastien. But after work, as the three of us were passing the bus stop on the way to the RER entrance, Valérie and Giulia each snagged an elbow and stopped me before a green-trimmed bus plastered with advertisements for *Lord of the Dance* and the Galeries Lafayette. "Where do you think you're going? This is your bus."

I frowned at the Galeries Lafayette ad. French supermodel Laetitia Casta beamed back at me from under the giant red heart on her head. Sébastien was so cute he could probably date Laetitia Casta if he wanted. "At six o'clock? I could walk faster, with all this traffic. I was going to take the Métro."

"Yes, but with a bus, we know where you're going." They smiled. "On foot or in the Métro, you can go anywhere you want, can't you?"

"I can't do that on the bus?"

Still holding on to my elbows, they both leaned in through the door to where the driver sat bored and blasé behind the wheel, his jaw showing a gray prickle. "This woman has promised to meet a man at the place de Châtelet. Can you make sure she gets off there and only there?"

The driver's hair slumped dispiritedly on his head, gray and obviously wilted from neglect. He eyed me, chewing idly on something tucked against a full cheek. "Of course." Disconcertingly, his bored expression didn't even change.

Passengers squeezed in around me with each stop as we crept our slow way down the car-jammed boulevard St. Michel. Some of them had washed, and some of them had not, and some of them had opted for enough perfume to try to keep you guessing. Odors clogged thickly, a traffic jam in my nose, which fought back frantically, trying to close up. We lurched forward and stopped, lurched forward and stopped, while horns honked everywhere. Occasionally I had the impression we lurched backward and stopped, but I think I was just hallucinating under the effects of claustrophobia and panic. I was going to be late for the first meeting. Maybe I shouldn't go at all. I could get off this bus. That driver had let a hundred passengers on and off already; how would he even notice me if I slipped out?

Imprisoned between masses of flesh and a smudged glass window, I enviously watched people stroll in and out of stores without a care in the world. I bet nobody was forcing *them* to go meet a gorgeous guy. We reached the bookstore Gibert-Jeune, with its yellow signs and vast displays of books, by the great bronze statue of Michael the Archangel that presides over the rose-pillared fountain where the boulevard St. Michel reaches the Seine.

The bus lurched its slow way over the first bridge across the Seine, the Pont St. Michel that joined the Rive Gauche to the Île de la Cité. The other bridges of Paris stretched to right and left, arches and curves marking points of history. The day was not so bad, maybe a light gray with a hint of blue in the sky. I could see, over the Pont du Change on the other side of the island, the slender column of the Fontaine du Chalet, topped with a gold angel. Only two more stops protected me from this meeting. I drew a deep breath and pressed the nearest red button.

The driver stopped and opened the doors to let more passengers on. I tried to blend in with the other passengers getting off, but just as I reached the doors, they whisked shut. Passengers piled up behind me, grabbing bars to keep their balance at the sudden halt.

"This isn't Châtelet," the driver told me.

Is it only in Paris that I would find myself having to convince a bus driver of my right to get off at the stop of my choosing? "I'm meeting him right there." I pointed over the straight stone Pont du Change to the plaza framed by two nineteenth-century theaters and the red awnings of cafés. "I'm going to walk straight across the bridge, I swear. I just want to collect myself."

He considered me for a steady, narrow-eyed moment, his expression as bored and cynical as ever.

"You'll be able to *see* me do it!"

He kept the doors closed another long moment as he weighed my character. "All right, but I'm watching you," he finally allowed, letting the doors swish open.

I walked across the bridge with the wind blowing through my hair, rushing cold over a barge full of sand below, and whipping around me without clearing my head. A pair of pigeons flew off the stone rail, heading for Notre-Dame and the easy tourist pickings. The bus lurched along nearly even with me, caught in traffic. I waved to the driver when I crossed the street to the fountain, just to make sure he didn't abandon his vehicle in the intersection and come after me. I could imagine him weaving through the gridlocked cars, picking me up under the arms, depositing me before my date, and returning to the wheel, all without a change in that jaded expression.

But he didn't. I went myself. Sébastien was sitting on the edge of the fountain, surrounded by crouching stone sphinxes, and he looked up at me and broke into a smile.

Six

A s I approached, he stood and looked down at me, dark eyes questioning, mouth smiling. He wore jeans and a beige sweater considerably classier than anything I owned. When he bent to exchange cheek kisses, a scent of vanilla teased my senses and my cheek pressed against skin that was a tantalizing combination of baby-smooth and subtle prickle. He had just scrupulously shaved, but without managing to eradicate the suggestion of darkness along his jaw. I rocked back on my heels, feeling dazed. I had touched him. We had actually touched.

Okay, that was way too much excitement for me for one lifetime. The butterflies in my stomach escaped and fluttered their little, brushed-velvet wings all up and down my nerve endings. I needed to apply some pesticide to those things, fast. I searched his face, hoping to see something horrible that would let me escape this relationship before I went into a meltdown of embarrassment and eagerness. What was that in his ears? Silver circlets? "Are you wearing earrings?"

He looked surprised at this start to the conversation but nodded.

"Is that new?" How had I missed them? I would have been truly convinced he was gay if I'd seen the earrings and so I had managed to ignore them?

"No, I got my ears pierced about six years ago."

"I've got four brothers." There was no way a girl from small-town Georgia with four older brothers could date a man who wore earrings. That was it, the relationship was over. I was saved. I'd just have to stick this first meeting out to be polite.

He grinned. See? I'd amused him. Just like the people in the restaurant sometimes did, only in my case not on purpose. "Do you have four brothers here in Paris?"

"Well . . . no." One of my brothers had visited Paris for twenty-four hours and the city had survived it, but that was the closest any of them had come.

"Well, I guess I'm safe, then." He laughed.

I frowned. "But they could fly over. If they have to." Yeah, right. My brothers thought that if I was stupid enough to leave the good old U.S. of A., I could handle my own problems. They'd taught me how to shoot, after all, and it wasn't their fault I'd chosen to live in a country where I didn't have the right to bear arms.

His grin softened into just a small smile, and he looked down at me with those brown eyes of his. Today they reminded me of some dark liquor just warmed in front of a fire. "They won't have to."

What did that mean? That he didn't have any dishonorable intentions because he didn't plan on seeing me again? He'd probably thought one of the other girls had left him the invitation, and now he was disappointed. Pilar. He'd probably hoped it was Pilar. I mean, come on, if he'd wanted to ask me out, he'd had plenty of opportunity to do so.

I'm not normally this bad on a date, but I did better with people I considered lucky to go out with *me* rather than the other way around.

He guided me toward one of the Australian bars popular in Paris, directing me courteously from time to time away from dog poop on the sidewalks. We installed ourselves in a corner of the heavy-beamed wood room—one where we were a step above and slightly removed from the rest of the bar but could see all of it. A wooden railing separated us from the bartender on the main floor, a vaguely reassuring barrier because the bartender was massively muscled and liked the looks of Sébastien. Boomerangs and Aboriginal Dreamtime lizards decorated our surroundings, in dot painting style.

I saw Sébastien notice the bartender's gaze without really paying it much heed. Was he so used to drawing attention he didn't know liquid stares and helpless smiles weren't normal human interaction? He probably didn't even realize someone was attracted to him until the person sat in his lap. Or left him an invitation on a table.

"What would you like to drink?"

"Oh—apricot juice. But I'm the one who invited you, shouldn't I get it?" I reached for my wallet.

He laughed. "No, you shouldn't." He left to get the drinks. "And you shouldn't keep your wallet in your jacket pocket like that, someone's going to steal it," he added when he got back.

Okay, can we all agree that men have no business telling women they barely know how to live their lives? I disgraced independent women everywhere by getting a kick of excitement from the remark. He *noticed,* he cared, and he spoke with such authority. And he was so darn cute. Off to my left, the bartender flexed his muscles and gazed at him longingly.

"You have *your* wallet in your pocket," I said.

"Trust me, no one is going to get his hand in my front jeans pocket without me noticing it."

I narrowed my eyes. "Are you sure?"

He grinned. "I'd dare you to try, but you'd probably run. You are so shy."

My jaw dropped. That was so unfairly true. "How dare you say that? I just asked out a man I never even met."

He blinked and stopped smiling. "You did? When was this?"

I stared at him. "Friday."

He'd been leaning forward on the table, so close, and now he sat back. "So who did you ask out?"

"You," I said, aggravated. "Hello!"

His eyebrows went up. "You didn't ask me *out*. You just left me an invitation to some party."

I felt as if I'd opened my mouth to talk and someone had punted a football into it by surprise. "That's not asking you out? Are we speaking the same language here?"

"I think so. You've got a really cute accent, though. Are you Canadian?"

It was tempting, but I haven't yet stooped to denying my country, not even in the most hostile of climates, like Paris. "No. American." I braced.

"Oh." He considered that. "I thought you must be Canadian."

"Why?" I asked suspiciously. "Because I seemed nice? Not loud, obnoxious, and arrogant?"

"No, because the invitation you left me said 'Maison du Canada.' I like fast food," he offered in the way of cultural conciliation.

Oh, for God's sake. Was he kidding me? Probably the one perk to dating a Parisian was that I'd get to eat well. "I hate fast food," I said uncompromisingly. I'd managed the *boudin noir*, but that was as far as I was willing to go in terms of eating horrible food, damn it.

He laughed and leaned forward again, meeting my eyes. Meeting a woman's eyes with attraction just peeking out is a European technique American men should try sometime. "Well, look at that. We have so much in common."

I still struggled to absorb the fact that after all the stress and work and crisis of courage, he didn't even feel like I'd picked him up. "What do you call it, then, my leaving you that invitation?"

"Trying to drum up more people to come to your dorm party. You were just being friendly, right?"

Anything I tried to say would come out as a sputter.

"But. . . ." He looked down at the table, rubbed its heavy wood with a finger, and looked back at me under his lashes. He had thicker, darker, longer lashes than I did, it pretty much went without saying. "Would you *like* to go out?"

I glanced around at our little slice of Down Under and back at him. "This isn't a date right now?"

He looked taken aback. "No. We're just having drinks. How could we have a date when we've never even properly met before?"

"I'm deeply confused," I said. I guess it was a good thing I hadn't worn those leather pants.

He studied his beer, traced the condensation on it, and peeked back at me. "So would you like to do something together Saturday afternoon?"

If we did, would that count as a date, or would it just be doing something together Saturday afternoon? If we hadn't even gone on a date yet, I could hardly quit now without trying, could I? He wasn't giving off any arrogant jerk vibes; in fact, the opposite. He was cute, likeable, and terrifying. I took a deep breath and reminded myself that Cambridge was only a couple of months away, and that between its start date and my contract's end date I had two weeks I'd planned to use traveling to Prague or maybe Italy. How messy could things get between now and Prague? "Yes. Did you have anything in mind?"

"Why don't we just meet at the fountain again and we'll figure it out? There's always something to do in Paris."

Out in the courtyard of the Maison du Canada, Adela dished her famous *ensalada de frutas* into plastic cups and plopped me firmly down amid more friends than I cared to share my heart with at the drop of a hat. Maybe I have latent misanthropic tendencies. "Tell," she said. Adela was wearing orange. I was a laughingstock for wanting to wear blue, but Adela got to wear orange. She claimed it was this year's black. "How did it go?"

"It went all right," I said as neutrally as possible. "This is good fruit salad, Adela. As always." Her *ensalada de frutas* tasted sweet and fresh, the perfect blend of fresh strawberries, oranges, and apples, with canned peaches for extra sweetness. I copied it so much that people occasionally called it "Laura's fruit salad," to Adela's great indignation.

"Thank you. Notice the use of peach syrup."

"Adela, I only tried pear syrup once. I told you I didn't have another can of peaches."

Her eyebrows curled. "Did I tell you that pear syrup was an acceptable substitution? No. Then you shouldn't have tried it. So what does 'All right' mean? Didn't you like him?"

"Didn't he like you?" Eva asked, slim and elegant in her gray suit. "Did he realize it was you leaving the invitation?"

You know, Eva dressed far too fashionably for me to like her. Cold chic, that's what she had. I'd never seen her wear a feather. And now that I thought about it, the delicate structure of her face gave her a rather sharp look.

"Yes," I snapped my teeth together. "He realized it was me."

"Of course, he would have been too polite to say otherwise," Eva mentioned. She smoothed back her hair—redundantly, because not a single brown strand of it ever strayed from her perfect coiffure. My hair frizzed all over the place. "Did he want to go out again?"

"Yes." I glared at her.

Eva shut her mouth in surprise and looked deeply disappointed.

"Really?" Adela looked unflatteringly surprised, too. Had *every* woman there that night been indulging in the fantasy that Sébastien assumed the invitation was from her? "So why did you say it was 'All right' and not fantastic? Was he boring? Was he annoying?"

"No, he seemed—great. But you know it's never going to work out. I never manage to date anyone longer than a few weeks, and anyway, I leave here mid-June. Remember?"

Eva brightened.

"You don't *have* to leave here mid-June," Adela said. Eva frowned at her. "I don't leave until the end of June. You could stay through then."

"If it becomes an issue," Eva said. "Which it probably won't. You know what? You should invite him to come out with all of us sometime so I can get to know him better."

I had very annoying friends. I glared at Eva.

"Well, never let a cute guy go to waste," she muttered, surprised at my attitude. "I'd wait until you were gone."

"He might just have a hard time getting over me!" I snapped, scowling. "And not want to be passed from one woman to another."

"After a month?" Adela asked.

"My, aren't we getting cocky after having one little invitation accepted," Eva said.

Seven

There was this weird freak of nature that Saturday: the sun came out. Sébastien and I didn't want to go inside for this unnatural nice weather, so we walked along the Seine. *Muguets,* or lilies of the valley, were everywhere, adding a sweet, delicate scent to the car fumes and cigarette smoke of Paris. People stood on streetcorners and passed through parks with buckets of the little bell-shaped white flowers to sell as a gift for happiness. *Ça porte le bonheur, les muguets.* It was the first weekend after the Fête du Premier Mai, May Day, and I thought of sinking ships.

Sébastien had taken my hand as we walked. I kept looking at it, not sure how it felt there. Nervous, definitely. But his hand was warm and strong and lots bigger than mine, and he really was very good at spotting dog poop and pulling me back and forth to make sure I didn't walk in it. I brushed a bug out of my hair impatiently. "Be *careful,*" Sébastien exclaimed. "You might hurt him!" The bug had fallen from my hair to my short-sleeved sweater, but he caught my hand before I could brush again and lifted the bug on his finger. "Look," he said. "See the green glints on its body?" He set the bug safely on a tree planted on the quay and watched it crawl off. I felt like it would be easier on all of us if he would act as I thought a Parisian should—cynical, cold, arrogant, and easy to break up with in a couple of months—but couldn't think of a delicate way to explain this to him.

We ended up on the Île de la Cité. Sébastien spread his jacket on the stones to prevent me from sitting in pigeon poop—a lot of poop hazards in Paris—and we dangled our legs over the water. My stomach tingled. It seemed it had been tingling for days. People chattered and laughed in the little island park just behind us, and at the tip of the island closest to the Louvre, a group of teenagers horsed around. "I think I like you," Sébastien said softly.

Well, that sounded tepid. I was from a small Southern town. To my worst enemies, I said more positive things than that. I sulked as a firefighter speedboat roared past.

Sébastien tilted his head, a little puzzled by my indifference to his bared heart. "What do you think? Do you like me?"

"Sure," I said nervously, with my natural gift for intimacy. Thank God we were doing this in French, a language where I could pretend I didn't know what I was saying.

He played with a strand of my hair, leaned in, and tried to kiss me. I remembered that the French had invented major art forms in kissing and that I was sure to come across as a clumsy amateur, panicked completely, and jumped up. "Oh, look, there's the Samaritaine, how'd that get there?" The Samaritaine is an enormous department store with a lovely Art Déco façade, and it doesn't really drift around Paris surprising people with sudden appearances as much as you'd think. "Because I just remembered I need to get something there. Some, uh"—what could a woman need suddenly?—"some Tampax." Damn it, wrong track, wrong track. "Some perfume. For my sister's birthday. Which was in

January and I've been forgetting it for the past four months. I have to run across right now, before I forget again."

Sébastien kept hold of my hand, stood up, searched my face a second with a kind of bemused calm, and tried again. I managed not to fall into the Seine when he lifted his head.

He made sure I didn't with another hand on my arm. He seemed to have taken on not letting me fall as one of his responsibilities in this relationship, rather like not letting me walk or sit in various kinds of animal poop. Which is really much more romantic than it sounds in a city like Paris.

He certainly looked happy with his lot in life, standing there on the edge of the Seine with a *Bateau-Mouche* passing by and all its tourists taking pictures of us. A little shy, a little eager, a little nervous, but mostly just happy. I think I was happy, too, but I was so giddy, scared, and—to be honest here—sexually excited that I couldn't tell for sure.

"So," he said, "what was it you wanted at Samaritaine?"

"Soap," I said, having remembered that I couldn't afford perfume and chocolate, too, "some nice soap."

Cambridge wanted the deposit for lodging by June 1. I pressed the form open, set it by my laptop, and stared at it. I thought of Kipling and C. S. Lewis and Magdalene College. A friend of mine had spent a semester at Cambridge. It was the high point of his life. He felt as if he were living poetry.

The phone rang—Sébastien at the dorm entrance to pick me up for our third encounter. Did I get to call it a date yet? Had yesterday been a date?

Like most Parisians, Sébastien didn't have a car, but today he had decided to take the Métro out to the Cité U to meet me and take the Métro back with me to wherever we went, rather than having us meet at some central point. This was a really sweet way for him to waste his time. Nobody liked taking the Métro more than they had to.

In the lobby, Sébastien stood waiting in a white tank that clung to those perfect abs and showed off his beautiful biceps. A bone surfer's necklace curled around his neck and rested in the hollow of his throat. It was enough to give a girl a heart attack. I couldn't *possibly* have the same effect on him when he saw me, could I? He held a bouquet of small decorative cabbages and bright sunflowers wrapped in yellow paper. Cabbages? He'd brought me a bouquet of cabbages?

"It reminds me of you," he said, smiling down at me.

I knew French people called each other cabbages as a term of endearment, but still, I didn't know how to take that. "A cabbage reminds you of me?"

"The bouquet. It's different and cheerful. It just caught my eye at the florist's."

"Oh." I wondered where he had gotten the idea I was cheerful instead of cynical, emotionally stunted, pessimistic, and depressive. Honestly, I had to start acting more sincere with men. "Thank you." I stood on tiptoe to greet him with the normal French kiss on each cheek, flushing deeply. I was used to exchanging cheek kisses with everyone by then, but it felt very different with him.

He pulled his head back, startled and offended. "Is that how you greet your boyfriend?"

"My what?"

"Your boyfriend."

"My *what*?"

We stared at each other, him hurt and me panicked. "We've only been out twice," I said. "And the first time didn't count, you said. Why are you saying you're my boyfriend?"

"Why are you saying I'm not?"

"We barely know each other! We could both still be dating other people."

Black eyebrows came together. "You date more than one person at a time?"

"I'm *not*—although plenty of guys have been interested, by the way, hundreds—but I could if I wanted to. Couldn't you?"

"I don't act like that," he said, offended. He frowned, eyes searching. "You do?"

"I'm not 'acting like' anything!" Geez, he was looking at me as if "tramp" might be written on my forehead. And I hadn't even worn my leather pants yet. "It's not like we're engaged! We've barely met!" Why was I having this discussion, when I wasn't dating anyone else, didn't want to be dating anyone else, and wasn't even sure I could handle dating him? My nerves were shot and I couldn't sleep anymore for the fizzing in my veins. But the jump from having drinks—*not* on a date— to girlfriend was a big one. Did this mean I should mention Cambridge?

"Come on," I said. "Are you telling me that you have considered yourself in a serious relationship with every girl you've ever kissed?" I held his eyes challengingly. "No one-night stands in your history?" That wasn't credible. He must have had women falling at his feet since he was about fourteen years old.

"That's different," he said impatiently. "I can't believe you're even comparing—are you going out with other men right now? Are you *kissing* other men right now?"

I folded my arms, a little awkwardly what with my bouquet of cabbages and all. Its yellow paper wrapping crackled madly. "I can if I want to."

"*I'm* not going out with other women."

I beamed, and he relaxed. "Well, I'm not either. Or other men. But that doesn't mean I'm your girlfriend!"

"Yes, you are," he said. "I don't understand the American dating system at all."

"That's okay, none of us do."

"Let's practice how a girlfriend says hello to her boyfriend again," he said and bent his head. "It's not on the cheek."

In the Métro, he amused the heck out of himself by pretending it was too crowded. "I'm so sorry," he said, backing me against the inside track doors—the ones that rarely opened—and squeezing closer, his hands pressed to the wall either side of my hips. "There are so many people." He grinned down at me.

It was a little crowded, but it wasn't that crowded. What a great game. "Oh, sorry." I bumped forward against him full-body and back and gazed up at him innocently. "I lost my balance."

He laughed and nudged closer.

"So where are we going?" I asked. I was really going to have to mention Cambridge soon. But it was such a non-issue. I mean, I almost never managed to go out with someone for longer than a month.

"My friends Éric and Virginie asked us over."

"What?" Had I dropped down the dating rabbit hole? "You're introducing me to your friends already?"

He looked confused. "What do you mean, 'already'? They asked us over. It's normal that I bring my girlfriend."

"Okay, try to remember that I'm not your girlfriend. We've barely met."

"Thank God I didn't grow up trying to date in the U.S.," he said. "I would have gone insane, too."

"What do you mean, 'too'?" I asked, and he "tripped," pressing me for a half second against the wall with his body before straightening and pulling back about three inches.

"Oops, sorry." He grinned. "I lost my balance."

"So, I bet your friends are French, aren't they?" I began uneasily.

"*Putain de merde!*" a male voice exclaimed behind him. "*Salope,* can't you watch where you're going?"

Sébastien stiffened and looked over his shoulder. I peered around him. A plump, silvery-haired woman with a big navy purse was flushing. "I'm sorry," she muttered. "I didn't mean to bump into you."

66

The male voice erupted in a string of curse words. I peered the other way around Sébastien to see a huge man, bearded and muscled but going to fat, slamming back into his little blue vinyl fold-down seat, spewing venom.

"*Monsieur,*" the woman's small, white-haired husband attempted to intervene.

"Fuck you!" the man yelled at him. "*Salop avec ta femme salope.*"

The husband stiffened and stood as straight as he could. He was a lot smaller than the burly angry man. Everybody here was, and everybody was looking the other way. I hated the Métro. I hated big cities. I hated the non-movie version of Paris.

"*Putain,*" Sébastien breathed and turned, keeping his body in place so that I was still behind him. "That's enough."

Everybody's jaw dropped, including mine, including the burly man's. I had never seen anyone help anyone else out in the Métro before, and I'd been on the receiving end of some of these scenes a time or two.

"What the hell business is it of yours?" the angry man asked. He was a lot bigger than Sébastien, I noticed. Sébastien was pretty tall, just shy of six feet, and he had some gorgeous muscles, but this guy was taller and wider and obviously nastier. At least Sébastien looked tough, not having shaved in a couple of days, and the muscle shirt really did give a salutary view of his biceps. I was the only one here who knew he protected bugs.

"You're getting on my nerves," Sébastien said. The tattoo that circled his left biceps flexed. "So why don't you shut up and leave the lady alone?"

I gasped. This could not end well.

"Nosy asshole," the burly man muttered, with a complete lack of self-perception. Sébastien held on to one of the metal bars and just looked back at him, saying nothing in response, waiting. The train stopped, and the man got up abruptly and flung himself off, still muttering.

I gasped again in relief.

"Thank you," the lady's elderly husband said.

Sébastien shrugged, acutely embarrassed. "I can't stand bullies."

He turned back to me. His jaw was still tight, a muscle in it flexing. But after a moment, his face started to clear, and he dropped his hand from the metal bar above his head to put it on the wall by my head, so that his arm brushed my hair.

"So it's a good thing you didn't bother to shave," I teased to lighten the mood. "Makes you look too dangerous to mess with."

He rubbed his prickly jaw. "I can't shave every day. I have delicate skin."

I began to laugh.

"I really do!" he said, offended. "It's bad for it to shave every day!"

I kept laughing.

He looked down at me with a gleam in his eyes and moved closer. My laughter did a little hitch in midstream. "Just trying to make sure everyone has enough room. It's not fair for us to take up more than our fair share of space."

"Sébastien," I said, "where did you get that little scar over your eyebrow and those tiny scars on your knuckles?"

I wasn't sure he was going to answer at first, but then he did. "From my awful teenage years. Not a good time."

"Did you get in a lot of fights?"

"I didn't have much choice," he said grimly. "When my parents divorced, they both went to live in the *banlieue*." *Banlieue* means, geographically, a suburb of Paris, but that's not really what it means. A suburb, in American, is a positive word, a safe place to grow up. *Banlieue* is just the opposite. It's where beautiful, lovely Paris stuffs all its racism and low-income housing. There are nice *banlieues*, but when people say, "I grew up *en banlieue*," they're not talking about the nice *banlieues*. Mathieu Kassovitz did a landmark film on the *banlieue* situation in 1995. The title was

Hate. "Where my mother lived was okay, I guess, but when I went to live with my father when I was thirteen, it wasn't great."

And here I'd just assumed that he . . . I don't know what I'd assumed. Gorgeous Frenchmen came out of Hollywood movies, they didn't get born and grow up in bad neighborhoods.

He touched the scar over his eyebrow. His mouth twisted ruefully, but his eyes were still dark. "That was actually a knife." He looked down at the back of his hand. "Probably some of those are from the same fight. I think I could have killed him. I was furious. My friends had to pull me off him."

He looked up and met my eyes. I'm not sure what he thought he saw there. I was just trying to figure out if this was a true story. I was always telling my brothers to pretend their scars were from knife fights defending a lady's honor. What were they supposed to do? Admit under questioning that they'd shaken up a beer bottle, tried to explode it with a slingshot, and got struck by the flying glass fragments of their own idiocy?

"I'm not *proud* of it," he said defensively. "I just—I don't know. To *pull a knife on someone.* When he did that, I just snapped. I'm not even sure how I got the knife away from him and got him down on the ground, but I do remember my friends had to drag me away." He was frowning deeply but then looked up and apparently imagined he saw something in my eyes again. "I've got a lot more self-control now," he said quickly.

I blinked. "Are you apologizing for losing your temper when someone pulled a knife on you?" I lost my temper when I got a run in my hose. And I wasn't going to start apologizing for it, either. I *knew* we weren't in the same league. It might be a good thing I was going to Cambridge before he could get to know the real me.

"Well," he said uneasily, "I was really mad. I think I could have hurt him. It wasn't a great moment. I moved away from there as soon as I got my *bac.*" The *bac* is the big test that decides whether French high school students qualify to go on to college or not, so he must have been about nineteen. Had he started living *on his own* when he was nineteen? I'd never met any French person who did that. Most seemed to live at home until at least twenty-five.

"Why did he pull a knife on you?"

"He was trying to steal this girl's moped, and I stopped him."

Lady's honor, lady's moped—it was pretty close. "Where did you move?"

"Up near République, in the Tenth. I have an apartment my stepfather helped me remodel in exchange with the landlord for a good deal on the rent."

So he had started living on his own that young. My eyebrows rose. "How old are you?"

"Twenty-four."

Twenty-four. I fooled people all the time by acting like a spoiled thirteen-year-old, but really I was twenty-seven. I changed the subject as fast as I could, before he could find out I was an older woman. I wouldn't want him to start expecting me to act mature. "So what about this one?" I touched the scar on his right wrist where it looked like he had broken a bone.

His mouth softened at my finger on his wrist, but then he realized what I was touching and coughed. "Oh. That."

"Another fight?"

"No." He cleared his throat. "That was a video game."

I choked.

"It was impossible! I couldn't manage to win it! They made the game too hard!"

"What did you do, hit the wall?" During my brothers' teenage years, I had on several occasions watched them glumly spending a Saturday morning with plaster and paint, repairing an explosion of temper.

"Yes, but it was the outside wall of the house. Concrete," he said mournfully.

I began to laugh again.

70

"I was a teenager!" he protested. "I have a lot more self-control now! And you can ask anybody about that game! Everybody will tell you they made it too hard!"

I was laughing so hard we nearly missed our change at Châtelet.

"Seriously," he said once we'd jumped off the train. He had hold of my hand and was leading the way through the crowds of moving people, letting the traffic break against his broad shoulders and keeping me in his wake. He looked over his shoulder to meet my eyes a second. "I don't get mad anymore. I just decided that wasn't the way to go. I don't even get mad about Risk, and I used to be a very poor loser."

"Oh, do you play Risk?" I said, interested. My brothers, all extremely poor losers, started me playing Risk when I was five. I grinned a little at Sébastien, provocatively. "It's a good thing you don't mind losing, then."

He raised an eyebrow at me over his shoulder. "I don't," he said and grinned cockily. "But then I don't lose," he murmured into my ear as he took my waist to pass me before him through the turnstile.

Eight

It's just because you're getting easy Mission Cards," Sébastien scowled. One best friend, Éric, slouched in his papasan chair giving me a searing look. A wiry bundle of nerves, most of them comic, Éric had failed his driver's license test the day before and was beginning to consider that my fault. Éric was the best friend whose father owned Le Relais; he was the waiter who was there all the nights Sébastien wasn't. I could only hope he didn't recognize me. Adela, one night he was waiting tables, had kept drinking half a bottle of wine and then sending it back as no good, assuring me each time that this was how French people behaved.

A second best friend, Fabien, pushed back his owl-round glasses and looked vaguely smug. Fabien was also twenty-four and already balding. Various pictures of him in mouse-ear frames decorated the apartment, thanks to his working for EuroDisney. Judging by his playing, he had not often won this game against Sébastien or Éric and was enjoying their come-uppance. The fourth in this tight circle of friends, Éric's long-term girlfriend and a part of their group since teenage years, looked thrilled. A woman so tiny she came up to *my* shoulder and had a face like a pixie, Virginie was a softie. There had been a couple of moments in the game when I might have faced a bit of a challenge if Virginie could bear to attack my weak spots, but she always chose to batter her forces against Éric's instead. I might have encouraged this choice a little by looking vulnerable every time she weighed her moves.

Vulnerability was easy, since they all seemed to think I was some kind of adorable babydoll with the cutest little accent. Every time I opened my mouth and they heard my accent, I could feel them subconsciously dividing my IQ by four. If that hadn't been so annoying, I might have let them win a couple of games to be polite.

"I don't understand this bit about Mission Cards," I said. "We used to play for world domination. I feel like I'm just getting warmed up and boom, the game's over and I've won again." I smirked.

"I don't understand how you could get so lucky three times in a row," Sébastien scowled.

"Yeah, it's amazing how that happens, isn't it?" I said drily. Luck played a clear role whenever I won against my brothers, too. "Plus, the dice were against you," I added with heavy sympathy.

He nodded, relieved I realized this. "That's true."

I slitted my eyes at him. He was cute, but he had his flaws. "It's the strangest thing the way men lose by luck and women win by it."

Éric ran a hand through his short brown curls and snorted. I felt relieved. Finally someone in this tight group of friends had understood something I said and even seemed to find it mildly humorous. All evening every joke I'd attempted had dropped like a dead weight on the conversation, with my funny accent and my inability to find just the right witty French word. They'd been very polite and encouraging about it, but kind of the way they'd be if a retarded child told a knock-knock joke.

"Men, on the other hand, only ever win by their superior skill."

Sébastien suppressed a grin. "This is true in my case," he said, straight-faced. "But of course I can't speak for all men and all women. That would be sexist."

DVDs crammed the shelves of Éric and Virginie's apartment around us. A giant plastic R2D2 phone sat on one speaker, and a newly acquired giant plastic Buzz Lightyear toy had been taken out for Sébastien to play with. I'd been expecting something a little more Art Nouveau and classy. That's what French apartments looked like in magazines. Here, fur covered most things, not as a design element but in tufts from their three animals. One of the cats had already bitten me, after snookering me into petting it for half an hour. American cats never bit me.

Magazine pullouts from different films—Frodo gazing at the Ring, Cameron Diaz winking—entirely plastered the walls of the toilet. I hadn't been able to find a sink, though, other than the one in the kitchen. Fabien had caught me snooping behind doors trying to find one, and he'd looked at me strangely, but I'd been too embarrassed to tell him what I was looking for. When I'd finally given up and used the kitchen sink, thinking I could do this discreetly, everyone had stared at me, appalled. Even Sébastien looked confused. Everybody looked away quickly, and Éric threw out a joke about something else.

Feeling like an animal that had wandered in from the barn, I folded my paws self-consciously. To be honest, in every Beauty and the Beast fantasy I had, I'd been the beauty. This was less because I considered myself a beauty than because Beast was so sexy before he turned into that wimpy prince, but still. The change of roles was discomfitting.

"You know, you can wash your hands in the bathroom sink, if you like," Sébastien breathed into my ear, under the guise of kissing me.

"Where *is* the bathroom sink?" I gritted back. "Under a poster?"

He walked with me down the hall and opened a second door I'd assumed was to a closet. Inside lay a treasure trove: not only a sink but a whole range of cleaning facilities, such as a bathtub, soap, and towels. "Where do you put the sink in American houses?" Sébastien asked, puzzled. "Not in the same room as the toilet, do you? That's disgusting."

I sighed. Why had Sébastien brought me here? What could possibly have attracted a gorgeous Frenchman to a clumsy American enough to introduce her to his friends? This group was so tightly knit. If you took the three guys from "Whose Line Is It Anyway?" added one of the female guest improvs to the mix, and had them grow up together, this foursome is what you would get. They didn't just finish each other's sentences. Someone would start saying something funny, a second person would twist it into something even more hilarious, and the third would add the last little cherry of wit that had everyone's sides splitting. This was not the kind of group to whom you brought *n'importe qui*. They were extremely nice to me, but what was I doing here? I was leaving the country in five weeks. Even if Sébastien called me "girlfriend," I was a fling.

Right? The too-good-to-be-true Sébastien and I hadn't discussed this, but I'd just been assuming.

74

"Have you told him you're leaving the country in about a month?" Valérie asked. We were sitting in the depths of a restaurant down the street from where we worked. A trellis of beams overhead featured silk vines, magenta flowers, and realistic birds in their nests. The place served a fantastic array of salads and drew a midday mob. I loathed American salads with a passion, but the things this restaurant produced were in no way similar. My favorite was chicken, avocado, palm hearts, and sweet corn on a bed of watercress. This meal could be finished off with the second best cup of hot chocolate in Paris, thick as heavy cream, dark as the real chocolate that was melted into it, and spiced with cinnamon. The owner—an eager, bitter little old woman with tight, scanty curls who dressed like Red Riding Hood's grandmother—stopped by with our pots of chocolate and more water.

"The first thing I said." I sipped my chocolate and closed my eyes a second on the lushness, breathing in chocolate and cinnamon. "When I was trying not to fall into something nasty in that toilet, I wrote, 'Do you, the most gorgeous man in Paris, want to go to a party with this clumsy, ordinary American? But don't break your heart over me, I'm about to leave the country.' Never say I'm not lacking in presumption."

"You could have told him since," Valérie reproved.

"When? A few days ago, we barely even knew each other."

"She does have to tell him," Giulia agreed with Valérie. "You're right."

"You act like he'll be traumatized when I leave," I protested. I wished we didn't have to keep talking about me leaving all the time. I'd been looking forward to it—Prague, Cambridge—and now it made my stomach feel all funny. "Do you honestly think someone that cute could fall for me?"

"Yes," Valérie said firmly. Valérie is a nice friend. "Which is why you have to warn him off."

Damn it.

"I'll tell him, I'll tell him," I said. At some point, I would.

I was having too much fun, the butterflies in my stomach couldn't settle down, and this was going too well. I decided to take control. The next time we saw each other, *my* friends were going to be there. Lots of them. Not Eva, but everybody else: noisy, difficult, and nosy, and turning this whole thing into a platonic friendly outing where no intimacy was possible and I wouldn't have to bring up Cambridge. Maybe I *should* give up on the Prague trip, as Adela had suggested. That would give me two more weeks here, and how often in my life would I meet a guy this sexy? Plus, most of my friends weren't leaving until the end of June; that would give me just a bit longer with them, too.

"So my friends and I are planning a trip to Giverny," I lied when he asked me out again. We weren't, but I'd have something arranged in a few phone calls. "Would you like to come with us?"

"Monet's gardens?" he asked. "They're supposed to be beautiful this time of year. I haven't seen them since my art class went there in grade school."

How can any American possibly compete with a European in terms of culture? As school trips, I went to see the local zoo's new gorillas. For kids who didn't have four brothers, I guess this was a fascinating rather than a redundant excursion. Sébastien, meanwhile, went to see Monet's actual gardens, designed by the artist, and source of some of the most sold notecards in the world. Come to think of it, when Sébastien heard the word "Monet," did a vision of a notecard or of a painting flash through his head? If a painting, we had a fundamental gap in our levels of civilization. I was getting better these days, what with my art history professor card and all, but I had a lot of distance to make up.

I had five friends ready to go out to Giverny that Saturday in five calls. About half an hour after the last one, Adela called back.

"But why aren't you doing something with Sébastien? You should ask him to come, too."

"He is coming," I admitted thoughtlessly.

"Oh."

I'd promised Sébastien we would meet him at the train station at noon, and Saturday morning my phone rang off the hook. Marina: "I can't make it after all. I've got a cold." Totally fake coughing.

Kam: "My fourth cousin flew into town without warning. Family is very important."

My best friend, Philippe: "Just forget it, Laura. I'm not playing buffer to your romance. Go with Sébastien and have fun."

Eva: "Laura, I heard you were organizing an outing. Why didn't you invite me?"

Adela: "I've got to study."

"Adela, you always say that, but you never study. Were you the one who told everyone Sébastien was coming?"

"I study! What are you talking about?! The professors just need to know their subject better. The questions they ask in the orals are ridiculous. They're not logical. Why would anyone have learned that?"

"Adela, I don't care about your professors! You've *got* to go! Otherwise, I'll be all alone with Sébastien."

"Oh, what a horrible shame," Adela said and hung up.

Sébastien found me in line, all by myself, in the nineteenth-century Gare St.-Lazare. *"Bonjour, crevette."* He leaned down to kiss me.

I blinked. "Are you wearing a Hawaiian shirt?"

He looked down at his short-sleeve shirt, white flowers against a black background, hanging loose over his jeans. "You don't like it?"

"Sure, but—is that legal in Paris?" If he could wear a Hawaiian shirt, why couldn't I wear feathers?

"It's black," he said. "Aren't you going to introduce me to anyone? You look like you're all by yourself."

"I have friends," I said. "I do. They just all abandoned me an hour ago."

He raised an eyebrow. When I tried to do this, I managed a rather comical curve over one eye. His eyebrow shot up into a diabolically elegant triangle. Tall, muscled, black hair, chiseled, perfect masculine face, long lashes, laughing dark eyes, and eyebrows he could raise independently . . . what the heck *was* this guy doing off a movie set? And with me?

"They wanted to leave me alone with you," I muttered, acutely uncomfortable. He was so sexy with that eyebrow, even if he was wearing a Hawaiian shirt, and I was so lame sometimes. My friends were lame. They should have come along and protected me. Okay, except for Eva, who was really dying to.

"I think I like your friends," he said and slipped an arm around my waist. "Two tickets," he told the woman behind the plastic window.

"I'll get it. It was my invitation."

He laughed and slipped his bank card across the counter. It was so annoying for him to keep paying when he had to be as broke as I was, if he was waiting tables nights to pay for school. I would have to pay with a card, too, but at least I was going to win the lottery one of these days. The immaculately coiffed, anorexic clerk stopped scowling at the sight of him and tried to catch his eye. "And it was a great idea, *crevette*."

At the second use of *crevette*, I finally paid attention. *Crevette* meant—shrimp. My friends had thought this was a hilarious joke when I was in grade school, too. I had never really hit my growth spurt. "I am not a *crevette*," I said firmly.

His mouth twitched. "Well, it's not like you're very big."

I gave him The Look. "Find another nickname."

"Hmm." He gave the clerk a friendly smile that made her swoon over onto the counter at an angle highlighting her cleavage. Oblivious, he typed his code into the machine she slid toward him—her breasts thrust up—and took the tickets. "What is *crevette* in English?"

"None of your business."

"Shrump. Isn't it 'shrump'?"

"I am not a shrump!" I exclaimed.

"It's not an *insult*." He dropped his arm from my waist to my hand and led the way to the quay. "It's what we call little children, like cute, tiny toddlers."

"You are deeply annoying me."

"I can tell. Do you know your nose gets all pink when you're annoyed? Just like a shrump." And he *pinched* it. I tried to bite his fingers off, but he was too quick for me.

"It does not!!"

"Okay, it's also often pink when you're not annoyed." He grinned down at me sideways, that melting fondue look in his eyes. "Little pinky shrump," he whispered.

I glowered and felt all excited inside.

Giverny was beautiful. It was stunning. It was like dancing under a shower of rose petals. The tulips were just fading, so there wasn't a single rose yet blooming in Monet's gardens, but it was like that still. It was sunny again and just at the cool limit of the balmy range. I couldn't figure out if it was sunny so much these days because it was May, or because nature had a crush on Sébastien. The latter was entirely possible.

We took the train to Vernon, and the bus from Vernon to Giverny to join the crowds of people flocking into these gardens. Flowers were everywhere: pink, white, yellow, blue, purple, more flowers even than people. Monet's prolific painting must have been a continual exercise in frustration, as the artist tried to capture what he gardened. Light played through the leaves and petals and dappled onto people and the water. Lilacs scented the air. Bees buzzed in the wisteria that curled around the Pont Japonais and dangled in thick clusters toward our faces. We sat on a bench under rhododendrons heavy with red-pink flowers until an older lady walked by and gave our bench an envious look. Sébastian leapt up to offer her our place. Long weeping branches of willow caught in my hair as we walked, and Sébastien caught the willow strands and eased them loose. The water reflected puffy white clouds and blue sky in a half-tarnished mirror. Azaleas of all colors surrounded us. A drunk and ecstatic yellow butterfly landed on the back of Sébastien's hand as he leaned against the bridge railing. He froze, thrilled, grabbing my arm with his non-butterfly-sanctuary hand and then pointing at his prize to make sure I appreciated the beauty of this moment.

When we left, we got ice cream cones from the vendor just outside the entrance and climbed high up a hill above the gardens. Grass grew thick and green well past our knees. Sébastien waded into it, while I held back. "It's warm enough for snakes to be out. Are you crazy or just from the city? Don't be wading into knee-high grass."

"There aren't any poisonous snakes in France. Well, there's one, but it's very rare and mostly in the south. Come on." He tugged on my hand. And for the first time in my life, I found myself wading through high grass without a dog to sniff snakes out and a stick to poke first. I felt as if I were in a book. People waded through high grass in books, but I always thought it was because the author was stupid, not because the books were set in Europe.

Sébastien stretched out the jackets we had carried just in case the temperature dropped, and we lay down on top of them, gazing down at Monet's pink house and the gardens. The sun was warm. We didn't talk much. Sébastien tucked my head against his chest and tickled me from time to time with a blade of grass or played with my hair, spreading it across his chest lock by lock. I fell asleep wrapped in a smell of vanilla, crushed grass, and springtime, with fingers running through my hair.

We woke from the chill. The sun was angling in the west, and "Shoot!" I sat up abruptly. Sébastien stirred and blinked up at me sleepily. "The last bus! It leaves at six!"

Sébastien took my wrist and checked my watch. "It left at six," he corrected. "We missed it. Laura, what is this giant plastic watch you're wearing? You need something small and elegant for your wrist."

It was a man's watch, one of those designed to resist multiple Gs and tell the time all around the world. I loved it. The ability to tell time all around the world was vital to my self-image, even if that feature didn't work right. "You don't think it makes me look tough and like I can handle anything?"

He made a slight, strangled sound and smoothed his lips out.

"The contrast of the chunky masculine on my delicate, feminine wrist doesn't hold visceral appeal?"

He said nothing. His lips trembled a bit at the corners.

Damn it. He probably went out with me for the comic relief provided by my sense of fashion. "Let's just stay focused," I growled. "We've got to find a way to get back to Paris."

We hunted through tiny Giverny for a way back to Vernon, the nearest town with a train station, and finally ended up walking the three miles to it. It wasn't a bad walk, even if I could have used a nice pair of American tennis shoes instead of my flimsy, sexy sandals about then. We did it hand in hand. When we got back, we still had three hours to wait for the only remaining train that day, so we walked along the river. There we fell asleep again, Sébastien keeping an arm firm around me because I was getting cold. We woke surrounded by gnats with big drops of rain plopping down on us. As the drops turned into a downpour, we ran across the bridge to the train station. Soaked, we sought refuge in a café across from the station.

"Pear juice!" Sébastien exclaimed at the menu. "I love pear juice." So I ordered it, too, and we drank sweet, thick pear juice while the roof developed a huge hole, and water poured through it, and pooled on the floor, rising closer and closer to our table. The café owner seemed to take this interior deluge in stride, although the waiter grew exasperated and kept trying to stem the flood with a perfectly inadequate bucket. Our train arrived before the café drowned, and we caught it back to Paris.

Sébastien didn't want me to take the Métro back to my place by myself at night, so he came with me, then of course came into my apartment and missed the last Métro back. He slept on my twin bed, somehow fitting me in with him. Really—he slept. Or I slept, and he kind of did. I'm not saying there wasn't a little bit of playing going on, because he refused to sleep with his shirt on, and as I've mentioned before, he had a gorgeous body. But I was getting in so over my head.

"I'm scared," I said. "I'm not ready for this."

So he finally wedged himself against the wall, since I was claustrophobic, and tucked me against him so I didn't fall onto the floor. I loved it, to spend the night tucked against those frequently tense and beautifully defined muscles. I don't think he slept much at all.

Nine

You've got the most uncomfortable bed in the whole world," he said the next morning. "And I want a shower and a toothbrush. Come back to my apartment?"

I folded my arms under my breasts. His eyes flickered down and promptly back to my face. "I don't think that's a good idea."

"Coward," he said without heat. "I'd kiss you, but without a toothbrush, that could be ugly. See you this afternoon?"

I couldn't go. I tried to get dressed and fumbled things and called my best friend, Philippe, to tell me how to dress. Super tall and thin, with the bluest eyes in the world and a nerdy charm that had slain the entire female population of the Maison du Canada, Philippe had told me he was gay a couple of days after we met at the start of the school year but sworn me to secrecy. We had spent the first four months at the house letting everyone there assume we were seeing each other, something that worked well for both of us. It upped *my* rep no end, since he was one of the cutest guys there, and cut out some of the more careless hook-up attempts. Meanwhile, no one thought to wonder about his orientation. A couple of months ago, he had finally relaxed and let the secret out. "And you know what," he had told me, stunned, "even Jack," a dorm resident who cracked homophobic jokes regularly, "only shrugged and said, 'That's cool.' "

"I told you," I answered. "Jack's not the problem. He's homophobic, misogynistic, and occasionally misanthropic, but basically he's a nice guy. *Adela*'s the problem. She's still mad at me for not telling her."

He had just laughed. Clearly he didn't realize how dangerous it could be to have Adela mad at me. Probably the whole setup at the restaurant, asking Sébastien out, was Adela's diabolic revenge.

"So what's wrong?" he asked now. "You know, someone made a poem about *torrides fesses* on your door." Torrid tushes.

I glanced at it. A niece had sent me one of those magnet poetry games in French, and I'd tried to weed out any words that could be used for pornography before I put it on a magnet board on my dorm door. Every couple of days I had to weed out a few more words. It was just amazing the combinations people could come up with. I began to suspect there was another set of words in the house and people were adding them when I wasn't around. "You wrote that, didn't you?"

"Well, I might have." He smirked and pushed back his rectangular glasses. "I'm a natural poet."

"Come in and tell me what to wear."

"You are such a stereotyper," he grinned. "You know, just because I'm gay doesn't mean I have a better fashion sense than you. Why don't you ask Adela?"

"Because your favorite color is blue, too, so you might let me wear it." He was wearing blue now, in fact, a deep blue pressed cotton shirt that matched his eyes almost exactly and made him look even cuter. It had been a lot of fun letting everyone assume we were together. Fun and *safe*.

Deep blue matched my eyes almost exactly, too, a fact that seemed to go entirely unnoticed here. I handed him his favorite peach-flavored candy, sent me by family from Georgia, and sat down on the uncomfortable wooden chair in front of my laptop, while he took the bed.

"So how's it going with Sébastien?" he asked. "Has he shown any signs of being curious about homosexuality?"

"Will you stop?"

"What? I'm just checking. I'd hate to waste a guy that cute."

"Yeah, you know, you and a whole bevy of females think that when they see him with me."

He raised his eyebrows. "Hey. You do all right."

I'm just surrounded by people who lavish me with praise, I'm telling you. When dating a sex god, a girl does not need to hear she "does all right," even if it's true. "So what do you think I should wear? This top—close your eyes"—I turned my back and did a quick change, trying to concentrate on clothes—"or this top?"

"The black one," he said. "Definitely. But straighten the neckline."

"Damn it. What's wrong with the blue sweater?"

"Black is more neutral. Do you have a necklace or something that will go with it? When are you meeting him?"

I glanced at my watch and swallowed. "In fifteen minutes."

Another lift of his eyebrows. "You're going to be late."

"Yeah," I said. Then I burst into tears.

"Oh, boy." He pressed his tail more firmly into the bed and gripped the edge of it with both hands, deeply uncomfortable. "What's wrong?"

"I don't know what to do! I'm leaving in a month. He's just so—okay, so I won't go to Prague. That's fine. But that only gives us two more weeks!"

"Have you paid for Cambridge, then?" he checked, surprised. "You didn't tell me."

"No." I sniffed and rubbed a finger under my nose.

Philippe glanced at my hand and looked pained. If I got anywhere near him with it, he'd be bolting for disinfectant. "Are you going to go to Cambridge?"

"I don't know!" I wailed. "Even if I don't, I've *still* got to leave by mid-August. I'm in the middle of my degree! So what good does it do to put off leaving for six more weeks? It will just make things worse!"

"I don't know." He stared at me. Long-term commitment was not part of our dorm way of life. We all knew we were only here for a school year. This was the year of the fling, the year of the hookup, whether you thought a fling was a kiss, as Adela did, or whether you thought it was a lot more, as most of the rest of the people in the house did. "Maybe you're getting in over your head."

"Right," I said. "Right."

Someone knocked hard and stepped inside without waiting for an answer. "Hi," Adela said. "Laura, did you know there's a poem about hot midnight flesh on your door?"

"Hey!" Philippe protested. "Did you steal *torride* from my poem?"

She spied the blue sweater dropped on my desk. "Laura, what is this? Were you thinking of wearing blue again? I can't leave you for a second, can I?" She broke off. "Are you crying?"

"She's thinking about not going to Cambridge," Philippe said reservedly. Philippe and Adela associated a lot, via me, but they had never embraced each other 100 percent. Maybe there wasn't room for two best friends in one woman's tiny dorm room. Also, only children such as Philippe had more trouble adjusting to Adela than I did. I had four older brothers and two sisters. The older sister could eat all four brothers *and* Adela for breakfast and still need chocolate and a Dr Pepper to wake her up. And people wondered why I'd spent half my adult life on the other side of the world.

Adela stared at me. Her brows shot down to form a thicket. "You're crazy," she said flatly. "Change your plans for a *man*? He's French!"

"You know, he was French before you made me ask him out, too. I just mention it."

If I expected Adela to recognize her own words thrown back at her, I underestimated her. "That's different! I didn't tell you to change your plans for him!" Also, as Adela's exams approached and papers came due, she was getting in more and more fights with her professors, a fact she blamed on them being French and out to get her.

"You told me to change my plans for *you!* You said not to go to Prague because you would still be in Paris."

"Laura. This is a guy. I'm your *best friend.*"

Philippe raised his eyebrows and slanted her a glance. Adela caught that, but she had a crush on him, so only smiled at him humbly and apologetically. Then she slanted me a mean look for daring to let Philippe think he was as important to me as she was.

"Anyway, I didn't say I was going to change my plans for him! I said I didn't know what to do." I started crying again.

"Will you *quit* that?" Philippe said uncomfortably. "Listen, can you just go have fun and quit thinking about changing your life? *Go to Cambridge.* Prague, it's up to you; you can do that some other time. But Cambridge is a once-in-a-lifetime opportunity. Sébastien is only a fling. A fling, by definition, ends. And can you get in touch with this guy somehow? Because there is no way you're going to get there on time."

I was forty-five minutes late. I didn't think he'd be there. Why would he be there still? But when I crossed the street from the café to the fountain, with no bus driver this time to egg me on, he was standing by a sphinx. One hand was in his pocket, and the other held a cigarette down by his thigh. He was gazing off in the other direction, face set and unhappy.

He turned and saw me almost right away, and his face lightened with relief. He started to smile but then didn't. He searched my face, his own somber, and he didn't ask what had kept me.

"I couldn't decide what to wear," I said. "I was talking with friends and lost track of time."

He nodded and smoked his cigarette, which was another flaw he had. Other than his being French, I'd found two. Then he took my hand and we descended the steps to the lower quay. Instant calm enveloped us, down below the sounds of traffic and the honks of horns, down here where no one was in a hurry. Hurried people did not take the lower Seine route. The smell of urine wafted out to us from under the nearest bridge, and we held our breaths as we passed through the tunnel of stench into the brightness beyond, upwind. Between the bridges, on the cobblestoned quays, the breeze was clean. The diesel smell of the trucks above had been reduced here to the occasional whiff from passing barges, blending with the heavy, wet smell of the river. It was another nice day. Paris was just busting her little heart out to give us nice days all of a sudden. You'd think she would have spent some effort trying to lure me in a lot earlier in the year, not just before I was due to leave.

One road did permit car traffic on the lower quay, but it was Sunday and that road had been closed to traffic, freeing the paved part for skaters, pedestrians, and cyclists. "Do you know how to in-line skate?" Sébastien asked.

"No." There could be few good reasons for that question. I gave him a wary look.

"It's the best way to explore Paris. You'd love it. You could come with Éric and Fabien and me some nights."

"I'd have to learn first." I did not have good memories of wheels on my feet. I'd tried skating once, before in-line skates were invented, in third grade for somebody's skating rink birthday party. I could still remember that party as one blur of strobe lights, repeated playing of "Celebration," bruises, and that wood floor. Pretty much all I had seen of that party was the floor when I fell face forward, the disco ball when I fell on my butt, other people's skates narrowly missing my head, and occasionally the tush of a friend who allowed me to hang on to her to try to learn balance. I think there had been cake at some point, blessedly allowing me to escape the floor for fifteen minutes without seeming a sissy.

"That could be fun," he nodded. "Maybe sometime this summer."

I flexed my hand in his and hunched. "I'm supposed to be leaving," I blurted out.

He stopped as if he'd run into a wall. There was a second where he didn't say anything and didn't move, and then he turned. "What? I thought you were going to school here and working."

"No, I'm going to school back home in the U.S. They just sent me here for a year. And the year's up June seventeenth."

He stared at me. "That's in three weeks."

I hunched my shoulders further and kicked a cobblestone. "I know." Couples passed us two by two, old and dressed in layers, in their forties and elegant, teenage and in jeans that showed the boy's underpants, which were made of more cloth than the girl's top.

"Why didn't you tell me this?" Sébastien asked.

"I didn't think it *mattered.*"

He dropped my hand. He looked as if I'd just slapped him.

"I mean, we've just barely started going out." Tears started to leak from my eyes, right there in public. "And I wanted to go to

Cambridge. I'm lousy at relationships. I'm just no good at this."

"Why did you even agree to go out with me if you knew you were leaving so soon?" Peripherally, I noted he still thought he was the one who had asked me out.

"Because you're so cute." I sniffled, tears leaking down my face. "I thought you'd be a jerk."

"A *jerk?* Why?"

"Because you're so cute!" How could he not understand this?

"You judged me before you even met me? Just based on my looks? Why did you go out with me at all, then?"

"Because you're so cute!" I yelled. "But I just assumed it wouldn't become much of anything because you're too cute to be anything but a jerk."

His jaw set. I leaked more tears. He hesitated, but then sat me down on a stone bench under a scanty-leaved poplar tree and gave the people eyeing my public tears a cool look. He gave me an even cooler one.

"The only reason you didn't judge me is because you didn't *notice* me!" I protested. "If I hadn't left you that invitation, you never would have realized I existed."

"What are you talking about? You came there nearly every day. Of course I knew who you were."

I did not go there every day. I might have gone there several times a week, but it was not every day. "Then why didn't you ask me out?!"

"I did ask you out."

"*Before* I left you an invitation," I said between my teeth. "You didn't even flirt with me."

He frowned, completely baffled by me. "You were a client. I didn't want to harass you. I'm not such a *jerk* as to hit on you when all you wanted to do was enjoy a nice meal."

What a feeble excuse. The French didn't object to sexual harassment. I knew because Valérie was always rolling her eyes over lawsuits that got reported in the "make fun of the U.S." column in

Le Courrier. Plus, someone as cute as he was could not possibly believe any woman would object to him flirting with her. "I bet you don't even remember the first time I came there," I challenged.

"Sure I do. You were with a part Asian girl."

My jaw dropped. Tory was actually Mexican American, but she did have an Asian look to her, especially if you weren't used to seeing as many Hispanics as Asians. "Do you remember what I was wearing?"

He shrugged. "Something black. You always wear black."

I thought about mentioning that I would wear blue if people would let me, but that might be too risky at this stage in our relationship. "I have black leather pants." Listen, when a woman owns black leather pants, she has to work it into the conversation any way she can.

He smiled a little. "Well, that would be nice to see." He stopped smiling abruptly. "Forget it. I can't believe you didn't tell me you were leaving in three weeks." He gazed at my face a long moment and then shook his head. "Shit." He turned, pressing his hands against the hard angle of the bench, and stared out over the Seine. *"Putain de merde."*

I sniffled. An awkwardly tall man, dreadlocks twisted into a turban around his head, clothes faded and baggy, came up and said something to me I couldn't understand. He seemed to be asking me if I wanted *du shit.* What? Sébastien answered quietly, shaking his head.

"Are you sure?" The man glanced at me.

"Yes, give us some room."

The man shrugged and slouched on.

"What?" I demanded.

"He was trying to sell you drugs." Sébastien brushed the incident away with a hand.

Me? I scrubbed at my eyes, taking that personally. The dealer had looked at Sébastien, with his earrings and tattoo and tough, unshaved look, and decided that *I* was the more likely drug buyer? Did I look like I was suffering from withdrawal or did the man just think a joint would do me a world of good?

Sébastien went back to staring out over the Seine. A *peniche* or houseboat crawled past on the brown river, a little blue Fiat locked in place on top of it. A red Converse shoe bobbed in its wake.

"I don't know if I *will* go," I whispered. "To Cambridge. But the thing is, even if I don't, I have to go back to the U.S. in mid-August. I have to finish my degree."

There was a long silence. Sébastien picked up my hand and studied it. He matched our palms so that mine grew very small against his, the tips of my nails reaching to just halfway between the creases of his knuckles. I noticed my pale polish was chipped, and my skin was dry and could really stand some lotion. Somebody who deserved to be in this story would have had a perfect manicure and silken skin. His hand looked large and dark around mine, already bronzing from the few days of summer sunlight. His hand flexed and closed around mine, and he stood. "Let's go get something to eat. I didn't have lunch; I fell asleep when I got back to my apartment."

Ten

We walked up to the rue des Rosiers, not because there weren't closer places to eat, but because any excuse was a good excuse to walk through the Marais and eat falafel.

"Falafel?" Sébastien asked.

"I didn't know what it was either before I moved here," I confessed. "Of course, I grew up in a small town in Georgia, so I don't know what your excuse is. It's good. At least it's good at the place we're going."

"No, I know what falafel is." Darn. If only I could keep my mouth shut, I might occasionally impress someone with my sophistication. "I'm just not sure why we would go out of our way to eat it. I was thinking we would just grab a sandwich from somewhere near the Seine."

"I'm trying to show you a culinary landmark of your city," I said. "Cooperate. Besides, why would you eat ordinary food when there's fantastic food within a couple kilometers' walk?"

I usually had no trouble in the Marais. It was one of my favorite places to walk: not only was it beautiful, but in the heart of this quarter no man ever commented on or tried to grab my breasts, my ass, my smile, or any other part of my person. Today, though, I got a few chilly looks for being so *gonflée,* that is having the nerve to bring such a cute guy into Paris's gay quarter while holding his hand and flaunting his heterosexuality. This was the only part of Paris where men walked hand in hand without hesitation, and we passed some extremely fashionable couples eating up the sidewalks with long, aggressive strides. Café tables spilled into our path, always a few feet beyond the café's government permit, and chalkboard menus stood between the short iron posts protecting the sidewalks from the street. These posts were set close enough together to prevent a car from parking between them, as no Parisian would hesitate to do should the space be free. Mopeds, however, could fit between the posts nicely; and here a bright yellow one, there a red tucked against a post as a backdrop to a menu. A Parisian mother walked by: super slim, with four-inch stiletto thigh-high leather boots, a black skirt with metallic pink dots glinting in a decorative splash near the hem, her hair dyed ash-blond and held back in a ponytail, her baby in a little black carrier at her chest, her head bent down to the child as she smiled and cooed while she walked.

We passed a house from the 1500s, tall and half-timbered; a seventeenth-century turreted mansion; a boutique featuring colorful lava lamps, bizarre chairs, and other kitsch and wildly modern things that baffled me but apparently not the throng of shoppers inside. Posters covered the burgundy front of a theater, advertising its plays and comedians. Someone was trying to start a milk bar, in tones of white and ice cream pastels. A milk bar? Well, come to think of it, it made a lot more sense than the water bars that were currently in style among society's absurd. I checked the menu, but it did not, in fact, serve fresh, creamy milk from different cows raised on different grass in different regions, which I would certainly have stopped to taste. No, it was mostly milk shakes and yogurt, and I snorted and continued on. I'd spent months trying to get a good milk shake in this city. I'd pleaded with the people making them; I'd shared the recipe; I'd paid extra. I'd gone to Baskin-Robbins, where you would think the staff would have been trained in the great American milk shake way. All to no avail. Eight ounces of milk and one minuscule scoop of ice cream in a blender do not a good milk shake make, although the combination does give you some fairly sweet, flavored half-and-half. I gave the Marais' Baskin-Robbins an embittered look as we passed it. Why put something that ridiculously pink in such grandiose surroundings if you can't get a good milk shake out of it?

Grandiose our surroundings indeed were. The fashionable quarter of France's golden age under Louis XIV, the Marais featured the greatest density of magnificent seventeenth-century mansions in Paris and was a shopaholic's fantasy of expensive boutiques. It had also been a Jewish quarter for nearly a millennium, and a conservative Jewish enclave remained in perfectly functioning symbiosis with the more recent gay residents. Thus the rue des Rosiers curved in a narrow arc filled with restaurants selling falafel through their windows, bakeries with pastries and breads of types never seen anywhere else in Paris, colored storefronts with Hebrew printed neatly in the windows. The line wasn't too bad in front of L'As du Fallafel for once. The name means "the Ace of Fallafel" but, in a beautiful play on words, also sounds like "Sick of Fallafel"—something that might express its highly successful owner's feelings some days. L'As du Fallafel is reputed to have the best falafel in Paris; some, in extremes of hyperbole, claim the best falafel in the world. Myself, I wavered between L'As du Fallafel where the brusque staff did indeed reveal how heartily sick they were of serving falafel to tourists through their window, and a neighboring rival with crispier eggplant. We went for L'As du Fallafel this time so that Sébastien could start with the most famous.

We ordered the *spécial*—three balls of falafel, cabbage, humus, grilled eggplant, and a special sauce—stuffed our bag with plenty of napkins, and headed back to the Seine. I was starving, but it would never have crossed Sébastien's mind to eat while walking or standing in the street. It would cross my mind, but if I actually yielded to the urge, I wouldn't be able to stick my nose up at other Americans in Paris. The potential for snobbery is a very important social control for those of us who lack willpower. "Let's go to the Île de la Cité," he said.

The Île de la Cité is not at the end of the world from the rue des Rosiers, but neither is it the closest park in Paris. I smiled. "Is that your favorite place?"

"I like it," he acknowledged. "It's calm. You're right in the heart of Paris and yet you're out of the city."

So we went to the Île de la Cité again. Neither of us had jackets this time, so Sébastien inspected the paving stones for the spot with the least pigeon poop and gave it to me, sacrificing his jeans on the less clean spot beside it.

After the first bite, he gave me a look of surprised respect. "You're right. It is good."

"Of course, I'm right. Try to remember that you may be the Frenchman, but you're the one who likes fast food."

He grinned and leaned back against the wall of the park that was raised slightly above the Île de la Cité quay. "Sometimes you just want junk." He took another bite.

Not even a drop of sauce curled over the back of his hand. "How do you do that?" I sighed. Bits of cabbage littered the ground around me, attracting interested pigeons, and sauce streamed toward my wrists.

His lips trembled. "How do you manage *that*?" he asked, gazing at my hands. I clung two-fisted to my pocket of falafel, trying to keep the thing in one piece.

I tried to lick a drop off my wrist before it could drip on my skirt. I failed. "*Everybody* makes a mess with falafel!" I protested. "It's famous!"

"Ah," he said and took another neat bite. Nothing dripped; nothing smeared on his lips or fingers.

"Did you get as much sauce as I did?" I asked suspiciously.

He studied the total mess I was making of myself and shook his head, bemused. "It's all in the way you bite."

Great, now I had to obsess over whether I was biting into my food correctly. This never happened when I dated people from my hometown. "Go—away," I said in a mean voice to a pigeon, venting. It eyed me sideways and waddled its fat gray butt closer to the cabbage. "Shoo!" I made an abrupt movement with my arm, losing a bit more cabbage in the process, and it fluttered up to land again a couple of yards away, watching and biding its time. Another pigeon came to join it. "Go over to Notre-Dame. I'm sure you'll find plenty of tourists willing to feed you for the privilege of having you perch on their arms for a picture." I shuddered. I don't let sewer rats crawl on me, and I don't let city pigeons do it, either.

"Yes, shoo it away," Sébastien agreed. "It's scaring the sparrows." He ripped off a crumb from his pita pocket and tossed it a foot or so from him. A little brown sparrow with dirty feathers pounced on it at once and hopped back an inch, eyeing Sébastien as a promising mark.

Sébastien tore off another bite and held it forward on the tips of his fingers.

I gave him an appalled look. "Are you going to let it *touch* you?"

"If it's not too shy," he said. "Look, I think it might come to me." He made a coaxing noise, crumb perfectly still on his outstretched fingers.

"It's filthy!"

"It's a sparrow, not a pigeon. Look at how cute he is."

Funny, I was thinking the same thing about him, sitting there with his hand outstretched trying to will a sparrow to him. "Look at how dirty its feathers are. I don't see how it could be any cleaner than pigeons, when it lives in the same city off the same things."

"You're scaring him with your negative attitude. Here you go, *petit.*" He clicked his tongue.

I coughed loudly, and the sparrow flittered back and eyed me cautiously.

Sébastien gave me a severe look.

"I'm just trying to protect your health."

"If I can survive taking the Métro every day, I can survive a sparrow." He tossed more crumbs to lure it back and then proffered another on his fingers. The sparrow crept back up, eyeing the crumb brightly.

"So let's do something tomorrow," he said while the sparrow ate from his fingers. I blinked. Tomorrow was Monday, and he should be in classes most of the day. "And the next day."

I studied him. He had his head bent, his concentration seemingly all on the tiny, half-tamed, filthy sparrow.

"You're leaving soon, and we've got to take advantage of every minute, don't you think?" he said. "I'll skip some of my classes."

A Bateau-Mouche, or one of its rivals, crept past, "La Vie en Rose" warbling from its speakers. *Quand il me prend dans ses bras, il me parle tout bas, je vois la vie en rose.* Tourists waved at us, as usual. I waved back, since I knew what it was like to want to be welcomed by this city. I took a deep breath and nudged

Sébastien with pseudo-confidence as if I flirted all the time, as if I knew this would be well received, which I didn't. "I think you should give me a kiss."

He hesitated a second. Despite what he'd just said, maybe he was still thinking about my imminent departure.

"Seriously," I blundered on. "It will make them really happy."

He glanced at the Bateau-Mouche. One eyebrow went up in that perfect triangle again. "You want me to kiss you to make tourists happy?"

I nodded firmly.

He rolled his eyes but then smiled a little and leaned in and kissed me. The Bateau-Mouche crowd cheered, cameras clicking like crazy.

In my room later, I stared at the Cambridge form for a long time. I just couldn't do it. I couldn't sign it and leave. It was the thing I had always most feared about relationships—that they would tie me down, cut off my options for travel—but I couldn't just walk away now. What did Cambridge have to offer that was better than this?

I checked off the box that said, No, I won't be able to come, and stuffed it in an envelope. That gave us another six weeks. We had ten weeks in all. Then I would be back in the U.S.

Eleven

So have you ... ?" Adela waggled her eyebrows.

This from a woman who had made a two-month scandal out of kissing someone. Or when Adela waggled her eyebrows lasciviously like that, did she mean a kiss? I didn't want to expose myself to possible judgment of my morals by asking. I was raised a strict Catholic, too, darn it. "Adela! He's French!"

"I know." She frowned. "Tell me again why you asked a Frenchman out? It doesn't seem like a very smart thing to do. I thought you were going to come back to Spain next year and meet some of my cousins." We were in Adela's room, where suitcases lay open on the floor. She had started packing, her school year over except for her exams. It gave me a queasy feeling in the pit of my stomach to see things disappearing off her wall into her suitcases. There were the lion masks Adela had insisted we make out of orange construction paper for some Dutch house party where we were supposed to wear orange in honor of the Dutch holiday called Queen's Day. All the other students there had just put on a bit of amber jewelry or an orange scarf or ignored the rule entirely. Disgusted, Adela had given them all a lion glare. "The Dutch," she had said. "We should have known they couldn't have any fun." Then she'd handed me her mask and pretended dressing as lions had been my idea.

"That's not what I'm talking about! The French! They have a whole kiss named after them! They're internationally legendary lovers! I'm not exposing myself to that kind of inferiority complex."

She squinted at me, as if she were trying to peer through my skull bones to find the missing cog. "You are so weird."

I am *not* weird. Why do people say that all the time about me? "So, Adela, if you had only a couple months with someone, would you, um . . . ?" I tried to waggle my eyebrows and Adela handed me a Kleenex.

"Go ahead and sneeze," she said. "It's the packing. It's stirring up a lot of dust."

I'd never been very good with my eyebrows. Sébastien's, on the other hand, were beautifully expressive. Darn it, every single comparison between us was revealing. "So . . . you know," I said, in lieu of eyebrow-messaging. I didn't want to come right out and say it, in case we were just talking about a kiss. "Would you?"

Wait, I told myself, you're asking advice from a woman who eats luxury displays and makes you dress up as a lion for a student party. Even you can't be that insecure!

"Of course not!" Adela said indignantly. "My father's daughter? But you're an American." She shrugged dismissively and handed me one of the lion masks to keep as a souvenir.

"So have you . . . ?" Philippe waggled his eyebrows. He had finer, more aristocratic eyebrows than Adela, so this made for a much less frightening leer. Philippe was packing, too, his Québec fleur-de-lys flag behind him, filling the wall over his bed.

"Philippe!" I have no privacy. "I'm still leaving in a couple more months, and there's no way out of that. I don't want to get any more involved and any more hurt."

"So if I correctly understand you, you gave up Cambridge to waste this chance, too?"

I glared at him. "You know what? You try acting consistently in this same situation! It's not that easy!"

"I wouldn't get in this same situation." He handed me a bag with four bottles of maple syrup in it. "There's no point me taking them back to Québec. And you'll be staying here, so I thought maybe you could use them. You remember the crêpe recipe I told you, right?"

"Right," I said glumly, staring at the syrup. I wondered if he really imagined me making crêpes Sunday mornings for my solitary self, in woeful imitation of all the crêpe breakfasts Philippe had sponsored for laughing groups of us.

Sébastien, who could do a pretty good eyebrow-waggle when he wanted to, grinned and didn't. Instead he asked me up for dinner in his apartment. Not being naïve, I braced expectantly for a little pressure. The great thing about pressure is you can do whatever you want with it: be turned off, since who likes to be pressured; or succumb in a moment of weakness.

His apartment was a minuscule place only about twice as big as his bed. It held a computer for his graphic artwork in one corner, a tiny kitchenette in another, and a lot of fur. It also smelled strongly of products used to clean and mask cat urine. The fluffy culprit yowled, then catapulted from one wall to the window and nearly over the wrought-iron railing to plummet six floors to his death before Sébastien caught him by the nape of the neck and hauled him back inside. He sighed, gazing at the striped beige demonball of fur with a mixture of affection and complete aggravation. "It was either take him or let him be put to sleep. What was I supposed to do?" He sniffed the air, sighed again, glared at his cat, and lit some incense.

"I'm just going to slip into something more comfortable. I've been in these clothes all day," he said and changed into a pressed white shirt. Apparently he was just too exhausted to button it, because he left it hanging open while he worked at the stove. He was making a simple pasta carbonara with *crème fraîche* and *petits lardons*. *Petits lardons* are something like bacon and something like ham but better than both for pasta carbonara purposes. "Could you help set the floor?" he asked. The apartment didn't have room for a table. "The dishes are right there." He nodded to a cupboard directly over his head.

Nobody ever built cupboards for normal-sized people like me. I had to stretch up on my tiptoes, and since he didn't move away from his sauce, my whole body brushed against his. He put out a hand to steady me and concentrated on his cooking. "The silverware is in there." He nodded to the drawer that was partly blocked by his hips. To reach it, I had to squeeze my arm between his body and the kitchenette. Muscles and shirt grazed against my arm as I did so, and the breeze from the window stirred the hairs on the back of my neck. He smiled a little, but he focused on the sauce. Was he *shy* about the fact that he was deliberately seducing me?

"You're doing this on purpose," I muttered.

"What?" He raised his eyebrows innocently. Then he looked out the window, and I swear he blushed a little. But he didn't button his shirt.

"Nothing."

After dinner, which proved to be delicious, he stood at the window railing, smoking a cigarette that he kept extended out of the apartment with one hand. The white shirt parted and fluttered against his flat stomach in the breeze from the noisy street outside. He made no move on me whatsoever the whole evening.

That was *fiendish* behavior. And he calculated all that. Every single part of it, except for the killer touch of shyness. That man played dirty. If I had even a modicum of emotional courage, I'd never have made it out of there.

I don't have any emotional courage, of course.

He took me back to my apartment. "Coward," he whispered after he finished kissing me there, before turning around and taking the Métro all the way back to his place again.

Okay, I breathed, kind of like I was practicing Lamaze. I could do this. I should do this—*carpe noctem*. Maybe the next time. I dressed particularly nicely as I'd been doing in extreme self-consciousness ever since I met him. "Let's go have dinner with my friends again," he said. "I want you to get to know them better."

Oh, boy. His friends seemed nice, and very funny, but having dinner with them a second time was still nerve-wracking. They'd been best friends most of their lives. What was he going to do for an encore, make me have dinner with his family? Surely not. I mean, the weekend before, he'd had to go to his uncle's PACS celebration, which was a *"pacte civil de solidarité,"* a wedding for same-sex couples, and he'd mentioned having me come along. But a brother of mine and his wife had happened to pass through Paris on a flying twenty-four-hour visit the same weekend, so I'd been able to duck both the PACS and having my family meet or find out about Sébastien. It was best to keep these two worlds safely separate.

In a soccer field near Éric and Virginie's apartment in their reasonably decent *banlieue* of Paris, the guys tried to throw boomerangs for a while with complete lack of success. Éric had just failed his driver's license a second time and needed something to console him besides Fabien's and Sébastien's open mockery. Then we took baguettes, ham, butter, and cheese out onto a pier in the canal. The water was dark and quiet, lapping against the pilings. I huddled against the rapidly chilling evening and gazed at the sky. Faint and far off a star showed, probably a planet, everything else faded out by the dull night sky over Paris.

"So I've got a game for you, Laura," Éric said.

I blinked, coming back from the quiet fringes of this evening. Sébastien kept a hand on some part of me at pretty much all times, and the others did try to include me, but despite my best efforts I kept drifting back out to the outskirts of this tight little group and all their fast-paced, slang-filled jokes. "All right." From his tone, it sounded like a game Éric thought he could win. Virginie gave him a tolerant look, confirming my impression. So he wanted revenge for Risk.

"I start a sentence with one word. The next person repeats my word and adds the second word. And we keep going around until only one person is left who can remember all the words."

I slid him a glance and didn't say anything.

"Claire used to be really good at this, remember?" he asked the group at large.

Virginie kicked him. Fabien pushed his glasses up on his nose and turned to me. "More to drink, Laura?"

I looked at all of them. Sébastien's face was carefully neutral. "Who's Claire?"

Everyone gave me a surprised look, including Sébastien. "His old girlfriend," Éric said. "They were together for six years. We all grew up together. You didn't know about her?"

Let me get this straight: there had once been five people in this intimate group, and the fifth person had been Sébastien's girlfriend? Whom he'd been with *six* years? He was only twenty-four. Six years was most of his dating life.

"We broke up about four years ago, *crevette*," Sébastien said. "I never mentioned her?" No, he hadn't. Did he think it was something I wanted to know about? If they had broken up when he was twenty, they had dated since he was fourteen. So she was not only his long-term girlfriend but probably his first serious girlfriend, and she and the rest of this group had grown up together.

"What, did you think you were getting a new car?" Éric teased me.

I tried to laugh and shook my head. No, I knew that. This was not the kind of guy girls left with nothing to do in the evening. It was pure fluke that I'd caught him unattached.

"*Parce que*, Sébastien, *il en a du kilométrage.*" Sébastien, he has a lot of mileage on him.

I stopped trying to laugh.

Sébastien frowned at his cigarette.

"He's tried out his machine," Éric said, in the throes of his own hilarity.

"*Ça va*, Éric," Sébastien said.

"They just fall at his feet," Éric said and shot Sébastien a glance. Come to think of it, how did the other two guys in this threesome react to Sébastien getting so much female attention? The suppressed jealousy had to come out some time. Lucky me, now was the time.

"Or something else to eat?" Fabien inserted firmly, speaking to me.

"Weren't we going to play a game?" Sébastien asked.

"I'll start," Virginie said. "*Alors.*"

"*Alors, il,*" Fabien said promptly.

"*Alors, il éternua,*" Sébastien said, and around it went in a circle.

Alors, il éternua dans. Alors, il éternua dans son. Alors, il éternua dans son lit . . . It was just a nonsense sentence: So, he sneezed in his bed . . . .

I lay back and concentrated on words. Words at least I had always been good at. Relationships, no; it was highly unlikely that I could live up to any experiences in Sébastien's past. But words I could handle. Sébastien patted his thigh. I hesitated, but then shifted to use it as a pillow, and he rested a forearm across my collarbone, rubbing one shoulder absently. Éric was good, I have to admit. He held out a long time, and all the others had long since dropped out, before I beat him.

"Let's play again," he said. So I beat him again. The fifth time, he finally gave up, and I gave him a small, mean smile. *Kilométrage?* Claire was always good at this game?

"She's evil," Éric said. "Why did you bring her here? I liked Claire better." He grinned at me.

"Suffer," I said. Sébastien squeezed my shoulder proudly. So the babydoll had performed well, I thought drily. Maybe I could graduate to my own piano grinder next. That was unfair, but what was fair? *Kilométrage.* I was so in over my head. I relented and explained: "They've done studies on children who learn a second language and those who don't. The ones who do can repeat a far longer string of nonsense syllables than those who don't. So, languages—that's what I do, you know?"

"That doesn't excuse Risk," Sébastien inserted.

I gazed up at his chin from my position on his thigh. "No, that's just because I'm lucky, remember?"

"I've learned a second language," Éric protested and switched to his. "I zpeak Inglizh verry well."

I didn't say anything at all for half the walk back to the RER station. We walked by the canal. Earlier, couples of all ages had filled this path, walking their dogs, carrying home groceries, watching the speedboats on the water. Now everything was dark and quiet. I tucked my hands into my jacket pockets instead of holding Sébastien's.

"Éric actually does speak English pretty well," Sébastien tried after a bit. "He just exaggerates his accent to make fun of himself. He's always making fun, Éric. He doesn't mean any harm by it."

"*Kilométrage?* That's not a very reassuring joke." I shoved my hands deeper in my pockets. "What are you doing with me?"

He sighed. "I'm going to kill Éric. I think he said all that on purpose to give me an even bigger challenge. As if you aren't complicated enough."

"Is that all I am? A challenge?"

His mouth tightened. "I'd like you to name one thing I've done since we've met that gives you a basis for that accusation."

I hunched my shoulders.

"Look, I went through a really bad year after Claire broke up with me."

Great, *she* had broken up with him. And he'd taken a year to get over it.

"And then, after that, I went through a phase."

"Have you had a real girlfriend since?"

"Yes, several."

Several. Well, I guess I'd been reading too much into the fact that he called me his girlfriend. I'd given up Cambridge for this? Oh, that's right, I was leaving soon anyway, so it didn't really matter how long he stayed with his girlfriends. "How long did you stay with the last one?"

He took a long draw on his cigarette. "Six months. We broke up a couple of months ago."

So when I'd first seen him, he had been with someone else. "If I'd listened to my friends and asked you out in February, would you have gone out with me?"

He looked at me. "Probably not," he said gently. "Since I had a girlfriend then."

I suppose I should appreciate that, since he considered me his girlfriend now. I didn't. "Were these other girls a lot prettier than I am?" Stupid, stupid, stupid.

He shook his head. "This is not a discussion I'm going to have."

I bet they were. Look at him. I'd always known he was too cute for me. Why couldn't he have just said, "No, you're gorgeous," damn it? "Why did you go out with me?"

"I just wanted to. You were so shy, all the time you were coming to the restaurant. You were so sweet and so shy, and I knew it must have taken all your courage to leave that invitation." His face softened just at the memory, as if something were melting inside him all over again. "And I just wanted to. *Crevette.*" He reached out and ruffled my hair. I noticed he didn't say I'd knocked him off his feet with my suave, sophisticated air and my overwhelming beauty.

We were nearly at the RER station now. We passed a couple of tweens doing wheelies on their bikes at an hour when they should have been at home in bed. "Why did Claire break up with you?"

He lit another cigarette. He was smoking way too much tonight. "She said I wasn't romantic enough."

I blinked and stared at him.

Five days later, the man who wasn't romantic enough showed up for my birthday with a floppy white Gund puppy, a bouquet of flowers, a pencil drawing of me warts and all, and brochures. I studied the drawing. It was of a photo of me from earlier that spring. On a trip to Rocamadour, my friend Kam and I had gotten lost on a short stroll through the hills of the Dordogne and ended up hiking for eight hours on an orange and a bottle of water. A smiling snail engraved on a concrete signpost was supposed to indicate the right path, and we searched desperately for it or even a road or any other sign of civilization. When we finally did find the snail, I dropped to my knees and embraced it, and Kam took a picture. Sébastien, flipping through my photos after I got back from the trip, had spotted this one and asked to keep it. At the time, I was touched. Now I studied the drawing he'd made from it, not sure how to take the fact that he had drawn me with a couple of pimples, my hair frizzing out all over the place, and tired but happy eyes. Somehow, I kept hoping Sébastien was delusional and saw me with perfect skin and perfect hair even after an accidental eight-hour hike. "What are those?" I pointed at the dots on my face suspiciously, just to make sure.

"Well, they were in the picture," he said. "Don't you like it?"

Of course, I liked it. He had *made* me a present. He had drawn me, as if I were worthy of art. No one had ever drawn me before. I wondered if he could erase the pimples.

He spread the brochures on my bed. "For London. For your birthday present."

I stared at him.

Those broad shoulders bent a little. "I don't want you to have to give up anything for me," he said, low. "I know you wanted to go to Cambridge. I know you love to travel. I'm sorry you have to choose. So I thought I would at least take you to London for a weekend. It's not the same as three weeks at Cambridge, I know, but at least it's something."

My heart hurt.

"We can go somewhere else if you'd rather," he said quickly. "I brought brochures for Brugge and Venice, too. But I thought of London first because you had wanted to spend the summer in England."

I grabbed him and held on tight. "You are amazing. I can't believe you're for real." And that might have been part of the problem: I really couldn't believe it. He was just too amazing to be true. Or at least, too amazing to be true for me. Which might explain why I had met him in a country on the opposite side of the Atlantic from where I was about to be living.

"Coward," I repeated Sébastien's word, staring at myself in the small rectangular mirror over the little sink tucked into an alcove by my door. Residents shared toilets and showers down the hall. I tried again to make my hair look right, but it was hopeless. The chalk in Paris water had destroyed it. The chalk coated my hair and dulled it, drying the ends so that they stuck out and refused to blend, taking away the bounce and leaving only the frizz. Despite extensive searches for a good Parisian stylist and the international conviction that there weren't any bad ones, I had found no one who knew how to deal with long, thick, fine, curly hair. One woman had bunched all my curls up in a rubber band, upended me, and blunt cut the ponytail, then straightened me and told me it was done. Another, when I requested a deep conditioning treatment, put me into a humidifier instead. Words fail me to describe the results of either of these methods on curls. My hair hadn't looked good since December, when the two-week stay at my parents' had helped get the chalk coating out and I'd been temporarily able to luxuriate in a silky feel again. I could see why most Parisiennes gave up and cut most of their hair off, slicking it down with straighteners if they were cursed with curls.

I sighed dispiritedly and noticed I was getting a pimple on my eyebrow. My *eyebrow.* Why, God? And don't even tell me it's the chocolate, God, that's been scientifically disproven. I bet none of Sébastien's old girlfriends or *kilométrage* got pimples on their eyebrows. Especially not just before romantic escapes to London. The phone rang, and I headed out with my overnight bag to join Sébastien.

We got off the Eurostar at noon at Waterloo Station, and we didn't stop exploring until midnight. We found the cheapest hotel we could, forewent taxis and even the subway as too expensive, and walked and walked and walked. We picnicked in the vast London gardens, stretched out on the lawn. There are almost no parks where people touch grass in Paris, and Sébastien was rhapsodizing on the experience of lying on turf when he froze. "Look, Laura! There's a squirrel!"

I glanced at the squirrel, which looked pretty much like any gray squirrel to me, and back at him. I had dated men in my hometown who shot squirrels. One of my own brothers used to shoot squirrels that came up to his birdfeeders, until he read that without bullets in its body a squirrel could live twenty years; then he felt horrible. Sébastien whipped out my camera and started taking pictures. "Here." He handed the camera to me. "See if you can get a picture of us together." He squatted, stretching one finger out toward the squirrel. He must have stayed that way half an hour, vainly making coaxing noises and trying to get the squirrel to come play with him. The squirrel looked at him as if he had lost his marbles, which was exactly how the men in my family would look at him if they ever saw this moment, and eventually hopped away. "Wow, a squirrel!" Sébastien sighed. "I can't believe it! A real squirrel!"

We walked from one end of the city to the other, went into the Tate Gallery, photographed Westminster, ate in a delicious Indian restaurant, contemplated the Eye of London but decided it was too expensive. We made our way through Soho at midnight and back to our room even later, where I fell into instant sleep out of exhaustion and remnants of cowardice. If Sébastien had any expectations about our sharing a hotel room on a romantic trip to London, he didn't mention them. He just sighed and grinned and borrowed the *Harry Potter* book I'd bought at a London bookstore earlier that day. The cover had looked kind of weird, but since the copies of it filled half the bookshelves in the store, I'd figured it must be some kind of local cultural phenomenon and decided to check it out.

"No, you can't have it back," he said on the train the next day. "You deserve to suffer, and I want to see what happens next.

I don't have as big an English vocabulary as I thought, though. What does 'Muggle' mean?"

Let no one say that I am easy. It was two more whole days before I showed up at Le Relais du Vin near closing time. Sébastien's face lit up when he saw me, as it tended to do. He installed me in the tiny corner between the bar and the front window. Louis, the wild-haired owner, smiled happily at me and went back to filling the small dishwasher under the bar with glasses.

"You should try this dessert," Sébastien murmured. He wore a black, pressed, short-sleeve shirt again, as he had the night I first saw him, but I could tell he was hot and tired and just longing to unbutton it and strip down to the black tank underneath. "*Poire belle hélène*. It's another of my favorites. Plus, the chef's gone by now, and this is one of the few things on the menu I can make." So he served me pears with pear ice cream, lavishly dripped with a hot chocolate sauce. It melted in my mouth, sweet and cool and hot all at once. I watched him move as I ate. Most of the tables were empty again by now, Sébastien taking care of the tail ends of lingering parties and hauling in tables from the cobblestoned street.

"Do you know what day it is?" I murmured, nervous and excited. I'd worn my stiletto boots again, and under my long black coat were finally and at long last my black leather pants. If black leather pants couldn't make up for failings in a certain department, what could?

"It's Wednesday, right?" he said.

"It's two months exactly since I asked you out."

"You asked me out?" he asked, confused.

I gritted my teeth. "Since I left you that invitation to the party."

"Right." He smiled. "That was a good day. Of course, I'd no idea how much work you would turn out to be." He pinched my nose before I could stop him and went off to bring someone a bill.

When he got back, I had a folded piece of paper under my hand. I hadn't written it in the toilet this time. I drew the line there. I slid it across the table to him. "It's another invitation."

He picked it up and unfolded it and then looked up at me, not quite smiling. "Absolutely," he said.

I hope I don't have to go into detail about what it was an invitation to do. Use your imagination. Anyway, I had no choice; he was holding *Harry Potter* hostage for my bad behavior.

Twelve

Adela was leaving for good, after only one year of her two-year DEA program. "That's it," she said. "I can't stand this city. Stupid stuck-up professors who think they know better than their students. Stupid stuck-up French who think they have the best city in the world. They don't even dress right." She sniffed, pure Seville. She would not be coming back after the summer. One of her professors had not appreciated Adela's mouthing off to her during her oral exam, and another had given an incredulous look at her final paper, provoking a heated argument with Adela, who "was only flesh and blood," in her own words. "I can't put up with that kind of thing." In any case, with the choice between doing the year over here or going to school in Spain, she was choosing Spain.

I watched Adela finish packing, feeling that lurching feeling you get just before you jump off a cliff—something I'd done quite a few times before in my paragliding efforts and actually found a lot easier. My paragliding instructor had insisted I shouldn't call it "jumping off" but "taking off," though. On the other hand, *he* always landed smoothly in the middle of a green field, and *I* always slammed full-body into the trees in the neighboring woods.

I went upstairs to find Philippe zipping up his last suitcase, only his toiletries and last-minute things lingering in his room. I walked down the hall to find Kam taping up her next-to-last box. Everyone was leaving. One after the other, within days, farewell party after farewell party. I was packing, too, but I wasn't going far. My time at the Maison du Canada was up. I had at last had to make an economical decision and sublet for half price from someone in another house, someone who was leaving only for the summer and wanted to keep her place. The Maison du Canada was right next door, but it would be filled with a flock of summer undergraduates here for their study abroad. They had already started filling the picnic tables in our courtyard, to the deep displeasure of those of us who remained. We graduates who had filled the courtyard all year clung to one table, the last remnants clinging to our last vestiges of our year in Paris. I had two more weeks here, and then I would be out in the cold. I could poke my head through the hedge, but I wouldn't see anyone I knew. Even my study abroad program was closing for most of the summer, Valérie and Giulia heading to Brittany and Rome for vacation. I had no job now to occupy my days and no friends left. I would be alone in Paris. I would have no one but Sébastien.

My friend Kam made me a poster for our year there, bits and pieces of things glued to the pink posterboard, "Dancing Queen" written in glitter across the top in honor of my indefatigability on the dance floor in our dorm parties and Paris clubs. Among other collage items meant to symbolize me, she had included lots of chocolate wrappers. I rolled the poster inside my beautiful seventeenth-century map of Paris and slid them both into the map tube along with posters from my favorite plays that year. I tucked all the memorabilia that so many people had brought back for me from their trips—little wooden shoes from Amsterdam, a tiny Italian flag, a Swiss coin—into a brown Maison du Chocolat box. I slipped dried flowers trimmed from each of Sébastien's bouquets into a blue tin from the Marquise de Sévigné (the chocolate shop, not the person). I tucked a candle with a Chinese pictograph wishing me joy from my friend Kam into a mint-green tin from Ladurée. I tucked *turrón* from Adela into the pink tin from Fauchon, smiling at the memory of the day we got kicked out of there.

The blue tin from Marquise de Sévigné had held sweet ground chocolate. The shop on the Place de la Madeleine had been nearly empty the day I bought it, and the man behind the little coffee bar had responded to my query on their hot chocolate by showing me how to make it from start to finish. I'd forced Paris to put up with me in the end, I guess, like a clumsy, tongue-lolling, persistent puppy who finally gets petted. All the packing up of experiences attested to it.

There was a knock on the door, and I opened it to find Kam, Philippe, and Adela there. Kam was the friend from Rocamadour, the one who had taken a picture of me hugging a snail. From what had once been East Germany, she was small and freckled, with fine pale hair that wisped out all around her head. She grinned. "We've got a birthday surprise for you. It's a few days late because you went to London."

They took me to the Parc André Citroën, a park about as weird and techno as you could expect from something named after a car manufacturer. The only pretty part of it was the square with water shooting up all over and children running through the fountain screaming with laughter. Above it floated an orange and yellow hot air balloon. "Remember?" Kam, the organizer, gloated. "You said you always wanted to go up in a balloon. So when I heard one was here, we got together. *And* guess what I found." She pulled out six cookies carefully wrapped in plastic film.

I gaped. "Oreos? You found Oreos?"

She nodded triumphantly. "Somebody sent a pack to a friend I saw when I was in Germany last month. So I begged him to let me have some, and I saved them for you! Happy Birthday!"

We went up in the hot air balloon and floated over Paris. It was attached, so we couldn't float far, but we could gaze at the Tour Eiffel from her level and look down at the city everyone but me was about to leave.

My heart hurt. This was the end of an era and the beginning of another, and I was going into it all alone. Almost all alone. Sébastien would be there.

But what did he know about living in a strange country for love? He had been born in a hospital only a couple of blocks from his current apartment. He had his friends, a solid wall of support around him.

"You have my friends, too," he protested, hauling my suitcases over to the new room for me. "They like you."

I shook my head. "It's not the same." They barely knew me. I barely knew them. They were *his* friends and probably secretly preferred Claire anyway. I was entirely dependent on him in too many ways.

"I don't see why you have to take this room," he said, flexing his arms after he set my suitcases down in the new place. It was about the size of my old room, but with hardwood floors. And, of course, totally empty of my experiences, which were all packed up now in my suitcases. I felt that vast sense of emptiness I always get when arriving in a hotel. "You should just stay at my place."

"We'd kill each other sharing your place. It's too small." Not to mention the cat's predilection for peeing everywhere. "No couple could survive that."

"We're just going to spend all our time in the Métro going back and forth to see each other," he protested. "You're going to be spending most nights at my place anyway. Right? This is silly."

"This way we'll each have our space." And I would keep this last lonely vestige of independence.

He rolled his eyes and pulled something out of his shirt pocket to hand to me. It was a tiny, handmade finger puppet he'd spotted in a shop window when passing through the Marais. He liked to bring presents I couldn't predict.

"Did I tell you?" he said. "I've got a job offer at the best graphic arts firm in Paris. And a couple of others, but I decided to go with this one. It's small, but it's the best, and I'll be able to learn a lot. It starts August seventeenth."

Two days after I left. So just when I was heading back to the U.S., to return to my long-term commitment to obtain a Ph.D., he would be starting on a long-term commitment to Paris, the dream he'd been reaching for ever since he went back to school as an adult and worked his way through by waiting tables. He would be illustrating for the best graphic arts firm in Paris.

"That's great," I said. Let's not think about the future, Laura. Let's just not think about it.

"They wanted me to start the beginning of August, but I asked if I could start two weeks later, so that I could spend those last two weeks with you," Sébastien said.

Kam drove back to Germany with an old boyfriend who had come down to pick her up. Adela and Philippe left from the airport, nearly at the same time. I went to the airport with them, toasted them off with airport hot chocolate, and watched them disappear into Charles de Gaulle's science fiction-style tunnels. I stood there, feeling scared and lonely. I was used to being scared and alone in a foreign country, but this was different. Usually the scared, lonely feeling was at the start of an adventure, when I'd first arrived and knew no one. Usually, I exploited the feeling by exploring, by doing everything everywhere until I knew people and we could keep having fun. Now I was scared and lonely in a country I knew. I'd already explored Paris. Sure, there was always more stuff to see, but I'd about had my dose. I was starting to crave the English language. Plus, now I was staying on for love, a far scarier reason than adventure.

"So how can you go at this no holds barred like that?" I asked Sébastien. "Doesn't it scare you, to know I'm leaving in August? Aren't you afraid of getting hurt?"

"Of course, I'm scared. But I know what happens when you rein yourself in," he answered. "I've seen lots of my friends do it, and I understand they want to protect themselves, but they miss so much. When you block out a relationship out of fear, you lose out on the world. I've taken some knocks, and I got really hurt with Claire, you know. But I would still rather lower my defenses and risk things than block out life."

I nodded, trying to pretend this kind of courage was something I could even remotely understand. We were walking up the medieval rue Mouffetard, having just visited my favorite ice cream place, the one that sold ice creams shaped like flowers. Sébastien licked a dollop of banana sorbet, his eyes half-closing in bliss as his tongue swirled erotically to catch a petal of yogurt-flavored ice cream and blend the two flavors together. I kept watching this motion out of the corners of my eyes. We passed a hippie ethnic store on our left, selling vaguely Andean scarves and various things with beads in them. *Le Petit Prince* held pride of place in the bookstore display on our right, angling for the American student market.

Sébastien grinned around his ice cream and slanted a glance down at my attempt at a thoughtful, courageous expression. "So, do you want to get married?"

I tripped, and he caught my arm before I could end up face-down on cobblestones.

"What?" I whispered. I wanted to shriek, but I was hyperventilating.

He grinned, watching my face. "And we could have little babies, and they'd be so cute."

I wrenched at my wrist. I did *not* do that marriage thing, nope, nope, nope. Even as a kid, I had not put Barbie in a wedding dress but rather had her kidnapped by pirates, dragged halfway around the world, and forced to submit to sexual desires. My parents must have got wind of this because they gave me a book written by nuns that explained what sexual desires were. And people wonder why I have hang-ups. My mom made me a wedding dress for Barbie to encourage me in the right direction, but I loaned it to my sister's Barbie and practiced having mine ride off on her Palomino into the sunset instead.

He burst out laughing. "I'm *joking*. You should see your face, though. Have you ever noticed that you're really terrified of relationships?"

Well, yes. I had noticed that, although I hadn't expected him to read me like a book. Damn it, I was four years older than he was; why was he the mature and insightful one in the couple?

He laughed. "Never mind, *crevette*. Your ice cream is melting while you worry about it. And I love the way you eat ice cream, so that seems a waste." He grinned, a flashing provocation, as he brought his ice cream cone back to his mouth. "We'll have to talk about it again some other day."

Thirteen

School was out, work was over, my friends were gone. French people were slowly drifting out of Paris while tourists filled up the empty spots. The maps posted at Métro entrances began to attract hordes of people in tennis shoes and shorts. I wandered the streets, even more purposeless than the tourists, who at least had all of Paris to see and only a few days to do it in. I went to museums again, chocolate shops, parks. It was a nice round, especially with the weather finally warm, but I didn't have anything else to do. No purpose. I invented purposes by sending queries to write articles or just writing them anyway and sending them. I studied, and I went to the library: St-Geneviève with its wide flights of stairs switchbacking up to the lone floor of this library that supposedly held two million books. Few books were in sight inside, just a long stretch of tables. I brought my requests for books to a librarian and waited fifteen minutes, then when they came took them to a table to look through them. It wasn't the kind of library I knew and loved back home, where I could wander the shelves and discover things I didn't know existed. I was really lonely, especially during the day when Sébastien was still working.

That obliged Sébastien to get creative. The first Saturday in July, he woke me up, grinning. "What are we doing?" I asked. It was actually a beautiful weekend, and I was game for anything. I thought.

"It's a surprise. You'll love it!"

"In terms of fashion, what kind of surprise are we talking about here?"

"Dress comfortably. You know, like for a battle or something."

I had originally imagined dating a Parisian meant most surprises would require sexy black dresses and include elegant restaurants, but I decided not to mention it. When I was battle-clad enough, we headed out to the Bastille, where he stopped across the street from the canal, looking very pleased with himself.

"What?" I said.

"Look!" He gestured toward the shop, which I slowly identified as Nomades, one of the primary skate shops in Paris.

My eyes widened in alarm. "You mean . . . that's the surprise?"

He nodded happily: "We're going skating!"

"Oh," I said. I checked his eyes to see how thrilled he was at having thought of this present for me. Pretty thrilled. "Oh, well . . . that's a nice surprise." I could probably survive it, too. I mean, maybe it would be really nice to learn, and surely I could manage a half hour of turning around in circles by the canal.

I thought it was sweet, rather than ominous, when Sébastien rented more protections for me than you see on football players: knee pads, elbow pads, wrist braces, helmet. But once I got the skates and protections on, we didn't stop at the flat space before the canal where other people were practicing skating. When I tried to brake, he grabbed my waist to keep me from falling over in the attempt and pushed me across the crosswalk toward the glossy techno-shimmer of the Opéra Bastille. Cars swirled madly around us and the Colonne de Juillet, a greened copper obelisk commemorating the site of the old Bastille prison that had been the first target of the French Revolution.

My voice rose to a full screech in protest: "What are you *doing*? I could fall in front of a car!" On cue, the light changed, leaving me with half the street still to wobble across. Horns erupted like wasps from a prodded nest; by the time Sébastien pushed me to safety, I was nearly deaf. "Why couldn't we practice back there?" I indicated the much safer, less populated space before the canal.

"Because I told Éric and Fabien we'd meet them here."

A long pause. "Why are you inviting your friends?" I said. "Won't they get bored? And won't I look ridiculous?"

"Oh, they might get bored, but they don't care if you look ridiculous. They'll just think it's funny."

That had been, oddly enough, my point.

"Besides, it will be a good chance for you to get to know Éric and Fabien better."

Oh, dear. He was inviting me another step into his life, a major step. He, his two best friends, and I were going to become a group that did things together, not just casual acquaintances.

I decided, therefore, to be tolerant. If three grown men wanted to drift around in circles for a while, laughing at me, that was their problem.

"*Circles?*" Sébastien said.

"*Circles?*" Éric and Fabien said. The looked disconcertingly competent in their skating equipment and only half-familiar: Éric, thin and wired; Fabien, a study in roundness above his shoulders, with his round face, round glasses, and balding pate. From his shoulders down, round-headed Fabien was paradoxically thin and gangly. I had learned he faced life with a slouch, from which position he could fling himself into extravagantly gawky slapstick routines at the slightest opportunity. I also knew now that he was saving up money to move to Québec, apparently having long nurtured dreams of freezing to death. Éric had just failed his driver's license for the third time. This time, he had lost a sideview mirror parking, nearly hit the examiner (with his fist, not his car), and was told he couldn't retake the test for a while. I got the impression he lived a little bit more on his nerves than his comic routine at first suggested.

"That's not how you learn to skate," Sébastien said.

Éric made the tongue-clicking French sound that means not only "No," but "No, and I've eaten snails bigger than your brain." Fabien, a kinder man, only shook his head.

"It isn't?" I said, as the three of them headed out and Sébastien pulled me after him.

"No, of course not. The *best* way to learn how to skate is to go for a *real* trip."

"What's a real trip?" I said, trying to grab hold of a traffic light pole to put a halt to this madness.

"Oh, you know, to the other end of Paris and back." Sébastien steered me away from the baby carriage I had nearly run over.

"I don't—I—don't you think I should learn how to *brake* before being around so many people?" I grabbed hold of one of those little black iron posts that conveniently dot the edges of so many Parisian sidewalks, in order to avoid hitting a lady bent double over her cane. Sébastien seized the seat of my pants and jerked me away from the whishing wheels of the car I had almost bobbled into instead. "Not to mention motorized vehicles?"

"Now don't start complaining," Sébastien said.

My jaw dropped at this injustice. "I'm not *complaining*; I'm trying to suggest an intelligent take on this adventu"—Sébastien jerked me to a halt, and my teeth sank into my tongue.

"Will you *brake*?" he said, exasperated.

"When I try to brake, I fall down!"

"Well, it's better than being run over by a car."

"Has it occurred to you that a place where I can be run over by cars isn't the best place for a first lesson?!!"

"She's getting into one of her moods again," Sébastien told Éric and Fabien. "Don't pay any attention to her."

If there's anything worse than a male who says things like that, it's hoping he won't let go of you while he does. I wobbled to the right to avoid a skating Asian couple and met the woman's eyes as we nearly ran each other down. If I understood Japanese, I'm pretty sure I would have picked out, "Are you absolutely insane?" in the words she cried out to her boyfriend as we passed. I wondered if he was welcoming her into his life, too. Over our heads, Sébastien and the Asian man exchanged amused, commiserating glances.

"And you should try letting go of me," Sébastien said.

"When I let go of you, I fall down! Into the path of speeding cars, other people on rollers, or old ladies!"

"You're supposed to fall down."

I would have stared at him in open outrage, only if I looked to the side I, naturally, fell down. "No, I am not! I'm not doing *any* kind of sport where I'm *supposed* to fall down."

"Everybody falls down, Laura," he said, exasperated. "That's part of it."

If I had even the remotest chance of accomplishing a dead halt that wouldn't have ended in permanent paralysis, I would have

121

done so. "Well, you certainly didn't tell me that before we started! I don't *want* to fall down."

"She's not usually like this," Sébastien apologized to Éric and Fabien. He leaned a little away from me in a sotto voce. "Must be that time of the month."

Suffice it to say that by the time we had gotten onto the Coulée Verte, the verdant Paris Greenway, and taken it up and down hills all the way to the Bois de Vincennes and halfway back, I was no longer in a tolerant mood. (Sébastien claims there aren't any hills on the Coulée Verte, but I've been there, and this is simply not true.)

Okay, so actually, a lot of the day had been fun, in its terrifying way, especially since all three of the men were a hilarious comic team, all bent on making me laugh instead of scream or complain. They also circled me vigilantly, especially Sébastien, so that I hadn't actually fallen that much, perhaps three or four times. Even when I did, they had usually tried so hard to stop me that they were under me when it happened. Usually the person under me was Sébastien, but on my best fall of the day, I took out all three at once.

But for a beginner, the whole trek was nearly a four-hour trip, so three-quarters of the way through it, I was exhausted, a fact that none of the guys seemed able to understand. "As slow as you're going?" Éric asked.

I used my hands to push myself away from a rock wall I still didn't know how to brake well enough to avoid. "You know, Éric, I'm getting to know you much faster than I'd like."

He laughed.

We rounded a bend and came to the longest and worst hill of the route. For a hill that Sébastien said didn't exist, it stretched on forever. "Sébastien!" I screamed.

He pivoted and skated back. "I'll brake for you," he promised, coming up beside me and holding out a stiff arm. And he did try. But it *was* a hill and not a gradual slope of land that even a baby could handle, as certain people still claim, so he couldn't brake enough for both of us. We flew ever faster until we nearly reached walking speed, Sébastien's wheels screeching against the pavement to no avail and me trying to get my own wheels to screech against the pavement to no avail, until I shrank backward out of this suicidal velocity and fell *fesses*-first onto the pavement, with a force that would leave dense purple bruises on all relevant flesh for a couple of weeks before they faded.

As my face crumpled in a way that would have made a three-year-old proud, Sébastien crouched beside me, betrayed by worry into exasperation. "What did you do that for? If you hadn't gotten scared, you would have been fine."

Things had been going from bad to worse, relationship-wise, for the past hour, but this was the last straw. "If you hadn't made me do this, I would have been fine, too!"

"Made you?" Sébastien drew back his head. A four-year-old who had just created his best fresco all over his mom's freshly painted walls couldn't have been more wounded at her reaction. "It was a *present*. You said you wanted to learn how to skate!"

"For fifteen minutes on a flat, enclosed, protected surface!" I yelled at the top of my lungs.

A cyclist rounded the corner at that moment, his face set warily at all the yelling. His expression lightened with comprehension when he saw me on my butt on the pavement, skate-chunky legs stuck out in front of me, and Sébastien crouched beside me, caught between concern and exasperation. "*Ça fait mal,*" the cyclist told Sébastien sympathetically. *That hurts.*

The worst of it was he clearly meant the sympathy for Sébastien and not for me. *Men.*

On the next hill, observers could see three Frenchmen holding on to the pants of one American rather like you might hold a toddler's diapers, braking with all their might in order to avoid reaching a speed that would make the American start screaming again—basically, anything over a few feet an hour.

Fortunately, that left none of them free to take a picture. It was just a good thing Virginie wasn't there with a camera. "Where is Virginie, anyway?" I asked when we were on flat ground again.

The guys flexed their hands to restore circulation, massaged their calves from all the braking, and exchanged glances. "Virginie doesn't really like skating with us," Sébastien admitted.

"Trust me, we wouldn't have had any fun with her," Éric said, disgusted. "The only time we tried to take her out, she started crying after only half an hour, threw her skates at me, and took the Métro home."

"She's a little bit of a *chouchoutte*, Virginie," Sébastien explained. A *chouchoutte*. Someone who likes to be pampered and babied.

"Darn it," I said, aggravated. "Frenchwomen are so smart. Can I be a *chouchoutte* from now on, too?"

Fourteen

Okay," Sébastien said next time. "This time I've got an even better idea." I looked at him warily. I still had a giant bruise on my butt from his last idea. "I think you need another birthday present. Didn't you say you wanted to go to Provence?"

I did say that. After a year in Paris, I had never been to Provence, and the lavender fields would still be in bloom if we hurried. Above all, I wanted to go to the Festival d'Avignon, the famous annual festival of theater productions. Critics were calling Isabelle Huppert's title role in *Médée* the best since Euripides first created it, and I wanted to see what they were talking about.

Sébastien had actually managed to get tickets for the most

talked-about play of the festival? And his old girlfriend had thought he wasn't romantic? I cuddled against him in the train with mushy heart and kept cuddling all the way to the Palais des Papes, where I learned that Sébastien hadn't, in fact, gotten tickets. He had just assumed we could buy them at the door.

I took a deep, calming breath and gazed at a woman in a nude leotard performing elastic contortions to elevator music on the steps of the Palais des Papes. We were surrounded by pale stone buildings that seemed sun-faded, irradiated with clear, dust-white heat and the resonating drone of cicadas.

"But that's okay!" Sébastien said, sunnily showing that he had not only found a silver lining but had done so without noticing the cloud. "My family's all down here visiting my grandparents at Chamaret. We can go spend the weekend with them instead!"

I was dating a man who thought spending a weekend meeting his *French* family for the first time was a wonderful birthday present, a perfectly acceptable substitute for the theatrical performance of the decade. "For my birthday?" I reminded him. We dodged a group of people in folk costume who were doing some hopping thing that involved smacking sticks together. Every conceivable set of steps or spot with good visibility was covered with actors performing something or trying to drum up enough of a crowd to start performing something.

Sébastien beamed. "I've been wanting you to meet my family. My mom, my stepfather, my little sister, and my stepgrandparents are there. This is a great opportunity, you can meet them all at once!"

"That sounds just lovely." I sighed and put away the theater pamphlets actors had been stuffing in my hand ever since we got off the train. A fiddle-playing hillbilly marionette bowed farewell to me from across the way. "How lucky for me you didn't think to get tickets."

Three hours later, in a stifling car driven by a mad Frenchman, we jerked, sped, braked, and swerved through that dry heat from Avignon, past still purple but graying lavender fields, clear green vineyards, olive trees, and truffle-producing oak fields. The mad Frenchman was Sébastien's stepfather, Jean-Charles, a man with dark, graying hair and a noticeable nose. Halfway to Chamaret, at the shocking realization that there might not be any good wine for dinner, we swerved into a vineyard to pick up a couple of bottles, naturally with a little *dégustation* first.

The grandparents' house was tucked below Chamaret, a sun-gold stone village just up the hill. Rosemary grew in profusion at the gates, and lavender fields stretched out before it. As I still flinch from the memory, I will draw a veil of silence over my traditional Southern attempts to help in the kitchen and the anguished discomfort these produced. Sébastien's mother, Claudine, kept laughing tensely, and her own mother-in-law, stout-chested Violette, openly growled at the way I cut strawberries. Thin and taut and very young, only fifteen years older than I, with a modish crop of tinted red hair, Claudine seemed exactly what I had expected of a Parisian mother, including the fact that she weighed less than I did and had better muscle tone. When I complimented Claudine on her tone and asked where she worked out, she laughed, pleased. "It's true I did a little gymnastics when I was in high school. Thirty years ago." It took a strong love of chocolate not to turn anorexic in this country.

We sat down to the table and its big bowl of salad, rich tomatoes fresh from the garden mounding up over its brim. The scent of them, that tangy, sun-filled scent of real tomatoes picked ripe, was making me salivate; but I knew another ten minutes would go by before I tasted them. The French meal is an art in savoring.

"Why don't you toss the salad, Laura?" Claudine smiled.

To excuse myself from accusations of gullibility, I can only say that as an American I didn't at the time automatically check every dish for ways it could be used against me as a weapon. I tried my best, but a couple of those luscious tomatoes spilled over the sides of the bowl and onto the bright yellow Provençal tablecloth. I fished them quickly onto my plate, but nobody looked unhappy about it. In fact, Claudine was grinning at her son. "*Pas bon à marier,* I guess!"

Not good marriage material. That was, interestingly enough, exactly how I had always described myself. I glanced sideways at Sébastien, who was trying not to laugh. He was the one who kept bringing up marriage, damn it. I looked back at his mother, my eyes starting to narrow.

Claudine gave me a broad smile, as if I'd just handed her the world and it was an oyster. "You've never heard that? In France, we say that someone who can toss a salad without spilling anything over the sides is *bon à marier.*" Good to marry.

"And vice versa," Sébastien said helpfully. He grinned at me. "Want to see me mix it?"

I passed him the fork and spoon. Catching my eye as he took them from me, he abruptly smoothed his mouth into a flat, deadpan-serious line and concentrated on the salad as if his life depended on it.

"You've always been good at that," Claudine sighed with maternal pride and what I considered a certain tendency to belabor a point, as Sébastien finished mixing the salad expertly, the tablecloth untouched. Everybody around the table was grinning now, except for me. I was remembering what twisted humor all those French movies seemed to have.

Claudine suddenly leaned forward, eyes sparkling. "It's such a good thing you made it down this evening. This means you'll be able to go with us on the old-car rally tomorrow!"

Naturally, I expected the worst. I generally do, even when activities aren't suggested by a Frenchwoman who can use salads to eliminate the unworthy from her son's love life.

Fifteen

The early morning sun was burning off the fog from the nearby riverbed when we headed out, Sébastien's mother and stepfather Jean-Charles in front, his little sister Justine tucked with Sébastien and me in back, behind the second windshield of a 1928 Citroen B14 Torpedo convertible. Jean-Charles and his father had rebuilt this red Torpedo by hand from a rusty heap, along with five other classic cars.

Burly, grumpy, and amused, Jean-Charles turned out to be a perfectly sane driver when behind the wheel of a car decades older than himself. Justine pulled a blanket out from under the seat and spread it and its dust across our legs against the chill of the early morning wind. As dark-haired as Sébastien, Justine was a slim, naturally bronze, preternaturally graceful and patient thirteen-year-old. If I were dating an American, I thought, he might chew tobacco, but odds were good I could feel more sophisticated than his adolescent sister and weigh less than his mother.

The fumes from the grandparents' 1952 Peugeot 203 convertible wafted back at us, mixing with the scent of roadside rosemary. I bounced on the edge of my seat and twisted this way and that, examining the tiny wood pegs that locked and unlocked the door, the system that folded and unfolded the second windshield. The twenties were my favorite decade; I had always wanted to be one of those jaded, flippant, and yet somehow life-embracing flappers. I had even tried to wear those straight Twiggy dresses during my adolescence, but at five-foot-three and with my overblown curves, I only ended up looking like a barefoot, pregnant housewife. Nudging Sébastien, I kept whispering to him to ask what this and that dial on the dash was for.

"Ask Jean-Charles," he said, a smile curving his sexy mouth. So finally I did. Chest swelling, increasingly pleased in that growly, amused way as I continued to pester him, Jean-Charles explained at length. Sébastien grinned and leaned back with his arm stretched behind me, teasing his little sister and watching the vineyards and tomato fields we passed in slow motion, at thirty miles per hour. I tried to look everywhere at once. Claudine twisted and grinned at my enthusiasm, as proud as if she and not her husband had been the one to rebuild this Torpedo with painstaking manual labor.

We met the rest of the car club in a gravel lot filled with classic cars, none less than forty years old. On the shady terrace of the only café in St. Pantaléon, a village that would almost fit into the palm of one hand, waiters bustled with our breakfast. Coffee, hot chocolate, juice, *pains au chocolat,* and some cream-stuffed pastry that was the café's specialty appeared before us. We quickly fell behind schedule as two dozen French enjoyed their meals, caught up with everyone's news, interrogated me on pink Cadillacs and means of getting them from America to France, and lamented the poor turnout. Jean-Charles, Robert, and the others shook their heads and muttered, slanting looks down the table at another gray-haired man obliviously immersed in his own conversation. The year before, they had had fifty cars, but then R. had gone and upped the participation fee thirty francs. That was the equivalent of almost five whole dollars more than last year's participation fee; no wonder people got mad and refused to come.

"Shameful," I agreed, hoping to keep the conversation away from the pink Cadillacs. I'd just run through the whole Bruce Springsteen song in my head and come up with not a single detail that would save me from sounding like a complete idiot. I escaped with Sébastien and Justine down to the old *lavoir* just below the café, an ancient stone half-building by the river, where laundry used to be washed. The sun was just penetrating into the *lavoir*'s coolness, and Sébastien and Justine amused themselves by dancing hand-shadows across the floor. The café's German shepherd scrambled frantically after the shadows, trying to dig through stone to get at them.

We bounced and jounced away from the café at last, the wind in our hair, people smiling and waving as we passed. At a couple of intersections, we passed so close to the car waiting to turn onto the road that I could see its male driver biting his lip with envy. Or was that alarm at getting behind twelve cars that wouldn't go over thirty-five miles per hour?

The oldest car's top speed was a perfect speed for touring Provence. In an open convertible, the scents of lavender washed over us off those endless fields of purple. Some of those fields had been cut by now, but many still had blooms to harvest. In our first real town, we slowed for a flock of people carrying baskets across the street. I turned my head, and as far down the side street as I could see stretched color after color: bright red peppers and tomatoes, yellow peaches, leafy greens, golden brown bread.

"What's that?"

"A market." Claudine turned to look at me. "You've never been to a Provençal market?"

"No." I craned my head to look back. "You don't think we could . . . ?" Well, no, I could hardly bring our caravan to a pause; everyone else here saw legendary Provençal markets twice a week. It was too late, anyway; we were rumbling over the baked gold span of a two-thousand-year-old Roman bridge toward a granite rock face. The river plummeted into a gorge below us.

The car in front of us stalled only half a mile later, scaring me. Was our cocky parade through Provence going to come to a halt so soon? The whole procession pulled over to the side of the road behind the problem car, and men thronged around the thin hood as it was folded up. The insides of the engine looked so simple even I might have been able to put them together in a third-grade science class, and they held the power of a super magnet. I had never felt any interest in cars in my life; I had once driven a full mile on a flat tire, all the time with this vague sense that my truck was riding kind of funny, before two sixteen-year-old boys in hunting clothes who had been flashing their lights at me for half a mile finally got me to pull over and changed the tire for me. But these classic cars were different. I found myself craning on tiptoe to look over the shoulders of the men gathered around the engine. I wasn't the only one. With a dozen men already at work on the problem—all classic car experts, as proven by the parade parked along the side of the road—not one but two modern car drivers nevertheless stopped to ask if we needed any help. "I saw you broken down and just wanted to check and make sure you had everything you needed." A hand sneaked out to caress the shiny curves of the vehicle. "I'm pretty good with cars. Do you want me to take a look at it?" A chin tucked in discreet but transparent craving toward the exposed engine.

"*Merci*," said the driver, which, by an odd but culturally significant vagary of French, means "no." His white head bent while he blew briskly through a detached fuel line. "Got a speck of dirt in it, is all." And off we went again.

By the third stall, I kept my calm. The younger generation, I thought disparagingly of the 1938 Renault Celta 4 and patted our 1928 Torpedo smugly. I had always thought things had gone downhill from the twenties. Besides, our Torpedo was a convertible and had *two* windshields: one for the front seat and one for the back. Beat that.

I wandered across the road to gaze at the nearly ripe apricots that weighted the trees. Some of the other classic car drivers and long-term passengers were starting to look disgruntled.

"Him again," Sébastien's stepgrandmother, Violette, shook her head in disgust, propping her elbow against the door of her 1952 Peugeot. Both round and barrel-chested, with a hefty way of moving, she had recently come out of the hospital after a major bout with illness and was much less aggressive these days than she used to be, everybody swore. "There's a man who can't keep his cars in order."

The owner of a red 1968 Fiat convertible popped up the rear of his car and pulled out a tool chest that had been somehow tucked against his motor. A one-armed man cocked open the hood of the recalcitrant Renault with his shoulder and plied a wrench. A collection of heads—38 percent of them gray and 60 percent silvery white—gathered once more around the obstreperous vehicle as phrases flew: "Carburetor?" "Air filter?" "No, maybe the spark plug."

Sébastien's mother took a picture of me and wandered over to my side of the road. "It's always like this," she said. "Fortunately these old cars usually don't take long to fix. Although I've known of at least one time when they finally had to tow a car back. Are you having fun?"

"It's wonderful!"

She smiled at that, but I kept my guard up. Last night's salad episode had marked me.

Our route wound into a small range of mountains, steep rock cutting up through the vines and trees. A herd of goats cropped grass on a long, green slope that curved downward toward a creek and then arched up again in a field of lavender, where a little stone house tucked in between two bushes. We must have stalled every fifteen minutes, and every time in a place no one could regret getting stuck in. I didn't regret it, anyway. I could have ridden in that red Torpedo and stalled every few miles from one end of France to the other and still been happy. We stalled by lavender fields, in river gorges, and in a village of golden stone about the size of a chessboard, with tiny bridges arching over a disciplined, finger-width river that had flowers growing along its banks.

"Having fun, *crevette*?" Sébastien murmured, pinching my nose.

I frowned and put my fists on my hips. "I am not a *crevette*." We had discussed this several times already in our relationship.

"Sure you are," Sébastien murmured. He grinned. "You have a pink nose again."

"I do *not!*" I said indignantly. "And if I do, it's only because you keep pinching it!"

He laughed. "Pinky shrump," he whispered in English as we climbed back into the car, his tone a caress.

By lunchtime, leisurely and heavy on olives, eaten high in the hills, everyone was relaxed, except for me, surrounded by salad-wielding French. I eyed the olive tapenade for potential traps, but nothing happened. Well, Sébastien's stepfather turned his full attention on me, and I think it might have slipped out that I had never seen *Bullitt* and didn't know what kind of car Steve Mc-Queen had driven in it. "A Buick?" I offered. Well, they both started with a B-U.

Sébastien covered his mouth, his eyes alive with laughter. Jean-Charles choked on his olive tapenade, cleared his throat of the crumbs, and tried to remain calm. "A Mustang. A 1968 Fastback Mustang GT 390. Are you writing this down? I want you to keep an eye out for one when you get back to the States."

"Right," I said. "Right. Mustangs would be Fords, right?"

Jean-Charles sighed. A few other men in hearing flinched, which seemed unfair, because I later looked it up on the Web, and I had gotten that one right. Jean-Charles was a nice guy, though. He changed the subject to something he thought I could handle—customs laws for shipping classic cars from the U.S. to

France—and poured everyone more wine. Bees buzzed thickly among the lavender in the restaurant's garden and occasionally flew through the open doors, over the tables, and out the other side.

"I hope we make good time," Claudine said as we headed off again. "We promised we'd be in St. Pantaléon at four for the festival, and if we're late we'll miss the *caisses à savon!*"

Soapboxes seemed a puzzling thing to be anxious about missing. "Why did we promise we'd be there at four?"

Jean-Charles grinned at me over his shoulder. "We're the starring attractions."

We were, too. The line of us swept into town at 4:30 and did a figure eight up and down cobblestoned streets, the drivers blaring their horns in a hilarious and enthusiastic cacophony of all the toots and honks invented over four decades. To my delight, the Torpedo had by far the best, something like a cross between a scream and a car upchucking.

We were almost too late, though. "Come on!" Sébastien's mother gestured urgently. "Hurry! We're going to miss the *caisses à savon!*" We ran past bales of hay and a bank of men clearly set up to judge a finish line, then around the curves of a twisty, near-vertical cobblestoned street. "Here's a good spot." Claudine stopped abruptly and pulled back from the curb as a clatter of wheels from above grew louder. "It's a tradition."

Two half-size refrigerators flashed past us. They were missing doors, welded together side by side, and packed with a team of two adult males and two adult females completely equipped in helmets and padding.

"They have this contest every year, who can make the best car without an engine. They give prizes for speed, and the funniest, and things like that," Claudine explained.

A six-year-old in a tiny little concoction I didn't even know how to describe came bowling down, his chin set determinedly. The purpose of those bales of hay became clear; they came between all those stone houses and the human bodies likely to ram into them. And a nice bulk of them protected the judges at the finish line.

"One year they had a bathtub, and the judges threw barrels of sudsy water on the driver at the finish line. Now, isn't that sweet," Claudine said as Super Papa came down at a slow and careful speed in something like a miniature wagon train, a little cart hooked on behind his *caisse*, three little kids buckled snugly into it. We knew he was Super Papa from his hand-scrawled T-shirt and a cardboard sign, where the title was followed by the carefully printed names of the children.

"How disappointing," Claudine said at the end. "It was much more creative last year."

"Really?"

"Oh, yes, one guy came down with a whole little café. The parasol came off his table, though." While I tried, baffled, to imagine a café-car, we went back down the hill to find all the contestants being hooked on to a long rope behind an SUV to be towed back up the hill for another go.

We wandered over toward the village café. Games for a *pétanque* tournament covered every inch of dirt that could even possibly be imagined flat, and I learned quickly to keep a sharp watch for flying metal balls when turning any corner. Conscious of Sébastien's family, I resisted riding the pink cow on the country-fair carousel.

On the café terrace, a serious discussion was under way. Subtly jerked chins indicated a World War II veteran in pink shirt and tie who was sporting a gray beret and a cane and hanging around over by some trees, watching the goings-on. The stalling Renault's driver braced firmly over his glass at the café. "He's a spy," he said tensely. "I know he's a spy. He's at every single last festival! Standing around watching everybody!"

Claudine, who seemed to be getting over my inability to mix a salad, caught my eyes, her own brimming with humor. It occurred to me that she might have been joking about the salad.

"What's the population of this village?" I whispered.

"Oh, I don't know, about a hundred and fifty people."

I looked around at the *pétanque* matches, the soapboxes being hauled uphill, and the little houses of golden stone. "They have a big spy problem, do they?"

If they didn't, they had too much local pride to admit it. Besides, Provence was famous for its Résistance efforts during World War II, when spies had been a serious danger even in villages like this, and apparently old habits die hard. The older drivers plunged into a debate over the pink-shirted gentleman's spy status with heated seriousness. Feeling unqualified for such a high-level discussion, I walked across the little stone bridge above the old laundry spot, and the spy called out to me a flowery compliment on what a pleasure it was to see such a beautiful, charming young lady at one of their festivals.

May I mention that I, personally, have always liked spies? They have all the moves.

Sébastien's family might not be so bad either, at that. I had never expected them to invite his strange American girlfriend into their world so readily. I had lived in several countries and traveled in more, and I had never had an experience quite like this. I had always thought a "successful" relationship would close my world and limit my options, but that didn't seem to be the case here. I felt embraced in something very special that not many outsiders got to see.

Now I started to wonder what Sébastien would think of my family and my world. And what they would think of him. My family, though, was on the other side of the world. And I was about to go back to it, while Sébastien stayed here.

Sixteen

The airport is horrible. Sébastien keeps shoving his hand across his eyes before anything can leak out. I bawl unashamedly. That's one of the things we don't have in common, our degree of self-discipline in public. Men with machine guns corral us at an unsafe distance from an abandoned piece of luggage. "How can we do this?" I cry. "We just can't do this. It will never work. I'll probably never see you again."

The airport is like some failed dream of the future. All of its once-shiny moon-colony ramps have, long since construction, grown worn and grimy. It's a pessimistic airport. It makes me feel that nothing can stay bright and beautiful. I refuse to say good-bye until ten minutes before my flight is due to take off, which is a serious miscalculation of how many moon-ramps lie between me and my gate. I reach my plane long after its doors should have closed. Flight attendants, pilot, and copilot all take a few minutes to scold me, but their voices dwindle off as I just sit in my seat crying.

Sébastien's first e-mail was waiting for me when I landed. More followed. Even though our phone bills mounted to four hundred dollars a month, we tried to communicate mostly over e-mail. Sébastien proved wonderful at love letters, pouring out his heart into them every day. Sometimes he added his artwork: a 3D teddy bear with a heart gleaming in his hand that became my computer wallpaper, a comic drawing of his cat Indy grinning from behind a pumpkin for Halloween, the flying buttresses of Notre-Dame as seen from the Seine where he had been sitting and thinking about me. He saw his family today and they sent me kisses. Indy had peed on his DVD player, which now no longer worked, and he was going to kill that cat. He loved his job, but he missed me.

I read the letters over and over. I looked at my books, all those books I had read and studied for my prelims, all those photocopies of articles I had analyzed, all those papers I had written. I didn't really like being a graduate student, but I'd always thought I should finish what I started. It looked like I had started two things.

"I miss you," I cried on the phone.

"*Please* don't cry," he said. "God, this is awful. Little pinky shrump, just imagine I'm there, holding you. See? I've got big strong arms and they're holding you and you're all warm and scrunched up against me, and now I'm starting to get distracted . . . ."

"*Awwwww.*" Heart-rending sobs from my end. "I don't know what to *do*. I can't stand this. You know we can't do this for years." And I couldn't ask him to come to the U.S. for me. I knew that. I had started this—I had left him that invitation, this poor innocent man in Paris who thought I was living there indefinitely. I was the one who had traveled to his world and started something I had no way of continuing. Now I couldn't ask him to travel to my world for me.

It was up to me.

"I miss you," Sébastien said. "I miss the way your nose scrunches up when you're trying to figure out whether avocado or grapefruit would go better in the salad you're making, and I miss the way you complain when I mess up your hair. I miss the way you slip into English when I tickle you and you say, 'Stop it, Sébastien, stop it.' I want you here so I can pinch your nose and hear you say, 'I am *not* a *crevette*.' Say it for me now," he begged. "Go ahead, say it. Say, 'I'm *not* a *crevette*.'"

"I don't know what to do," I said. I did know what I had to do. I had to choose between a fairly useless Ph.D. and Sébastien.

"But if I come to Paris, where would I live? I wouldn't have any money, I wouldn't have a job, I wouldn't even be legal this time. I'd be trying to find a way to get a visa and get a job."

"Here," Sébastien said. "With me."

"But we'd *kill* each other in that little apartment. We'd break up in no time." And I would have given up my Ph.D. for a romance that failed.

"You say we'll break up if we try to live in opposite countries for two more years, too."

"It will just die," I said. "The relationship will die. Two years apart is impossible." And two years was an optimistic estimate of how much longer my Ph.D. would take. We could spend summers together, of course, and nine months out of the year apart. I started crying again. "I miss you so bad."

"Maybe I should come there," Sébastien said. The idea clearly terrified him. "But I need a year of experience before I try to land a job with a U.S. company. I can't come there fresh out of school."

"No," I said. "You love what you're doing. I can barely stand what I'm doing. I know the choice is clear."

"I don't want you to do anything you'll be unhappy with," Sébastien said. "I won't ask you to do this."

I stilled and huddled into myself. "You don't want me to come back, do you? You don't want to try to share your tiny apartment with me either."

"No. *No,*" Sébastien said. "Are you crazy? Quit twisting things like that. I just don't want you to be unhappy, and I'm afraid you'll be unhappy."

So was I. Paris and I—well, let's just say we could still use some good couple's therapy.

All through the night, two questions gnawed at me until I felt like one giant perforated ulcer, and they led to a horde of other questions, all of which seemed to be attacking me. The first was, what if it didn't work? That is, what if I gave up a career, smiles, and sunshine for something that proved to be a flash in the pan?

Could you know someone well enough in four months to uproot your life for him, or was this just another way of fleeing real relationships, rushing into something that could never work? Was I pretending to risk something for love when I was really just indulging in some romantic fantasy with an exotic foreigner? The tall, dark, handsome Frenchman, for God's sake. If I changed his name to Raoul and made him a wealthy count, I could star in my own Harlequin. I knew I had read too many of those when I was growing up; they had given me a false idea of what was humanly possible.

The second question, or set of questions, was even worse than the first: what if it *did* work? What if I found myself, long-term, dealing with this foreign culture, a culture I found difficult at best, a culture in which I seemed always in the wrong, always less refined, and always spoke with an accent that rendered me dismissable? But this set of questions promised difficulties I could barely contemplate. With optimistic pessimism, I preferred to concentrate on the fact that it probably wouldn't work and on the question of whether I should be changing my life for love. Honestly, what self-respecting woman changes her life for love?

So granted, sitting in graduate classes in America analyzing the silence in the language of Victor Hugo was an idiotic career that I had been hating passionately for some time. But hey, the university had paid me half what the Economic Policy Institute considers poverty level to do it, and at least working on a Ph.D. had some *prestige*. I'd even been able to turn on the heat once every year or two when I'd scraped enough money together to afford it. In Paris, I wouldn't have heat, since Sébastien's apartment didn't have a radiator and we wouldn't be able to afford more than the bare minimum of electricity. And I definitely wouldn't have prestige; I was an American.

I don't know. I just wasn't sure it was entirely rational for a woman to be giving up the noncareer she hated to go live in Paris with a gorgeous, sweet, romantic Frenchman who could cook, albeit mostly with cream. At least analyzing Samuel Beckett or Céline was *something*, even if it was likely to require expensive meds. In Paris, I didn't have anything but love. Well, okay, and great chocolate. But still, that's a hell of a lot of pressure on love.

The next morning, I found an e-mail he had written long into the night. Pages and pages, all his hopes and fears for us, how his heart had leapt with joy and fear at the possibility I might come to Paris, how it broke his heart with hope that I might come and fear that I might be unhappy, how much he missed me. At the bottom of it, he drew a comic caricature of himself on one knee, his hands stretched out wide, clutching flowers, saying, *"Je t'aime."*

I went to talk to my professors, to tell them I was leaving. They were remarkably sympathetic for some of the most successful academics in their field. "Why in the world," said one, "would you choose a career in academia over a love affair with a handsome Frenchman in Paris?"

My jaw dropped. "Are you supposed to tell me that?"

"No, but how hard a choice can it be?"

I decided most professors in French literature went into their field out of a highly developed sense of romance and then just got trapped by all that literary theory. Either that or I was a lousy student and they were seizing on the chance to get rid of me without hurting my feelings. We agreed that I would finish the semester and take the oral part of my prelims, which would qualify me to leave with a Master's, so that the time I had spent here on my degree wouldn't be totally wasted.

And then I would go back to Paris. Paris. Oh, boy. Paris without friends. Paris without the money to live anywhere but in that tiny apartment with Sébastien. Paris without a job and without a work permit, with nothing to do those cold, rainy winter days but look for a job, or use my bogus art history professor card, or sit in that claustrophobic apartment. Paris, that pain-in-the-ass, snooty little city that thought all she had to do was give you a few views of the Eiffel Tower, nice museums, and great fresh bread. Then she expected you to get down in dog poop and kiss her manicured toenails in gratitude while some stranger walked up and pinched your butt. Paris. I had some fond memories of Paris, now, but we had progress to make before you could call our relationship anything but dysfunctional. And I wasn't sure life as an illegal alien trying to find a job and living in a minuscule apartment was the best way to make that progress. Still, I bought my tickets—refundable, in case I backed out in a last minute of sanity.

I wanted only one thing from Sébastien first.

Seventeen

I wanted him to come to the U.S. for Christmas, and meet my family, and see my world.

A meeting between future in-laws has always been considered a scary business, but this one promised to be particularly traumatic. The overwhelming majority of my family was male, Southern, and hard-core Republican. The rest of it was just Southern and extremely conservative Republican. And not to put too fine a point on it, but as I've already noted, Sébastien was French. He was also adamantly opposed to the death penalty, believed in national medical care, and had once publicly described Georgia's use of the Confederate flag as obscene. Fortunately, his public on the occasion had been French.

Let's just sum up some of his physical details, while we're at it. Elegant, fastidious about his clothes, Sébastien shyly spoke an accented English taught by British professors, an education that left him woefully unprepared for two weeks of Georgia redneck conversation. To top off these handicaps, he had been perverse enough to get both ears pierced and have that Polynesian-inspired design tattooed around his right biceps. If a beer can or an American flag had been tattooed there, God knows, some common ground might have been possible, as long as the earrings went. But no. Those damn French never had known how to compromise.

And what if he told my parents he was an atheist, for God's sake? I sternly forbade him to mention this and pretty much everything else he believed or didn't believe, and I even hinted he might want to take off his earrings, but he said he must come as who he was or not come. This showed unfortunate strength of character on his part.

To be perfectly frank, when I had started dating him, Georgia seemed so far away I'd forgotten to include what my family would think of him (or he would think of my family) in my criteria for selecting a boyfriend. In a family my size, this is always a mistake. I mean, we had a slight compatibility problem here. My family was going to think he was a highfalutin Parisian snob. My oldest brother had threatened to shoot anyone my niece dated who sported earrings, and he made a practice of cleaning his shotgun whenever potential boyfriends were around. And Sébastien was going to think my family was a horde of barbarians. My oldest brother was a horde of barbarians in and of himself, and that was before you started counting the next three.

Of course, Sébastien *was* the only French male I'd ever met who knew how to fire a handgun, so he might show *some* promise for getting along in the Southern world. But it was a slim hope. Besides, my brothers had never accepted any male brought home by any of their sisters, ever. And one sister had been married for fifteen years.

The closer we got to it, the more the idea of Christmas, that whole beautiful family season, with one boyfriend and four brothers arriving at our parents' home one after the other, was starting to stand all my nerves on end. My parents seemed a little tense

143

about it, too, which was understandable, because they'd seen me and my brothers get into way too many fights already. "He's *French*," my mother said.

"I'm *sorry*," I said defensively. "I didn't mean to. You know. It just happened."

"What should we serve him to *eat*?" my mother asked, looking panicky. My mother looks a bit like the Queen of England, but she doesn't have the royal nerves under pressure.

No one knows better than I the phobia of exposing anything culinary to a Frenchman's chauvinistic palate. I don't mean to criticize anyone else's manners, but for people who have fits if you can't finish everything they load onto your plate, the French sure are quick to express disdain for anything you offer *them*. Once in Tahiti, when I served my French friends there my most fêted cake covered with rich, gooey icing, two of them actually gagged on the sugar, a reflex for which I have never forgiven their entire nation. So I gave my mother a quick dose of therapy: "Don't worry. As long as you don't make any cakes, you should be fine. He's dying to try real Southern food, that's all he's talked about. Biscuits, cornbread, cookies, brownies, some good grilling, fried green tomatoes. I think fried green tomatoes are the real reason he's making the trip over here."

"It *was* a good film," Mom admitted, distracted.

"Food," Dad said. "You think food is a problem?" He had attended a philosophy conference in Paris when I was a baby and never quite recovered. My dad was a white-haired Socrates, half his sons' size, confident, and troublemaking. He had the brightest blue eyes in the family, and usually they were puckish with mischief. But right now, they held the tense, suppressed look of a man on the brink of desperation. "What *wine* should I get?"

I guess it's a good thing I never became a psychotherapist, because I couldn't think of a single encouraging thing to say in response to that. "Don't even try; you're doomed," seemed negative. I remembered Sébastien's tendency to compare American beer unfavorably to his cat's little carpet accidents and smiled a malicious smile. "He said he wants the authentic Southern experience, Dad. I'm sure he'd love a nice cold beer."

My dad looked at me incredulously, and right then I knew that one-week conference in France twenty-seven years ago had scarred him even more than I thought. "He's *French*," he said despairingly.

Sébastien decided to bring his own wine, ostensibly as a gift but more likely in self-protection. "Don't go overboard," I told him on the phone. "My brothers are mostly beer drinkers, you know; and you can only bring two bottles through customs, anyway."

"Umm," he said.

"I'm warning you. When I bring back wine with me, they don't even drink it all. A few sips, and the bottle gets shoved into some corner, half-full."

"That wine you pick out at the big tasting shows?"

"Yes." I loved the frequent wine expositions in Paris, and I went to a lot of effort to pick out the most interesting reds and whites for those in my family who wanted to become wine connoisseurs.

"Umm," he said.

They didn't even stop him in customs. All those trips when I had stayed up until 3:00 A.M. trying to figure out how to fit a couple of extra hidden bottles into my luggage in such a way that they wouldn't break in transit, and he just *told* them how many bottles over his limit he had and strolled on through without being stopped or taxed or anything. Sometimes I could just about kill the French.

I was too happy, though, to kill him then. His summer tan had faded, and he seemed more nervous and excited than I had ever seen him. Other than that he had not changed. We grabbed each other and held on as tight as we could for a long time.

145

My parents' house was about an hour west of Atlanta, near the Alabama border. My parents built their house to be as far as possible from unnerving things like civilization, so we wound and wound our way down country roads, with Sébastien peering through the windows into the dark. The red dirt road to my family home had been paved over at some point during my youth, and the rickety wooden bridge had been replaced with a concrete one high enough to be passable when the Little Tallapoosa River was high. My parents' driveway, however, had been left untouched, and we jounced and bounced up it in a way that explained why I was the first and last person in my family ever to try getting a small foreign car. The winter-bare branches of trees arched all around us as we reached the house, and Sébastien got out of the car to stand among a jungle of SUVs and pickups and stare overhead at the stars.

"You should see them in Texas," I murmured. Meaning the stars, although Texas pickups were something, too. "Really, you should."

Set in the middle of Georgia woods, on a ridge over a brown Georgia river, was the house that my parents and older siblings had built when those siblings were tweens and young teens. All was quiet, in a way that seemed to give Sébastien an earache. In Paris, there was no such thing as silence.

Only a couple of logs still glowed red in the fireplace, and heat still escaped from the dining room's Benjamin Franklin stove. Everyone was already home for Christmas and asleep, but they woke up bright and early the next day and filled the house with loud voices and uncontrolled boisterousness from one end to the other. I'm the sixth of seven children. All the females in my family had turned out really small and all the males really tall, except for my father; he had passed genes for gianthood on to his sons but been trapped eight inches smaller than they by polio when he was seven. We all had big voices, though, and knew that the only way to make ourselves heard was to just keep talking and get louder. Everyone usually participated in at least three conversations at once, while our mother wailed that we were giving her a headache and why couldn't one person talk at a time.

Introductions went tentatively. I could tell my brothers were making a real effort, in spite of the earrings, because they didn't shoot Sébastien and they even kept speaking to him. I'm sure Sébastien was making an effort, too, because he hid the fact that he didn't understand a word spoken in that molasses-and-music drawl. I would have liked to help out and translate for him occasionally, but my oldest and biggest brother, the alpha wolf, stopped that in its tracks. "No French," he barked.

I glared at him. "Don't you think you're being just a tad xenophobic?"

"No." David folded his arms over his enormous chest smugly. "I don't like people saying things I can't understand."

Sébastien started out his before-dinner, Christmas Eve presentations with the cautious gift of a corkscrew. "Now, I was sure you all had one," he lied, "but this is a style I really like." It was a nice piece of work, too, with the simple elegance of a tool with one purpose in life: no frills, no experimentations, only the best. My father and brothers, who routinely compared their latest Swiss Army knives and Leatherman tools when they got together—some kind of phallic ritual, I guess—passed this corkscrew from hand to hand. In their eyes, I saw a first gleam of appreciation.

And I noticed something else. All twenty people in my rambunctious family had gathered near the table to watch. No one was saying, "Let's eat already," and no one was wandering off to the bathroom or lingering in the living room over a game of chess. I hadn't even had to herd them to make a good show. I had just said, "Sébastien brought some wine for dinner."

The last two bottles I had snuck at great risk through customs had been slipped onto my brothers' wine racks and never commented on again. I scowled.

"First, I have an aperitif," Sébastien said, breaking the wax seal and uncorking it with that no-nonsense smoothness I had appreciated when I first saw him and which my brothers watched with calculating admiration. I could see them anticipating exactly how many bottles they would have to open before they attained that smoothness.

I took a glass of the aperitif to be supportive but needn't have bothered. Everyone of age in my family, and a couple of people who would have been of age in France and were too polite to correct Sébastien's mistake when he served them, took a glass and exclaimed how good it was. Some even took seconds, and they stood around talking, sipping, and enjoying it *just like French people*. There was food on the table, and they weren't rushing to eat.

I eyed Sébastien warily, hoping he wasn't secretly seeing himself as some missionary among the savages, leading them to salvation. It would be about like a Frenchman to be entertaining that kind of fantasy among Americans.

Everyone greeted the wine he brought with equal enthusiasm, and Christmas morning over breakfast I found Stefan, the youngest and normally most reserved of my brothers, interrogating Sébastien in his most carefully pronounced English on how to choose wines.

"Y'all come up to our place tomorrow," the oldest of my brothers said. He pointed his big, callused finger at me. "But no talking French."

The road to his house *hadn't* been paved over yet, and David's gravel driveway was even longer than my parents'. By the time we reached my brother's big, gray-blue house among the woods, Sébastien was looking at me thoughtfully: "Your family has problems with urban life, don't you?"

"I *told* you Paris was too crowded."

Once inside the shield of trees, a long lawn swept out to meet us. Up stone steps above the house, a white gazebo stood by a fishpond; beyond it lay herb and vegetable gardens. Rosebushes David had once planted with a construction crane curved up the drive. All of this was a winter ghost of its summer self, but still beautiful. We all credited such taste to David's tiny, blond wife Annette, having no other possible explanation. We'd grown up with David, after all.

No sooner had we stepped out of the cars than David landed on Sébastien. "Say-bas-tee-YON!" he called. We hadn't managed to persuade him to stop martyrizing Sébastien's name and to use its English version like the rest of the family. "That's not his name," he had countered. "Say his name again, Laura? There you go; that's what I'm saying."

"Say-bas-tee-YON! Come with me." He grabbed his keys and marched toward his truck, custom-made to be the biggest in the Southern states. I checked to make sure his new shotgun wasn't anywhere in evidence. "Honey," he called to his wife Annette, "we're going to get some wine."

"Shall I come along?" I asked nervously.

"No, you'll only start talking French again. We'll do just fine."

They arrived back in an hour, Sébastien grinning from ear to ear, both arms wrapped around a paperbag chock-full of wine bottles. My redneck brother was similarly loaded. "I thought we should stock up while we had an expert around," he said. "Now, Say-bas-tee-YON, explain to us why these are good wines."

11:00 A.M., the day after Christmas, and the kitchen island was soon sporting half a dozen bottles as Sébastien gave a short lesson in tasting.

"Hmm." After various tastes, David looked thoughtful. Even pricked by suspicion. "You know, Annette, I wonder if that wine we picked up from Alabama is actually any good? And that jug of wine that guy at the liquor store told me was as fine as all that fancy stuff? Let's see what Say-bas-tee-YON thinks of it."

The appalled look on my poor Parisian's face when he saw that jug of "as fine as the fancy stuff" wine was priceless. He nevertheless summoned up the courage to taste it. "It tastes, ah, very similar to glue," he said as politely as he could. "Glue? Isn't that the right word in English, Laura?" he checked, as laughter erupted around him.

"Don't worry, we understood 'glue,' " my sister-in-law said.

The Alabama wine came next. After he sipped it there was a lengthy and puzzled pause. "It is meant to be wine?"

That brought another explosion of hilarity.

"I'm serious!" Sébastien protested. "I was just checking." He tried to explain the technical reasons for which he had genuinely thought it might not be meant to be wine, but no one would stop laughing long enough to listen.

My big brother David had adopted a look of outrage at these aspersions on his wine cellar, but his lips were crinkling at the corners. He burst out laughing, too. "I just got a new shotgun, Say-bas-tee-YON," he said, clapping Sébastien on the shoulder. "Why don't you come out and shoot it with us?"

I'm pretty sure the emphasis on the "with" is why a Frenchman should never leave civilization without a corkscrew and some wine. But I think Sébastien's acceptance was really sealed—accent, sharp clothes, earrings, and all—when he outshot my biggest brother with his own shotgun the whole afternoon. "I guess I was just made to be a redneck," he said with a grin. He seemed to be having the time of his life.

See, now, that's such a scary thing to say. But what most shocked the women was when he and my brothers became such an inseparable fivesome that my brothers washed dishes. They had never done this before. The women cooked for two days, sat down to eat, then cleaned late into the evening, while the men drank beer; no fits of fury on the part of myself and my sisters had ever changed this lifestyle. Sébastien had started helping with the dishes the first day, but it wasn't until after the shotgun episode that a world shift occurred. The next day at my parents', we women were still sitting at the dining-room table, and our jaws dropped when we heard the sound of running water in the kitchen. We peeked around the separating wall to see four brown heads and Sébastien's black one. Yes, there my brothers were, blue eyes twinkling as if they were enjoying themselves, filling every last corner of space, big bodies brushing past each other as one of them scraped and stacked dirty dishes, Sébastien washed, and two others dried and stored. After he felt Sébastien had done more than his fair share, the youngest and most evolved of my brothers actually put his hands in dishwater himself.

I came out after they were done to find Sébastien lingering in the kitchen watching the bird feeder. "I can't believe you grew up in a place where you could see so many squirrels," he said enviously. "You're so lucky."

I just stared at him, still thinking about the dishes, dumbfounded. He hung up his dishtowel and set me on the kitchen stool, his hands resting on my hips.

"So, will you marry me?" he asked.

I laughed, but uneasily. Something in his tone was different this time, and he was looking me straight in the eyes.

"No, I mean it," he said. "Will you marry me?"

I blinked rapidly. "Are you asking me to marry you in my parents' kitchen while my brothers are only a couple of rooms away?"

"Well, I was going to ask you on top of the Eiffel Tower at night," he said defensively. "But then your friend's boyfriend went and did that. How did he come up with the same idea?"

Let me think. How *had* another man come up with the idea that proposing on top of the Eiffel Tower at night would be a romantic thing to do? Wait a minute—the engagement he was mentioning had occurred in July. Had Sébastien not, in fact, been entirely joking all those times in the summer he had said we should get married? "So you went straight from the Eiffel Tower to the kitchen thing? You didn't have any other intermediate ideas?"

"It just seemed like the right moment," he said, with a tiny embarrassed shrug. He still had a happy, eager smile lingering around his mouth, but his hands flexed nervously on my hips. "I like the fact that your family's around. And a kitchen—well, I mean, a kitchen is the heart of a home, isn't it?"

I sighed. Americans give Parisians this reputation for romanticism based, I think, on the fact that for most of us romance and reality are separate and conflicting modes of thought. Sébastien's sense of romance was very grounded in the real.

He nudged my legs with his hips. "So? Will you?"

"I don't know," I said. The crazy thing was that I *didn't* know. I would have thought my first instinct would have been a definite no, per my antipathy to marriage and ties, but somehow "No" wasn't what I wanted to say. I had already quit school and was moving to Paris for him, which was proof of something: a guy like Sébastien and a feeling like ours wasn't something you said "No" to, except by such an unbearable act of emotional cowardice you would regret it all your life.

His face fell, and he eased back a pace.

"I mean, I really don't know. I'm not saying no," I added hurriedly. "I mean—this isn't my only chance, is it? I have to grab you now or never?"

"No. You can think about it." But the smile had drooped all away.

"I just—we only really met eight months ago. And for nearly four of those months we were on opposite continents."

"I think those months apart count for something," he interrupted firmly. "They showed we can stick together, even when things are tough. Those months were *hard*. And we're still together."

"Yes, but I'd just like—I think we should go ahead with my plan to live in Paris with you for a while. I think we should see how that works—if I can really live there, and if we can really live together."

He blinked a couple of times now himself. "But you're not moving back to Paris for a couple more weeks."

"I know."

"You're going to make me wait *weeks*? I thought you wanted to think about it overnight."

"I kind of wanted to think it over a couple of *months*. I don't think two people from different countries should get engaged without seeing if at least one of them can live in the other's country!"

"But you *can* live in my country," he said, confused.

"It was tough sometimes. And that stay in Paris was temporary, one year, and just for fun." It had also, like all my other sojourns abroad, been financed by a grant that had both given me an income and permitted a student visa. In a sense, the other times I had lived abroad had therefore been like dipping into a swimming pool with little floaters on my arms to help me swim. Moving to a country where I had no source of income and no legal right to develop one was like jumping into a violent, stormy ocean without a life preserver. I wasn't sure I was that strong a swimmer. "Permanent commitments to places are different. Can we just see how it goes first?"

He took a deep breath, although he was still hurt, I could tell. "All right," he said. "All right."

I nodded, and we were quiet for a moment. "By the way," I said to change the subject and because certain cultural differences had been worrying me, "you seem to be handling my brothers' more barbaric habits all right."

"That's what you call barbaric?" Sébastien looked worried. "I don't know how you're going to take my father's side of the family, then."

Eighteen

I hadn't actually known that it was possible to be more barbaric than my brothers, so that was disturbing. Maybe I should get to know his family a little better before making a decision on the marriage proposal. Hey, when it came to stalling commitment, any excuse worked for me.

"That will take a while," Sébastien said as we put off separation in the Atlanta airport. That wrenching pain of missing someone was setting in, but we were trying to ignore it.

"Why? How many family members do you have?"

"Close, you mean? I guess a couple hundred."

"Really. When you start talking about your extended family, who does that include? Half of France?"

"Well, and some of Sicily. A great-grandfather. But you only need to meet about a hundred or so of the family to start off."

"Do I. And how many of those hundred are on your father's side?"

"Good God, Laura, I'm not going to introduce you to anyone on my father's side before the wedding! They play rugby."

Playing rugby did seem ominous, now that he mentioned it, but an announcer started calling passengers to board before I could ask any more questions. We focused on all the mushiness we needed to get out of our systems. We were not getting any better at this. Red rimmed Sébastien's eyes by the time they began calling his name specifically and not just his row. "Damn it." He shoved a hand across his eyes. "I swore this time I wasn't going to do this."

I just cried. And I already had a ticket to follow him only two weeks later.

Packing was hard. Outside, the ice storm had passed, and the Georgia January sky was balmy blue. I was wearing a tank top, and I was trying to force wool sweaters into a suitcase originally bought to hold bathing suits and sunscreen. I had been lured into graduate studies in French via Tahiti-French Polynesia and had been doing just fine with the South Pacific thing until I made the mistake of leaping at my university's offer of a year in Paris. They didn't warn me about the weather, it goes without saying.

Imagining you share a language with the British can be a perilous thing. Growing up, I had assumed "sunny France" to be, well, sunny. No one had explained to me that British authors described France as sunny because they had glimpsed blue sky there a couple of times during the Hundred Years War. Therefore, on my first trip I had wasted a great deal of space on things like short-sleeve shirts and other items you could bring out in Paris only one month a year. For a while there, I'd thought that dating Sébastien had cured the weather, but then I'd spent the Fourteenth of July freezing my tail off while we tried to watch the fireworks with his friends on the Champs de Mars. Trust me, five adults in sweaters and jackets huddling together for warmth is not something you'd see at a Fourth of July celebration in Georgia.

"Everyone told me the weather here got nice in May!" I wailed, shivering madly as blue, white, and red flares went up behind the Eiffel Tower. Although our two countries share the same patriotic colors, the French refer to theirs always as the *bleu, blanc, et rouge,* exactly the opposite order of our *red, white, and blue.*

"It does," Éric had answered, offended. "But this is July now. We'll start to get more and more cold nights."

"Anyway, it's America's fault for not signing the Kyoto Treaty," Virginie said. "We never used to have such bad weather. The Gulf Stream is moving."

I could never complain about anything French without the French pointing out how it was my fault.

"You know, you wouldn't complain so much about the cold and rain if you'd dress properly," Valérie had once said to me, around the first week of October when any normal country would have brisk, balmy, clear blue days. That had been at the start of my first year, and therefore my first winter, in Paris.

"What are you talking about? I'm wearing a jacket and gloves, inside, at my desk, and I'm still freezing."

"You call that a jacket?"

"You don't?" I clutched it, alarmed. I had been there only five weeks by then, and I kept hoping this extraordinary cold spell would snap.

"Well, it's fine enough for August and maybe some Septembers, but now that we're into October, you're going to need a proper winter coat."

I looked down at my cropped leather jacket. "You mean this doesn't count? Wait. *October* is winter for you?"

She rolled her eyes. "Besides, if you were wearing a real sweater, you wouldn't even need a jacket inside."

I unzipped my jacket triumphantly to show her my cropped, V-necked, cotton sweater.

She gazed at it a second in disbelief and then closed her eyes: "You know, Americans take a lot of work."

One of the Parisian instructors, in a gray cashmere turtleneck, paused long enough to shake her head. "Are you wearing *blue*? I'll never understand your country." No kidding. Every time Texas executed someone under twelve, she had a screaming fit, go figure. And always at me, and I wasn't even *from* Texas, a defense she seemed to consider splitting hairs.

Remembering these scenes, I gazed grimly at the contents of my suitcases: several black sweaters, various black turtleneck shirts, several pairs of black pants, several black antiperspirant deodorants, and so many containers of black dental floss that my teeth could survive a nuclear winter. Okay, the deodorants and dental floss were white, but they did fill up every spare corner. On one previous extended stay in a French territory, I had been deeply embarrassed at having to ask family members to mail me dental floss, and I didn't intend to give them any more ammunition to use against me in the annual Christmas reunion reminiscences. This French territory had been Tahiti, a little bit more remote than Paris, but still, a girl couldn't be too careful.

Once I fit all the dental floss into my suitcases, it didn't leave much room, so I packed all my shorts, T-shirts, and tennis shoes in boxes and told my mother if I didn't come back within two years or took up smoking and being rude to complete strangers, to give them to Goodwill. I tucked my orange teddy bear into my carry-on, so that we didn't risk getting separated at such a perilous moment. My father had brought Teddy back for me from his conference in France when I was a baby and given me a French-English picture dictionary to go with him, so that Teddy and I could learn to talk to each other. Poor Dad. He said he had learned from that and was only ever going to give his grandchildren safe presents, like firearms. Despite being born in Paris, Teddy had still turned out to be a boon companion, so packing him seemed like an optimistic gesture. You can't abandon all hope.

One of my favorite jokes is the one where the guy falls off a cliff and catches himself on a shrub halfway down. He looks down and sees rocks and stormy waters a long, long way below. He looks up and screams, "Help! Is there anyone up there?"

"Yes," a calm voice says. "It's Me. God. I'll take care of you. Just let go."

And the guy looks down at those rocks far below again, looks back up, and shouts, "Is there anyone else up there?"

Falling for Sébastien and choosing to do something about it was like falling—or jumping on purpose—off that cliff. Going back to the U.S. to my Ph.D. program was like catching myself on a good, solid branch on the way down. Everything Sébastien did, everything he was, could count as that calm, sure response that said, "Let go." And leaving my Ph.D. program and getting on that plane was letting go.

The stupid plane flew too fast. This could have been good, because I would see Sébastien sooner, but Sébastien had no idea. So it was just bad, because it gave me one hour less before I set foot on Paris concrete again and thus plunged headlong into the rocks and stormy water below.

My flight arrived in Paris at 8:00 A.M. Sébastien met me outside customs at nine, exactly five minutes before my plane had been scheduled to arrive. By that point, I was in near hysterics. "You got here on time!" I said. "How could you get here on time?"

"Laura, I didn't *know* your plane would get in an hour early and you would be sitting here waiting for me. I thought getting here at your arrival time would give me an hour's margin while you got through customs."

"But if you really loved me, you would have wanted to see me so badly you would have gotten here an hour *earlier* than my arrival time, just in anticipation. You don't really love me, do you?"

Sébastien looked at me and sighed. "You're having a nervous breakdown about this decision to come to Paris, aren't you?"

"And leave my life," I sobbed. "I left my whole life, and you *got here on time.*"

It was a bad moment, but we did eventually manage to get through this coldhearted punctuality of his and escape the airport. Grayness hovered a few feet overhead as we stepped outside, so cold it felt as if any minute the droplets of mist in the air would turn into ice. This came as no surprise to me. Sure, it had been sunny all the way across the Atlantic and even over Normandy, but just after I got my hopes up, I had seen the bowl of clouds collected over Île-de-France.

"Guess what?" Sébastien said happily, glad to proffer a new subject, now that the one on how little he truly loved me had been exhausted for the next three minutes. "My family has a surprise for you! They decided to postpone their Feast of Kings get-together until tomorrow so they could get a chance to meet you. Wasn't that sweet?"

It was probably just a minor flaw, but I had noticed before that my almost fiancé had a tendency to pose trick questions, most of them to do with his family. On the one hand, I had always wanted to participate in a real French Epiphany celebration, and I *did* have to meet more of his family someday. On the other, it sounded like a gathering where a lot of people would be forming their first impressions of me. The average Frenchmen I passed in the street had never acted as if their impressions of me were all that good. "When you say 'family,' could you be more precise?"

"Well, my grandparents, of course, can't wait to meet you. Then there's my uncle Titi, his partner, Bruno, their dogs, my aunt Martine, her husband, Jacky, and their children, Julie and Gaëlle. And, of course, my mom and Jean-Charles and Justine, and their dog, whom you've already met. I don't know yet if there will be anyone else."

"Wow," I said. "All of those future in-laws at once. That's nice." I wondered if I had to impress the dogs, too. Probably. I wouldn't trust anybody who couldn't get along with *my* dogs.

Sébastien hefted a seventy-pound suitcase in each arm, an act that reminded me I was at least going through all this for a really sexy guy, and slanted me a look distinctly lacking in sympathy. "Until you have to taste wine from Alabama at eleven in the morning, I don't even want to hear about it."

Nineteen

Sébastien's apartment, now ours, was on what the French call the fifth floor to make it seem more accessible but which would be the sixth floor in the U.S. There was no elevator, but one of my suitcases wouldn't fit in most Parisian elevators anyway. I wouldn't even fit in most Parisian elevators, and it's nothing to do with the chocolate.

We could hear Indy caterwauling as we came in from the street, and he still hadn't stopped by the time all the wheels had fallen off my suitcases and we had finally bumped them up to the top. The striped beige cat crouched in the middle of the floor and gave one last defiant yawl as we came in, before stalking off. I could tell Sébastien had thoroughly vacuumed before I came, because the layer of cat hair clinging to everything was only two inches thick.

Sébastien set my suitcases down, which effectively took up the only remaining floor space in the apartment. I looked around in something approaching desperate terror.

The apartment was nineteen square meters, smaller than most American cars. Our tiny refrigerator was tucked under two stove burners, in a minuscule kitchen unit against one wall. I had good memories of that kitchen unit and of Sébastien cooking there in an unbuttoned white shirt, but still, it was a small place to live. Two enormous windows let in the day's gray light and saved the apartment from being completely claustrophobic. The bed took up half the space, while a small table a foot high, my suitcases, and a computer occupied the rest. The table had been added in my absence; we used to eat sitting on the floor with our plates in our laps. The computer was also a foot off the floor. Sébastien didn't want to have to try to fit chairs in.

When we opened the windows a crack to get rid of some of the cat smell, the noise of the traffic below immediately boomed into the room like a freight train. Memories of this street's unfortunate acoustics came flooding back. Something about it amplified every sound: delivery people blocking the street at seven in the morning while commuters pounded on their horns; former sleepers leaning from the window to tell them to shut the *putain de merde* up; that Peugeot's alarm that seemed to go off every single morning at 3:00 A.M. and go on for hours and hours. Of course, there were some good memories mixed in with all this, and not just the night someone threw a brick through that Peugeot's window, or else I wouldn't have been in the apartment at 3:00 A.M. I would have been in my own old place at the Cité U. But. I sighed, turned around to put down my carry-on, and discovered Indy in the process of peeing in the only corner left.

I put a hand to my temple. We were both just out of school; we both had no savings and even quite a bit in student loans to pay off; and I had no job and a long, excruciating job search to go before I could get one, get a work visa, and start earning money. So this was our apartment for the immediate future, if our couple could survive it.

"Are you still glad I came?" I asked Sébastien.

"Yes," he said.

So we went to bed and slept until it was morning again and time for me to get up and face the in-laws.

The Feast of Kings, or Epiphany, officially takes place on January 6, but in France any gathering in January is an excuse for a *galette des Rois,* and the possibility of a *galette des Rois* is an excuse for a gathering. The flaky, almond-intense *galette des Rois* is a French tradition that dates well back into the Middle Ages, and some historians trace its roots back to Roman times. It is now the key element of the festival of Epiphany, or the visit of the Three Magi. Although traditionally the first *galette des Rois* is shared among friends and family on Epiphany itself, or very close to it, people continue to share *galettes* at every occasion up into February. While there are various classic recipes, one of the more common ones is that of a thin, rich, flaky tarte filled with almond paste. Inside this "king cake," as Louisianans have translated the expression for their Mardi Gras version, is baked *a fève,* which literally means a dried bean but rarely is one anymore. Whoever gets this *fève* is King or Queen for the evening and must choose a consort, both to be crowned with the paper crowns the baker provides with each *galette.*

I liked the idea of a *galette des Rois* but remained leery about the gathering business. "You know," I hissed to Sébastien as we rode in the back of the car with Claudine, Jean-Charles, Justine, and their dog to his grandparents' house, "my family might drink beer, but at least you only have one grandmother of mine to meet. I'm about to meet your second set of grandparents, and I still have *two more to go."*

"Well, and then my great-grandmother," Sébastien said. "But I have only two brothers, and neither carries a shotgun. Hey, Mom, did you know Laura was raised in the woods?"

Slim, delicately boned Claudine, with her cropped red hair and tiny sapphire earrings, hesitated and glanced at me in the rearview mirror. "You mean . . . by wolves?"

Okay, now, my table manners weren't *that* bad. On the other hand, when I was a child I did have four teenage brothers who used to feed me dogfood sandwiches, something that wouldn't have worked on a smarter little girl because my parents only bought dry dog food. And when four teenage males gathered around the dining-room table, things could get pretty ugly. "Not exactly."

Claudine twisted around. "Séba, has she met *any* of your father's side? You're going to have to have a pretty big wedding to accommodate all the family. Have you calculated all the guests?"

"I figure about one hundred and fifty will be able to make it," Sébastien said.

As his mother nodded and twisted back around, I poked him. "What are you talking about? *If* we get married, I thought we agreed to do it in the U.S. Haven't you told your mom that, yet?"

"I'm not going to tell her that *today*," Sébastien said, appalled. Then aloud, "But Laura still hasn't officially agreed to marry me yet, Mom."

I froze like a deer in headlights, feeling sick to my stomach. Instant nausea was a natural human reaction to such a statement to a semifiancé's mother, but I should also mention that Jean-Charles was in top competitive French driving form today, and there *was* a big wet golden Lab in the car.

"No!" Claudine twisted her red head again, apparently not in the least troubled by carsickness. She fixed me with brown eyes only a shade lighter than her son's, her gaze unwavering as Jean-Charles accelerated at top speed to within an inch of someone's bumper. "Why not?"

"Umm . . . we haven't known each other very long," I stammered.

Claudine continued to gaze at me in polite inquiry.

"Only eight months," I tried.

Jean-Charles braked on a dime and roared something at the driver he'd been tailgating. Claudine's gaze did not waver.

"I'm not sure I can take a lifetime involvement with the French culture?"

Claudine frowned. Maybe she didn't know the French were so difficult.

"Are we very far?" I murmured to Sébastien. "Because otherwise, we need to stop so I can throw up."

Sébastien's maternal grandparents lived an hour outside of Paris, in a small, old stone house with a huge and at that moment soaked garden. The mist had turned into rain during the night, and now rain poured down on verdant green lawns, and poured, and poured, making it clear it had no intention of stopping that day and probably not even that week. Sébastien's grandfather, a small, stocky man with a luxuriant shock of gray hair, came out with an umbrella over his head to open the gate for us. The golden Lab jumped out and quickly started tracking mud in the entrance hall. We had barely arrived when she was joined by two others of her race, who leapt from the back of an old Fiat, followed immediately by shouts to behave. "Olive! Hermine! *Descendez! Ah, ces chiens! Bonjour!*"

The two men climbing out of either side of the Fiat could not have been more different physically. Sébastien's uncle Titi—small, stocky, and dark—had a diamond stud in one ear. His real name was Jean-Pierre, but people always called him Titi, the French name for Tweety Bird. Barring any sudden sprouting of yellow feathers, I was going to have to assume that was for his personality. Though his hair was cropped short and had not yet grayed and his mannerisms were far more ironic, he resembled his father in a younger, more robust form. His partner, Bruno, sliding out of the driver's seat, topped him by a foot.

At thirty-five, Bruno was the younger man in the couple, but his hair was pure white, classily cut, and silky, just long enough for him to toss it expressively or run his fingers through it, as he did as soon as he stepped out of the car. "*Et voilà la petite Laura!*" He seized me for kisses on each cheek, confused when I stopped after two. "No, no! Here it's four!"

He passed me to Titi for more kisses, and then Sébastien's grandfather René caught my shoulders and held me there to look at me. "*Et voilà la petite Laura!*" he said as well, with four warm kisses. His eyes sparkled with pleasure. "*Mais elle est jolie!"* he complimented Sébastien. Pretty, hmm? I decided I liked him.

The dogs were banished to the entrance hall, since they had already covered it with mud, anyway. The rest of us crowded into the kitchen, where Sébastien's tiny, round, and round-faced grandmother Pierrette was washing dishes. Shyer and quieter than her husband, but with the same attentive kindness, she dried her hands on a dishtowel and gave me four *bises.*

The kitchen and dining room were one and the same room, one that seemed much too small to hold the nine of us. It seemed even tinier when another small table was pulled in from another room and pushed against the rectangular dining table, a tablecloth thrown over them both to hide the crack. "There are four more people coming," Titi explained cheerfully, his diamond stud catching the light. "My sister and her family later, when we get to the *galettes.*"

"Oh," I said, having forgotten them. Always eager to be introduced to new future in-laws, that was me.

"They're bringing the *galettes,* so they'd better get here," Claudine said as she pulled food out of sacks: smoked salmon, pâté, and even a pressure cooker, which unsealed to reveal a pot full of rabbit.

Pierrette turned back to the dishes again, although I was a little confused, because it looked as if she was taking the clean dishes from the dish drainer, rewashing them, and putting them back in it to dry. Jean-Charles installed himself at one corner of the table and proceeded to dominate it with his size and growly, humorous presence. Titi and Sébastien started picking on Justine, who continued to be preternaturally patient, and Bruno moved to center stage, telling some hilarious story from the last party all of them had attended. It involved mimicries of Titi in an advanced stage of inebriety.

René put himself in the middle of everything, bouncing on his toes with the pleasure of the gathering of people around him. He turned to me constantly to make sure I felt welcome in his home. My eyes kept being drawn to his thick, lush, dark gray hair. That a man in his mid-sixties should have such an amazing head of hair seemed symbolic of his love of life. I had never seen anything like the vivacity of his dark eyes or the energy he exuded: flirtatious, joking, eager for everyone to be happy, showering compliments around him like sunshine on that unremittingly rainy day.

Remembering Claudine's query about wolves, I concentrated on not doing anything barbaric and on getting through the first course. The first time I ate one of Claudine's meals, the first course had been a salad she asked me to mix. Enough said.

The second time I ate one of Claudine's meals, she had served sausage. I had comfortably finished half the slices of it on my plate when Sébastien held up a sausage-laden piece of bread and regarded it amorously. "Mom, this is delicious. What's in it?"

He wanted to know what was in *sausage*? Was he crazy or just trying to sabotage me? I turned to glare at him but then remembered: the first time he had spoken to me, he had described the contents of blood sausage. He was worse than crazy; he was French. In his sanest moments, he would not only want to know, discuss, and think about what was in his sausage, but salivate over the details.

"Oh, that? I think it might be horse. It's horse, isn't it, Jean-Charles?" Claudine checked with her husband.

Jean-Charles did, indeed, believe it was. Yum, yum, yum. Nothing quite so good as horse.

Beauty, screamed my next bite of sausage as I bit into it, *Black Stallion.*

This Feast of Kings was my third meal prepared by Claudine, and I already knew what the first course was: smoked salmon. I hate fish. I've hated it since the day I was born, and I used to have to eat it raw all the time in Tahiti, where people kept serving me *poisson cru* as a special treat every time I went anywhere for dinner. What kind of culture serves innocent guests raw fish, I ask you? What kind of culture serves innocent guests horse, for that matter?

The slice of smoked salmon Claudine put on my plate flopped all the way across it and hung limply off the edges. The appalling odor of salmon rushed up at me.

I took a deep breath and dug in, smiling and chatting while I worked my way through it. I only had three stomach-wrenching bites to go when Sébastien glanced over at my plate. "Mom! You didn't give Laura salmon, did you? Fish always makes her want to throw up."

There was a tiny pause. "My meals nauseate you?" said my French potential mother-in-law.

I ground my foot hard into Sébastien's toe under the table. "What?" he exclaimed loudly. "You shouldn't have to eat something you hate!"

"I had already eaten it," I pointed out between gritted teeth. "What was the point of bringing it up *now*?" I smiled weakly at all the people on whom I was trying to make a good impression.

"*Non, non, non,* he's absolutely right," Claudine said, plucking what was left of my salmon off my plate and putting it on Sébastien's. "What would you like, instead? I think we have some sausage."

After that, the second course of rabbit was a relief. It didn't scream *Thumper* at me or anything. About eight hours into the meal, Sébastien's Aunt Martine arrived with her husband, children, and two *galettes*. These eight hours, from 11:00 A.M. to 7:00 P.M., had been relieved only by brief breaks between courses to stretch our legs. With the pouring rain, stretching one's legs consisted mostly of huddling on the threshold of the house freezing to death, surrounded by people smoking cigarettes. Exceptionally, no one was smoking inside. This was for the health of Pierrette, one of the few people not smoking. René, spry and happy, rolled his own cigarettes with a particularly dark and rich tobacco, making what the others called *des brunes*.

Eager to be a queen, I sat on the edge of my seat when the *galettes* were set out, filling the room with the scents of butter and almond paste. I concentrated on willing a *fève* to come to me. Everyone else tried to get Justine to climb under the table and crouch in the mud we had all tracked in. "You're the youngest, Justine! It's your job."

She held firm. "I'll cover my eyes." While Sébastien cut the slices and Justine named whoever should be served the piece just sliced, I watched suspiciously for any cracks in her fingers. I've read Shakespeare—when a crown is at stake, you can't trust anybody.

Needless to say, I didn't get a *fève*. Needless to say, Bruno did. It took us forever to find the second *galette's fève,* and people were starting to accuse the baker of forgetting it, when Titi spotted it tucked under the edge of Justine's plate. "*Cheater!*" he said, outraged. "*You* got it?"

"*Not* on purpose," Justine protested, only to be drowned out by the uproar of accusations. Bruno, who would probably have befriended Richard III, put a paper crown on her head anyway, and she held the other in her hand a moment, stymied at which male relative to name her king. She finally chose Sébastien and offered her crown to me, but I shook my head. If I couldn't be chosen by the *fève* itself, I was *not* going to accept any hand-me-down queenships, thank you very much.

A *fève* was once, in its linguistic and historical origins, a dried bean baked into the cake, but *fèves* have long since developed into little figurines in an infinite variety of motifs. Our *fèves* were generic examples from whatever bakery was most convenient to Martine's route, but they provoked rich reminiscences. The stories of the different *fèves* people had seen ranged from exquisite handcrafted creations of great elegance to, er, erect penises.

"*Zob!*" Bruno cried out at that memory, riveted with inspiration. He sprang to his feet and swept up a fourth crown to place

168

on his head, where it balanced precariously on top of the one he had won on his own account, the one he had stolen from his consort Titi, and the one Justine had been too cool to wear long. We had now been at the table for at least ten hours, and alcohol had flowed. Bruno executed a sexy hip movement to get things started.

"Oh, no." Titi buried his head in his hand.

Bruno ignored him and burst into full-throated song.

En revenant de Paris, jusqu'à Nantes,
Oh! lala, oh, lala, lala, lala, lala,
En revenant de Paris, jusqu'à Nantes,
Tiens, voilà mon zob, zob, zob,
Tiens, voilà mon zob, zobi!
(Coming back from Paris to Nantes,
Oh, lala, etc.
Look, here is my zob, zob, zob!)

"*Zob!*" Bruno directed his hysterical audience, waving his knife like a conductor who had sipped a little too much during intermission. "*Zob! Zob!*" cried everyone else, including Titi. René, standing on his tiptoes, bellowed "*Zob!*" at the top of his lungs with every refrain, laughing with delight, his eyes gleefully alive.

J'ai rencontré trois jeunes filles charmantes,
Oh! lala, oh, lala, lala, lala, lala,
J'ai rencontré trois jeunes filles charmantes,
Tiens, voilà mon zob, zob, zob,
Tiens, voilà mon zob, zobi!
(I met three charming young girls, etc.
Look, here is my zob, zob, zob!)

Sébastien and Jean-Charles pounded the table with each resounding "*Zob!*" Justine covered her mouth to try to stop laughing so hard, and we all swayed back and forth as we sang the one part I could master, *"Zob! Zob! Zob!"*

I do think it was perfectly natural of me to assume *"zob"* was a nonsense word, like the *"Oh! lala"* part. I mean, grandparents and grandchildren were present. Grandparents and grandchildren were *singing* it.

"No, actually it's slang for penis," Sébastien corrected me, with a grin. "Children's slang."

I paused. "Excuse me, but have I been singing, 'Weenie! Weenie! Weenie!' at the top of my lungs for the past fifteen minutes?"

"Well, yes," Sébastien said blankly. "So?"

True, no one else seemed to mind. Claudine was singing with the best of them, and René, bouncing on his tiptoes, infected everyone with his joy. He had quite a considerable collection of his own dirty songs, I discovered, as Bruno finished up his performance and Jean-Charles and René launched into a new one.

It was funny. I had come still expecting a standoffish reception and gotten something else entirely—enthusiasm, joy, welcome. A real feast of kings.

Twenty

The standoffish reception came from the government.

Immigration counters seemed to get higher with each office I was shunted to, until I had to stand on tiptoe to peer over today's, in a dull, faded room of cheap plastic and linoleum. A habit of dislike added ten years to the pale face of the dark-haired woman behind the counter, who had a job from which God himself couldn't fire her but which she could never learn to like. She looked meticulously over every page of the file I handed her, flared her nostrils, and handed the whole thing back. "You need four copies of the form establishing your grandmother's maiden name."

"That's interesting," I said, "because yesterday you said I needed three."

She had waved a list of requirements at me and refused to let me keep a copy or even touch the copy she held, but I remembered the number three clearly. I wondered if the government was really that stingy in its photocopy allowance or if she had just not wanted me to have written proof of actual requirements.

Her nostrils flared yet wider as she looked at me with pure hate. I tried not to take it personally. She had looked at the other people before me in line with hate, too. "Four," she repeated.

"Well, is there perhaps a place I could make a fourth copy?" I asked, looking at the photocopier directly behind her.

"Down the street," she said, staring me straight in the eye.

"And when I come back from the photocopier down the street, will I have to wait another two hours in line?"

"Yes."

"And you're closing in half an hour."

"Yes."

Well, that answered one question. She could, in fact, say a word other than *"Non."* She couldn't seem to adopt an expression that wasn't negative, though.

I drew a deep breath and tried to make my Southern smile at her, but even I could tell it looked more like I was baring my fangs. "I guess I'll be back tomorrow then."

"We're closed tomorrow," she said. "It's Wednesday, you know." As if it was the most natural thing in the world that not only did civil servants in French immigration get most of the days of the year off in holidays or vacation, this office also got Wednesday, too.

"Thursday, then."

171

She opened her mouth but had to close it again. It was February, one of the few months when the French have to work every Thursday, so she knew I had her.

I went past the other people waiting on plastic chairs in this miserable gray room, down the twisting narrow stairs. Just by the stairs was a photocopier where you could make copies for the equivalent of eighty cents apiece. Broken. Out on the street, it was raining, a cold, bone-aching rain that poured straight down, and the cars driving by sprayed water up onto my legs. I tucked my stack of documents under my coat and slogged to find a photocopier, then down slick steps into the Métro, which was packed with dangling wet umbrellas and the grim faces of all the other people wishing they were somewhere else with fewer people and better weather. Thank God for Parisian bakeries and chocolate, we were probably all thinking.

Damp and spattered, I made my way up the five flights of stairs to our apartment, from which wafted a smell of cat piss. Something crunched under my boot.

I looked down and at first thought that Indy had been using his contributions to the litter box as toy balls again. He seemed to do about anything when he was bored. But when I bent closer, the squished brown thing suddenly took on a drastic resemblance to the antidepressants I had brought back from a weekend trip to see friends of Sébastien's in Belgium: chocolate from my favorite Belgian chocolatier. Yes, yes, I know we were too broke for me to buy expensive chocolates. Even Citibank was starting to think we might be too broke to buy expensive chocolates, and that was a bad sign. But some things are essential.

On the table, the sealed plastic sack inside a second plastic sack had been pulled out and ripped open, and I found the round Belgian truffles in every corner of the room. Had Indy eaten the truffles, they might have at least poisoned his liver as he deserved, but no. He had just played with them and covered them with cat hair.

Being dependent on chocolate to keep me going in tough circumstances, I ripped off my coat, sat down on the bed, and buried my face in my hands. I stayed that way a long time, and then got up, put my coat back on, and went to the Louvre. I had no job interviews of my own that day, despite my best, most humiliating efforts; and I had six more hours to kill until Sébastien got home from his fantastic job for the best graphic illustration firm in Paris. I was writing articles, sometimes sold and sometimes not, and I was trying to get taken on as a restaurant reviewer for a local English language publication—a job that paid only in meals but would be a lot of fun. But those did not really fill the hole this move had created in my life. I wasn't mad that Sébastien had the job he loved and colleagues he raved about while I seemed to have no hope of ever working again, really, I wasn't, but . . . it didn't seem fair. And I was damned if I would sit six hours alone in that tiny apartment with a cat who had just destroyed my chocolates. One of us would have to go out the window.

Besides, there's no better place to be on a rainy winter day than the Louvre. In the Louvre, light, space, and beauty are concentrated to such intensity that visitors wallow in a daze, drowned by it. Pale and vast and filled with the soft natural light of Peter Rice's skylight—a light that maintains its luminosity no matter how gray the day outside—the Cour Marly alone is the most blessed architectural feat in the history of urbanity. Pale stairs climb up three plazalike levels, and live trees intersperse with dramatic statues, heightening the sense of a sunlit, peaceful park. Best of all, even at the height of tourist season, I never see more than a half-dozen people in all this space at one time. I would have thought most of Paris would have a pass to the Louvre, as I did, just so they could go into the Cour Marly whenever they wanted, sit, and close their eyes. Sometimes I could stay there an hour without moving, just feeling the space, the light, the gentle echoes, like a waterfall in the background, of those few people moving around, looking at the hearts and souls of some of humanity's greatest artists, poured into physical form for us to keep.

Most of the people in the Louvre gathered in the other wing around the Mona Lisa. I went there, too, sometimes. Although I am a Philistine when it comes to the Mona Lisa and wish she would get that damn smirk off her face, I can't walk through her room without having all the hairs on my arm stand on end. There's just something about her. More importantly, on the same side of the museum, the Victory of Samothrace soars up above the stairs in winged, headless, armless victory, her whole body one dramatic lift, erasing my depression every time I see her.

As a foreigner trying to find a job and a work visa in Paris, I needed Victory of Samothrace therapy frequently. I'm not saying it wasn't a beneficial lesson in humility, seeing my credentials dismissed with raised, contemptuous eyebrows and being turned down with hauteur for jobs far beneath the qualifications I had established on the other side of the Atlantic. I'm sure it was good for me. But I wouldn't wish it on anyone except French civil servants.

The worst part was staring at the walls in that apartment, wishing I had something useful to accomplish. Maybe I should have been happier with nothing to do in Paris for months, with endless time to linger in cafés, the Louvre, the Musée d'Orsay, go to concerts, the theater, explore. But I shouldn't *have* endless time to linger and explore; I needed a *job*. It sounded so easy to friends who didn't do it, to give up a boring graduate program for true love in Paris; but unemployed and often afraid, there were days I hated Paris more than any other place on the planet.

"So guess what happened to me today?" I asked Sébastien, sitting on the bed while he washed the dishes. I'd made dinner, timing it for just when he got home. What a good little woman I was, to be sure. But what the hell else did I have to do?

"Oh, boy." His hand flexed around the skillet handle, and his mouth set. He didn't look at me. He worked from ten to seven officially, but usually that ran over to 7:30, so that he got home at 8. Before my installation in his apartment, he got home to a place of relaxation. Sometimes he went out for a drink with the guys from work, and then he came home and worked out, and maybe played an hour of video games to relax. Now he couldn't do any of that: he didn't want to go out with friends and leave me by myself even longer, he didn't want to work out with me only a few inches away in the small space, and I didn't want him to play video games instead of talking to me and reminding me why I had sacrificed so much to come here. I needed some positive reinforcement, and he was the only positive reinforcement I had.

"I had another job interview this morning. And the interviewer sniffed and said, 'We're looking for people with teaching experience.' "

He frowned. "I thought you had teaching experience."

"I do. Four years teaching languages in a high school and one year teaching at one of the best universities in the U.S." As a graduate instructor, but on a CV, that was just "instructor." I had even volunteered teaching ESL in the evenings to Hispanic immigrants for a while, so that not only did I have second language teaching experience, I specifically had English-as-a-second-language experience. "But she said, 'Well, we mean experience teaching English to corporate clients.' Which is so much B.S., Sébastien. Most of the people working for them are British teenagers trying to get a few months in Paris. She just wanted to make sure I was grateful for their miserly offer of five dollars an hour, not counting transport time back and forth between different factories."

"But she did offer you a job?" Sébastien asked quickly.

"Oh, of course. They all offer me jobs, if I can survive on the SMIC." Minimum wage. "But they won't sponsor my work permit. I have to find someone who will sponsor my work permit. Or I have to get the government to give me one without a sponsor."

I laughed, a tad hysterically. "She asked me what a Fulbright was and why I should mention it on my CV."

Sébastien glanced at me warily. "What is a Fulbright? Isn't that when the government paid for you to study in Tahiti?"

My teeth snapped together. "It's not need-based." A *bourse* in French was a scholarship, but all it suggested was that the French government had given you a handout, as it did so many people. Merit wasn't implied. "Do you see me as *anything* but a half-wit babydoll with a cute accent?"

He scrubbed the pan with unnecessary force, focused on it, looking grim. "I'm not the one putting you down, Laura."

"Your countrymen are! And I'm so sick of them."

"I didn't force you to come here."

"No, but what other choice did I have? Do you think we would have managed if I'd stayed over in the U.S. for years to finish my degree and we only visited? It was either I move, or you move, or nothing. And you wouldn't move, and I didn't want to choose nothing."

"This is exactly what I was afraid of. This is why I told you to make sure you really wanted to do this. I didn't want you feeling you'd sacrificed everything for me."

"I *did* sacrifice for you! And claiming you didn't ask me to is just a cop-out! Would you have come to the U.S.? Would you have preferred to let us just die a natural death through separation?"

"It would have been better than watching us die through you learning to hate me!"

I gasped and took a deep breath, wanting to cry. "Tell the truth, Sébastien, would you have come for me?"

He looked grimmer and grimmer. "I just started my career. I have to get some experience before I try the U.S. market! I have to build a portfolio, for God's sake."

"You don't really love me, do you?"

"*Putain de merde.*" He shut off the water and opened the floor-to-ceiling windows, leaning over the rail as cold air flooded into the already chilly apartment.

In a split second, I was screaming at him, screaming out all the cold, wet days and the humiliation and the uselessness, all the times I went to museums to try to find the silver lining in this situation, to try to fill my empty, lonely days. I grabbed my jacket midscream.

"Where are you going?" he asked, pale and frighteningly grim.

"Just leave me alone! I don't want to be near you! I don't want to talk to you!"

I ran out of the apartment, slamming the door behind me. I ran down all those flights of stairs, up which I daily trudged after fruitless job searches, carrying sacks of groceries or laundry to try to give myself some use in our couple. Out in the street, all the stores were closed for the night, locked behind grills and corrugated metal panels.

We lived halfway between Belleville, the heart of ethnic Paris where one only occasionally saw a store sign in the Latin alphabet, and the place de la République, the vast roundabout that filled with crowds on every occasion Parisians could imagine to form one—concerts, Gay Pride parades, endless demonstrations. We were used to seeing white vans filled with riot police parked up and down all the side streets. None were there now. The street was empty. My boots sounded dully into nothing. I passed a homeless man, curled up in cardboard under the eave of a theater. I knew I could have it worse. In Paris, there was always proof I could have it worse.

On our street, half the stores were called by ethnicities and no other name: the *Arabes* or tiny *épiceries* that functioned as mini-supermarkets; the *Chinois* restaurants that were mostly run by Vietnamese; the five *Pakistanais* dime stores, where dark-skinned men would sell me a ten-franc pack of rough pink toilet paper, liquid for blowing bubbles, and packs of nails, but not superballs, because the superballs might give me a headache. ("It's the petroleum products," said a twinkling young owner.) Behind a barrier of interlaced steel, the video *Anal Vixens* still held pride of place in the *papeterie* display window, among magazines and postcards. Our favorite florist had pulled her sweet-smelling gardenia in off the sidewalk and completely covered her store in corrugated metal, but at the base of the hill, a few stores past the bakery, McDonald's still shone its golden beacon of artery-clogging food into the night.

To my left at this intersection stretched the smooth, gray stone promenade that followed the underground canal all the way to the Bastille and, more importantly, one of the last Parisian chocolatiers to still make his chocolate on the premises and fill the street around him with the scent. Sébastien and I walked down that way some days, for the market. Mostly I walked it by myself while he was at work. To my right, the Canal St. Martin surfaced, the old-fashioned streetlamps glowed off its dark waters, and a dozen little bridges arched over it. Often, often, when Sébastien came home and wanted to relax, he went out for a walk with me along the canal instead. During the summer, people used to take over our favorite bridge, couples sitting all up and down its steps, drinking beer from a nearby bar out of plastic cups. But now it was winter and empty, except occasionally for a homeless man asking for a cigarette. We often walked along the canal at night and stood on that bridge, huddled close under one umbrella as we gazed at the dark water, dimpled with rain, the streetlamps reflecting off it and the golden warmth of apartment windows stretching away under barren winter trees.

It was one in the morning. I headed up the canal alone, and a flake fell down and caught on my eyelashes. I tilted my head back in astonishment and discovered the whole sky filled with flakes, drifting down in the light from the lamps and the windows. It was snowing, big, thick flakes, rare in Paris, where the city holds the heat at a couple of degrees higher than the surrounding countryside. I walked and walked along the canal, with the flakes swirling slowly past the lamps and into the water.

Although it was late at night, nobody bothered me at all. Two men coming out of a bar called out, "It's snowing, it's snowing!" delightedly. And that was the most human contact I had. Cars still whisked past on the moistened streets, but there was a sense of magic stillness to the city, as if we could all escape out of it into its movie version.

Twenty-one

I stood on that bridge for a long time, watching the snow. Stood on it until my heart started to ache at the fact that Sébastien wasn't there to share it with me. Finally, I started back, determined to find him and try to make up so that I could drag him outside and show him the snow.

A figure sitting on the steps of a bridge three bridges down lifted his head as I passed, and I realized he wasn't a homeless man but Sébastien in a hastily donned sweater and jacket. He didn't say anything. He didn't need to. I knew he had followed me, even though he was as angry as I was, to make sure nothing happened to me alone out here at one in the morning. Our eyes met. I hesitated, beset by anger at him again for making this hard time necessary by being so wonderful. But I *knew* that wasn't fair. I turned and sat down beside him on the steps. The concrete froze right through my jacket to my butt instantly. I peeked sideways. Sébastien had more snowflakes caught in his long lashes than I did. He reached out and shook a handful of my hair, knocking flakes loose.

"I feel like you're breaking in my hands," he said, low. He brought his hands back to clasp them between his knees and stared at them, not at me. "And that it's my fault, because I tried to hold you in them in the first place."

179

A car passed, whooshing slowly, its lights swirling snow.

"I feel like the most important thing in my life, us, is slipping through my fingers and shattering as it hits the floor. And there's nothing I can do to stop it." He flexed his fingers helplessly against the backs of his palms and just stared at them.

I put my hand on his knee. Then I realized he wasn't wearing gloves and moved my gloved hand to cover his bare ones.

"You know, I used to hate Paris, too," he said. "All the noise, the way people can be so obnoxious, the stress, the gangs that hang around causing trouble for people. I spent most of my teenage years in fights, you know. What really taught me to love Paris was when I started in-line skating. I used to go out skating late at night when things got too much for me, and I would skate for hours, through streets that were so empty and quiet. I learned Paris that way, every part of it."

He seemed to be trying to sell—or maybe give was a better word—something he loved to someone he loved, which made it worth at least a try from me.

Unfortunately, my sole experience with in-line skating had been with him and had not implied I would be good at all-night excursions. We looked at each other. "*I'm* game to try again," I said defiantly.

"You yelled at me for four hours straight the last time."

"It wasn't yelling," I said, offended. "I was just—expressing my fears."

Sébastien examined a snowflake thoughtfully. "Why don't we try you on a scooter first?"

I took to the push scooter immediately. You had to be pretty gifted to fall off it, and as an American in Paris, I was used to being taken for an idiot anyway. Besides, scooters were highly fashionable that year. Really—like feathers the year before.

We would head out nights after we ate, around 10:00 or 10:30. It didn't matter if we were in the middle of the week.

Sébastien might go to work the next day on very little sleep, but he could lose sleep to stop my breaking in his hands, to offer me his world, and invite me into his self. On the weekends, sometimes his friends joined us and teased me infectiously about my scooter; but during the week, it was always just the two of us.

We coast down the steep slope of our colorful street. Sometimes an *Arabe* or two is still open, casting warm, golden light into the dark street. At the intersection of McDonald's and the Canal St. Martin, I let go of my sense of orientation and follow Sébastien as we cut through Paris at night, past revelers grouped outside nightclubs, across République, its statue silhouetted against the yellowish gray of a city's night sky, down rue Turbigo, where all is quiet except for the regular swish of cars, and on, through the gray and black and streetlamp gold of Paris' night streets, until we come out into the open at l'Hôtel de Ville, Paris' palatial city hall.

Imagine. It's early February, and here, on the exact spot where the guillotine once dominated the city, Paris has set up a temporary public ice-skating rink, which stretches across the vast open *place* or plaza before the Hôtel de Ville, squeezing up against the fountains and nudging pedestrians off to the far edge. The big clock above us says 10:30.

The Hôtel de Ville itself is lit at night, with the gentle richness that has earned French illumination such fame. We cross over the bridge. To right and left, as far as we can see along the Seine, stretch other old and famous bridges, each with its own special character, each lit with fantastic delicacy and charm, glowing warm and magic against the water. In the far distance, down the Seine, the Eiffel Tower is copper and proud against the dark sky. At night, *la Tour Eiffel* is the undisputed queen of the city and knows it.

On the Île de la Cité, we turn right at a corner featuring an elegant clock dating from the Renaissance and follow a smooth sidewalk along the edge of the river, past the Conciergerie, its two conical medieval towers a silhouette of great age against the low sky. No stars hang above. In all my time in Paris, I've spotted a star only twice, faint and far off, unable to compete with the city lights. When Sébastien came to my country home at Christmas, he didn't even know his constellations. I made a note to myself to teach them to him one day.

Two gendarmes are standing watch outside the Conciergerie. We nod to them, and one of them grins broadly at my one-legged chugging and gliding on my scooter and makes a comment to his colleague just after I pass. I assume he's jealous. Sometimes you have to suffer the envy of lesser mortals to be as fashionable as I am. Besides, the day Parisians don't make comments on whatever catches their eyes, the world will end.

It's smooth gliding down to the end of this sidewalk, until we reach the Pont Neuf, the oldest bridge in Paris, built in 1604. The statue of the equestrian Henri IV rises above us, less obviously green at night than during the day. Down the stairs behind this king, the Vedettes Parisiennes are still running, one of several companies along the Seine that escort tourists up and down the river in boats. We rattle over cobblestones to the statue side of the bridge, then cross over to the Left Bank of the Seine. The sidewalks are better on this side, Sébastien assures me.

The Eiffel Tower suddenly fizzes like a bottle of champagne: lights sparkle and dance up and down it. Cynical Parisians stop in their tracks, point, and exclaim with delight. You would never imagine that they had seen this before, that every night for a year now, for ten minutes on the hour, the Eiffel Tower had gone off like a magic act. It was 2001, and that's the way Paris wanted to be at the turn of the millennium: glorious, exciting, and fizzing like champagne. Sébastien and I, too, have seen the Eiffel Tower go off countless times, but as always, we stop and watch it. I seize the handlebars of my scooter with pleasure; Sébastien grins at me and slips a wind-chilled hand under my hair, against the nape of my neck.

All the stress seems to have drained out of the city, leaving it hushed and calm. All the stress has drained out of us, too, allowing our energy and happiness to expand and fill us. All the ancient, famous buildings and bridges that are gray stone in the day have become luminous gifts, golden against the night. The people we pass are few and on skates themselves, or strolling, in no hurry. They, too, have lost their daytime grimness. It is quiet, and yet it feels as if the true life of the city has emerged.

Sébastien races ahead on the smooth sidewalk, then circles back to meet me, to catch my waist and either push me very fast or pretend that I should drag him like a train engine drags cargo cars. We pause, laughing, near the Pont des Arts to listen to musicians playing. This straight wooden bridge crosses the Seine just in front of the entrance to the Louvre's smaller, interior courtyard, a place of intimate vastness, with a round fountain that draws those who sneak away from the larger daytime crowds in the main court around the Pyramide. The smaller courtyard is cobblestoned, though, and the skating crowd tends to gather in the smoother, larger one, behind the Pyramide. When Éric and Fabien and other friends come with us, I sometimes sit and watch over discarded coats while the guys play pickup roller-tag with strangers in the great courtyard.

When it is just Sébastien and I, we are more likely to linger near the Pont des Arts, although we don't actually skate and scooter onto its teeth-chattering wooden boards. With a row of benches down the center and old-fashioned streetlamps stretching up and down it, the Pont des Arts draws throngs. Bands play on it, people meet on it, tourists sit and write in their journals on it, Notre-Dame and the verdant tip of the Île de la Cité visible in one direction, the Louvre to the side, and the Eiffel Tower in the distance. It is a superbly romantic spot.

Tonight a group of amateur ragtime musicians are busking in the middle of the bridge. When they pause for a break, I sneak a head start and race Sébastien toward the next pedestrian bridge, just past the Musée d'Orsay. The museum's old train station clock glows an eerie green above us. This newer bridge, with its steeply sloping, neo-technical metal, appeals to almost no one and is therefore empty. Without Éric and Fabien along to provoke suicidal races down its often rain-slickened slopes, we pass it by.

A faint mist has started to fall, emptying the streets still further. We head on past the gold dome of the Invalides, yet another magnificent seventeenth-century building that borders the Seine, and cross back over the Seine to the Right Bank at the glitzy Pont Alexandre III, in order to follow the good sidewalks. The first stone of the Pont Alexandre III was laid in 1896, the giddy nineties, by the Tsar Nicolas II. With its bronze, copper, and gold, and its thirty-two ornate clusters of streetlamps—more than a hundred lanterns in all—the bridge always appears dressed up for an evening of luxury. It is, with the Opéra Garnier, the most ornate monument in Paris; while during the day it looks a little gaudy, at night it is in its element.

It is raining a little now, light drops. We could turn back, or we could catch the Métro home, but we don't want to. It is too much fun to be going on, to share moments as we pause and look at things, to pretend to race, under the rain.

To our right, where the gardens of the Tuileries meet the place de la Concorde, La Grande Roue de Paris sparkles and glitters like some garish, grand country fair. This great Ferris wheel was set up to celebrate the year 2000 and then caused considerable legal problems when its owner refused to take it down again.

We could turn on to the Champs-Élysées, but since the whole avenue is about as interesting and authentic these days as a Twinkie, we stick with the Seine. The Eiffel Tower starts dancing with lights again as we head toward it, and we reach Trocadéro about fifteen minutes after midnight. The Eiffel Tower looms up over us so that we can see the nuts and bolts of it, see it for the grandiose architectural triumph that it was. It is another turn-of-the-century construction that is at its glamorous best at night, looking almost clumsy and uncomfortable during the day, like a six-foot-plus supermodel among average people. But at night, dressed up in lights, she is superb.

We reach Trocadéro and climb up the stairs to its heights behind the Musée de l'Homme at one in the morning. We are leaning against the wall, looking out over the night-silent fountain at the great copper Eiffel at exactly 1:00 A.M., just when the lights that give it that dominant copper gleam at night go out. Simultaneously, the ten-minute-on-the-hour champagne sparkle bursts and fizzes up and down it. I have until then only seen the sparkle on hours before 1:00 A.M., always with the regular lights still on. This new view is strange and haunting, the Eiffel Tower stark and black against the skyline, a white fireworks display of joy dancing up and down it.

The light rain changes to a rain in earnest as we leave Trocadéro, too late to catch the last Métro. By the time we reach the Louvre again, we are soaked and laughing, vainly scraping water back off our faces. We take refuge for a few moments in the empty, vaulted Cardinal Richelieu corridor of the Louvre, gazing through its immense glass windows at the calm beauty of the Cour Marly and the Cour Puget, their marble statues close to us but aloof at the same time. Then we head on, past Châtelet and home. We glide side by side while the rain falls on the dark streets, and streetlamps and car headlights make them glisten.

There are many things that can make someone love Paris: the witch-house display windows of a *salon de thé* called Charlotte de l'Isle and the thick, almost Spanish hot chocolate there; the exotic island ambience of Maison de la Vanille and the frothy *laits frappés* they serve, drinks of whipped milk that are much more refreshing than milk shakes; the flower-shaped ice cream at

Gelati d'Alberto on rue Mouffetard. I can even think of some things that aren't food, like the river and the gardens, the theaters and the museums, the Canal St. Martin. But I think I began to love Paris exactly the way Sébastien thought I would, on those nights with him gliding through it.

Maybe the breaking and making points of a relationship are the same thing, and it just depends what you do with them. If you're going to let go of that bush halfway down the cliff, maybe you just have to fall and not keep clutching at any root or branch to stop you on your way down. Maybe, when it comes to relationships, you've just got to risk it all with blind faith, even when it seems crazy and impossible and like you have too much to lose, including your familiar life. Everything, after all, is crazy and impossible, especially romance, which makes no logical sense whatsoever and seems to require an extraordinary belief in something intangible. It's just a thought. I have them occasionally.

I took a deep breath when we got back from the last of these excursions and sat Indian style on the bed in front of Sébastien. It was the last excursion because I wrecked my left knee on that cute little scooter. I was also flying back home the next day; I'd finally managed to get a work permit, but I could only pick it up at the consulate in Atlanta. This would be our third parting in an airport in six months, and even though this particular separation should last only a week, we weren't getting any better at it.

"So," I said. I took another deep breath and had to grab something for support. "Where's my teddy bear?"

We found him covered with cat hair under the computer; Indy had apparently attacked him in our absence and had a battle with him all over the apartment. To think that a year before, I had actually liked cats. I dusted Teddy off and returned to my position in front of Sébastien, clutching the bear in my lap for some pretense of security. "So," I tried again, "will you marry me?"

Sébastien looked confused. "Laura, how much reassurance do you need? I've been asking you every day for the past three months."

"I know," I said. "That's why I'm asking you this time. I thought it was only fair."

He paled, which was a bit unflattering, but I understood. Getting engaged was a fraught moment even for a normal couple, and we weren't normal because, as I have mentioned, Sébastien was French. He occasionally seemed to think I wasn't too normal either, but that's the French for you—judgmental. Up until now, our cross-cultural couple had been a romantic adventure either side could abandon at any time. Once we both said yes, we would be saying we could handle this intercultural romance long-term and committing ourselves to doing so. I still felt like this was saying I could climb Mount Everest when I'd never hiked more than ten miles and had a deep fear of snow, heights, and energy bars.

"So . . . will you?" I squeezed Teddy hard.

"Yes," Sébastien answered. Still pale, he grasped my hand in a surge of excitement, lips softening into a cautious smile, watching me as if to make sure I meant it.

Twenty-two

René started vomiting sometime while I was on the plane. They took him to the hospital the next day, when he didn't stop. He didn't want to go. He never wanted to go to the hospital, never in his life, which was too full of living for places like that. But he didn't have enough energy to fight it. "What's wrong?" I ask Sébastien on the phone.

"I don't know," Sébastien says. "They're running tests."

I pick up my visa at the French consulate in Atlanta with amazingly little trouble after everything that preceded it. Two weeks later, I'm back in Paris, and the tests have come back.

"He's riddled with it," Sébastien says quietly to me. We're in the RER B coming back from the airport, a grim, empty ambience for this kind of conversation, with the RER car's torn vinyl blue cushions, its graffiti, its stale odors and endless concrete tunnels. "Liver, lungs." I can see his grandfather, eyes merry as a boy's, saying, *Mais elle est jolie!* as he embraces me, rolling his dark, rich, insidious *brunes* to smoke with his family outside under the rain. "They'll try chemotherapy," Sébastien says and stares at his hands, locked together between his knees. He rubs his thumbs together, uselessly, not knowing what to do. Neither do I. At the Feast of Kings, that tiny, happy man had pulled me into the family, bouncing on his toes with all his energy. This is horrible news. Yet I lack the presumption to cry. I have met him only a handful of times; Sébastien was rocked in his arms as a baby.

René's hospital is simple and clean, with a disquieting absence of technology. His room has a little balcony, and the setting is beautiful. His room looks out over green sloping hills to the red tiles of a village framed in its green-nestled distance by nearer trees. Among the paved paths of the park below and the old stone houses converted into different components of this hospital, humans and animals wander at will: goats, geese, rabbits, tired men and women pushed in wheelchairs, patients trailing IVs and their healthy family members.

On our very first visit, René still has that gorgeous, thick hair of his, the hair that Sébastien inherited. It thins quickly to a few faded wisps as the chemotherapy leeches the energy out of him. It seems like no matter when we visit he is tired but happy to see us, and there are family—second cousins, grandnephews—stopping by. They make my acquaintance courteously, and then I press my back into a corner or hover on the balcony, feeling useless and extraneous to the heart grief of this situation.

"La petite Laura," René always greets me.

Titi, if he's there, mocks his father in that brusque way that always makes René laugh. *"La petite? Elle est aussi grande que toi!"* Which is true—René might be stockier, might have *been* stockier, but he is about my height. We all wait and talk and try to make jokes to cheer René up, and René tries to let us, sinking back into tiredness between laughs. And we all feel totally helpless.

In Paris, meanwhile, I discovered that having a visa that entitled me to work didn't yet mean I had the right to do so. I had more lines to stand in, more offices to visit, more paperwork to wait for, and as the final obstacle, a mob of fellow visa-starved foreigners to fight my way through. The office in which the work permits were handed out was about the size of our Paris apartment, and the quantity of people desperate to get this final stamp easily topped a hundred. No one outside the room could hear her name when called, mangled beyond recognition; and if you missed it, the women behind the desk would *not come back to you* later. The crush was incredible. A massive stranger tucked me behind him protectively and along with the other big men developed a system: whenever someone's name was called, everyone immediately yelled it to those outside the room, and the men passed the person hand to hand up to the desk. I kept waiting to see someone walking on people's shoulders, in a *Crocodile Dundee* moment.

I survived that experience with only a few bruises, thanks to the giant stranger, and started my new job teaching English May 2. It wasn't a good job, it wasn't an interesting job, but it was a job. May 31 I got my first paycheck and discovered my employers were skimming 16 percent off my salary by pretending it was a government deduction. A French pay stub is a complicated thing, and they didn't know I was living with a Frenchman who could interpret mine for me. I had been incapable of admitting in a professional interview that I was giving up my Ph.D. at a stellar university to come live with a Frenchman I had picked up on a whim in a restaurant and that that was why I was looking for a two-bit job teaching English. I had actually pretended to a passionate interest in ESL. I swear.

While I was trying to work the salary deduction problem out, I focused on keeping the romance alive. I was engaged now, which I found frightening. What if living together and making an actual commitment to each other killed the sense of romance?

Sébastien sighed when he heard this new line of relationship paranoia. "Are all Americans this insane, or did I just get lucky?"

"It's just me," I said. "Quit making cultural stereotypes based on the actions of one person."

"You do that to me all the time!"

"I'm an *American,*" I said, annoyed. "I'm culturally entitled to judge the rest of the world out of complete ignorance anytime I like. So when you say you got lucky, do you really mean you don't feel lucky anymore, to be dating me?"

Sébastien clutched his head.

"I'm annoying you, aren't I?" I said. "Does that mean you don't love me anymore?"

Anyway, when I finally got accepted as a restaurant reviewer, I knew it was perfect. What better way to feed a romance than at Parisian restaurants?

"You don't think you're just a tad obsessed with food?" Sébastien asked.

My jaw dropped. "You're French! How can you say that?" I couldn't trust these people about *anything.* No one ever wore berets either.

He laughed. He loved the idea; he just liked picking on me more. When I received my first assignments in May, he bragged to all his friends about the job his fiancée had managed to bag. We both loved to discover tastes and places, and I hated to write but persisted in doing it anyway. I couldn't quit my day job, because the publication didn't pay me anything beyond expenses, but I'd take meals for two at Parisian restaurants over ten cents a word any day. Restaurant reviewing would be a romantic culinary adventure *à deux.*

"So are you ready for"—I peered at my list—"The Grouchy Bear?"

As soon as I saw that name among my first review assignments, The Grouchy Bear joined my favorite French restaurant names, right up there with The Crazy Elbow and The Fools Across the Way. We found the bad-tempered *ours* in the Halles, not very far from Le Relais du Vin, where we first met.

The owner meandered out to greet us in a red plaid shirt long since washed down to a dusky rose, an ancient blue beret cocked on his graying head, and a faded blue work apron covering him from waist to knees. He could have been working a market stall in the fifties Halles. Nostalgia for the pre-Pompidou era suffused the inside of his classic, dark wood bistro. Original, turn-of-the-century wood Métro benches formed the seats, and three large ceramic scenes depicted the way the world had been before officials took it into their heads to destroy the old markets of the Halles to make room for the street-side drug trade. When this bistro was founded, the unpleasant Halles area was still the living heart of a vibrant city, and as in Le Relais du Vin, these walls were a lovesong to that past. The whole place could seat sixteen recently showered, nonclaustrophobic diners.

Marcel, the owner, clapped Sébastien on the shoulder as we sat and leaned in close. "You two look like you could use my room for the night."

We stared at him.

"It's upstairs." He leaned in closer and lowered his voice. "Keep it quiet, I don't need to tell you. This is all *au noir*." On the black market.

"Well, we . . ."

"I was going to give it to them"—Marcel waved a hand over his shoulder at a kissing couple who pulled apart enough to give him wary, harassed looks behind his back—"but you have the advantage." He leaned down to whisper in my ear: "You're smiling."

I looked behind him. Glasses covered the bar, drops of red or occasionally gold lingering in their bottoms. Napkins were scattered here and there, crushed between half-empty bottles. This wasn't a good sign in a bistro, where the glasses are normally whisked away the second you set them down.

"Thanks, but we live quite close to here," Sébastien said. "République."

Marcel drew back, baffled at why that would make us forgo an illicit tryst above a bistro. He caught my eyes to see if I was going to take this unromantic prosaicism sitting down.

195

"*Merci*," I agreed with Sébastien, having mastered the paradoxical French word for "No."

He shook his head in faint disgust and wandered back toward the bar, leaving us among the debris of previous diners: a half-full wine bottle, two empty glasses with red stains in the bottom, a glass of red wine, crushed napkins, bread crusts, and stained paper place mats. We waited ten minutes before Marcel thought to start clearing off our table. He caught up the full glass of wine and wandered over to the next table to sit down and drink a toast to them from it.

Sébastien bit back a grin. "You know, tonight might not be the best of nights to eat here," he murmured.

"The review's due Monday. I don't want to be late on the first one." Besides, I liked Marcel's style. It seemed a shame to waste it and come back when he was sober.

Sometime before Monday, Marcel got our table cleared off. To celebrate, he snapped three clean wineglasses down in front of us and eased the cork off a bottle of champagne that cost twice what my publication had allotted for this meal. "*On va fêter ce soir!*" he said and squeezed in beside Sébastien. Sébastien met the wall with an *oof*. Old Métro benches aren't known for their roominess, and Marcel wasn't small.

Not one of those sissy flute men, Marcel filled the full-bellied red wineglasses to the brim. "To smiles."

I never would have thought it possible when I was scaring women in the streets almost two years ago to find myself toasting smiles with two Parisians. Unfortunately, a bistro owner's work is never done, and Marcel only had time for a few swallows before some starving diners succeeded in a desperate attempt to catch his eye. He abandoned his champagne on our table and wandered agreeably over to sit and drink with them instead.

"You know what," I said, "I don't think he's picking up someone's unfinished glass each time. I think he *actually has his own glass of wine or champagne on every table.*"

Sébastien did an expert scan of the glasses on the other tables. "I think you're right. I hope you're not too hungry."

Truthfully, I was pretty much always hungry—there was way too little snacking between meals in this country—and by the time Marcel got back to our table, I was plotting a major distraction to steal somebody else's bread. Sébastien kept a firm hand locked around one of my wrists under the table.

Marcel took our order eventually, but only got as far with it as the next table before he had to sit down for a drink. He was persistent, though, and toast by toast, he slowly worked the room toward the kitchen. Just when I was getting excited, some bastard at a sidewalk table waved dramatically, and Marcel wandered past us out the door. I stared after him with my mouth open like a baby bird suddenly bereft of a worm.

Sébastien and I slid deeper into our increasingly-less-charming-and-more-uncomfortable Métro benches, wondering if it would be remotely acceptable to get up and walk out of the restaurant if the owner had given us a bottle of champagne more expensive than our intended meal but forgotten to let us eat. "The review is due the day after tomorrow," I said. "I've got to eat *something*. I can't tell them I couldn't do the first one because the owner wouldn't feed us."

A miracle occurred, in the form of the chef, a strained-looking man about our age who appeared in the kitchen doorway, weighted down with plates. The chef had given up hope of anyone coming to carry his creations to their intended tables. He must have spotted a kindred look of strain on our faces when he passed, because his eyes narrowed in suspicion. "Have you ordered?"

"We did a, er, very long time ago, but I think maybe we should order again," Sébastien said delicately.

The chef pressed his lips together in an alarming gesture of internalization and shot one glance at the owner before asking us what we wanted. Sébastien was impressed. Didier at Le Relais would never have shown such self-discipline.

We were even more impressed with the food when the chef brought it out to us some time later. A baked Camembert rested on a bed of walnuts and greens for the first course, later followed by *confit de canard* with *pommes sautés,* all traditional bistro food and all set apart from other bistros by its quality. I had expected at the very least burnt-black potatoes at this point. The cook was going to get an ulcer if he didn't vent his stress on something.

Out of solidarity, Sébastien took it upon himself to serve as waiter for our table. As he leaned into the kitchen to get water and offer an encouraging word to the cook, Marcel made another of his peripatetic stops beside our table and gazed at those broad shoulders.

"You know, I like him much better than your last guy," he said approvingly.

Since he had never met the last guy, this approbation was kind of like having an Oracle open his mouth to let the voice of God approve my choice of fiancé. "Thanks, so do I."

"Although"—the Oracle cocked his head—"he's not really my type, frankly."

Then again, Delphi was always getting the Greeks into trouble. "That's all right, he's mine."

He eyed me, head still cocked. "You sure you don't want that room for the night?"

"Really, we live only four Métro stops from here. Twenty minutes on foot."

His look said that was a poor excuse.

"Could I order a glass of wine?" Sébastien asked, returning. Wine seemed a request Marcel would enjoy handling.

"You haven't finished your champagne yet!" Marcel pointed out indignantly.

"But if we're going to *eat,*" Sébastien coaxed, "we'll need wine. Would you want us to drink champagne with a meal?"

"Fine." Marcel puffed air into his lower lip, in one of the many variants of the French considering-the-options expression. "What kind did you want?"

"This red you recommend looks good."

"Good choice." Marcel wandered back to the bar, picked up the half-full bottle that had been sitting on our table when we arrived, and wandered back with it. "Just help yourself from this."

Well. There was no technical *reason* we couldn't get our glass of wine from an unfinished bottle abandoned on a table, since it wasn't as if the diners would have spat in it. We might have objected when he charged us the full price for the bottle later, but since our meal still didn't come up to the value of the champagne we had just drunk, what could we say?

We were not the only ones to receive such liquorous generosity. I had been wondering for some time what the non-French-speaking English couple the next table over was making of this. Apparently one thing they had made out of it was that they were ready to leave. Pursuant to this goal, the Englishman approached the bar to wrestle a bill out of the owner.

Marcel beckoned him behind the bar and handed him an unopened bottle of vintage wine. The poor Englishman took it with an expression of half-credulous pleasure. "For me?"

"*Non, non, non!*" Marcel waved his hands. "For them!" He gestured to two women sitting at a far table.

The Englishman stared at him, baffled, a reaction Marcel blamed on the language barrier. Abandoning words, he went into an elaborate and half-mocking mime, full of good-humored contempt for inferior English wait skills. He pressed a corkscrew into the Englishman's hand—hard, to make sure the silly Brit didn't drop it. He dramatically gestured opening the bottle, elbows waggling. He gestured pouring the bottle, with exaggerated care. Then he clapped the Englishman on the back, turned him, and pushed him toward the table.

I had to admire the English desire to humor natives. The

dazed diner stumbled over to the table and actually performed wait service for the ladies.

"No one's ever going to believe me about this," I told Sébastien. "They always think I'm exaggerating when I tell these kinds of stories."

"Well, weird things do seem to happen to you more than anyone else."

"No, I just like to brag." I speared a bit of meltingly tender *confit de canard*. "Other people are more discreet."

"Yes, not everyone thinks of weird things as some kind of life achievement. Would you like a bite of tripe?"

"Sébastien. There were edible things on the menu, you know."

"It's delicious." He sliced another odd-textured bite and closed his eyes as he chewed. "I don't know when I've had better."

"Just let me pretend you're eating something else, all right? Don't keep telling me what it's called."

Freshly appalled at how many things I insisted on missing in life, he went back to his meal.

Our dessert was sweetened *crème fraîche* and a bowl of lusciously ripe strawberries, by which I don't mean the American supermarket fruit. Ours needed no extra sugar. Finally, stuffed and replete and desperate to get off those charming little benches, we steeled ourselves to pay the bill.

The task had been beyond many. Several diners had abandoned it altogether, either promising to return the next day or stuffing an approximation of what they owed under their plates. We couldn't imitate them. I had to have a proper bill to get reimbursed, so we tracked Marcel down at another table, where he had managed to squeeze in with four other diners. The diner crushed to the wall was starting to turn purple.

Marcel paused in his toast to his fellows and got briskly down to business. "Tell me what you ordered."

"Baked Camembert salad."

He scrawled a row of zeros on a napkin.

"Andouillette."

His head snapped up. "Andouillette or andouille?"

"Ah, you're right, andouille, sorry."

He shook his head, narrowing his eyes and waving a minatory finger. "Because it's not the same thing." He added another row of zeros. The pen wasn't working properly, so he circled over a few times, tearing the napkin.

"*Confit de canard.*"

He nodded sagely. More zeros.

"Strawberries and *crème fraîche* for both of us."

000×2. He carefully totaled up the zeros. "Oh, and then that bottle of wine you had. Let's say three hundred francs. That suit you?"

I looked at Sébastien, who is in charge of handling his more difficult countrymen when necessary. He laughed, although I'm pretty sure I detected a note of alarm in there somewhere. "We've got to have a real bill."

Marcel sat back, dismayed at our impractical behavior. "That's going to cost you more."

"That may be, but we've got to have it."

"Oh, fine." Marcel waved a hand, utterly disgusted with us. A few smiles could not make up for both romantic staidness *and* monetary profligacy. "Go ring it up yourselves, then."

"All right." Sébastien grinned. He did, after all, know his way around a restaurant cash register. He slipped behind the bar to encounter an amazing sight. The cash drawer stood wide open, and money people must have forced into Marcel's hands lay scattered all over the counter.

"Wait, wait, wait! You're not doing it right!" Marcel laughed and came around to squint at the cash register. Sébastien indicated the next key to press.

Before Marcel could touch it, another couple tried to slip behind us out the door. "No, no!" He reached to snatch at them.

Misunderstanding, they gestured to the cash they had tucked

under a plate to indicate they had paid and tried to squeeze past me. From the panicked look on their faces and the fact that they didn't say a word, I got the strong impression they were yet another non-French-speaking tourist couple that had wandered into this tempting little corner to find themselves bogged down like ants in honey.

Marcel grabbed a bottle of vintage Calvados from the top shelf and thrust it at them. "But you can't leave yet! You haven't even tried this!"

The couple shook their heads frantically and fled into the night.

Sébastien firmly pointed at the next key, and we persisted in this way until our bill finally got totaled up. Marcel pointed out with disgust that it was fifty francs higher than what we would have paid his way.

"I won't hold it against you, though. I'll still let you have that room if you want it."

"Maybe another time," Sébastien laughed.

Marcel stared at us in shock. "You're just going to go back to your apartment?"

"Well—yes."

"When you could *take a black market room over a bistro* for the night?"

"Well—yes."

"And people wonder why there's such a high divorce rate these days." He stood in the doorway, shaking his head in despair, as we slipped our arms around each other's waists and headed off.

At least he had a clear conscience. He had gone down fighting for young love, and if our couple failed, it would not be for lack of his trying. It's funny, but despite how uncomfortable those Métro benches grew, it was the most heartwarming experience. With government and employers doing their worst to ruin our chances, it was nice to know there were still complete strangers willing to give their all to further love.

Twenty-three

Anew blow hit Sébastien's family: his grandmother Pierrette had breast cancer. From her hospital bed, she wrote long and careful love letters to her husband, which her children carried to his hospital bed. Her family flocked around her, her children Claudine, Titi, and Martine traumatized by this sudden onslaught of mortality in their parents, who were only in their sixties. But the doctors said it was operable, relieving everyone's worries. I thought how this discreet, sweet woman with her obsession for washing dishes was going through probably the most terrifying medical problem of her life but that it was all in the shadow of her husband's mortality. René was going to be released soon. Nobody even pretended this was because he was cured. There was just no point in him wasting what was left of his life in a hospital.

On my work front, meanwhile, things got worse and worse, even as Paris warmed into an enticing summer. My employer promised to correct the "error" in my June check but didn't. When I pointed this failure out to them, they admitted they had never intended to correct it; I would just have to accept what I could get because, as a foreigner in Paris, I had no other choice. By July, we were in serious dispute. Despite everything else going on, Sébastien's family tried to offer me the good side of their lives to counterbalance. For Claudine, this meant cherries, which might be why I was getting along so well with my future *belle famille*. *I* think most of the best things in life are food, too. I think also that in some ways it was easier for Claudine to help her son and his fiancée to happiness rather than dwell on her parents and approaching unhappiness.

For the last two weeks of July, every telephone exchange with them concerned René, Pierrette, and the ripeness of the Burlat cherries in Claudine and Jean-Charles's backyard. They lived in the suburbs of Paris, although not one of the bad "projects" suburbs, and had a house and garden. Just before the end of the month, Claudine called Sébastien. "Ça y est. We're saving them for Laura, but you've got to get out here this weekend. We're supposed to get rain Monday, and that will make the cherries split."

So I was up in the cherry tree on a Saturday morning, blissfully filling sacks and sacks with beautiful *cerises,* when Jean-Charles stopped below me. He wore a paint-splotched T-shirt and baggy shorts, his gray hair flying every which way around his head. A professional restorer and remodeler of houses, he was a stocky man with hidden strength in arms that easily moved things serious weight lifters couldn't handle. Baggy, paint-splotched clothes were his favorite attire. "I don't hear you whistling," he called up. "You know, in France, cherry pickers are supposed to whistle to prove they're not *eating all the cherries.*"

I coughed a cherry pit out of my mouth discreetly and tossed it into the bushes behind my back. Of course, as my white shirt had been indelibly stained in various places with cherry juice, this wasn't very convincing. "Maybe you should whistle when you walk by, too," I counterattacked. He had already culled a half dozen of the darkest cherries automatically and was popping them into his mouth as we spoke. So when he exclaimed, "Oh, there's a nice one!" I naturally assumed he was talking about a piece of fruit. I turned, hoping I could grab it first.

A big fat brown snail was oozing its way up the Burlat cherry trunk. Jean-Charles dumped cherry pits out of his palm hastily and snatched it. "One for my collection." He grinned and disappeared into the back of the garden.

I didn't follow him because I didn't trust Jean-Charles. He kept telling me things about his culture that turned out to be true. It was unsettling.

Take snails, for example. Everyone knows the French eat snails. I tried one in French Polynesia and decided that eating snails was similar to putting gold leaf on perfectly good chocolate. Neither tastes good, both have a lousy texture, and both are clearly priced for showing off rather than for their culinary value. But Jean-Charles never ate anything just to show off, so either he was playing with my mind about French-snail stereotypes and was going to put on a beret next, or . . . he genuinely collected snails?

I chose not to have my leg pulled and went back to picking cherries. I would find it more reassuring to take the French culture on as an in-law if, even once, Jean-Charles turned out to be actually pulling my leg.

The next morning I was sunning myself on a bench he had made, contemplating attacking the cherry tree again, when he passed en route from the tool shed to his remodeling project in the kitchen. He stopped, grinning at me as if I were his sister and he had a big bug in his hand. "So, do you want to see my snail farm?"

Well, actually, I did. Maybe I hadn't yet fully grasped what getting married to a Frenchman would mean and still hoped seeing a snail farm would be a once-in-a-lifetime opportunity.

I followed him behind a flower bed to an old plastic paint tray set on top of a plastic crate that was turned upside down over an old plastic bucket—not a store-bought plastic bucket, which wouldn't have suited Jean-Charles's sense of frugality, but one that had once held some kind of remodeling project goop. Behind the bucket towered two oil barrels, which saved Jean-Charles fifty dollars a year off his water bill by collecting rain. I was still looking around for the snail farm when Jean-Charles picked up the paint tray.

Glistening pale flesh oozed up around the holes in the plastic crate as half a dozen snails tried to squeeze their bodies through the bars of their cell. Jean-Charles flipped the crate right side up and plucked these escapees off without even an instant's hesitation about touching them. He dumped them back in with the rest, and I peered down at nearly a hundred snails, crawling over each other at the bottom of the bucket, crawling up the sides, drawn into their shells, or sprawled out sloppily. Or . . . doing some other things, I think. I'm not an expert on snail interactions, but I'm pretty sure I glimpsed snails in more positions than I was old enough to see.

"I put them in there to fast," Jean-Charles explained.

I eyed him sidelong. My previous experience with fasting consisted of Good Fridays, Ash Wednesdays, and any week prior to wearing a bikini, and these acts seemed entirely too ritualistic for the mob of slime below me.

"For a couple of weeks," he added. "Not less than a week. Empties out their intestines."

If one thing is vital in the process of preparing snails, it is, as I would learn, emptying out their intestines. "You see that slime they leave when they move?" Jean-Charles asked, no doubt referring to the sticky brown-green, unpleasantly puke-colored trails on the bucket and other snails' shells. "You don't want to eat that."

No, I didn't. In fact, now that I got a closer look at the raw material, I was beginning to regret that snail in French Polynesia.

"Slime," Jean-Charles said, "is not one of the better flavors. Which you'd know if you ever got a mouthful of an improperly cleaned snail." He poured the snails from the bucket into the plastic crate as he spoke.

"It's good I have you here to help me; this is usually a long job." I jumped, but he didn't notice. "First we have to wake them

oped a sado-masochistic streak, because I felt aggrieved to have missed it.

Fortunately, even an American in Paris could be satisfied with the exquisite unpleasantness of the next step. The snails might be washed and cooked, but they were still in their shells. We had to get them out, in the process separating the part we wanted to eat (I use the "we" loosely here) from the part we didn't.

Jean-Charles brought out the equipment to do this, making me feel culturally underprivileged. Never, in not a single American kitchen, had I ever seen little two-pronged forks designed exclusively for popping snails out of their shells. "Don't watch too closely," Jean-Charles said as he demonstrated this instrument. "It's never nice to get a face full of dead snail juice." He stabbed his fork into the dead snail flesh, forced it halfway out, and just when things were looking too easy, pressed his thumb down on the second half of the snail and ripped the two halves apart. "Hepatho-pancreas," he said. "Don't want to eat it."

I stared at this, then at the bucket of nearly a hundred snails, feeling queasy. Jean-Charles paused and raised an eyebrow at me: "You asked how snails were prepared." I *had*? I couldn't remember this at all. "So you're going to help, right? There's a lot to do."

I took a deep breath and plunged my tiny fork into a snail corpse. Popping it out was easy enough, but it took me a long moment before I could squish my thumb down on the hepatho-pancreas and rip away. I quickly rid myself of the hope of a *clean break*. The two parts separated easily enough, but bits of innards and stringy things dangled and curled.

"You've got the cutest expression on your face, *crevette*," Sébastien said from well out of snail juice range.

I gave him a dirty look. "Why aren't you helping? And I am not a *crevette*."

"Do you see anybody else in the family crazy enough to do this? I was raised by Jean-Charles; I've had all the experience with snails I need for a lifetime, thank you."

"Not easy, snails," Jean-Charles admitted. "That's why they're so expensive in restaurants. Plus, anybody who's willing to prepare them has to be well paid."

"No," I said. "You're kidding me."

He grinned. "*Normally,*" he admitted, "the person who prepares the snails never eats them."

"Really? I wonder why."

"But *I'm* not going to do all this work and not enjoy them. They're delicious."

As I settled into a rhythm with the snail-innards-ripping part, I could focus on the question that had been needling me ever since I had watched snails vomit the day before: what could possibly have inspired the first Frenchman to think, "Look at all those snails ruining my garden. You know, I bet if I starved them for two weeks, made them vomit for a few hours, washed them repeated times, boiled them, ripped them out of their shells, and cooked them again in the right ingredients, they'd be delicious."

"Probably the siege of Paris in '70–71," Jean-Charles responded promptly. "They ate anything that winter, even rats, even the two elephants they had in the Jardin des Plantes!"

Although I later did some research and found references to snail recipes at least a hundred years older than 1870, I still think he had the right idea: famine. Perhaps the main reason the great Paris siege famines of 1870 and 1590 get so much attention from casual historians is that they reduced the bourgeois and aristocrats to eating rats, too. The average French peasant underwent extreme famines regularly. Someone had to try snails at some point; what awed me was that they had figured out how to make them taste good. I had to hand it to my prospective culture-in-law. Other regions have gone through famines, and possibly other people have eaten snails out of desperation over the course of history; but only French peasants could turn them into an internationally known delicacy.

The rest of the snail preparation was comparatively easy: we had to wash them again several times and then simmer them for an hour and a half in water, garlic, herbs, cloves, and white wine. Next we had to squeeze them back into their shells, which Jean-Charles had boiled clean as a surprise for me. Normally he just stuffed the snails into little white *pots à escargots,* yet another thing you don't often find in American kitchens. We smothered them with enough garlic-parsley butter to make anyone but a Frenchman gain weight, popped them into the oven long enough to heat them through and let the butter melt, and then . . . *à table.*

"This is the life," Sébastien said happily, gazing at his gastropods. "I don't know how Laura survived until now. Do you know, when I was in the U.S., I saw this documentary on American sandwiches? You would not believe what those people eat. They even showed a sandwich that combined bacon, peanut butter, and bananas."

The Elvis! *That's* what my mother could make Sébastien the next time he visited. Sébastien really did need to experience a bit more of the U.S. soon, if you asked me. I didn't want to keep hoarding all these culturally enlightening experiences to myself. Sometimes, especially when those culturally enlightening experiences included snails or hours waiting for my number to pop up in an immigration office, I couldn't help feeling selfish.

I took a deep breath and poured the snail and its butter into my mouth. Interestingly, now that I had spent hours torturing snails and mutilating their bodies, my tongue, even through rivers of butter, could identify every part of this one as I hurried it through my mouth. Fascinating anatomy lesson, really.

"It's the sauce that's delicious," said my skinny mother-in-law-to-be, dashing a shot of melted butter down her throat.

"Yes, but couldn't you have put it on *chicken?*"

Sébastien's family looked at me with polite tolerance and shook their French heads. "It just wouldn't be the same."

"That's my point."

They all exchanged glances. "Maybe she didn't get a good one," Jean-Charles said doubtfully. "Here, try another."

"Another one?"

"Where's my camera?" Sébastien asked gleefully.

"Wait for me!" Justine ran to get her own.

"You know, when I agreed to marry you, I never intended to become a zoo exhibit," I told my fiancé. I took a deep breath and picked up the second snail, recalling vividly the impression of an eyespot on my tongue from the last one. I dumped the snail into my mouth and tried to concentrate on its butter and garlic while Sébastien and his sister captured a whole series of grimaces on film.

Sometimes you have to impress your future in-laws any way you can.

The next day we went to see the grandparents, both released from the hospital and back at their own home, in the village near Paris where all their friends lived. Pierrette looked paler and older, but she was moving around fine, while René seemed wasted by the chemotherapy. He had only a few wisps of hair left. He was very tired, and yet there was something still spry in his eyes. When we drove up, he was polishing an old car with his sweatshirt sleeve. Jean-Charles had gone down to Provence soon after the diagnosis to pick up one of his classic cars, a beige and brown Citroen C4. He had made the slow journey back up to Paris, several careful, thirty-mile-per-hour days of driving in a car built in 1931. All along the way hotel owners took their cars out of private garages to make sure his could be kept safe, in order to let *Papy*, René, keep the car in his garden storage house. Nothing was ever spoken about this. Jean-Charles said he just wanted to have the car around him, and he appreciated his wife's father letting him use his garage for storage. But everybody knew why, as we saw Papy tenderly buffing the round rim of a headlight.

Papy and I, we ride together in the back of this 1931 car, in style, lavender sprigs tucked by his head in one of the old-time potpourri holders, as we make our way by backroads from the grandparents' house to Titi and Bruno's huge, old stone farmhouse for a get-together. I'm not sure why I get to be the one to ride with him; maybe just because I love those old cars so much, and they all spoil me. The moment holds too much. He knows, as we do, that his life has been leeched out of him, so suddenly and so completely. But his eyes are sparkling with delight, and he bounces on the rear seat of that old car. Riding like a king.

Twenty-four

A week after the snail lesson, I was back in immigration offices. Progress had been made, though: I could actually rest my chin on today's counter while wearing flat shoes.

"Let me see if I've got this straight," said the woman on the other side of it. "Your employer was skimming 16 percent off your salary?"

"That's right."

"Did you talk to them about it?"

"Of course." Well, it had started out as talking. "But they said tough luck and if I protested they would get my visa revoked."

"They can't do *that*," said the woman, outraged. When you pit a company and an employee against each other, the average Frenchman automatically reacts on the side of the worker, even an immigrant worker. It's one of the reasons there are so many strikes.

"That's what I thought. But it's okay, I've already found another job."

"What do you mean, 'you found another job'? You left your old job?"

I checked. "Well, yes."

"You can't do *that*," said the woman incredulously. "You signed an eighteen-month contract."

I paused. "Was I clear about the fact that they weren't paying me my contracted salary?"

"Well, yes, but you can't just walk out because they aren't paying you according to your contract."

I tilted my head to one side and stared at her, the way our family's collie used to stare at humans when they were particularly unfathomable. It didn't seem fair that I had ended up in the role of the dog and the French in the role of the humans, though.

"It might adversely affect the company," she explained.

"That was my hope. If I timed it right, they might even lose a major client they were trying to land."

She pressed her lips together. "Your company can't change your pay from a signed contract, and you can't leave your company just because they don't pay you. What would happen to the economy if we had these kinds of things going on? You should have let us mediate it."

I got cold chills at the very idea. "Sorry. I didn't realize I could take down the whole economy by quitting a job. Besides, wasn't ending serfdom one of the key goals of the French Revolution?"

Her lips tightened further. "Well, they also behaved very incorrectly, so don't worry, that letter they sent trying to get your visa revoked . . ." She made a pffing sound of contempt and flicked her fingers. "Now what's this you were saying about finding another job?"

"Yes, as a translator." I had decided English-language teaching was just a scummy job to have in Paris, something almost everyone else who had ever done it confirmed, and I was ready for another field. Long-term, I wanted to work as a coordinator of a study abroad program, and I had gotten some positive nibbles. Those positions opened up slowly, however, so I needed to do something in the interim.

Her brows drew together. "But your visa is as an ESL teacher."

"But now I want to change, and it says right here that I can change jobs if I want to." I stood on tiptoe and stretched a finger over the counter to indicate while she looked deeply offended at having her space so invaded. Still, I had high hopes of actually having something in writing, with an official stamp on it and everything.

"Why, look at that!" she exclaimed, intrigued. "Right after that, it even tells you it will take only two weeks to get the form to change those jobs approved. What will they tell you people next?"

"Well, I know it's July and I shouldn't properly expect anything even to be looked at until mid-October, since no one will be in the office until then, but couldn't you make an exception? I need to work."

"I can't promise anything. And you can't take a translator position. This visa is for an English-language teacher."

"What about the changing jobs clause?"

If nature had ever produced anyone stupider than an American, she clearly didn't know who it was. She stared at me and spoke very slowly. "You can change *jobs*. You can't change *type of employment*."

"I hate your country," I told Sébastien when I got home.

He looked at me warily. "You aren't going to start about gun laws again, are you?"

Once, after explaining a postal-worker joke in an American movie to Sébastien, I had indulged in a long and articulate fantasy about how many French civil service workers, particularly in visa offices, could be eliminated if it wasn't so hard for people to get hold of a lethal weapon here when they needed one.

"No," I said. "But I've received an offer of a good job teaching back at my old university in North Carolina."

Sébastien stilled, half an avocado in one hand. He'd been making dinner.

"I'd really like to take it. It would triple our joint income, which would save me from total bankruptcy, and it might also let us afford wedding rings. It might also save me from jumping off a bridge in loss of self-worth. The job situation as a foreigner in Paris is really hard to take. Have I mentioned it?"

"At length," Sébastien said. "Your comparison between yourself and edible larvae, in terms of the Parisian hierarchy, was particularly illuminating. But I love my job. What do you want us to do? Live apart for the next nine months? That was awful the last time. Go ahead and get married now, which would solve most of the visa problems? Or do you want me to leave my job?"

We discussed this over and over, long evenings in late July and early August walking along the Canal St. Martin or sitting by the Seine playing Abalone, a strategy game for those capable of thinking in two dimensions (Sébastien) or just really fond of pushing around marbles (me). Not far from us, a group of drummers boomed rhythm into the night, and passersby collected to dance around them.

A man wandered up and, before we realized he wasn't just peddling drugs or mooching a cigarette, grabbed a handful of marbles in drunken delight. The rest went flying and hit the brown Seine with a plop.

"See?" I said, once Sébastien had encouraged the man to leave. "See? This kind of thing would never happen where I come from." That was because the only creatures that wandered close to the river where I grew up were a herd of cows, but it was too hard to make an argument for the superiority of my country if I kept bringing in those little details. I don't know why I had started wanting to go back home; for years I had sought every opportunity to live somewhere else. But after seven months trying to find a professional foothold in Paris, I felt battered and needed to retreat, and when animals retreat they go back into small spaces they know well. I could have said, "See?" and laughed. See? This would never happen in my tiny former world. The world is crazier here; I have more contact with reality here; I see more life here. That was what I *wanted*, right? To live a full life, to see the world? But I didn't. I wasn't in that frame of mind.

"The thing is," I said, "I desperately want to have self-respect again. I feel like I'm dying of other people's contempt here."

"You have a thin skin," Sébastien said. Born and raised in a big city, he couldn't believe how I let other people affect me. "You need to stop caring what they think. Why do strangers' opinions of you become your opinion of you?"

He had a good point, but I needed a breather. Maybe if I had time for my thin skin to heal, scar tissue could build up and thicken it. "The thing is," I said, "the thing is, you don't think that, so far, I've been doing most of the risking in our couple?"

His face fell. "You know, I do a lot for our couple, too, Laura, even if you don't realize it. I try to make you happy. I've changed my life completely for you."

Not as completely as I had for him, I couldn't help thinking. But I wondered if I could really know that, if I could really judge his efforts from my perspective. That apartment had probably seemed a nice, cozy size before a second person moved into it. "I know," I said. And I did know. "But the thing is, the thing is . . ." The thing was, up until now, the question in our couple had been, Can *I* do this? Can I open heart and soul to the possibility of love, no matter how dangerous and fraught with Frenchness? Can I change countries, strive for jobs and a visa, try to adapt to his family and culture? Maybe I had done my share for a while. Maybe we should experiment with another question: Can *he* do the same thing?

"The thing is, maybe it would be good for us if you tried living in my culture for a while. So far things have been a little one-sided."

His face changed again. He watched a barge move slowly past, piled high with gravel, tiny, ridiculous Smartcar latched on top of it, ready for its owner to drive out and explore wherever he moored. I had always thought the barge life would be awful, partly because I could get seasick in a hammock, but Sébastien found it fascinating. "I'll say," he responded. "Do you *realize* how much of the world you've seen? Okay, I've taken vacations in Spain and England, but I've only ever lived in Paris."

I looked at him a moment, the warm light of the streetlamp falling on the clean, strong bones of his face, the five o'clock shadow he could never shave off, the lashes longer than mine. For the past five years, people had been telling me how envious they were of my adventurous lifestyle, how much they wished they could live all over the world as I did. Not a single person ever tried it, though. A lot more was involved in moving to another world than simple adventure. Maybe Sébastien needed to know what it was like so that we could properly understand each other. But was he one of those people who could only dream about moving to another country, or could he really do it?

"I want to take this teaching job in North Carolina," I said. "That will last nine months."

He nodded, staring at the lights of his city reflected on the murky Seine water. "I'd like to get a few more months experience at this job so that I'll have a full year at it." It was a good job; to land a job like that straight out of school had been an exceptional achievement. He had been so proud, and he had kept trying to let slip enough information, without showing off, so that his family would realize how proud they should be of him, too. "What if I follow you in October?"

I nodded. Neither of us said anything for a while. We were afraid, and this was a fear we had faced too many times before. Every time we separated, there was a possibility we wouldn't get back together again, that we wouldn't be able to keep making the leap across cultures. This was a real test moment. When push came to shove, could Sébastien give up home and culture for me as I had for him? Why would anyone give up anything for me, let alone someone who had so much going for him and who could have nearly any woman he wanted?

"At least you won't have the same trouble I did with visas and work permits," I said, to focus on something positive. I had memorized a lot of patriotic poetry when I was younger and considered myself an expert on my own country.

"I can believe *that*. No bureaucracy could be as bad as the French one."

"Right. And we're talking about America here. We're much more open to immigrants."

Hey, that's what it said on the Statue of Liberty.

We went to see his mother for lunch to tell her. She was upstairs in the pharmacy where she worked. A green neon cross glowed above the automatic glass doors. We slipped past the little metal turnstile, the pristine shelves full of medicines, the mother and child waiting to fill a prescription, and up the stairs to Claudine's apothecary. Women moved around in white medical coats down to their knees. Machines and counters filled the maze of small, old rooms. The floor of this ancient building smelled of medicine and, richly and thickly, of herbs. The open window in Claudine's workplace looked down on a small stone courtyard. Big antique containers from apothecaries of a century or more ago filled the shelves above her main counter, blue and green ceramic jars with golden stoppers, marked with names of plants in Latin. Several white ceramic mortar and pestle sets, of various sizes, spread across the counter.

"I'm just finishing up," Claudine said. "Look, Laura, I'll show you how I make pills." She filled a bronze mold of hundreds of half-capsule shapes with yellow powder and slipped it

219

in a machine. There was a stamping sound and she pulled it back out, flipped the fresh-minted yellow pills out onto a counter, and counted them into a plastic container.

"You *make* the medicines here?" I asked.

"It depends on what it is. Some medicines come already in their packages, but we're known for being one of the pharmacies in Paris that still prepares things from scratch."

The malpractice suit potential in that boggled my mind. This was really a different country.

We went to a little crêperie around the corner, a small quiet restaurant in tones of yellow, with paper place mats. Over *bolées* of *cidre doux*, clay cups without handles filled with a yellow-orange froth of cider, Sébastien told her. "I'm going to move to the U.S. with Laura."

Claudine stared at him for a long moment, a slight crunch to her eyebrows, as if his words were slowly being deciphered into something meaningful by clumsy machinery in her brain. All at once, tears filled her brown eyes and spilled over. She ripped off her glasses and wiped them away, turning her head away from both of us. Hand pressed against her cheek, she stared out the window, half hiding her eyes. She didn't say a word.

"For a year, I think," Sébastien said.

Claudine looked at me for one second and then back at him. This was horrible. I had tried and tried to get Sébastien to tell her over the phone, or tell her sometime while I was hiding somewhere else, say in the Louvre.

"You're moving across the world?" she said. "Now?"

"In a couple of months. I want to do a full year at my job."

Her mouth worked. "*Mon père, ma mère, et maintenant mon fils.*" My father, my mother, and now my son.

"*Maman,*" Sébastien said. "I'll still be there. Just over the telephone."

She flexed her shoulders, then brushed her hand across her eyes with a hard shake of her head, and put her glasses back on.

"So"—she smiled at us—"that will be fun for you, won't it? To see a little bit of the world? But what will you do there? How will you live? Do you speak English well enough?" Her eyes opened very wide. "How will you manage to organize the wedding here while you're over there?"

There was a long, uncomfortable silence. Sébastien said nothing. He was not happy with the solution we had come up with. "I think we'll have to get married in the U.S.," I said finally. "There's a forty-day residency requirement for marriages in France, and it would be hard to reestablish that in time to get married next summer, if we spend the school year in the U.S. Plus, in France you have to publish banns and all kinds of things."

Claudine just looked at me. After at least a full minute, she turned her head to look at Sébastien. Then, stiffly, back to me. She knew whose fault this was. She said almost nothing the rest of lunch and barely touched her crêpe. Claudine could force smiles and chatter in the worst of situations, so I knew things were bad.

"Well, that's that," I told Sébastien when we finally escaped, my crêpe sitting like so much glue in the bottom of my stomach. "Your mother's going to hate me now. Wait until she tells the rest of the family; they'll probably never even speak to me again."

Twenty-five

Oddly, a few days later Titi called. I flinched and nearly hung up when he identified himself on the phone, but caught myself. If he didn't believe my story about Indy accidentally stepping on the hang-up button, it would just make things worse. Like the

221

time I hid in the apartment and pretended I wasn't there while an enormous, rugby-muscled man rang the doorbell insistently for half an hour, and he turned out to be Sébastien's father. I discovered this because Sébastien finally showed up from work and let his father in, making it pretty hard to hide the fact that I'd been there the whole time. Boy, *that* had been an awkward evening. But trust me, Sébastien's father does not inspire door-opening confidence in a female home alone who doesn't know who he is.

"Our village is having its *fête* the weekend before you leave," Titi said. "You and Sébastien will come, won't you? It can be your *bon voyage* party."

Claudine called to repeat the invitation a couple of days later, worrying me by still being on speaking terms with me. It didn't seem normal. "You can't leave France without participating in a village festival," she said. "You've got to come."

I swallowed the bait.

Bruno and Titi actually lived in Paris; but some eighteen months before, they had bought a stone farmhouse centuries old not far from Paris, in a minuscule village near the beautiful medieval town of Provins. On one of our first visits out there a few months before, we had ridden a slow, rattling old train to Provins. Bruno and Titi picked us up at the station and took us on a tour of the city before we left. Gray and covered with moss and lichen, intact ramparts framed two sides of the old part of Provins, and bright banners hung over the gateway. We walked along the old defense ditch at the base of towers of all shapes—round, square, octagonal—and then climbed up them to look down at the town. Inside the walls, little shops sold honey and *spécialités à la rose,* rose-flavored local specialties whose recipes had been brought back from Arabia by Crusading knights. Kids roared up and down the cobblestoned streets on their mopeds, girls clinging on behind the boys.

From Provins to their little village, we rode with Bruno and

Titi through rolling wheat, corn, and rapeseed fields, dotted with groves of trees and stacks of wood left from the *tempête,* the driving gale-force winds that had ravaged France at the turn of the millennium more than a year before. Their farmhouse, stone in shades of browns and grays, was two thick stories high, with a roof of gray, round, mildewy tiles on one side and bright, square, new orange-red ones on the other. "*La tempête,*" Titi said, lips pressing together at the memory. "A few months after we bought it."

The stone farmhouse had needed a complete overhaul even before the *tempête* hit, so it was still in major restoration, a project carried out by Jean-Charles, Bruno, and Titi. The first night I spent there with Sébastien was unusual in that we were the only overnight guests. We slept on the second floor, a three-year-long restoration project that served as a communal guest bedroom. It could be reached only from a door in the outside wall of the house that opened onto age-rounded, warped wooden stairs. Our bed formed an island of pink comforters amid thick black tentacles of electric cords, crumbling stone spackled with fresh gray concrete patches, lots of dust, and all kinds of work things, including a toilet and other equipment someday to be installed in an upstairs bathroom. An additional stack of ten mattresses against one wall showed how many guests Titi and Bruno were ready to receive at any given moment. In a pinch, they often fit two to a mattress, and teenagers slept on cushions. The old stone house was cold and humid, and the sheets clung a little to my skin whenever I moved. When I had to go to the bathroom late at night, I groped through dust for shoes and a flashlight and probed my way down slanting steps without a handrail. My feet crunched on gravel as I circled around the outside of the house, under the stars, and found my way through a kitchen crowded with excited dogs to the bathroom.

We spent that first weekend with them working on the unkempt two-acre garden. On weekends, holidays, and five weeks of vacation every year, Bruno and Titi battled to hold their own against new weeds, and attack years of neglect. As I helped them do this, I felt part of the family. It was wonderful to be away from the city. While Titi and Sébastien pulled up weeds and Bruno worked on the upstairs restoration, I rode the lawn mower under apple trees, around plum trees, and over dog droppings, feeling worthwhile again. Somehow, Sébastien's family and the things we did with his family were becoming what I loved most about life in France. I had come a long way from the person who had once thought Paris would be a great place if it weren't for the people.

When we got to the farmhouse the day before the village festival, Titi and Bruno's friend Colette was riding the lawn mower, Claudine and Justine were picking zucchini, and Jean-Charles was pruning half-dead apple trees. The sun was out, burning away smells of must and filling the air with the scent of the honeysuckle that formed a corridor from the kitchen to the outdoor dining area. Colette, the oldest and yet spryest of us all, with a big-tipped nose and the exaggerated expressions of a born comic, wasn't related to Titi and Bruno; but the English word "friend" didn't seem to cover her relationship to them. She was family, their scrawny, freckled mother hen.

"Wow," Sébastien and I exclaimed, as we did every time we came there. "This place is fantastic."

"It is nice," Bruno said proudly, flicking his white hair back. In the frequent masquerade parties he, Titi, Jean-Charles, and Claudine organized, Bruno favored roles that showcased the real him, like Louis XIV. The stone farmhouse with its grounds was his Versailles. He turned toward me. "Did you know this is where we had our big PACS ceremony? A huge celebration, one hundred and fifty people who stayed for two days."

"I heard about it," I said. Bruno and Titi had gotten PACSed almost as soon as a law passed allowing legal "marriage-

224

equivalents" between people of the same sex, and they had celebrated it in extravagant fashion.

"It's the perfect place for that kind of thing," Bruno explained, smiling at me. "PACS, huge birthday parties, weddings. I'll have to show you pictures."

"Okay," I said. I had seen many of them, but I was game for another round. Whenever I looked at pictures of Bruno and Titi's PACS, I felt as if I should ask for autographed copies. The event was that famous. How many stories had I heard of *two days* of feasting, the baker delivering sacks and sacks of bread to replenish the supply, Sébastien rolling out champagne in a wheelbarrow, René supervising the *méchoui,* the long, slow process of roasting a couple of lambs over open coals? Titi had spent the entire week beforehand cooking in the kitchen of the old farmhouse. When they brought out all the desserts he and the local baker had made, it had taken four men to lift the eight-foot-long, foil-wrapped board, laden from end to end. Bruno had cried as he tried to give his speech, and people had danced for ten hours without stopping. All of these stories and accompanying pictures spilled out again that evening over dinner outside at Titi and Bruno's huge teak table, where everyone relaxed and lingered until 4 A.M., surrounded by tiki torches.

"That sounds wonderful," I repeated wistfully. "I'm only sorry I missed it." I had been invited, but my brother David visited Paris that weekend, and I had to protect the city. Also, at that point Sébastien and I had been dating only a month, so I had met none of his family, and it had not occurred to me that doing so could be a pleasant experience. They were French, after all.

"It does look like fun, doesn't it?" Claudine said, exchanging very pleased glances with Bruno. Titi gave them a minatory look. "The next time they do something like that, you've *got* to be here."

"The next time?" I said, surprised. "You only get PACSed once!"

225

"Oh, there are plenty of other occasions to throw a party," Bruno said airily. "Birthday parties, New Year's Eve, *weddings*. You never know."

The village festival the next day bore no resemblance to an ambush. We joined the crowd in a large yard behind the single building that served every possible government function in the village: school, city hall, *salle des fêtes* or party hall. White paper tablecloths covered two long rows of tables under a sagging white tent top. A homemade dance floor had been nailed together in the center of the yard, and the aroma of roasting pig filled the air. I wanted to embrace the whole day, to plunge into my last experience in France for a while. I couldn't put my finger on when, but mixed in with the bad, I had somehow been seduced by snails, drunken restaurant owners, skating along the Seine, Sébastien's family. Now that I was leaving what I didn't like in France, I was suddenly, acutely aware of how much I loved. Leaving France had become painful.

Claudine was watching my face. "We could do something like this for your wedding, if you want. But even better. Something like Titi and Bruno's PACS."

"We could?" My image of a large U.S. wedding was of something formal and fussy and not very enticing. Nothing like this. "But I already promised my mom we would get married in the U.S."

"Do you know, it was so sad when Mamie realized she probably wouldn't be able to see her only grandson married," Claudine told Sébastien. "She tried not to cry, but one tear rolled down her cheek despite herself. You're her first grandchild to get married, you do realize that?"

Since Sébastien obviously realized that, I had to assume she was mentioning it for my sake. "I *wish* we could have a marriage in France, too," I said. How could anyone not want a celebration where you wheeled champagne out in wheelbarrows and danced on a wood floor thrown together in the middle of a garden? But a guilt trip over Pierrette was not enough to make me want to break my own mother's heart. My parents were more than two decades older than Sébastien's parents, and they were simply not going to get on a plane and fly to some foreign country at their age.

"Do you?" Claudine beamed at me. "Bruno, why don't you ask the mayor if we could borrow this dance floor for the wedding? It would be perfect for it."

"A French wedding on top of a U.S. one would just be too complicated," I said. And we didn't have any money. Nine months of an instructor's salary was not going to redress the past year's financial catastrophe, let alone give us the resources for two big weddings.

Bruno nodded thoughtfully. "Well, if you decide you want to do it here, you're welcome to use the farmhouse. That goes without saying."

"And we'll all help," Claudine said. "But you know that."

The auto-da-fé note to this village gathering, two suckling pigs impaled on spits, rotated gently over coals. The pigs looked very much like the nursing children they had been a couple of days ago, little feet curled up under their chins, an iron rod coming up their anuses and out of their mouths, flesh orange-black from a night of roasting. Crowds flocked to this infanticide. "How cute!" they exclaimed. "They look delicious! Almost done, do you think?"

"That's a good way to feed a lot of people," Bruno suggested. "If you wanted to have a wedding here, we could roast *cochons au lait* like that. Or lamb."

"No," Titi said immediately. "It takes forever. You have to think about who would watch over it while we're all at the ceremony."

A shadow fell on their faces. "Papa always did that," Claudine murmured. René had been too sick to come to this village festival, although it was the kind of thing he loved. She tilted her head up to the sky and gazed into blue. "He would have loved to dance you around at your wedding," she murmured to me. "He really loves you."

I blinked rapidly. René loved everybody. I didn't know he loved me in particular, and I hadn't known how much that would matter to me. "I would love to have him dance with me at my wedding, too," I said, low. I could imagine it: René twirling me around on a wood dance floor like the one patched together in the center of the yard, his eyes glowing with joy. I could see him bouncing on his toes by a *méchoui,* being everywhere at once in Titi and Bruno's vast garden, trying to make sure our wedding was beautiful and perfect for us. In my vision, he had all his hair and energy, as he had the day I met him at the Feast of Kings.

We all looked around at something other than what was in our heads. The hundred people gathered around us had to surpass the actual population of this dilapidated village, but everyone had invited friends and family from all over to come enjoy the fun. The day was beautiful, sunny and hot, and all but one person seemed to be having a wonderful time.

That one person, Jean-Charles, watched the rear corner of the stone building with feral alertness, rarely taking his eyes off the 1931 Citroen C4 that gleamed there. Jean-Charles had brought the beige and brown car over to show off at the festival but now acted like a miser who had displayed his gold in a weak moment. I can only imagine how insulted he would have been if the car *hadn't* attracted attention, but there was no need to worry about that. The crowds were circling like vultures.

"They keep *touching* it," he growled. "What's the matter with people? Any minute now, someone's going to open the door and take it for a drive."

"Surely not." I patted him on the arm.

"I'm not exaggerating! When I brought it up from Provence a few months ago, I actually came out of a restaurant once and found a kid behind the wheel. His parents had put him there and were taking pictures! Look at that!!" Jean-Charles half rose. "That man just ran his hand the whole length of it!"

Claudine grinned at him and caught my eyes. "He might bring the Torpedo up in the spring. He's thinking of driving the old cars for weddings occasionally."

Of all the cars Jean-Charles and his father had in their collection, the 1928 Torpedo remained my favorite, and that was saying a lot. "For . . . weddings?"

"Um-hmm." She set her chin on her hand, smiling at me. "Wouldn't that be wonderful, to ride to your wedding in one of those cars?"

Yes, it would. "Could I wear a twenties-style wedding dress?" I asked eagerly, seeing myself with a miraculously stick-shaped figure, berouged lips, a cloche hat, and a jade cigarette holder.

"Of course you could!" Claudine exclaimed, her eyes lighting up. "You would look *wonderful* in a twenties-style dress!"

My jaw dropped, and I decided I definitely loved Claudine. Nobody had ever been able to share my twenties vision of myself before.

Bruno leaned forward excitedly. "Could we *all* dress up in twenties style?"

"Yeah!" I leaned toward him, just as excited, then sat back, trying for a cooler head. "We couldn't ask our guests to do that. Everyone wouldn't be able to find the right clothes."

"I'm sure they could manage something, if they tried," Bruno said sternly. His gaze grew lost in the middle distance. "The twenties. Do you remember those little boater hats men wore?"

"And the flapper dresses!" I said eagerly. "Do you think I could have a jade cigarette holder?"

Claudine looked at me blankly. "*Non, non, non.* I was thinking of those dresses with bustles and little lace collars and S corsets for you. Isn't that the twenties? Those flapper dresses just wouldn't suit you."

Damn it.

"But you would look *wonderful* in a lace collar," Claudine tried, sensing she was losing me.

I scowled.

A dozen feet from our table, a sixty-something gentleman installed himself behind a synthesizer, and a teenager picked up an accordion. They burst into a polka, and Bruno grabbed me, over my protests that I didn't know how to dance the polka. He solved that problem by holding me in a very firm grip while he danced it. Trailing my stumbling body around the floor, Bruno danced the polka, a Viennese waltz, a fox-trot, and various numbers I didn't even recognize. Sébastien regularly tried to cut in, but Bruno ignored him. Only when the musicians paused and put on a CD mix did I get a break: Bruno had to let go of me to pull off his shirt and wave it over his head, per the instructions of a popular song that year. Over by the spit, organizers finished pulling Babe into pieces for our main course, and we returned to the table, breathless and hot. Claudine laughed through gasps for air. "That's so much fun. French weddings are kind of like this, don't you think, Titi?"

"Our PACS was like this, anyway," Titi agreed, tugging on his diamond stud. "But with more champagne. Remember how you danced, Sébastien?"

"I remember the wheelbarrows of champagne," Sébastien said, flexing his shoulders.

"I asked the mayor if we could borrow that dance floor," Bruno said. "Just in case you two decide to have the wedding here. But she said they had borrowed it from another village."

"A dance floor?" Jean-Charles waved a hand dismissively. "I can put together a dance floor for you. Don't you worry about that."

I leaned closer to Sébastien and squeezed his thigh. "It *does* sound fun," I whispered.

His face lit up. "Really?"

"How would we manage two weddings on two different continents, though?"

"We could manage it," he said. "Look at all the organizers we've got around us. They'd *love* to get their hands on our wedding. They love nothing better than to throw a big party."

I looked around me. "It *does* sound fun."

When I looked back at the others, Claudine was watching us, smiling happily and nudging Bruno.

Justine tapped my shoulder. "Do you want to go sign up for the stilt race?"

"There's a *stilt* race?" I sat straight up. "Yes!"

We found a portly gentleman in loose shorts and an untucked shirt registering contestants at the other end of the pavilion. "Are you here for the stilt-walking contest?"

"Of course!" Not that I had ever touched a stilt, but that didn't seem a good reason to shrink from entering a top-speed race to me. Justine knitted her hands together and hesitated uncomfortably when she saw the sign-up sheet. There were two categories—under fourteen and over fourteen. She had turned fourteen only a few months earlier.

I grinned at her. "Don't consider yourself a child?"

She looked demure. "I don't want to take advantage of anyone."

I stared.

She coughed delicately. "I mean, I, um . . . I've had a lot of practice."

"You're a *stilt-walking* expert?" Why didn't my family produce these kinds of talents? "How did that happen?"

"Summers in Provence. My grandfather made me a new set every year because I kept growing out of the old ones."

I watched her sign her name under mine in the adult category, deeply impressed. We just didn't encourage such vital skills in the U.S.

"Good for you," the portly gentleman said heartily, pleased to have his first two adult entries. "Do you have any stilt

231

walkers at your table? We don't have enough people in the adult category."

As it turned out, everyone at our table of Parisians had stilt-walked at least once. I would have thought their skills would be confined to how to call a taxi, but I had noticed before how close some Parisians were to something rural and peculiarly *authentic.* Valérie, only thirty-two, often casually referred to daily trips to collect milk from a nearby farm when she was growing up in Brittany. Suave Bruno, at thirty-five the third highest ranking executive of a major French hotel chain, could, from personal experience, tell you how to kill and dress any barn animal you cared to name, including quite a few that weren't barn animals in the U.S. What's more, this was *good cocktail chatter.* I swear. Everybody but me always had something to contribute on the subject.

Despite this familiarity with the *terroir,* or land, many hesitated to sign up for the stilt race, repeating phrases like "look ridiculous" and "fall flat on my face" so frequently that I started to think maybe I should have given both some consideration myself. This cowardly spirit forced Titi and Bruno to take matters into their own hands. When the portly gentleman came around to drum up the competitive stilt-walking spirit, they blocked frantic grabs for the pen with their bodies and signed up every single person at the table.

Passions ran high, or maybe it was alcohol, as Justine established a clear lead, someone else's child cheated, I trod diligently but woefully behind, and Bruno proved himself competitive to the point of self-extinction. He was so determined not to fall off his stilts that he would keep clutching them as he fell, rigid as a board, until his face slammed into the ground and broke the fall for the rest of his body. By the time the adult stilt race ended, he had so many bruises on his face it looked as if he had entered a boxing contest; and he was complaining heatedly to the organizers about having left such hazards as bits of gravel and race course markers lying around, since anyone could see these could take out an eye.

I, of course, got eliminated in the first round. That brat, Justine. "Can we have a stilt race at our wedding if we have it in France?" I asked Jean-Charles when I sat down on the edge of the dance floor with him. *"That* would be cool!"

"Hmm." He obviously didn't want to say no and discourage me but had to admit: "We'd have to make a lot of stilts."

Justine won, of course, and the embarrassed organizers handed her the adult prize—a bottle of fine champagne. She accepted the bottle with good grace and regifted it to Bruno, who needed it. Then everyone went back to dancing.

Children skipped among the gyrating adults: a vivacious *métisse* child with soft, dark curls, who danced with every single person on the floor; a tiny redheaded girl who attached herself to Sébastien, thumb in her mouth and head tucked down to stare up at him with enormous blue eyes. Whenever she shot her arms straight up at him, Sébastien would laugh and pick her up to dance with her in his arms until she wanted down again. A very sketchy adult male gyrated among the children, too, repeatedly attempting to bump and grind Justine and her even younger-looking cousin until Jean-Charles, Titi, Bruno, and Sébastien turned on him en masse. Sébastien passed the redhead to me, and I carried her away from the scene to her mother. When the sketchy man *persisted,* it looked very like we were going to have a fight right there, but the mayor's husband finally ordered him to leave. It was midnight by then, and the stars were bright overhead, as they never were in Paris.

I would miss this place and these people, I thought. Well, maybe not sketchy males, but everyone else. I really would.

"Your wedding's going to be just like this." Claudine smiled at me.

"Including drunk men who try to grab parts of your body, probably," Sébastien muttered, glowering. The loss of his little dance partner had wounded him deeply.

233

I seized Sébastien's hands. "Let's do it," I said. "Let's have two weddings, one in the U.S. in July, and one in August, here. It will be fun." I really said that. And I wasn't drunk, I swear.

Sébastien spun me around the dance floor, he was so happy. I stumbled the first steps and then caught up with him, laughing as we whirled around.

Twenty-six

I was halfway over the Atlantic before I realized I'd been had. Sure, the PACS sounded wonderful, and the village festival had been great fun. Who wouldn't want to have a wedding with two days of dancing and feasting under the stars at a stone farmhouse built before my country was born? I had, however, forgotten one essential difference between those two events and our wedding feast: in the first two cases, *someone else had done all the work.* Caught up in the excitement, I had agreed to throw two big weddings on two different continents exactly five weeks apart from each other. Was it just me, or did that sound suicidal? "Does that sound suicidal?" I asked a recently married friend in the U.S. She handed me her therapist's business card.

"Does that sound suicidal?" I asked my sister Anna.

"You know what bothers me?" She frowned. "When I go see my therapist, all she ever wants to talk about is you. You, you, you. She says you're a fascinating case study, and she'd really like to meet you. Meanwhile, what do you think that does to my psyche that my own therapist would rather talk about my sister?"

Maybe I should give this whole double wedding thing some more thought.

However, I had other things to worry about first. Could Sébastien, too, give it all up for love and a woman who could cook but didn't know what side of a plate to set a wineglass on?

"I told you that I would," he said over the phone. He sounded slightly impatient for someone who had only answered this question twenty times the past week. There you go, impatience—I'd found a third flaw. "And the wineglass issue isn't really as important as you think it is."

"Oh, so left or right, it doesn't matter?"

He sighed heavily. "I'll set the table."

"See, here's the thing. You're so gorgeous and so sweet and so French, and you're going to give up everything to come to the land that invented Twinkies? For *me*? Why? It doesn't make sense."

He laughed. "I'd explain it to you, but it's pornographic, and making you blush over the telephone is just an exercise in frustration."

"That's such a nonanswer. That doesn't explain *anything*. Do you know one of my sisters thinks you're just using me to get a visa?"

He laughed until he choked. "What, because this is one of America's immigration problems? The horde of French people just dying to live there?" He laughed so hard he started to wheeze. "Excuse me, I've got to get some water."

"Well, I *know* it's ridiculous." My siblings had obviously never lived in France. "I'm just trying to explain how incredible it is, even to the people who know me best, that anyone like you would do something like that for *me*."

"I've always had a weakness for women who are *chiante*." *Chiante* means a pain-in-the-ass. "My mom's that way, too, so I must have imprinted."

"Your mom is not *chiante!*" I said incredulously. "She's a sweetheart. *Just like me.*"

He laughed.

235

"Well, at least Americans are normal," I pointed out. "And easygoing. It will be much easier for you to adapt to my country than it was for me to adapt to France."

"That's what you say," he agreed. "That Americans are so polite and friendly and welcoming."

"Yes," I said confidently. "So have you bought your ticket yet?"

A moment of silence. "No."

A longer silence.

"I'm waiting for my paycheck," he said defensively. "So I can afford it. *Don't start crying.*"

I covered the phone with my hand and sniffed hastily. "I'm just worried you'll decide not to come."

"I told you I'll come, and I'm going to come. And guess what else?"

"What?"

"Fabien is going to move to Québec! He's been dreaming of it for forever, and saving money, and they've finally processed his immigration papers. We'll be leaving almost on the same day."

I remembered the threesome braking with all their might to escort me down a hill on skates. "How is Éric taking this?" That was, how was he taking the sudden vast hole opening in his life, his two best friends from childhood moving across the world? He was the only one who wasn't replacing the friends with a new adventure, who was going to be right where he had always been but minus the two people he did everything with.

There was a long pause. "Well, none of us are taking it very well, shrump. But—that's life. *Sometimes things have to change.*"

When he hung up, I lay awake all night, imagining how he must be feeling as he left all his friends, left his family, came to a country that had never held much interest for him, and where he knew no one . . . all for me. I had at least had practice at it, from so much traveling; Sébastien had never done it before. Would he be able to do it? Would he be okay?

236

A week later, he called back, troubled. "I got my tickets. But they won't let me take Indy."

"What? You can take cats on an airplane."

"No. Maybe it's something to do with the new security measures, but they won't let me take him. I'll have to leave him with my mom." I could feel the frown in his voice, the worry. "But he's my cat. I've always taken care of him."

"You're still going to come?" I asked fearfully. I mean, *I'd* choose me over Indy, but then Indy had tried to eat my teddy bear, so I bore a grudge.

"Yes," he said. "I got my ticket. I'm coming. I just . . . feel bad about Indy." Maybe he had counted on having Indy as his one friend.

Two days before his flight, his grandfather went back into the hospital.

I closed my eyes, feeling sick to my stomach. "Do you want to postpone your flight?" I made myself ask. Don't be selfish, I told myself. Even if you know this is the breaking point, this is the moment when he backs out—for a very good reason—and never gets up the courage again to come.

There was a long silence. "No," he said at last. "No, no one knows how long he will be in the hospital, and he could be in and out for a long time. Hopefully he'll dance at our wedding. I'm his first grandchild, you know. He wouldn't want me to cancel my flight. The last thing he would want would be for us not to get together because of him. He just loves you."

Two days later, he came down the escalator into the baggage claim area, pale and excited. As soon as I saw him, I felt sick to my stomach again. A sudden sense of responsibility will do that to you, when you're not used to it. I hadn't had one for a long time; I'd been looking out for myself and no one else. But now I had

237

taken a man out of his happy life, his happy family, his world that he loved, and lured him here. I had sort of liked the idea of myself as a luring siren up until now, when I started worrying about him smashing up against the rocks below. Any pain he suffered because of this decision, any unhappiness he felt, would be my fault. I wondered if Sébastien had felt the same way, when I moved to Paris for him that January, when he got to the airport to pick me up and I was crying. How hard had that been for him?

Sébastien wasn't crying, though. He hugged and kissed me hard and for a long time, before he looked around the baggage claim area, trying to figure out what America was going to hold in store for him. He looked smaller here, partly because he was in such good shape compared to the people around him and partly, I think, because he himself felt suddenly so vulnerable. But then he grinned and kissed me again and hoisted his luggage with one easy arm.

When we got to our new apartment, there was a message on the answering machine from his mother. He called her back right away. His grandfather was dead.

"*Mon père et mon fils, le même jour,*" Claudine said, crying. With my arm wrapped around Sébastien's waist, holding him, I could hear her through the phone. "I lost my father and my son the same day."

"*Maman,*" Sébastien said softly. "*Maman.*" And nothing else, because what could he say? She cried and cried, and Sébastien pressed his chin into the top of my head and tears slowly soaked through my hair.

He would not dance with me at our wedding now, René. The man who had embraced our couple at the start would not get to celebrate with us. I kept thinking of the last time I had seen him, on the trip to the stone farmhouse when he had ridden in the back of that old car like a king. In Bruno and Titi's gardens, he had watched Justine and Sébastien and me play Frisbee and looked delighted when I threw one to him. He played with us until he got tired, which happened quickly, and then sat and threw fallen apples to the dogs, undeterred by the slobber when they brought the fruit back for more.

I don't know how many things Sébastien thought of as he sat there on the mattress beside me—our only place to sit so far—while the crickets hummed through the window. He started life in America with sorrow, caught on the other side of the world while his family mourned.

I think, when I came to France for Sébastien and was unhappy, it must have been hard for him. A lot harder than I ever realized before.

Twenty-seven

To distract himself from grief for his grandfather, Sébastien plunged into America as enthusiastically as he could. This was when I learned that some of my assumptions about America were based on complete ignorance. How could I possibly have guessed Americans were as difficult as Frenchmen? No one except the French and citizens of some two hundred other countries had ever mentioned this before, and it was disconcerting to realize I would have to start taking these oddballs into account. America had always been the place I returned to when I wanted a dose of sanity, an idealization that awed Sébastien. "You think your country's sane?"

"Well . . . I did."

It was unfortunate that we had started this conversation on Sébastien's first trip to an American supermarket. He stopped dead at the beginning of the cereal aisle, where rectangular boxes lined up to form a flat wall of garish colors. He walked away from me, all the way to the end of the aisle and back. "Laura, it's all cereals."

"Um-hmm."

"The whole aisle."

"Yep."

"Wow." He rubbed his hands together. "Can I get some?"

"Sure. It's about time you started eating a healthy breakfast. Just coffee is really bad for you. Try the chocolate-coated sugar pops."

He came back with his arms full and began opening and trying bowls of cereal the moment we got home from the store. The produce section proved a less happy occasion, though. He recoiled. "You're not going to buy tomatoes that look like that, are you? Wouldn't you rather pick them up at a market?"

"Yes," I said wistfully. "I would. Unfortunately, there aren't any markets around here at this time of year. In the summer, you can find a couple of farmer's markets, although they're about half an hour away."

He looked at the tomatoes, then at me, aghast.

But it was in the cheese section that his morale collapsed. "Good God," he said. "It's all vacuum packed and in plastic. Don't you have any laws to protect human rights in this country at all?"

"We *can* get good cheeses. There's a specialty market near here. Not as good as in France, but still a good selection."

"Can we go there next?" he asked anxiously.

"Okay, but first I want to get some frozen fruit. I haven't had a good smoothie in more than a year. Your countrymen just don't grasp frozen drinks."

"That's because when something's that cold, you can't taste it." He broke off, his head cocked to one side. "I knew there were purple potatoes, but red and green?"

I followed his gaze to the package of frozen fries, splashed with images of crinkle cuts in virulent shades of red, green, blue, purple, and yellow. "Oh. Hmm. I'm not sure there are. They might add food coloring to, uh, I guess make it more appealing. They do that to a lot of kids' foods. You noticed the purple and green ketchups?"

He looked at the package another long moment and then back at me. "Explain to me again how you managed to think your country was sane?"

"Let's go get your cheese," I said.

We really did have a store with a nice cheese selection for the South, not only French cheeses but some from Spain, Italy, Greece, and Israel. Sébastien was a bit surprised, both by that and the wine section. "You mean other countries besides France produce wine and cheese?"

"Yes."

"That you can actually eat or drink?"

"*Yes.*"

He opened his hands defensively. "Well, who knew?"

I was picking out a slice of Spanish manchego and attempting to impress the cheese clerk with my sophisticated knowledge of European cheeses when Sébastien came back from the French cheese section. "Laura. The Camembert's been pasteurized."

"Oh, has it?" I darted a glance at the clerk to see if he understood French and lowered my voice. "Is that bad?"

"Is that *bad*?" Sébastien's nostrils flared, and he stared at me as if he'd discovered he was marrying a black widow spider.

I looked from my manchego to his face and past him to the vast cheese selection. "Umm. I think cheese has to be pasteurized to be imported into the United States."

He gazed at me in utter despair for a long moment before turning and walking away toward the bakery section to see the bread in store for him.

I was pretty sure that wasn't going to make him feel any better but decided not to stop him. It was like a bandage—better to rip it off in one fell swoop.

While these questions of adaption were serious enough, on one point I had made a grave error: finding a job in America was *not* easier for a foreigner than finding one in France. My country was, if anything, less receptive. For some reason, at different points in time, we had both assumed that when our governments said "No work permit without an employment contract," that meant if you *did* have an employment contract and no criminal record, then you could get a work permit. American companies disillusioned Sébastien on that one as quickly as French companies had done me. "We're not even trying that again. It could be years before they finish sending back our paperwork and finally let you start work. But if you somehow find a work permit without us, we'd love to hire you."

This catch-22 meant Sébastien, jobless, was soon going as stir-crazy in the U.S. as I had in Paris. Worse, actually. I had at least had Paris, to love and hate. Sébastien was rapidly discovering that Americans didn't have many sources of entertainment other than television and other things that flickered on a screen. And he was a big fan of both films and video games, but—"You can't *walk* anywhere," he said. "There's nowhere you can just go, stroll around, look in shop windows, watch people, just *changer les idées*. Don't you guys ever have any human social contact with complete strangers?"

"Well . . . we have malls," I said, and took him to one.

He came away utterly disgusted. "That was the most horrifying thing I have ever seen in my life," he said. "Do you realize there was not one bit of creativity in the whole place? That every shop was selling the same thing? And it's so *ugly*. Where do you go when you want to just stroll around and enjoy life?"

I drew a blank on that one. "I guess I'd go take a walk in the woods."

He looked at me.

"I'm seeing your point here," I assured him hastily. "A certain human interaction issue, yes."

Meanwhile, I had fallen in love with my teaching job, which meant that now I was the one who had a wonderful job while Sébastien braved the job search humiliation and afternoons without the Louvre to go to. He wasn't mad at me because I had a wonderful job while he had lost his for my sake, but . . . it didn't seem fair. Not one to sit on his tail, Sébastien ordered a high-speed cable connection and started doing freelance graphic illustrations for companies in France. If a foreign national earns money while in the U.S., he is required to pay taxes on that money, so we went down to the local tax office to get his legally required Tax Identification Number. The first trip we picked up forms and talked to someone about what was required. The second trip, Sébastien brought in everything they said they required and came back to tell me they had changed their minds and needed something else. The third trip, I went with him again and, sick of bureaucratic lines, sat in the car grading papers.

After a considerable time, Sébastien came back out. "They won't let me give them the forms," he said.

"What? What did they come up with this time?"

"They say they can't accept applications from foreign nationals who don't have visas."

I looked at him blankly. "But you do have a visa. It's right there in your passport."

"I showed it to her; but she would only say she needed to see a visa, and if I didn't have one, I'd have to apply through their center in Philadelphia."

I double-checked the instructions that came with the forms. Yes, the I-94 visa visitors get when they pass through U.S. Customs and Immigration in the airport was very clearly marked as one of the types of visa that qualified. Maybe it was a language problem. Sébastien speaks English very well but, to his deep frustration, his Southern auditors don't always understand him. I tried to explain to him that Southerners didn't understand most Northerners either, but it wasn't effective consolation.

"Let's go back in. I'll talk to her and see what exactly it is they need."

Sébastien looked annoyed. "I'm telling you what she told me: a visa."

"Yes, but it doesn't make sense. There must be some kind of miscommunication."

We went back into the office and up to the little window behind which a short dumpling of a woman sat in a navy-blue suit. "Hi," I said in what I thought was a friendly manner. "I just wanted to see what was going on. My fiancé says you can't take his application here?"

"Yes, ma'am, I already talked to him, and I don't need to talk to you," she said flatly.

I blinked and tried to keep my tone friendly. "I just wanted to see if there's some kind of language misunderstanding, because it's not clear."

"Ma'am, I *told* you, I have already talked to him, and I don't see what you have to do with it. We don't process any foreign nationals' tax identification number requests if they don't have a visa."

"He does have a visa." I opened his passport and showed it to her.

"Yes, he showed me that, but he has to have a visa."

"This is a visa." I pointed at it, trying to draw her eyes down to the green slip.

She lifted her head high and refused to look at it. "Ma'am, I'm getting tired of this conversation. To process his application from here we need a visa, and that's all there is to it."

"This *is* a visa. An I-94 visa, which is listed on your own forms as an acceptable visa." I drew out the forms one of her coworkers had given us on the first visit and pointed to the line. "I don't understand what you need, if this isn't it."

"Ma'am, I am sick of this conversation; you are wasting my time. I told him, and now I'm telling you, even though it isn't any of your business, that he needs a visa for us to process his application. I don't see what use it is for you to make me repeat it a thousand times."

"But it *is* a *visa*! Will you at least look at it?"

"Ma'am, now you're getting downright rude. I don't have anything more to say to you."

I drew a deep breath. "Ma'am, can I have your name, please, and the name of your supervisor."

The fact that she gave both of them correctly scared the hell out of my vision of American bureaucracy. It meant the whole past conversation had been perfectly correct from the point of view of her governmental agency and that of her supervisors.

I nevertheless called her supervisor in Raleigh. "Ma'am"—I thought I'd start the conversation off right—"I am calling on behalf of my fiancé who is trying to apply for a tax ID number here in your office in Durham. Now, I don't know if it would be appropriate to make accusations about discrimination against foreign nationals, and I don't know exactly how high it would be appropriate to start making those accusations; but your office won't let him file his application."

"Ma'am!" exclaimed the woman on the other end of the line. I was getting very sick of that word. "We handle thousands of applications from foreign nationals. We deal with foreign nationals every day. In no way are we prejudiced against them. What did she say was the problem?"

"She said he needed a visa. So he showed her his visa, and I showed her his visa, and all she would do was repeat that he needed a visa."

A pause. "Well, it would have to be an acceptable type of visa, like the I-94, for example."

I gritted my teeth. "It is the I-94."

Another pause. "Well . . . you know, ma'am . . . I think it would be much more efficient for you to just apply by mail through Philadelphia. You know, that's all they're going to do at the local office anyway, is accept your application and then mail it on a few days later. You'll save so much more time bypassing them."

"Evidently, but that doesn't give your local office a right to refuse the application without putting themselves in a very dubious legal position."

"Ma'am," said the woman who had just claimed her local IRS employees were practiced hands at foreign national applications and in no way prejudiced, "it's a question of comfort. Our employees *do* handle lots of foreign national applications without any prejudice, but they aren't necessarily . . . *comfortable* about it. So of course they can make errors. I really do suggest you apply by mail through Philadelphia."

She hung up, and I stared at the phone, dumbfounded. "I'm glad to know the U.S. is so much more open to foreigners," said Sébastien, the smart-mouth.

"It was that damn Emma Lazarus poem on the Statue of Liberty," I said. It occurred to me that I got most of my facts about America from other Americans. Was it possible these sources could be biased? "It gave me entirely the wrong impression. Do you know I memorized it when I was a kid? I was so proud to have a country with the Statue of Liberty 'lifting her lamp beside the golden door' and telling all those ancient lands to keep their storied pomp because we would take their people."

Sébastien patted me on the shoulder. "The French built the Statue of Liberty. I'm just mentioning it."

Twenty-eight

By November, I was beating my head against my desk.

"You're going to hurt yourself that way," Sébastien said, deep in the 3D airplane he was modeling for a French newspaper that wanted to do an article on the Concorde accident. He was trying to get the light on the wings just right.

"Maybe we should just get married," I growled.

"I love it when you use that romantic tone of voice." He poked his head out from behind his monitor and gave me a wary look. "Are you saying—now? A civil service? I thought you loathed the idea of a civil ceremony."

"I *do!* It's so sordid. It's so—I want us to get married in a *church.* With all our families there."

Sébastien retreated behind his monitor again. He knew that tone of voice.

"I hate the government! I hate all governments! Stupid bureaucracy. Why do they make it so impossible for two people from different countries to live in the same place? *I don't want to get married in a civil ceremony!*"

Sébastien poked his head out from behind the monitor again, tentatively, like a groundhog just barely peering out of its hole. "We could still have the church ceremony. But you've got to admit, having a civil ceremony soon would help immeasurably with all these visa problems. In both countries."

"I don't see why the government should be able to *force* us to get married before we're ready!"

He scooted his chair so that he was now firmly out from behind his monitor and set his chin on his hand, gazing at me steadily. "You don't want to marry me?"

"In *July*," I said. "In a *church*. And in *August*. In a *church*, if anyone in the diocese of Meaux ever answers all our e-mails and calls. But not right now in a government office!"

"So you don't want to marry me—yet."

"It's not that!" I wailed. Maybe it was that, a bit. Could we just see how we could handle a stable routine for a while? Away from this constant menace of separation and financial disaster? And "financial disaster" was not a joke at this point. At least Sébastien was able to work for French clients long distance, but it would take him a while to build up enough of those to earn a living. We'd be doing a lot better if he could work for a graphic arts firm here. "It's the government office part! That's so cheap and sordid!"

He frowned, puzzled. "Well, you have to get married in a government office in France, so don't expect me to understand. I mean, people can do a second ceremony in a church if they want, but priests are so difficult, most people just skip it."

I frowned even more deeply. I think something had happened to me when I was shopping for a wedding dress, because I had ended up with a gown that was white and all lace from the top of its very short bodice to the end of its very long train. Since I hate lace and used to want to be married in a simple cocktail dress, this choice confused many people in my family, including myself. But with a dress like that, I wanted all our families and lots of dancing at a nice summer wedding in Georgia and another one in France, and I didn't want us to be already legally married when it happened.

"Fine," I said furiously. I glared at Sébastien. "Fine. I'll do it. I'll schedule a ceremony for us in Georgia the day after Christmas. That way at least some family can come, although there's no point, because this *isn't* going to be our real marriage. And I'm not wearing my real wedding dress! This is just a fake, paperwork thing to satisfy our asinine governments. And I hate our governments, and I am *not* going to be happy about this!"

And, by God, I wasn't. Sébastien weathered daily crying jags and harangues against governments that continued as we headed down to Georgia to partake in the Christmas festivities. "It kind of reminds me of that time I tried to teach you how to skate," he said. "Only every day. For a month."

"You, too?" Fabien said from the back of the car. Missing family but without enough money for a ticket back to France, he had decided to fly down from Québec to join us for Christmas, apparently for the primary purpose of tormenting me. "I was wondering if it was just me. But she's not always like this, is she?"

"It's hard to tell," Sébastien said. "In Paris, it was French immigration and the weather that set her off. But I'm hoping that once things get straightened out, she'll settle down and become a normal person."

Fabien looked dubious. "Well, she did act kind of normal the first time I met her," he offered at last. He thought about it another moment. "Although she washed her hands before eating. In the kitchen sink. Just before I'd caught her trying to sneak looks behind all the doors in Éric's apartment. Maybe normal is too strong a word."

"I was looking for a bathroom sink!" I exclaimed, driven. "If you people would put a sink in the same room as the toilet, I would never have been reduced to the kitchen. Besides, explain to me why it's so bad to wash dirty hands over dirty dishes that will *later be washed in very hot water,* rather than touching food with dirty hands."

Fabien pushed his round, geeky glasses up his nose and gazed at me with his brows knit. "You might want to give this for-life decision some more thought," he told Sébastien.

But Sébastien had stopped listening, absorbed by the sight out his window. "Laura, why is there a giant butt hanging over the road?"

Fabien leaned forward and peered over his shoulder. "Wow," he said. "And I thought the South was pretty conservative."

"It's not anyone's butt," I said with extreme patience. "It's a giant peach. You know, as in Peach State. Georgia has the best peaches in the world, and South Carolina thinks it does, so sometimes you see enormous peaches, often over outlet stores. I think they might be used as water towers," I added doubtfully.

Sébastien sat back. "This is really an amazing country," he told Fabien. "Just this morning, the news showed a picture of a sixty-foot Christmas tree someone hung over the interstate a couple of weeks ago." I coughed and kept my eyes fixed on the road ahead. "Can you imagine that? A *sixty-foot* Christmas tree. Hey, Laura, can we take Fabien by the gas station that has that pink papier-mâché elephant outside bigger than the whole building?"

"No," I said. "It's in the other direction. But if you're good, I'll show you a shack that's entirely covered in tires."

Down in Georgia, big David was waiting for Sébastien. "This time I've got a really good wine for you to try," he grinned. "Kind of an American specialty, you might say." He disappeared for a moment and came back with a small flask filled with a liquid of a poisonous red color and very clearly marked MD 20/20.

"David, you can't give him that," my brother Stefan said. "He might die."

"No, no, let me try it." Rising to the challenge, Sébastien took the flask and unscrewed the cap.

By that time, rumor had flown round the house that David was actually feeding Sébastien Mad Dog, and the whole family rushed to the kitchen. Cheers went up as Sébastien tilted his head back and took his first sip. He paused, rolled it around on his tongue, swallowed, and took *another* sip, this time to gasps of horror. Was he insane? Had one sip of Mad Dog short-circuited his brain? "You know, it's not bad, actually," he said. "Reminds me a bit of a cooked wine, something you'd drink before dinner."

He handed the flask back to David, who looked down at it and shook his head. "You know, I do try, but I don't think I'll ever understand wines." He looked up again, not to be crushed for long. "Hey, Say-bas-tee-YON, Fabio, have you ever been crane-swinging?"

In the yard of his crane operation, only one of David's cranes wasn't out on a job, and that one was occupied. "Don't worry about it," he called from its cabin, as he lowered a sixty-foot Christmas tree from a two-hundred-foot perch. "I had to check on the strings of lights on this thing, anyway. I think one of them has gone out."

"How could he tell?" Fabien whispered, craning his head back. The closer the tree got to the ground and to us, the more we could see how big a sixty-foot Christmas tree was.

"Not sixty feet," David said. "There's no need to exaggerate. The tree itself is only forty feet. It's the star on top that adds another twenty. Those reporters never get anything right."

"I'm sorry. Did he just say, 'There's no need to exaggerate'?" Fabien checked his English.

David and "his guys," as he called his employees, had welded metal square tubing together, strung it with some fifty strands of heavy-duty outdoor Christmas lights, and run a two-hundred-foot power cord up the crane to light its twelve thousand watts nightly. David set all that on the ground calmly enough, as if it was fairly typical Christmas decorating, and replaced it with a bulky rigging sling. Only he described it as a swing.

"Of course, sometimes we have to take the people out of the swing and drive it over to pick up a railroad car or something. I don't know if we can actually accuse the boys at this plant nearby of smoking dope, but it's amazing how often they get a train started down one track, then flip the switch too soon and send the back wheels of the last car down a different track. Of course, sometimes they've got good reflexes. They stop it before it actually derails, and they get the little wheels turning in their heads. 'Wait a minute,' they say, 'we can back this car off the track and get everything fixed right without them calling David

251

in to make fun of us. But before we hit reverse we have to *flip the switch back* to the track it was supposed to go down. Okay, go ahead and flip it, guys. . . . Whoa. Whoa. Damn. We've played hell now.' And so about once every year I have to get the people out of the swing and drive down there to lift the railroad car out of the gravel and back on the track. Then I can come back and let the kids play in their swing again."

"Is it safe?" someone asked.

David looked thoughtfully at the load line, probably wishing we'd get the little wheels turning in our heads, too. "Well, now, those railroad cars weigh about 250,000 pounds, but we only pick up the back end; so it's true it hasn't been tested to above, say, 125,000 pounds. I didn't like to suggest to my wife and daughters that wouldn't be enough for them because Annette gets touchy about that kind of thing, so I go ahead and let them play in it. But it's up to you. Who's first?"

How sweet, I thought. David kept trying to share his culture with Sébastien, too. And he did it exactly the way Jean-Charles had shared snails with me, with a grin and a challenge. "Not me," I said. I appreciated the gesture, but David liked to be in trouble, something an eighty-ton crane facilitated. I had clear memories of the time he had put his wife in a tree for fifteen minutes and pretended the crane had broken so that he couldn't get her down.

"Me," said Sébastien, who had, after all, already drunk Mad Dog today and lived. He climbed into the makeshift seat. "Now get a good grip," David said. "Here, Dana, you want to swing him?"

"*Dana?*" Sébastien said, as David's little blond eleven-year-old daughter climbed up into the cab, took the controls, and raised him six feet off the ground.

"This is why we never bothered to fix that old swing at the house," she explained, grinning, and rotated the superstructure of the crane. Sébastien swung in a slow arc thirty feet to one side, rose above the rooftop of David and Annette's business, and then dropped back in a long sweeping glide of sixty feet to the other side. By the time Dana ended his ride ten minutes later, Sébastien was grinning from ear to ear.

"Hey, Say-bas-tee-YON, do you want to learn how to control the crane?" David called. Of course, Sébastien did. "Now it's real simple, Say-bas-tee-YON. You just do this, this, and this. All right, Dana, your turn. Hop in the swing; Say-bas-tee-YON is going to swing you."

Thus Sébastien learned how to operate an eighty-ton crane, its boom stretched to 175 feet, with his instructor's eleven-year-old daughter dangling from one end of it.

"Laura," he said afterward, "I'm glad you told me Americans were normal, so that I would know."

Due to the aftereffects of Christmas dinner and having twenty people in the house, the septic tank broke down during the night before December 26. No one was allowed to use running water the morning of the fake wedding, including the bride.

I sat down in the kitchen and did what I like to think any normal person would have done in those circumstances. I began to cry.

"Oh, honey, now . . ." My dad looked alarmed and retreated until his back pressed against the counter.

"I don't want to get married!" I bawled. "I never wanted to get married! I'll be a *Madame*! Do you realize that? Just because I'm marrying a stupid Frenchman, I'll be a *Madame*! If I were marrying an American, I could be a Ms., but no, the French are too sexist for that, so I'll never be a *Mademoiselle* again!" I was pretty sure that just as soon as the judge pronounced the words "husband and wife" my breasts would sag, the skin around my eyes and mouth would turn into a map of the Alps, and I'd acquire grocery sacks and strollers, in permanent unattractive grafting to my person. I didn't think *Mesdames* were allowed to wear stiletto boots and balance in toilets asking cute guys out. This might have shown a fundamental misunderstanding of French culture, but there you go.

"Honey, if you really don't want to get married, then don't," my father said, his eyebrows drawing together. He looked somewhere between fuddled, anxious, and firm. "This is the time to make that decision."

I felt a jolt of panic at this support. "I mean I don't want to get married in a stupid office!" I caterwauled. "We *have* to get married! It's the only way we can stay together. I just don't think I should have to get married in a stupid office by a stupid judge because governments are so stupid! It's obscene! I hate governments!"

Some people might have thought all was said on that subject at that point, but little did they understand my powers of repetition. My brothers came into the kitchen and left. My mother came into the kitchen and left. My sister came out and left. My father pressed as far back into the corner of the kitchen counters as he could and stuck with it, looking desperately stressed.

After about forty-five minutes of this, a door down the hall opened. Sébastien stalked into the kitchen, his hair looking absolutely ridiculous, like a squooshed fuzzball on the top of his head. He had pulled on his white dress shirt but not yet buttoned it. He knew very well what seeing him in an unbuttoned white dress shirt did to me. He stood with his feet braced in the kitchen and looked at me with flaring nostrils and deep impatience. "I see I'm going to have to get up and take care of this."

"This" sat on the kitchen stool and cried.

"Have you finished?" he demanded.

I cried.

"You're hurting my feelings," he said. "Don't you want to marry me?"

"Well, I do," I sniffled. I was pretty sure. It was hard to tell, though. I didn't think married men walked around in unbuttoned white dress shirts deliberately to undermine female defenses. They probably sometimes did it accidentally, while getting dressed, but it was the deliberateness of the gesture—the knowingness—that got to me. Okay, that and he was really built. Would his muscles all sag the instant the judge said "husband and wife" or would all the sagging be one-sided? Marriage made women sexless blobs but men got to stay sexy, everybody said. "But not like this. Not in a stupid government office because of a stupid—"

He waited me out patiently (well, he looked kind of impatient, but he did wait) until my next pause. "We've talked about this. It's either this or I'll have to go back to France and you have to stay here until after what you like to call the real wedding."

I knew. That was exactly the problem. I couldn't stand another six months apart. Neither could he. It was heartbreaking, those separations in airports. It was horrible, it felt each time as if somebody were reaching inside us and ripping us to pieces. "If I get married, I'll be *old*. And ugly. You won't, because you're a guy, but I will."

"What?" he squinted, baffled.

"You *know* married women aren't sexy."

He just stared. "I'll never understand your culture in a million years."

"That's right, you're French, you probably believe in affairs."

His head came up, brown eyes cool. "No. No, that I don't believe in. I saw affairs rip apart all the families I ever had." He started buttoning his shirt, which was a real shame. I noticed my dad had escaped. "That's a stupid thing people say about the French anyway. They only think that because tourists never meet anybody but slimy people. Who else is going to walk up and start hitting on a tourist in the middle of the street—a nice guy? Unless you really *don't* want to marry me, quit trying to pick a fight and go get dressed. We're going to be late." He stalked out of the room.

I sat there and sniffled a second and glowered after him.

Finally I got up and went to find my dress. A few minutes later, his hair straightened, he caught me in the living room, whirled me around, went down on one knee, and kissed my hand. "You look beautiful, *crevette*. Will you marry me?"

When we got out to the car, I discovered he had decorated it with all the leftover Christmas ribbons from the day before.

"Because in France," he whispered, "we always decorate the wedding cars with ribbons. Are you crying again?"

To Sébastien's everlasting bemusement, one of my brothers actually wore an American-flag tie to this fake wedding. Not a blue tie with a small American flag printed discreetly on it; no, the whole tie was an American flag. This display provoked a second brother into tying an American-flag bandana around his head to make some kind of political point, but I managed to get him to take it off by threatening to have hysterics again.

"And *then*," Sébastien said, when recounting the day to his mother, "the judge put us against the wall as if we were about to be shot and read us our rights, every other word of which was 'God,' but I guess we have different ideas of a civil ceremony in our country."

Afterward, everyone decided it would be nice to go out to lunch together, in honor of the occasion. Unfortunately, the day after Christmas in a town with a population under twenty thousand, not much was open, and we ended up in what Sébastien called "some kind of run-down fast-food joint," but which was a very nice sandwich place really. Okay, so the murals on the walls hadn't been finished in five years, and the unmatched wobbly tables and chairs had come from garbage dumps. It still had the best sandwiches in town, although none of the waiters knew how to pronounce the focaccia they used in them. While waiting for his wedding dinner of pot roast on a bun, Sébastien drew out and examined the plastic bag presented to us by the judge's assistant and filled with what the assistant had described as wedding gifts.

He held up one after the other in a deeply puzzled fashion. A small package of Folgers coffee. Paper napkins. Anti-aging cream.

"You know, in France, we don't give anything remotely like this to people on their weddings."

"That's because it's not the real wedding," I said. I was getting tired of explaining the difference between a legal wedding and a real one to everyone I knew. People seemed remarkably dense on the subject. "The real wedding is in July, in a church."

Sébastien put his chin on his hand and sighed. "Are you telling me we don't even agree on when we're married?"

"Oh, that's not cultural; that's just her. We think you're married," my brother Stefan reassured him. "Don't we, Larry?"

"Of course," the second to the oldest of my brothers said. David wasn't there, which was why he and Stefan got a chance to talk. "We're delighted to welcome another man into the family. You about all done there, Seb? Because we've got to dig up that septic tank before it freezes tonight."

They didn't get it done that night. It took my father, three brothers, Sébastien, and even sometimes Fabien two full days of hacking through cold Georgia clay into the darkening hours of the night. It was just a good thing that wasn't our real marriage, because as honeymoons went, I'm pretty sure Sébastien was disappointed.

I was, too. My strict Catholic mother agreed with me that a civil ceremony wasn't a real marriage, and she made us keep sleeping in separate rooms.

Twenty-nine

This civil ceremony might have made having the right to be on the same side of the ocean *possible*, in some far-distant future. It did not, however, make it easy. One of the many forms Sébastien now had to file was called an I-485 Adjustment of Status application. Nothing about this form was clear, and I tried calling the INS (Immigration and Naturalization Services) number to get an answer to a question I had about it. I pressed button after button on my phone as I fought my way through a byzantine maze of automated options, heard more electronic repetitions of "America the Beautiful" and "The Star-Spangled Banner" than I ever want to hear again, and finally reached a busy signal. After I tried fifteen more times, I got through to a human voice.

"Mmbzeybex," said the human voice.

"Hello?" I checked, startled. I had expected something more along the lines of "INS, may I help you?"

"Right," the male on the other end responded.

"Ah . . . hello. I'm calling about form I-485, the Adjustment of Status application."

"Okay."

"I have a question about the medical exam. My husband is applying, while in the U.S., and I can't tell if he needs to take a medical exam beforehand or not. In the instructions, it's not clear."

"You generally need to do what the instructions say."

"Umm. Yes. But in the instructions, it's not clear. It says, 'If you are filing your Adustment of Status application with the local INS office, or if you are an asylee filing an Adjustment of Status application with the Service Center, one year after you were granted asylum, do not submit a medical report with your Adjustment of Status application. Wait for further instructions.' My husband is filing with the local office, but he hasn't been here a year. Of course, neither is he an asylee granted asylum. Does the 'one year' apply to all applicants or only asylees? There's either an incorrect comma or a vocabulary error in that sentence, but I don't know which. Does he need to have a medical exam before applying or not?"

Thirty seconds of silence followed on the other end of the line. "I'm sorry. What did you say?"

Granted, it was complicated, but that was my point. I repeated myself.

Sixty seconds of silence followed on the other end of the line. "I'm sorry, you're going to have to go through that again. What did you say?"

I repeated myself again but dropped the bit about grammatical versus vocabulary errors, since I feared I might be going over his head.

"So," he began right away, which was promising. Then he stopped, and another sixty seconds of silence followed. "So what do you want to know exactly?"

"If he needs to get a medical exam before applying or not," I said. I didn't lose my patience because people had recently told me if you lost your patience with the INS, they had you deported. "Does he need the results of the medical exam with the application, or is that something he will be sent to do later?"

Again there was an extraordinarily long stretch of silence. "So you want to order an Adjustment of Status form, is that it?" the man on the other end said out of the blue.

I stared at the receiver, deciding he must be drugged. "No. I have the form. I want to know if my husband needs to get a medical exam or not."

"Okay. Sorry. Umm . . . let me think a minute here." He wasn't kidding about the minute. I sat at my desk watching the clock hands tick around. "So you want to know what exactly?" the man said.

"If my husband needs to do a medical exam or not."

"So you want to be admitted to the U.S.?"

I ripped out a large chunk of hair. "I live in the U.S. I am a U.S. citizen. I want to know if my husband needs a medical exam to adjust his status or not."

"Well, generally . . ." The silence this time lasted two full minutes. I had a clock right in front of me, and I am not exaggerating. "Where are you applying now?"

"Through the local INS office in Charlotte."

"Well, generally, if you submit forms, they'll tell you."

"Tell me what?"

"Just, you know."

I swear my voice stayed patient. "If I don't submit the right forms, they'll reject this whole application."

"Well, maybe they won't," he said chirpily.

"But if they do, we'll be delayed six months and have to pay another six hundred dollars to have the application reconsidered."

"Yes, well, okay, then," said the guy on the other end. What, did he get a commission?

I drew a deep breath. "So should we do the medical exam ahead of time or not?"

"That's what you should do then," the man said and hung up.

We didn't get the visa problem sorted out by the time the July wedding came around. We did, however, reach an interesting stage: Sébastien wasn't yet considered a legal resident of the U.S. but still had to pay a hundred dollars and make a request two months in advance in order to leave it and visit the country of which he *was* a legal resident. His work permit arrived the third week of June, after he had spent eight full months trying to fill the gaping holes in his life with freelance work and classes. By that time, we had been living on one salary for a year and a half, with student and credit card debts up to our ears, and I couldn't even look at bridal magazines; if I read one more article on frugal brides who whittled their wedding bill down to twenty thousand dollars, I would start shooting everyone involved in the bridal industry. Our weddings would be homegrown.

We spent a lot of time on the fourteen-hour round-trips between my teaching job and my parents' house. The approaching wedding and presence of French people made my parents decide that many things let go for decades needed to be fixed in the next few months. We spent Spring Break ripping out the concrete of a fountain that had not functioned in fifteen years, digging several feet deeper through hardened Georgia clay, and rebuilding a new version of the fountain. Early birds, my father and I often found ourselves digging on it together in hours so young that no one else even noticed they existed. Around eight, Sébastien would come out and set to as well, breaking the clay with a pickax, sinking the shovel in, hauling hundred-pound rocks away, and then hauling them right back to the same place they had started in when my sister and mother changed their minds and decided they looked decorative.

"Your fountain," my father kept calling this project, as if I'd gotten everyone into all this trouble. I preferred to think of myself as the victim.

"It could hardly be mine," I finally said. "You first built it when I was a baby."

"But I built it for you."

I paused with my shovel thrust the inch I could get it into red clay. This was a story I didn't know.

"I went to France when you were just fifteen months old, and I saw this beautiful fountain in front of a museum, I think it was in Nice. I was sitting there drinking orange juice because it was the only thing I could figure out how to order when this couple walked across with their little daughter, about your age. And I thought, 'What am I doing here in this strange country when I could be home with my baby daughter?' So I gave the little girl my orange juice, went home, and built a fountain for you."

I looked at our hands red from the same dirt we had been digging together. I could imagine the scene twenty-eight years ago. My father, young and thin and adventuring in a strange country, missing me, the little blond toddler I knew from pictures, then coming home and building a part of France for me. And here we were, father and daughter at 7:00 A.M., rebuilding this fountain for my wedding to Sébastien, himself now in a strange country. Moreover, I would be living between France and America the rest of my life. What had I been doing in a strange country when I could have been home with my family? I looked up the drive toward Sébastien, coming out of the house. What was he doing in this strange country when he could be home with his family?

"It's funny," Dad said. "I brought you that orange teddy bear you still take everywhere back from that trip, too. As soon as you got old enough to understand where it came from, you decided to learn French, to speak with it. You were always begging me to take you to Paris when you were little, before you got distracted by all the other countries you wanted to travel to. Isn't it funny, what gets things started?"

Multiple trips from our apartment to my parents' place had everything almost ready, and ten days before the wedding, we had the countdown days planned to a T, without any spare time for breathing or sleeping. Then my sister called. "You'd better get down here early. Mom and Dad just had two of the oaks in the yard cut down, and we'll have to clear them away before the wedding."

"*What?*"

"One of them dropped a branch a week ago. They were afraid another branch would fall on your guests and kill them."

"*What?*"

"It's *possible.*"

Once off the phone, I explained to Sébastien why we were leaving the next morning.

"What?"

"Trees," I repeated, precisely. "My parents decided to cut down a couple of trees."

"What?"

"Trees."

"Why would they decide to do that a week before the wedding? We don't have enough work to do already?"

"They were afraid a branch would fall on your family."

Sébastien gazed at me. "Didn't you and your six brothers and sisters run all over those woods every day for two decades? Odds

262

are good my family could survive a couple of hours there without getting decimated by falling branches."

"They brought out some tree expert last week after a branch fell. He said the trees had to be cut down; they were rotten and would start to kill people right and left if my parents didn't remove them."

"Did he say they had to be cut down a week before a wedding?"

"The guests," I reminded him. "Your family's safety."

"I don't mean to be critical, but have you noticed that every time we go to your parents' they have a backbreaking project for me? Septic tank, fountain . . ."

We left the next morning and got halfway up my parents' driveway. We couldn't go farther. Trees blocked the rest of the way. I got out of the car and stared in hysterical hilarity. I think both of us, up to that moment, had been envisioning these trees as, well, somewhat smaller. The two red oaks that had bordered my parents' drive now lay sprawled from one end of the two-acre front yard to the other. With the trees on their sides, some of the bigger branches slanted twenty feet or more into the air. The oaks had grown for over a hundred years in Southern semitropics before being cut, and the enormous spread of their branches covered pretty much everything.

"We didn't want any of your guests to be hurt on our property," my dad explained, coming out to meet us as we picked our way through the mess.

"So I've heard." I ran my hand over the stump of one of the trees, three feet in diameter and solid, beautiful red oak from one end to the other. "Tell me again how much that tree guy charged you to cut down these rotten trees and save your guests? I'd love to have his address."

By my side, Sébastien was alternating between laughter and slow shakes of his head. "And you thought my mom's salad test was tough," he said. "I've drunk wine from Alabama, competed with shotguns, dug up a septic tank, and now I have a football field full of trees to clear in less than a week. Does your family know that in traditional fairy tales the suitor gets to stop after three tests?"

"Oh, you're not a suitor anymore," my father said. "You're family! We're just treating you like one of the kids."

"Oh," Sébastien said, speechless with pleasure at being so embraced into the bosom of the family.

We put on our oldest clothes and set to, my father and Sébastien on chain saws cutting up the branches, my sister Anna and I hauling them away. If there's a month you don't want to clear trees in Georgia, it's July. The first day, Sébastien peeled down to the scantiest clothes possible and even so could not believe this experience. "Laura, even my underwear is soaking wet," he said.

"Yeah." I didn't have much energy for more syllables, and sweat-soaked clothes weren't the same news flash to me.

"I can't *believe* you complained about Paris weather."

"I told you we didn't want to get married in July! May, I said. But no, you said Justine wouldn't be out of school until the end of June and we had to wait for that."

"I didn't think we would be clearing trees for the wedding!"

David came down on the weekend with a five-foot chain saw to attack the main trunks and was joined by Anna's fiancé Ken, who had to be rethinking his decision to join the family at that point. Stefan and Larry flew in a few days before the wedding and started log-splitting contests to get those three-foot-wide trunks into disposable morsels. "May I never again," Stefan said grimly, hoisting a mallet, "have to try to split green red oak."

We stacked all the wood to burn throughout several winters, a criminal waste: the red oak was so solid and beautiful from one end of those hundred-foot-plus trees to the other that anyone who had ever made furniture would have killed us. We went to bed aching every night, got up at six in the morning, and cleared. We usually broke around 5:00 P.M. from sheer exhaustion, showered off filth, and went to run wedding errands for the next few hours. "We've got to get this done at least three days before the wedding, so the branch cuts on my arms and face have time to heal," I mentioned. "Also so I can throw the flowers over my shoulder. Right now my arm hurts too much to bend it that far back."

"We should have eloped," Sébastien said.

"You were the one who wanted a white dress and family!" At the very beginning of our wedding plans, I had argued for a simple blue sheath dress and a tiny ceremony in New Zealand. Sébastien, however, had insisted on a fancy white gown and family. I tried to throw this fact up at him as often as I could.

"I was still getting to know your family at the time." But he laughed when he said it. This guy was just too special.

"How did you end up with me?" I asked out loud, baffled.

"Because that night you said you would marry me, I felt as if my whole world had exploded wide open and this new, beautiful horizon stretched all around me," he said and turned his chain saw back on. The roar cut off conversation, and the keen-sweet, sunny smell of fresh-cut green wood filled the air.

I remembered that evening. It was after a skating/scootering trip, the night before I left to get my visa for France. I had been clutching my teddy bear, sick with nerves, still harboring a secret fear of marriage reducing my own horizons to family vacations in Disneyland—or, even worse, EuroDisney—and he was thinking something that beautiful. People ask me all the time why someone like Sébastien ended up with me. It's not very complimentary, but I understand where they're coming from. And all I can say is, I honest to God do not know.

We cleared away the last branches Wednesday before the wedding, just in time to head to the Atlanta airport to pick up Sébastien's family. Many giant logs still waited to be split, but we had rolled them into positions to act as seats and tried to pretend they were deliberate.

Despite their insistence on a wedding in France, all the major organizers of the French wedding had decided to fly over for the U.S. version, too. My belief that we might have to choose one country or one culture over another was something they just kept refusing to accept. I liked their attitude, but it seemed to take a lot more energy and flexibility than I suspected I had. I had been insane to take on a wedding in both cultures. Trying to juggle two weddings and families on two continents in one month might be my breaking point.

Sébastien's Aunt Martine and her family joined Claudine, Jean-Charles, Titi, Bruno, and Pierrette for the trip. "Wait a minute," I said when I first heard their travel plans a few months before the wedding, eyes narrowing. "Weren't your grandmother's tears over her inability to travel one of the reasons we're having *another major ceremony in France a month after the U.S. one?*" I was already getting a little stressed by then.

"Laura," Sébastien reproached. "Can't you just be happy she can make it?"

"Sure," I said, "I can be happy." I could, too, because it would be good for Pierrette to travel with her family. She had taken the loss of her husband hard.

I looked at the list of things still to be done before the Georgia wedding and, next to it, the dartboard to which I had pinned various photos of bridal magazine editors. "I have a major wedding, a road trip with ten in-laws, an intercontinental flight, and another major wedding to do in less than four weeks; but with sufficient medication, I'm sure I could be happy with anything. Has your mother found a priest in France yet, or does she still want us to manage that?"

"She found one. She went and talked to the bishop, who said he had been getting all our messages, by the way. I guess he just didn't feel like responding. Anyway," he brushed away the question of a priest for the ceremony, "those are minor details. My family will be here soon, and I can't wait to show them the U.S.!"

The French were planning to take advantage of the wedding to spend two weeks in the U.S., traveling around the South and maybe taking in Las Vegas, Los Angeles, Texas, New York, and the Grand Canyon while they were at it. Over the months prior to their arrival, I tried many times to discuss with them the feasibility of this plan: "I'm going to name a length of time spent in a car per day. You tell me whether it's a road trip or a daily commute to work."

"Right, fine. You know, we do drive to work and when we go on vacation, Laura. We're used to making long trips."

"Half an hour."

"A commute. If there's no traffic."

"Two hours," I said.

"Trick question! It's neither. That's the time we might drive on a weekend to go see someone, like Titi and Bruno near Provins."

"Umm," I said. "Three hours."

They laughed. "Definitely a road trip. These are too easy."

"Six hours."

A puzzled pause. "In one *day*?"

"Eight hours."

"Why in the world would anyone drive eight hours in one day? When do you eat?"

"Ten hours."

"Isn't that illegal?"

"Sébastien," I said, "convince your family they need to focus on the South for their trip. When I say the South, I don't mean New Orleans or Florida. They'll be lucky if they get from Savannah to Tybee Island."

They eventually yielded to my advice, although Bruno has never forgiven me for keeping him away from Las Vegas. Meanwhile, on our end, we arranged for rental cars and hotel rooms. These ten people—three siblings, their mother, and their significant others and children—had made a pact to spend every minute of two weeks together, sharing three hotel rooms and two cars.

"Wow," I said to Sébastien. "That's really impressive. Are you sure?"

"Of course."

"All ten people want to spend every waking and sleeping moment together while traveling in a strange country for two weeks? All ten people in the same family." Twelve for a week of that, counting us. Oh, boy.

"Um-hmm."

"And that doesn't worry you? I mean, you don't think they'll kill each other?"

"Of course not! They'll have a wonderful time!"

"Wow," I said. "Don't tell my mother, all right? She'll start in again on how she failed as a parent."

The wonderful time started out a little negatively. Since they took the most economical fare they could find, they had been traveling for eighteen hours by the time the flight landed in Atlanta, and we expected them to be tired. When their plane had been on the ground for over an hour and they still hadn't appeared on the escalator into the baggage claim area, we thought they would be even more tired, and that they might possibly be lost. "I don't understand how this kind of thing happens to people in Atlanta," I said. "It's a very clear airport, really."

"Laura. There are five Métro stops between their gate and baggage claim. That's half of Paris. They probably got out and are wandering around in one of those malls you call a terminal, thinking that they went too far and reached downtown Atlanta and that it looks exactly like in the films."

Two hours after their plane was on the ground, we began to worry. I found an airline representative for the third time and finally persuaded her to tell me if our guests had gotten on the right flight. Yes, the family was somewhere around. Where, she didn't know, but no one had mentioned any passengers falling off in midflight, so in Atlanta they were.

Three hours after their plane landed, they finally appeared at the bottom of the escalator. I almost didn't recognize them, they looked so washed out from exhaustion. "Did you get lost?" I asked. "Customs problems? It was the champagne, wasn't it?"

"Did *we* get lost?" Bruno said bitterly. "No. Our luggage got lost. Or, I'm sorry, misdirected. They sent it to Puerto Rico. They think."

"*All* of your luggage?" Sébastien said.

"All ten bags. Well, fifteen, counting mine."

"But that's okay." Titi held up a plastic packet and regarded it with deep irony. "They gave us this."

"It's so cute." Martine pulled out her own and displayed a toothbrush the size of her thumb, similarly sized toothpaste, shampoo, soap, conditioner, and a piece of blue flannel.

"Useless at a wedding," Claudine said. "But cute."

"Pajamas," Titi explained as I touched the flannel tentatively. "It took me a minute, too."

By the time they were installed in their hotel it was 10:30 at night, which made it 4:30 in the morning their time, the exact time they had gotten up twenty-four hours before to begin this trip. As they were washing up, I wondered where twelve people could eat in a small Georgia town at this hour. Thank goodness for Waffle House, my old friend from college days, its bright yellow sign beaming at me from across the parking lot. The French had come for the American experience. What could be more perfect? Sébastien had loved it the first three or four times I had taken him there, after which he had asked me if I knew of any American experiences that weren't greasy.

Titi and Jean-Charles finished washing up first and joined Sébastien and me outside the hotel, lighting up cigarettes the instant they got out the door. Bruno followed a few minutes later, cigarette already lit despite Sébastien's promise to talk to him about indoor smoking. They all gave deep, shoulder-heaving shrugs, the kind miners might make when coming out into the light after a twelve-hour shift.

"Now," Bruno said, slumping onto the bench beside me, "for a nice cold beer."

"Oh." I looked around the town, much of which was visible from where we sat. Surely there must be somewhere within a half-hour radius that would be open and serving alcohol at eleven on a Tuesday night, but nothing sprang to mind. I hated to be the bearer of this news, but: "Waffle House doesn't serve alcohol."

"Oh." Bruno looked briefly disappointed, then made a moue of acceptance. "Well, wine, then. Whatever."

"Um," I said. "They don't serve *any* alcohol. No wine, either."

All four men stared at me, as if my words, though in French, had no sense in the language in which they were spoken. They simply could not be processed through a French brain.

"You have restaurants that don't serve wine?" Bruno précised, with great care.

"Um. Well, quite a lot of them, really."

"I didn't know," Sébastien interjected hastily, as all eyes began to turn toward him.

They hesitated, came back to me, then refocused on the parking lot, so as not to seem too accusing of any one person. "I feel that," Bruno said very carefully, "it should have been mentioned. Before we came."

"I didn't think of it," I said plaintively.

"It should have been thought of."

"How could you possibly not think of it?" Jean-Charles asked, appalled.

"Look, I told you to get a French guidebook! They warn you about what sandwiches have Cheez Whiz on them, too."

"That's not a myth?" Jean-Charles asked, distracted. "You actually eat that?"

"Then a bar," Titi said. "Surely you have bars."

270

"It's almost eleven on a Tuesday night," I said. I was feeling some injustice here, given that Titi and Bruno's little village didn't even *have* a restaurant several days a week, nor any bar within forty minutes, the reason they maintained a very good cellar. "Besides, didn't people want to eat more than anything?"

They all looked at me.

"I guess we could go back into Atlanta," I said.

Atlanta was an hour's drive. The women of the group would unite in a block so cold it would freeze the South Pacific.

"Well," Jean-Charles said, "there's always the champagne for the wedding."

"No!" I jumped up. "You got it unbroken from Paris to Milan to Atlanta, you got it through customs—how do you guys *do* that?—sorry, the point is, it's not going to get drunk now."

A very unhappy group of French males followed the women into the Waffle House. Our party took up three red vinyl booths, and Jean-Charles, Titi, Bruno, and Martine's husband Jacky ended up together at one of them. Although the significant others of all men were present, appearances suggested four unattached French males were in the room, and our waitress took an instant liking to their table. In her forties, with hair only starting to lose its sprayed stiffness now toward the end of her shift, she leaned forward and tried to offer them a friendly welcome: "Soooowowlooooyaaaaaaaaaaallstaaaaaaaathotel?" Unfortunately, they had studied an archaic version of English in school that had consonants in it and could only gape at her.

"So how long are y'all staying at the hotel?" she repeated to me when she got to the only table with someone who spoke her language.

"At least through Sunday."

She smiled. "Well, you have to tell them to come back."

"Could you bring us some grits?" Sébastien asked eagerly. "A big bowl."

"Grits?" Claudine repeated.

"You just have to try it," said Sébastien, who had taken to grits with enthusiasm. "It's a Southern specialty."

Once the giant bowl arrived, we passed it from table to table so everyone could try some of its contents. Busy showing our table and the table behind us how to eat grits, Sébastien and I didn't realize we had left the four men to blissful experimentation. They dug in happily, apparently quite pleased with the dish, and only paused when their server returned.

She gazed down with the deep calm of a career waitress. "I don't think I've ever seen anyone put steak sauce on grits before."

They smiled up at her, clueless. She reached across their table for the sugar and proffered it, still speaking as if they could understand her: "This is what I put on it."

They did hesitate, but only for a fraction of a second. After all, in a strange country, advice from natives was not to be sneezed at. They poured sugar onto the mess of steak sauce and grits.

"Now that's what I call traveling," Jacky said when we left. "Enjoying the local specialties, meeting indigenous peoples . . ."

"And all this time we thought we'd be eating hamburgers and fries for two weeks," Jean-Charles said. "You know, your country's cuisine has unexpected creativity."

"They always like things so sweet in America, though," Titi said. "Have you noticed?"

"Is there *nowhere* we can get a beer?" Bruno pleaded.

When we left them, it was after midnight, and they had not slept for three countries: Paris–Milan–Atlanta. We figured we would give them what was left of the night and the next day to recover from jet lag and rejoined them the next evening, after a day of wedding preparations finished with a little light wood-chopping. When the teenagers let us in, their hotel room furniture featured rows upon rows of soggy dollar bills in various stages of drying. "From when they threw each other into the pool," Justine explained.

"What?"

"I think Papa started it, and then of course Bruno and Titi had to get him back."

"The hotel clerk tried to get us to stop because it was 3:00 A.M., but they convinced him it was perfectly okay," her cousin Julie added. "They didn't get arrested or anything. That was later."

We found Bruno and Jean-Charles playing tennis in the back parking lot beside the pool, where Claudine, Martine, and Pierrette all sat. Martine and Claudine turned their faces to the sun and baked, Martine's straight red hair spilling over the lounge chair; Pierrette sat under a parasol, covered in a hat and layers of cloth.

"I know where you can find beer here, Laura," Jean-Charles said, backhanding the ball to Bruno. "So you'll know in the future. Gas stations, which I find just a bit strange. You know, your country's not as puritan as it makes out to be, is it?"

"Where did you get the tennis rackets?"

"Oh, those. You know, there's the neatest store just across the road. Some kind of Karl-Marx or something like that."

I looked down the road and spotted the Wal-Mart. "Did you even *think* about Jean Bové when you went in there? What's the point of his spending five years in prison for bulldozing McDonald's if you're going to cave in to globalization and big business the second you set foot in America?"

"Yes, but you can find *everything* there."

"Explain to me how you got arrested."

"*Almost* arrested," Bruno said regretfully. "We never actually saw the inside of a jail."

"We went into Atlanta," Titi began.

"We *tried* to go into Atlanta," Claudine interjected from the pool. "It took us a few hours. You could have warned us that your road signs are totally insane."

"Yes, explain to me again how they can put you on a circular road and tell you it goes north," Jean-Charles said. "We were lost for hours."

"But we managed to get there, eventually," Claudine continued. "We ate at this nice little restaurant, and we thought everything was going okay; but when we asked the waitress how to get to Centennial Park, she called the police on us."

"Were Bruno, Titi, and Jean-Charles dancing on the table or anything at the time?"

"No, no. I mean, they thought about it, but it being their first day in America, they were trying to behave. When that policeman walked up, our hearts must have jumped right out of our mouths. Americans are so *severe,* we thought. Just for asking directions?"

"But I can't believe how nice your policemen are!" Martine raved. "The waitress had called the police officer to give us directions! He came to the restaurant just to do it and was *glad* to. You would *never* find that in Paris. Plus, those funny little safari hats."

The safari hats finally clued Sébastien in. He'd been reading the tourist brochures: Atlanta had established a hospitality team of Cultural Ambassadors who wandered around tourist spots and remained on call to help lost visitors. The French contingent was not pleased at his explanation.

"You mean we *weren't* almost arrested by an American cop?" Jean-Charles's face fell.

"You still would never find that in Paris," Martine said loyally. A big *Gone With the Wind* fan, she had nothing but positive expectations of this trip, and even staying out of jail couldn't ruin it for her.

"Speaking of things you wouldn't find in Paris," I cleared my throat. "My brother David has invited all of you up to their place for the Fourth of July tomorrow." I harbored deep fears about how this first meeting of both sides of the family would go. They couldn't even speak the same language. "He's almost sure to have his friend the sheriff there if you want another try at getting arrested."

Thirty

David's tiny, superbly competent wife Annette subscribed to *Southern Living* and *Martha Stewart* and habitually prepared twenty different dishes and four different desserts just to have a few American family members for Sunday dinner. Her reaction to the challenge of receiving twenty Americans and *ten French* for that most American of all days, the Fourth, emptied surrounding supermarkets for the next week.

The guests gathered on a vast deck pierced by trees, high up above ground that plummeted toward a creekbed. Familiar with the French rule about never helping oneself when a guest, I worried they would starve before plenty and explained the American-buffet nature of Annette's appetizers several times. "Just help yourself. Don't hesitate."

I didn't realize my error until an hour or so later, when Martine wandered up, plate in hand. "This is delicious. Who says Americans can't cook? That was a wonderful meal!"

I looked past her and saw that the other French did, indeed, look quite replete.

"That wasn't the meal. Those were appetizers. *Hors d'oeuvres.*"

"Really?" She clutched her stomach, alarmed. "But they covered the whole kitchen table and all of the counters."

"That's the main course." I pointed to David, who had just opened his smoker and was starting to pull briskets out of it. Cameras flashed. All ten French photo albums of the trip contain multiple shots of that moment: the great deck looking over a creek in the heart of a Southern forest, and big David angling in toward the meat, smoke whirling around his head as he pulled great chunks of beef out of black depths.

The men gathered around this scene in deep excitement. "*Ooh-la-la*," my sister Anna said triumphantly, listening intently to their conversation. She had her long, kinky-curly blond hair tucked behind her ears and was wearing brand-new white Keds in honor of the guests. She wanted them to know Americans could be classy, too. "See? I understood something. I told you I was good at French in high school."

In fact, all of my siblings had limbered up their high school French by this time, and the French had limbered up their high school English. These preparations didn't make for a vast range of conversational possibilities, but they were actually managing quite well as long as everyone kept dodging the gesticulating plates and glasses. It's hard to communicate in two non-shared languages without using your hands.

I wandered over to the smoker after the feast, to find David deep in explanations of grilling to his French male audience. David's remnants of high school French concerned mostly pronunciation, which was why he tried so hard to get everyone else to pronounce Say-bas-tee-YON's name right; but the fact that no one could understand him hadn't slowed him down.

"Cooking a perfect steak is really easy," he said, holding out a big hand and sticking out a finger. "First, you got to get Annette to marinade the steak—never try to cook a good steak without Annette. Then get some beer from the basement." He showed the beer he was holding in his right hand, to make sure the French understood that part. "Use wet wood." He pointed to the wood and a pitcher of water, gesturing with his hands to indicate combining the two ingredients. "Start the steaks on the grill, and when the fire goes out, put 'em over on the smoker and add more wood. Then get some more beer from the basement." He held out his beer as exhibit A again. "Set the steaks on a clay pot next to the smoker and start the propane grill. When the propane grill goes out, cuss, then get another beer. Go split more wood and put it on the fire, then listen to Daddy awhile and calm down. Take the empty propane grill off and put it in the back of the pickup truck. DO NOT tell your wife, 'Don't let the door hit you in the butt on your way out, honey,' when she walks in with an attitude because the steaks are not done yet and because she got the rest of the meal done half an hour too early."

Annette, who had just delivered a tray to one of the tables, put her hands on her hips and looked at David. Crisp and clean despite the heat, in a pale blue shirt and shorts, she showed no signs of stress from preparing an enormous banquet; but she did narrow her eyes at her husband.

He held up a hand. "That is," he corrected himself, "DO NOT be smart with your wife when she very *sweetly, politely, tactfully* comes out and asks you why in the hell the steaks aren't done yet. . . ."

Annette started toward him, and David ran to hide behind his friend the sheriff.

The French men all grinned.

While David tried to get his friend the sheriff to arrest Annette for spousal abuse, I took a moment to gaze around in delight. I had honestly thought that these two groups of in-laws would never truly be able to meet and mingle. I had been wrong. Martine's little, gray-haired, irascible husband, Jacky, former chocolatier for the famous Parisian chocolate-maker Christian Constant until he developed multiple sclerosis, was telling Dana her "Death by Chocolate" beat anything he had ever made; long-haired, Scarlett-wannabe Martine was trying to get Annette's coleslaw recipe out of her, and Annette seemed like she might actually be willing to give it; and the French men were discussing whether it would be better to take a smoker back on the plane, try to find one in France, or have Jean-Charles make one from scrap. Making one from scrap was exactly the kind of thing David would do in a pinch, and he forgot Annette's arrest to eye Jean-Charles with appreciation. It was another kind of Feast of Kings. The two worlds had met, and they were getting along like a house on fire. To see *them* do it, bridging two cultures looked as easy as pie. I reached for Sébastien's hand, feeling more optimistic than I had since we first started visiting immigration offices.

Because the French would take their turn at frenzied wedding preparations in only a few short weeks, they were excused from this round and used the afternoon after the rehearsal to tour small towns in the surrounding area. Meanwhile, every family member on the American side worked at a frantic pace. My parents and aunts organized things at the house. Anna made bouquets, crouched in skimpy pajamas over a mass of greenery spread out over my mom's sewing-room floor until just a half hour before the wedding. I did *not* take a picture of her with her butt sticking up in the air in those tiny pajama shorts; that was our older sister Mary Kay, who had descended on the gathering the day before and immediately started causing as much trouble as she could. Mary Kay was the eldest sibling and the reason I could take Adela in stride. She had hair as kinky-curly as Anna's, but had recently dyed it pink in an anti-aging move. She claimed the pink was on purpose, but we weren't sure; she had been known for self-dying accidents when she was a teenager. Nieces ran everywhere, doing hair, helping with bouquets. My mother's friends from church, women in their seventies I had barely seen since I was a child, whipped up food in their kitchens and hauled the dishes over to the church hall. Not a hair on her stylish blond head out of place, Annette ran decorations, a major operation that required every other able body in the family, including her two daughters, David, all five of her brothers-in-law, Mary Kay, and me.

"I can't believe all the work your family and your family's friends have put into this," Sébastien murmured to me. "We could never have managed it without them."

"I know," I said, awed myself at the energy and love being put into making our intercultural love story work. "And when I first introduced you to them, I thought they were going to shoot you."

The church for our wedding was about as far away from any actual town as it was possible to get, probably due to Southern Baptists. When I was growing up, friends who really cared about me would invite me to their revivals. They didn't want me to go to Hell for staying a Catholic.

This small Catholic community had been founded in Georgia when a Yankee Carpetbagger decided to import Hungarian and Slovak Catholics to grow Tokay wine and brought in—who better?—French to supervise. When State Prohibition hit in 1907, forty thousand gallons of wine stocked in cellars somehow disappeared overnight, and most of the Catholic families just drifted away, as any intelligent Catholic would when wine was outlawed. A few stayed, maintained in the faith by a missionary priest's monthly visits to their old one-room schoolhouse. When that property was sold in the early fifties to finance a new church, news hit local papers that moonshiners had been hiding liquor under the altar all these years. The priest and parishioners all acted deeply shocked, but come on. Forty thousand gallons of wine and then moonshine? Who's kidding whom here?

Anyway, the Catholics obviously felt some need to keep a distance from teetotaling Southern Baptists and so built their new church out in the middle of farm and forest, on land donated by actress Susan Hayward and her family. All the time I was growing up, this was the greatest place. Peacocks wandered in the cemetery and across the parking lots, spreading their vast tails and losing feathers we children ran to collect. In fact, having read that peacock feathers in a house meant the girls in it would never marry, I used to keep some in a vase in self-protection. Ironically enough. The priest, who arrived a month before my

279

birth and stayed until retirement two decades later, kept Irish wolfhounds by the half dozen, somewhat smaller donkeys, and pretty much every other kind of animal life that ever piqued his interest or got abandoned on his doorstep. Some of the wiliest parishioners would openly "donate" unwise animal acquisitions, such as a herd of goats, to the church. We ate some of the goats at Easter feasts, to my father's annoyance, since he had to help prepare them. Come to think of it, maybe my philosophy professor father and top executive Bruno could swap notes on killing barn animals.

To the aggravation of some of the more aesthetically inclined parishioners, the priest also put up a cheap portable road sign where he maintained the statistics on "Children Murdered since Roe vs. Wade." Around it on the hillside above the cemetery Susan Hayward had so elegantly landscaped, he stuck white crosses for every million dead babies. In case anyone is imagining the ordered, poetic beauty of the white crosses in the Normandy cemeteries, don't. It was more like a pincushion. There are some classic pictures of him being hauled off, head and knees still bent in prayer, from an abortion protest by two policemen.

This priest was great. Sometimes he would just suddenly, out of the blue, on a Wednesday morning when everyone was trying to fit church in before work and school, decide to sing High Mass in Latin. I *loved* High Mass in Latin; it was like he brought back all the power and mystery to a world that otherwise bore very little resemblance to my fantasy books. I think that's what Monsignor felt, too. Other times, a Mass reading would make him think about sacrifices in the Judeo-Christian tradition, and he'd be off for twenty minutes on how the *blood* spurted *up,* his voice moving into a joyful cadence. Second-generation Irish, he sang "Danny Boy" at every single potluck dinner and sang it so well that as a kid I actively looked forward to the moment he wandered into the center of the church hall with a mike. Increasingly fat and rambling as he got older, he was always kind to parish youth and was robbed frequently by the stray criminals he took in off the streets. Whenever I went to Confession, he would recite from the other side of the shadowy screen, "Oh, my Jesus, oh, my Jesus," as if I was breaking his heart, and then remind me my mother was a saint, an absolute saint. He had started that with my older brothers; it wasn't anything I did, I swear.

Monsignor died three years before our wedding, and the new priest swept all the animals and white crosses away in a wave of fastidiousness, but I still "saw" them when I stepped out of the car in my lace gown into the suffocating humidity. It was my real (if not legal) wedding day, and this was my history. My first idea, the New Zealand church, would have solved our cross-cultural difficulties by removing us from both cultures to a place where neither of us had anything. Sébastien and his family's insistence on France for at least one ceremony, though, had somehow made this church my only choice for another ceremony. My home, where I came from, where I still kept expecting Irish wolfhounds to run up and jump all over my dress.

I realized suddenly that this sense of home was why I had been willing to make all those fourteen-hour round-trips here rather than choose a church in North Carolina. I wondered how many things Sébastien didn't fully realize and couldn't articulate, how many unnamed layers of richness and belonging like this church were behind some of his needs for France.

The French and other guests new to the church didn't see peacocks and Irish wolfhounds, but they still saw a long country road and then, framing the entrance to the church, Stone Mountain granite and giant magnolias, in bloom for the wedding. The far side of one of those magnolias was bare, since one of my brothers had plundered it when we ran short of flowers in the church hall, but that was our little secret. From the parking lot, guests could only see white flowers against glossy thick green leaves and catch whiffs of sweet scent when a breeze stirred the stifling air. Green slopes curved down and up again on either side, the valley and hill of the cemetery to the left and the donkey's old grounds to the right.

Inside the granite church, pine rafters warmed, and sun filtered through stained glass so rich and beautiful it looked as if it didn't belong here. The windows, created by one of my father's closest friends, outshone the whole church. Red carpet stretched all around us, which I, used now to the stone floors in Europe, found a little tacky and which the French, used to stone floors in Europe, loved. The ceremony flowed without a hitch. Claudine, all pretty in pink and still thinner than I despite my corset, proudly walked her son down the aisle; my mother, regal as a beaming Queen Elizabeth could be, walked me.

My father gave a homily about strawberries. "Boy, your father has got you pegged," Sébastien whispered. "If anyone wants to hold your attention, talk about food."

First Man and First Woman got in a fight, and she left mad. By the time First Man realized this wasn't a good thing, she had such a good head start and such a good grudge on that he couldn't catch up to mend things. He followed her and followed her, but she wouldn't stop striding away, and he could never get to her. So God created all kinds of things to help slow her down— forests and lakes—but nothing worked. Then God brought out the great guns: he made strawberries. That stopped First Woman, all right. A patch of good strawberries would me, too. Eating the luscious red fruit softened her mood, reminded her of the sweetness of human love, and gave First Man time to catch up; she even shared some of her strawberries with him, just like I sometimes share my chocolate with Sébastien. The two made up and lived happily ever after and, in good Catholic coda, populated the earth.

My father completely missed the moral of this story—that good food can resolve most problems. Instead, he said, "Now, I'm warning you all—and especially you, Laura and Sébastien—that from now on whenever you eat strawberries, you'll remember this story and know again that the only thing sweeter than the taste of strawberries is human love. And you ask yourself, Is there someone waiting now for me to catch up? Or should I wait for someone who is trying to catch up with me?"

That was oddly moving, and something for both of us to do a lot of thinking about. In our relationship, one person was always in a culture alien to the other—far ahead, in a sense, of the other who had no chance of catching up. I looked at my father suspiciously. "I'm stealing this story from the famous author Andrew Greeley, who adapted it from a Cherokee tale," he explained to everyone. I felt relieved. It's always disorienting when a parent starts sounding wise all by himself.

Sébastien was so excited and happy the heat of it swelled his hands, and it took me much pushing and shoving to get his ring on his finger. The church laughed. "We're married!" I whispered to Sébastien, feeling as if those thousands of butterflies that had been in my stomach so long were about to take flight and carry me with them. "We're really, truly married!"

"Oh, *now* we're married?" he whispered back. "Thanks for keeping me posted. I never know, with you." His eyes were shining.

Things turned bacchanalian immediately after the ceremony. Sébastien and I danced and danced, and kissed repeatedly as demanded by our glass-clinking audience. I even gave a spectacular karaoke performance of "Born in the U.S.A." with an invisible guitar, and I wasn't even drinking, because I didn't have time. I just felt that happy. Sometimes, when people start sending me pictures in the mail of these moments later, I wish my happiness could express itself in less embarrassing fashion, but there you go. At least I wasn't the only one. The French and American families and friends interlocked in chains, dancing all around the church reception hall, led by Mary Kay in her midnight-blue bridesmaid's dress and pink hair. As a joke, my siblings had installed my Parisian-born orange teddy bear in pride of place, wearing a tie for the occasion; David grabbed the bear and danced rock-and-roll with him. I had never even seen David dance before, let alone with a teddy bear. Another brother got so drunk he tried to beat Teddy up for some imagined slight, but we made peace between them, and the dancing continued.

"See how normal my country is?" I asked Sébastien happily. "I told you so!"

"They do seem to be acting normal for once," Sébastien said, watching my brother pat Teddy's head apologetically. Teddy's midnight-blue tie—made from one of the wedding decoration ribbons—was a little askew.

Annette had created a French garden theme for the decorations, then filled in the vast windows with the stolen magnolia blossoms; scents of French lavender and Southern magnolia blended with the sparkly aroma of champagne. The families disappeared for an hour together and entirely destroyed our car, coating it with French and English good wishes in purple and white foam. Titi even signed his name to his contributions, although he later claimed that was a frame.

"We don't *do* that in France," he claimed, wounded. "We use pretty ribbons to make the car look nice."

I narrowed my eyes at him, remembering that one of Tweety Bird's traits had been his ability to maintain total innocence in all situations, even ones in which he completely demolished his opponents.

After a symbolic getaway, we met our two families at my parents' house. The idea was to let close family and friends unwind together at a barbecue. Melt turned out to be a more accurate word than unwind. We had expected it to be hot, but we had not counted on it being the hottest day of the year. Temperatures over ninety degrees could kill off a tenth of France's population, and it was over one hundred degrees this evening, in humidity like a sauna.

No one alive could be outdoors and not sweat, even in the shirtsleeves or sundresses into which everyone had changed. In the deepening dark, humid as only a Southern night can be humid, fireflies came out all around in the forest, and we lit tiki torches filled with citronella oil to keep away the mosquitoes. Crickets sang all around us. Everyone sank onto giant, unsplit logs under a magnolia tree, around the Nice-inspired fountain. No one could have found the remotest resemblance between this setting and Nice, but I had a strange sense of coming full circle, or maybe spiraling back around, not closing the circle but coming back above an old event as the spiral continued. French and Americans talked back and forth to each other in languages the other didn't understand. Mary Kay had brought out her Spanglish and seemed to be doing quite well with it.

We were married, I thought. We still had the French ceremony to do to seal both cultures into the deal, but we were married. I leaned back against Sébastien, who was beaming like a fool, and just felt happy. I would wait until tomorrow to think about whether I could handle a second wedding on top of this one without going stark raving mad. Maybe we should have had the French wedding first and the Georgia one second; if I had exploded under stress with my family, they would have taken it in stride as normal behavior.

Around eleven, David grew deeply concerned that anyone should drive in his condition. He declared himself over the base of a red oak stump that came up to my shoulders and his navel, his podium decorated with empty magnum bottles, plastic cups, a Brita water pitcher, and a cooler of ice. "NO DRIVE." He shook his head and open palm emphatically to emphasize the NO. "Jean-Charles, NO DRIVE." He elaborately nodded his head yes: "Claudine—drive. Bruno, NO DRIVE. Titi, NO DRIVE. Gaëlle—drive." Pointing at himself: "David, NO DRIVE. Annette—drive." He gave that some thought and repeated: "David, *NO DRIVE*."

I picked up the water pitcher to refill it, and David got distracted briefly from the No Drive lecture. "You know, Laura"—he wrapped me up in a bear hug—"I love you. And I like Sébastien, I really do. I don't know if he realizes I like him because sometimes I can come across kind of . . ."

"Oh, no, David," I mistakenly tried to reassure him. "Sébastien really likes you a lot. In fact—"

David stopped that nonsense by holding up an open, impatient palm, bigger than my head. "I don't care if he likes me or not. I just want to make sure he knows that *I* like *him*."

He nodded elaborately, looking around at the crowd of family and new family all gathered in the humid night. "You know when I realized Sébastien was a good guy? Now this might seem to you a kind of—I don't want to say a *crude* reason but a"—his hand was making low, as-far-as-he-could-stretch-it-still-standing gestures toward the ground, rock-bottom—"a—a—"

"Primitive?" I suggested. "Basic? Fundamental?"

"I don't know, but you see what I mean." He made some more of the rock-bottom gestures. "Was when I took him out to shoot that shotgun with us."

I blinked at him with profound respect. I remembered Sébastien outshooting him, but that David could admit his real reason for liking his French brother-in-law out loud, without a trace of self-mockery, gave me new insight into what it meant to be a man's man. A real man, you know, from the South.

"And he did all right on the shotgun, you know; he was hitting some . . . but then"—respect leaked into his voice—"I handed him a pistol, a kind he'd never even shot before, and I lined up some bottles out there. I told him we'd each start from the outside and see who got to the middle first, and—he *hit* 'em." He nodded, reliving the moment. "And I said to myself right there, a man that can pick up a weapon he's never shot before, and shoot with it, shoot like that, well, he's a good man. A good man. I guess you're going to say that seems silly, but—you got a good guy."

Thirty-one

When my sister got married, she and her new husband went off together to Costa Rica and spent a week exploring active volcanoes, swinging from trees in rain forests to explore their inner baboons, and sharing other romantic adventures. She got married to an American, but that probably has nothing to do with it. When my best friend got married, she and her new husband chose New Orleans for five romantic days in a bed and breakfast with lots of lace and dogs. She married an American, too, but that's probably just coincidence.

Nevertheless, I mentioned the coincidence as we were driving to meet Sébastien's family in Savannah, where they had preceded us because we had lingered a couple of days to clean up the mess left from the wedding.

"That's funny," he said. "The first time *I* got married to an American, I had to spend two days in the freezing cold with her brothers, digging through this god-awful red substance you people call dirt, to fix a septic tank."

"Okay," I said, "now you're getting off the subject. What I'm trying to say is—"

"How much nicer and more relaxing it will be to travel around with ten of my family for a week," he beamed. "I know. I've *missed* them."

I sighed. He had once introduced me to his mother as a birthday present, so I guess I could have predicted this conversation, if I'd been facing the truth. Funny, the aspects of a loved one's personality that you just don't pay attention to until you realize you won't be relaxing on a beach in isolated calm after a year of wedding planning.

"But that's okay," I said out loud, determinedly. "I may be so exhausted I'd like to spend a week in a coma, but this is my chance. For once I get to share some of my culture with your family, in thanks for all of their culture they've shared with me. I've got this great place to take them. They're going to love it."

By the time we met the French contingent in Savannah, they had been wandering loose in the South for two nights and three whole days, and they had discovered *Super* Wal-Mart, had their photos taken as curiosities in several small towns, and about gotten their fill of Waffle House.

"You can eat somewhere else, you know," I said. "It won't hurt my feelings."

"Yes, but it's just like a film. And besides, there aren't really many other choices in Macon." Macon, roughly two hours from my parents' house, is a city south of Atlanta whose primary purpose seems to be to serve as a shopping outlet for a nearby military base. The French had stayed there the first night after the wedding.

"Yes, can you go over the decision to stop in Macon with me again? I mean, I've been there myself, several times; but it was under duress. There are giant strip malls closer to my parents' house, you know."

"Well, we'd been driving for over two hours; we had to stop somewhere for the night. Plus, it has the same name as a town in Burgundy, so Jean-Charles called it a sister city. Speaking of Jean-Charles . . . have you talked to him yet?"

"No."

"I believe he wants to speak with you. You might not want to go find him."

Unfortunately, on a road-trip honeymoon with ten of the groom's family members, I figured I would have to face my father-in-law sometime. We went ahead and braved his hotel door.

Claudine opened it. Jean-Charles, Titi, and Bruno froze in mid-jump on one of the beds, twisted, and tumbled down on top of each other. Titi, who ended up on top, posed immediately as if he were riding in a rodeo. Jean-Charles, recent victim of a talcum powder dousing, started shaking his hair to share the powder with the other two. Bruno, crushed on the bottom, writhed out from under them enough to lift his head and fix me with a stern stare. "We need to talk."

Titi tumbled off and stood with his hands on his hips. "Three words. No Beer Sunday."

I stopped dead and tried to back out of the room but unfortunately bumped into Sébastien. "Oops," he muttered in my ear. Then out loud, perfidiously, as if he hadn't discovered this calamity himself the hard way a year ago, "You can't get beer on Sundays, Laura?"

Three men rose up on the bed like the wrath of God. "We thought the cashier was crazy—"

"She kept picking our beer up and setting it back in the cart—"

"Saying, 'No Beer Sunday, No Beer Sunday!' "

"Then we tried to go back and get wine—"

"And no, not that either!"

"No Wine Sunday!"

"So then we went to another store so we wouldn't have to deal with any religious fanatics—"

"They said the same thing!"

"And there wasn't anything *but* beer and wine in the whole store, they didn't even have any alcohol, so what were we supposed to do?"

"Is your country completely nuts?"

"And that left us with nothing to drink for the whole day! We could have died! Jean-Charles almost had to drink water!"

"Fortunately, a couple of hours later, we hit on the idea of getting a cup of coffee instead."

"We were at this lake where we'd been paddle-boating around—"

"And we went to the little refreshment stand, and—"

"No coffee," I said, resigned.

"*You knew?*" Bruno flexed his hands.

"Well, you could have gotten coffee other places! Of course you can't expect them to have it in a little lakeside refreshment stand!"

"Yes," Bruno said, "we can."

"Actually, I'm not sure it's fair to let them think they can get coffee other places," Sébastien stipulated. "Most of the time, that isn't what they would call coffee."

"You told us this was a developed country!" Jean-Charles exclaimed. "Well, all right, Sébastien never went that far, but still, we expected the fundamentals. Not only do you not have any good wine, but you've outlawed it on one day. No Beer Sunday. I couldn't believe it."

"So the next day we had to buy three coolers and fill them up with ice and beer because God only knows what you've done to the other days of the week. We barely had enough room in the cars for Bruno's luggage! We had to throw out some of the cereal we bought at Super Wal-Mart! Have you ever tried the Oreo cookie ones?" Titi added to Sébastien, briefly distracted.

"Well, the whole country isn't like that," I proffered weakly. "You can buy beer in other states on Sunday."

"Then why didn't you get married in another state?"

"I'll never understand American government. You can change something as important as that according to what state you're in?"

I started to tell them that in the U.S. you could change the *death penalty* according to what state you were in, but then thought better of it. Self-preservation was still a minor interest of mine. "Well, and, er, county, yes."

"What's a county?" Titi asked suspiciously.

"A very small local division of government. There are 159 of them in Georgia. Also, I need to explain to you that in the U.S., beer and wine are considered alcohol. Now as to what you keep referring to as 'alcohol,' meaning gin, rum, and all that, I know it's legal in certain counties in Georgia; but I'm not sure which ones."

Bruno took a deep breath, still flexing his hands in an ominous fashion. "What else do we need to know before we travel any farther?"

My country was so normal compared to theirs that it took me a moment to come up with anything. "Well, on a scale of one to ten, how do you feel about spiders and alligators?"

"Reserved," Claudine interjected. "Why?"

"Because weren't we planning on going to the Okefenokee Swamp?" I had wracked my brain for months before their arrival, trying to come up with fascinating American cultural experiences I could share within range of the French idea of driving distance. I don't know why, but Super Wal-Mart just never occurred to me. The Okefenokee did, though, and I felt sure it would be perfect. The Okefenokee Swamp was exotically Southern American even for me, a deep, strange, wild, wonderful place.

"You keep saying that word," Bruno said. "Swamp. What does that mean?"

I thought for a minute. "*Étang.*"

They all gazed at me, baffled. "Is it really worth taking time out of our trip to go see an *étang*? We're not here very long, you know."

"Oh, you'll love it," I said. "At least . . . hey, how could you not? You don't have anything like it in France, I promise you. It'll be an adventure."

They all exchanged dubious glances, including Sébastien, who had never seen the Okefenokee *étang* either, but who tried to take my word for it that it would be worth the trip.

"So what do the alligators have to do with an *étang*?" someone asked me as we were driving the two hours south of Savannah to the Okefenokee. "Do they keep them in cages there or something?"

The roads back into Okefenokee Swamp, each one smaller than the last, wound and wound their way into ever remoter country-side. Gas stations lost their ability to take credit cards at the pump and then disappeared altogether. We sank into forests of pine and opened our windows to the scents and the heat, which buffeted in through the windows, fighting the air conditioner.

The air was like glue. Once parked, the family waded through it to look over wooden rails at endless black water and cypress trees hung with moss. They seemed a bit surprised. But then, it's hard to *expect* the Okefenokee, no matter how well described, I thought.

Sébastien gazed around at the black water glimmering through trees in all directions. "Laura, this isn't an *étang*."

"It isn't?"

"*Étang* is the word for an artificial body of water considerably smaller than a lake, but bigger than your parents' fountain pool."

"Oh," I said. "That would be a pond. I thought it meant swamp. What's this, then?"

He looked dubious. "Well, I guess you could call it a *marais* because that's usually the word for standing water like this, but I'm not sure we have a word for a body of standing water this size in Europe."

"*La Belgique?*" I suggested. "*Les Pays-Bas?* Without the dikes, I mean."

"Smart-ass. Go explain to my family that this isn't really a pond, not even to an American."

Most of his family was leaning over the railing of a wooden bridge, gazing at several very large turtles sunning themselves next to a big log. "What do you put in it to make the water so black?"

"Are there a lot of factories near here?"

"No, that's natural, from tannic acid," I explained. "Makes it particularly hard to see alligators, I find."

"Well, the guide will point them out to us," someone said easily.

I paused. "The guide?"

"We're going to go on a tour of the swamp, right?"

"Well . . . I thought we'd go into it a little ways, yes. You can't really explore the whole thing, or even a fraction of it, in a day."

"Is it safe to go out in a boat in there? Where do they keep the alligators? What if one of them got loose?"

I opened my mouth and closed it, wondering if I hadn't quite properly explained the venture we were setting out on.

"Oh, don't be silly; even if they did get loose, I'm sure the boat will be too big for them to do anything to us," someone else said.

I opened my mouth and closed it again. The log in the water below them did, too; but since they were all now looking at me, nobody noticed, and I decided not to mention it.

"The alligatorsaren'tkeptincaptivity," I mumbled very fast and low. "They just swim around wherever they want. And, well. There's no guide. And, umm, the boats are canoes. Didn't some of you learn how to canoe at summer camps?"

There was some low-voiced conversation as they probably tried to figure out whether this was my way of removing all the in-laws from the picture of my honeymoon. I bet Jean-Charles was starting to rue the day he had ever made me prepare snails, yessirree Bob. Claudine might even be feeling a qualm or two about that salad.

They all glanced at Sébastien, who was considered responsible for interpreting my bouts of insanity and judging whether they would prove harmful to members of saner cultures. "It will be great," Sébastien said firmly. He was the only one who had noticed how many teeth the log below had, and he was looking excited. "Let's go."

Jean-Charles was the first to nod, probably assuming that no one to whom he had graciously taught the snail art could mean him any harm. Or perhaps just accepting my challenge-gifts the same way I accepted his. "Sounds like fun."

Claudine, Bruno, Titi, Justine, and Gaëlle all agreed. The four others decided to wait at the entrance on the off chance we came out again alive.

The yellow flies and mosquitoes attacked before the six of us even got into the canoes, despite liberal applications of every brand of mosquito repellent we had. As a layer of winged things settled on my skin and sank their suckers in, I realized my last visit to the Okefenokee had been in autumn. It made a difference in terms of wildlife.

The twenty-year-old untying our canoes grinned up at us. "How do you feel about spiders?"

I shrugged. "Okay."

"Good, then look." He pointed above my head. "You'll see lots of those goldens in there."

I looked up at a golden spider in a web only six inches above me, its graceful legs stretching out to cover a span bigger than a large man's open hand.

"What is *that*?" Claudine asked.

"A spider," I translated what the canoe-handler had told me rapidly. "Err—very, very rare." So rare that a couple more hovered above Bruno. "And perfectly harmless, except to children smaller than they are."

I hurried down to the first canoe. The others walked under the golden spider, still staring up at it. "You know, in France, we don't have any spiders that can catch bats for breakfast," Bruno said. "I don't mean that as a criticism or anything. I just mention it."

We wanted each two-person canoe to have someone in the stern capable of steering, which put Jean-Charles and Justine in a canoe, Titi and Bruno in another, and left two possible combinations. Sébastien and I could split our steering abilities between two canoes, or we could stay romantically together, somewhat like a honeymoon couple, and leave Claudine and her niece Gaëlle in one boat to figure it out.

"It's a good thing I learned how to canoe last vacation," Gaëlle said. Dark-haired, with a sharp little face, she looked very credible except to people who had seen her in the wilds before. "Took to it like an expert. Trust me. I'm perfectly capable of doing this."

Claudine must have considered no lengths too great to further our romance because she looked at Gaëlle a moment and then descended into the bow.

"Remember, don't get out of the canoe!" the canoe-handler called after us.

Just in case we didn't hear him, there was a sign to that effect as we rounded the first bend. Claudine noticed it particularly, because she ran straight into it and had to push at it with her paddle to get them turned around again.

"Tata, you have to steer!" Gaëlle called to her aunt from the stern.

"It's not working!" Claudine said. "I don't know what to do!"

I hesitated, wondering if I dared correct anyone's belief that you could steer a canoe from the bow, or if I had best keep out of it. Keep out of it, I decided. After all, before my intervention with the Okefenokee idea, they had all been planning on spending a day at the beach. Perversely, I wanted to spend a day at the beach, *too*, but kept feeling they had to see more of America than that. It was my gift to them, for all the aspects of France and themselves that they had gifted me.

Jean-Charles and Justine started a race. Bruno and Titi plunged paddles in pursuit and clanged against Gaëlle and Claudine's canoe, doing a slow eddy in the middle of the channel. I smacked my sandaled left foot and lifted a hand dripping with blood.

"And we thought the mosquitoes were bad," Jean-Charles huffed, out-distancing us. "Do the yellow flies work in cohorts with the alligators or something? Once we lose enough blood to the insects, we don't offer any resistance?"

At that, something plopped in the dark clear water up ahead, and everybody tensed, staring at the ripples, until a turtle poked its head out. It dived for cover again as Claudine and Gaëlle backed its way, Gaëlle still shrieking at Claudine to steer. Bruno and Titi tried to avoid them, but their canoes clanged together once again.

"I'm trying!" Claudine said. "But it doesn't seem to make any difference what I do!"

"Well, yes, it does, clearly," Gaëlle said, "that's why we keep running into things. *Tata, watch out!*"

They grounded against a boggy island. Shallow water is a secret blessing in terms of steering, though. When Claudine used the old tried-and-true technique of pushing against the swamp bottom with her paddle, they were soon redirected, out in the middle of the channel again, and heading into the opposite bank.

"*Tata!*"

"This isn't working." Bruno and Titi exchanged long-suffering glances. "I guess we should change canoes. There, that bit of ground looks stable." Bruno nodded to the densely vegetated bank, so thick with leaves, grass, and branches that his foot would sink in it to mid-calf before hitting the ground he couldn't see.

"Don't get out of the canoe!" I yelled.

The hysterical bride thing was getting a bit old by then, so they just rolled their eyes at me. "What, are you afraid we'll get eaten by an alligator?"

"No, I was more concerned about poisonous snakes."

"There are *poisonous snakes around here?*" two female voices shrieked.

I abruptly remembered the dearth of deadly animals in France and strove for a nonchalant, this-is-normal tone. "Well, sure. Rattlesnakes and copperheads and water moccasins." I tried to think of some good news. "You don't really have to worry about the coral snakes much, because they don't have good teeth. They have to gnaw on you a while to get the venom in, and who lets a venomous snake gnaw on them?" I thought of Sébastien with the squirrels and added as a precaution, "Umm—don't be letting any red, yellow, and black snakes gnaw on you while you try to get someone else to take a picture. I'm serious."

"Exactly how many poisonous snakes do you have? Are we surrounded by them?"

"Well," I said. "I don't know about *surrounded*. There are probably a few around us on the banks somewhere, but that doesn't mean you . . ."

"Tata, *quit running us into the banks!*" Gaëlle shrieked, paddling frantically and burying them farther in grass.

"And the water moccasin swims, so it's usually in the water." Okay, I probably shouldn't have added that, but they *had* fed me horse.

Everyone jerked his paddle out of the water. Bruno and Titi replaced theirs right away and looked tolerant, convinced I was trying to scare them. "Claudine, I'm sure it will be fine. Laura wouldn't have led us into a place where we could actually get bitten by snakes."

"Ah . . ." All heads turned toward me. I smiled feebly. "Well, I grew up in a place where I could get bitten by snakes." During the NO DRIVE speech, Claudine had been sitting on the exact spot where my mother had once reached down to wrench out a weed and come up with a copperhead instead. I guess I was close to the *terroir,* too. "Around my parents' house, I nearly stepped on a copperhead two or three times a year." Completely unreceptive silence greeted this explanation. "So, um, I didn't think about it."

Everyone just stared at me.

"That's probably true," Sébastien admitted. "She didn't think about the pasteurized cheese, either."

"I *told* you to get a guidebook! I can't think of all these things."

They laid their paddles across the canoes and folded their arms.

"It's just a question of paying *attention,*" I said. "Look at me. I've seen lots of copperheads and haven't gotten bitten yet. I know only a couple of people on my road who ever got bitten." Somehow that didn't seem to reassure them nearly as much as I had meant it to. "I'm just saying I don't recommend strolling around in vegetation where you can't see what you're stepping on."

I started paddling as hard as I could to distance myself from accusing stares. A few minutes later, I heard the clank of canoes, much splashing, and even more squealing. "Watch out!"

"Bruno, be careful!"

"No, don't move! I'm going to fall!"

I twisted to find the two canoes locked in the middle of the channel as the four people in them tried to rearrange themselves so that Bruno and Claudine were sharing a canoe, with Bruno in the stern, and Gaëlle and Titi were sharing one, with Titi in the stern.

"I can't look," I said.

Sébastien flinched as one of the canoes wobbled particularly dramatically. "Laura, if my mother falls into the Okefenokee *pond* and gets eaten by an alligator or any other form of American wildlife, this will not have been a successful honeymoon."

"Yeah, I know," I said. "No one will ever believe I didn't do it on purpose."

"*Chut!*" someone said. "Is that an alligator?"

We all turned to look, Claudine and Titi frozen with legs in two different canoes. We had drifted to a point where the swamp opened out into a large pond. And there, at the opposite end from us, was an alligator. A part of an alligator, to be precise—we could only see a partial curve of his tail above the water, and that part of his tail was six feet long. I remembered the guide telling us to keep an eye out for the biggest alligator in that part of the swamp, an eighteen-footer that hung out in a pond . . . a pond around about here, now that I thought about it.

Claudine and Titi settled into their canoes very quickly. "Let's go get a closer look!" Jean-Charles said excitedly.

"Maybe we can wake him up and see him swim around!" Bruno agreed.

"Umm," I said. I had been pretending I was a tough American for a couple hours now and hated to give up the role, but I hesitated at annoying an alligator three times bigger than any of us. "I don't know if that's such a good idea."

"Oh, look at that one!" Justine exclaimed. On the other side of the pond, a younger alligator dropped off a tuft of land and into the water, giving us a good look at his teeth as he did so. He was a tiny ten-footer. I'm a five-footer. I just mention it to keep things in perspective.

He submerged under water and then rose up until only his snout and beady eyes showed, fixed on us. A growling, hissing sound started, and we all jumped as we realized it was coming from him. "What's he doing?" Gaëlle muttered behind me. "Why is he coming this way?"

As the tough American in the group, I couldn't stoop to a mutter, but I was wondering that, too. Without a pause in his hissing growl, the alligator headed directly toward us, his beady eyes fixed.

Ten feet from us. Five feet. Soft, suppressed screams began to eek from the canoes. It was now only two feet from Claudine, having fixed on her canoe as the closest. "Laura!" she whispered. "Help!" See, that's the problem with the tough American act. At the first sign of trouble, people expect you to wrestle alligators. The alligator made another growling, hissing noise, its loudest yet, and dove.

Dead silence. "Is that good?" someone said.

"Where did it go?"

Under our canoes was a sure bet, given its direction. We all peered down into the black water, which reflected back our own faces like a crystalline mirror. The canoes suddenly felt extremely flimsy. I'd heard of whales turning boats over by emerging under them, why not alligators with canoes? And whales were nice; they swallowed people whole and let you come out again in three days, like Xena and Jonah and Nemo. I was pretty sure alligators didn't have that kind of attitude. I hadn't watched *Crocodile Dundee* and *Tarzan* for a long time now, so I was fuzzy on the details of death-by-alligator, but I bet it involved a lot of teeth.

We all glanced over at the giant tip of tail at the other end of the pond. It still hadn't moved. It might, though, if people were up-ended into its pond. That would be two alligators with teeth against eight people with paddles. That didn't seem like good odds.

The smaller of the two alligators resurfaced on the other side of our canoes and turned to face us again. Deep breaths were drawn all around. "Maybe we should leave," someone suggested. "Aren't alligators an endangered species? Horrible to disturb their habitat like this."

"Right," Jean-Charles said. "Right. They probably wouldn't let me take new alligator skin boots through customs anyway."

We fled and regrouped with the yellow flies at a safe distance. I sighed, gazed at my own hand totally mottled with blood from oozing yellow-fly bites, and accepted the failure of my cultural gift. "Do you want to go back to the dock now?"

The French looked at me and at each other. Between the mosquito and the yellow-fly bites, they resembled plague victims. They hesitated only a second. "Of course not," everyone said at once. "We're just getting started! Lead on!" And without waiting for me to do so, Jean-Charles drove his paddle into the water and headed down an unexplored bend of this Georgia swamp. Bruno raced after him. We stayed out there for hours, as our flesh became a mottled mass of yellow-fly bites.

"That was wonderful!" Claudine said firmly when she at last got to climb out of her canoe. "What a great idea to show us that!"

"Fascinating," everyone else agreed.

And it was with the greatest possible delicacy that over the ensuing week my French in-laws redirected all my cultural offerings to Savannah, Charleston, beaches, and Super Wal-Mart.

But here's the worrying thing: the whole trip, they didn't kill each other. Four people per hotel room and per car, twelve people in all, traveling around in a foreign country with twenty-four/seven exposure to each other for two weeks—and at most they had a couple of spats. Once Pierrette cried a little at one of those spats, and they all then apologized to her *and to me* for it.

What that meant was, no matter how overextended I felt, with all these weddings and honeymoons and country-hopping, I had to keep things under control. If I lost it even once during the wedding preparations in France, they would never understand.

Thirty-two

We hit French ground running, adrenaline pumped, ready for one last mad bout of action. We ran all the way to the ancient stone farmhouse, where we arrived just in time for aperitifs.

The heart of Sébastien's family awaited us in the garden around Titi and Bruno's teak table, under the white parasol: Claudine, Jean-Charles, Justine, Titi, Bruno, Colette, and Pierrette, or Mamie as Sébastien and her other grandchildren called her. I, too, was calling Pierrette Mamie now. I wasn't one to call my husband's family by their relationships to him. I called Claudine "Claudine" and not "Maman." But somehow I had started using "Mamie" after Pierrette leaked tears of stress that morning during the wild trip with eleven family members through America's South. Okay, so she was forty years older than I, had never been out of her home country before, had lost her husband less than a year before, and was recovering from her own bout with cancer; I could still cling to the knowledge that I wasn't the *only* person overwhelmed.

"Great, you're just in time for the council of war," Jean-Charles said. "Who wants what to drink?"

"I should probably try to keep a clear head if we're going to talk wedding plans," Sébastien said. Sébastien was so happy to be back in France he could hardly stand it. He kept looking around and taking big gulps of air.

Jean-Charles nodded sagely and poured him a glass of *vin de noix*, the homemade green-walnut wine his father had sent up from Provence. "I had a hard time thinking straight on what they serve in America, too. Especially on Sundays."

The weather was hot and clear, a good augury for the outdoor wedding feast. In the year since the *fête villageoise*, the garden had grown less ragged. The gnarled and disheveled look that still lingered only added to its charm. Prickly, crackling weed life crowded against the wire fence marking off Titi and Bruno's two acres, and beyond that stretched fields of fading golden wheat stubs. "Don't worry," Claudine told me. "I got plenty of sheaves before they cut it."

"Hmm?"

"Farmers don't mind if you cut just a little. We stopped along the edges of different fields and took only the most beautiful sheaves. It will be perfect to decorate your wedding."

I brought my gaze back from the fields and stared at her. Claudine wore snazzy black capri pants and a black spaghetti top, both of which fit her slender self like a glove. Gold circlets sparkled in her ears, a sapphire gleamed in the hollow of her throat, and she waved a cigarette in one hand, a glass of Riccardi near the other. She looked far too elegant to be talking about stealing wheat sheaves or using them to decorate anyone's wedding.

"Wheat is for good luck," she explained, while I tried to fit wheat sheaves into my idea of wedding decorations. "*Ça porte bonheur.* You've got to have it. And I've already bought all the silk flowers and ribbon in your colors."

I swallowed my *orgeat*, a Provençal mixture of water and syrup of bitter almonds that no one else drank; Titi and Bruno had added its components to the liquor cabinet especially for me.

"That's wonderful. Thank you so much. I don't meant to pry, but what are my colors?"

"I'll show you," she said happily and disappeared into the farmhouse, coming back with a plastic bag. She reached into it with the triumph of a magician grasping rabbit ears and pulled out silk flowers and ribbons in a dark, intense blue and an extreme sunflower-yellow.

For a country that seemed to think gray and beige were flashy colors, let me just say that these were a jump. The blue I could figure out, since everyone knew I liked blue. I was infamous for it. I had trouble with the yellow, though. "That's a . . . particularly nice shade," I said. "Vivid."

"I knew you'd like it," Claudine beamed. An orange butterfly circled around her head and headed back to join the throngs around the lush purple *arbre à papillons,* or butterfly tree, that half shaded the table. "It reminded me of you. It looks so cheerful." She handed the sack across to me. "Now all you have to do is figure out how to make it all look pretty. I've got the wheat sheaves in the house, and you can experiment with everything in your spare time."

I looked at the material in alarm. Most people don't trust me with aesthetic decisions, and handing me wheat sheaves wasn't a good place to start. "We'll have to do it together," I said. "I'm sure you've got better decorating ideas than I do. You've got a much better sense of style."

I escaped to get the first course, zucchini straight from the garden that morning, sliced very fine and drizzled with olive oil and minced garlic. A grill smoked on the old, pockmarked patio, waiting for the second course of chicken.

"Okay, I've got my list ready." I uncapped my pen. "What needs to be done?"

"We need to make decorations and wedding favors," Claudine started.

"Wheat sheaves," I noted. "Right."

"We have to finish the upstairs of the farmhouse," Bruno added to Jean-Charles. We expected thirty or more people to crowd the communal guest room the night after the wedding, and Bruno and Jean-Charles had been working hard every weekend to prepare. We had already marveled at the spotless new bathroom and toilet room and the fresh whitewash on the walls, but the floor still needed to be tiled.

"And the cars polished," Jean-Charles said. "Plus, I'll have to make sure they're in working order." Jean-Charles had not been able to bring the Torpedo up from Provence for the wedding and had returned instead with a car suitable for a gangster, an opulent blue and burgundy 1928 Citroen C6. The men were delighted when I let them have that one and chose for the bride's car the more discreet brown and beige C4. I liked the memory of Sébastien's grandfather riding in it beside me, welcoming me into the family. The men, who didn't have that memory, liked pretending to be Al Capone.

"Laura and Sébastien, *your* top priority is to go see the baker, preferably yesterday, and pick out your *pièce montée*." The *pièce montée* held the role in French weddings that a wedding cake did in American ones, but instead of sugar and chemicals it was concocted of *petits choux,* custard-cream-stuffed little puffs. These could be fitted together in classic conical towers or in any other shape we wanted. "While you're at it, make sure you order enough bread delivered here that weekend. Then you need to go see the church organist," Claudine told me as Sébastien fled to grill the chicken.

"I thought we didn't have any choice about the music."

"She said she wanted to talk to you about what you want." Claudine shrugged. "So maybe she changed her mind. She lives only a couple of villages over; the priest said her place was easy to find. That reminds me, you need to meet the priest."

My lips twitched as I wrote *Meet the priest* third on my list after bread. Nothing like the French to keep things in perspective. Or at least these French. At some point, the French had started acting like individuals, but I still figured if I made enough sweeping statements, I could get them to stop.

"And pick out the church," Jean-Charles said. "I like St. Remiel. It's beautiful."

"Wait a minute. What happened to the church we put on the invitations? The wedding is in two weeks, and we don't have a church?"

Claudine laughed. "Oh, the priest gave us a few others to choose from. It's true St. Remiel was nice, but I liked the entrance of that other one he showed us. Which one was it, Jean-Charles?"

"What about the pews in the one at Sandrillon?" Titi argued. "Those were nice."

"Are there any redeeming characteristics to the one we actually told a hundred and fifty people to go to at 11:00 A.M., August tenth?"

"It's horrible," Claudine said frankly. "And about seven centuries younger than the other three choices."

I wrote down *Pick out church* and put a star beside it. With only two weeks to go before the wedding, it seemed like a priority up there with the baker, even in France. Plus, I liked the idea of wandering among village churches almost a millennium old, picking out which one would host our wedding. It was a pity we hadn't done this before sending out the invitations, of course, but if we did things like normal people, where would be the fun?

"August sixth we can't do anything," Sébastien warned, returning to the table with the chicken. "Anna, Ken, Sue, and Dwayne are coming in, and we promised to pick them up at the airport and show them around Paris." My sister and her fiancé as well as our two best American friends had decided to join us again. Two weddings on two continents just to make them accessible to both families, and people kept choosing to attend both.

Our families stubbornly continued to demonstrate that an intercultural marriage didn't mean a choice between two cultures but a choice of both. I, meanwhile, kept wondering if a choice of both wasn't going to lead me to a nervous breakdown. I remembered telling Adela a long time ago that getting married would limit my life to trips to Disneyland. Well, at least I couldn't say that had happened yet.

"And you need to meet the mayor." Claudine grinned.

"The mayor? Why?"

Claudine clapped her hands together. "It's a surprise! She's going to marry you, too."

"She's *what*?"

"When we were having trouble finding a priest, she offered to do a pretend civil ceremony."

"But we did find a priest. So . . . ?"

"Well, I don't want to hurt her *feelings*," Claudine said, astonished at me. "Besides, as soon as she suggested it, I knew you'd love it. You can have the complete French experience, a civil and a church ceremony, just like you did in the U.S."

I sat blinking.

"Imagine that!" Claudine said happily. "Four weddings!"

"I am."

"Most people only ever get to have two."

"Well, one, where I come from."

"And you get to have four! Isn't that wonderful?"

"It's . . . that's . . ." I met her hopeful, happy eyes. "When are we going to do this?"

"The same day, of course! A real civil ceremony would have to come before the church wedding, but in your case, it doesn't matter. We can fit it in after if that works best."

I tried not to think about the reaction of my American family and friends when they got here in a few days and learned we were having a fourth wedding. It didn't seem like something I was likely to live down before the next family reunion. If I collapsed from the stress of a cross-cultural couple before the next family reunion, they'd use the four weddings in my eulogy.

By the time we reached dessert, night had fallen, and the tiki torches were all lit. Bottles of wine were scattered all over the table. I went to get a tray of sliced fruit, and Bruno carried out his accompanying *fondu au chocolat.* We dodged hissing geese, and my foot squished on a plum.

It was hard to avoid running into plums right now. Everywhere I walked, they begged me to pick them before they fell or the bees got them: green-gold oval plums with juice that spurted out all over; purple plums that were unreliable, sometimes sweet and sometimes mouth-puckering acid; golden plums, round like a ball and brushed with orange, bursting sun-hot sweetness into my mouth.

Only two plum trees weren't quite ready for harvest. Among plums, one species was the pride of all gardens, a queen who *se faisait désirer,* let people wait for her, let herself be desired. This was the fabulous *mirabellier,* with fruit worth its weight in gold in a city market in any ordinary summer. Some people said the *mirabellier* had its best harvest every seven years, and if so, this was the seventh year. Titi and Bruno's two *mirabelliers* were a mass of tiny, deepening gold jewels that were not quite ripe. On the other side of the wire fence behind them, almost a dozen others lined a lot of land that had been for sale and unvisited for years, branches bowed under the weight of their fruit.

"Now about the food," someone said as we dipped into the fondu.

"*Brochettes,*" Jean-Charles suggested, meaning kebabs. "They're not very expensive, and we could do half a dozen different kinds, with different meats and combinations."

Heads cocked. "But how would we get them all cooked?" somebody said. Nobody thought to ask how we would get them all prepared. I don't know why.

307

"That's the beauty of it," Jean-Charles said. "The guests would cook them. We could place grills all around the garden, and that would create gathering points, where people would meet and talk."

"Great idea!" someone exclaimed, and the echoes ran up and down the table. On the sixth bottle of wine, preparing enough kebabs to feed 150 people for two days seemed easier than making enough roasts and chicken for the same and serving them cold.

"Can we borrow enough grills?" I asked, ever focused on keeping out of debtor's prison. "I don't want to have to buy them."

Rapid brainstorming ensued. How many people did they know who had grills? Could we maybe find some to buy somewhere cheap, like at a flea market? Jean-Charles brushed all ideas aside with his hand. "Oil drums."

Even on the sixth bottle, this was a little cryptic. Everyone stared.

"We can burn them out to get rid of any drops of oil clinging to the sides, cut them in half lengthwise, and set them on something, concrete blocks maybe, so that they don't burn the grass and don't roll over. Then all we have to do is find enough grills to lay over them. You can always find something like that." He opened another bottle of wine.

"You *can*?" I said.

"I'll take care of it," he said, as a veteran flea-market scavenger. "And we'll burn wood down to coals in them. Then at night, when it gets cooler, people can gather around them to warm up."

"So that's settled," Bruno said from the end of the table. "More wine down there? Now about the rest of the food . . . . "

Thank goodness we had hurried to get here, because the planning proved time-consuming. Not nearly as stressful as I had thought, but a definite time sink. Before we finished plotting, stars shone bright and clear overhead, as they never did in Paris, and everything seemed possible. It had nothing to do with the alcohol; that's just the way Sébastien and his family made things feel. Now that the sun was gone, the night grew cold, and I tucked my hands and sandaled feet under my legs and shivered. Having learned the hard way what kind of summer weather I was used to, Claudine and Titi kept coming back from trips into the house with more wool sweaters to push over my head. By midnight, we had finished making wedding plans and were remaking the world. *Refaire le monde* is a peculiarly French expression used to describe energetic discussions over wine that last until 6:00 A.M. God might have done it in six days sober, but even a Frenchman can't do Him better in one night without wine.

The females yielded first, one by one, and climbed upstairs, for our first night sharing the communal sleeping quarters. Even Bruno and Titi would be sleeping up here until they got a restoration project cleared out of their bedroom. Ensconced on mattresses on the floor, comforters pulled up snug around us, we heard the men begin to sing. "Oh, Lord," Justine said out loud. Claudine pressed her head into her pillow and snickered. Titi and Bruno's mother-hen friend Colette, being of stronger stuff, started to snore.

Tiens, voilà mon zob, zob, zob,
Tiens, voilà mon zob, zobi!

We giggled ourselves to sleep to lullabies about weenies, only to be wakened four hours later, as day was lightening in the east.

"Jean-Charles, not the dogs!" Claudine exclaimed, starting to laugh again.

Ah, so that was what had just galumphed over me.

"Why not the dogs? The dogs love us! The dogs want to be with us! Bruno! What are you doing?" I peered out from under the covers to see Bruno in his underwear trying to climb into the wrong bed. "That's my woman, go find your own!"

At six in the morning, he, Bruno, and Titi all found that hilarious.

"*Non, mais!* Bruno! *Va-t-en! Casse-toi! Dégage!* Go away!" Titi said, as Bruno climbed into the right bed and presumably tried to embrace him, oblivious by this point to the fact that there were some ten people in the room, plus dogs. Titi, either remembering the audience or not a fan of drunken passion, was adamant in his rejection, though. "You stink! *Tu pues des fesses! Tu pues du bec! Tu pues du cul! Tu pues l'oignon!* You stink from the butt! You stink from the mouth! You stink from the ass! You stink of onion! Go away!"

Sébastien, also in his underwear, had crawled under the covers with me and was shaking so hard with laughter it felt like being enveloped by an earthquake. I remembered, a long time ago, thinking the French were all gloomy, cynical, manic-depressive, and snobs to boot.

"Bruno! You stink from the ass! You stink from the beak!"

I know Bruno eventually gave up, because Titi eventually shut up, the dogs eventually calmed down, and we women eventually ran out of hysterical laughter and fell back asleep. I dreamed of being attacked by a horde of kebabs wielding yellow bow whips, but I think everyone else slept peacefully.

Thirty-three

Meeting the mayor didn't prove hard. She lived directly across the minuscule street from Titi and Bruno. When we spotted her blond hair moving around under her plum trees, we hallooed over the stone wall a few times and then went around to join her on the terrace.

A robust woman, with a fair, easily flushed face and frizzy blond hair fluffing out around it, she welcomed us with friendly competence. We swapped delighted stories about how well the plums were bearing this year, and she photocopied our birth certificates and proofs of our previous weddings. She did not at any time break out into guffaws at our organizing a fourth wedding ceremony, although her lips twitched from time to time. She asked a few questions so that she could get her facts straight for the speech, she said. Her lips didn't twitch that time at all.

We found the curé easily enough, too. An old, well-fed man with a flushed face and a slight stoop, he reminded me of my childhood priest, and in fact was near the same age old Monsignor would be now if he had not died three years before. At eighty-two, the curé should long since have retired, but the Church needed all the priests she could get. After following him from Mass to Mass all morning, only to have our promised post-Mass conversation replaced by a forgotten Baptism each time, we finally hit on the idea of waiting outside the presbytery where he lived with an old woman who made his meals. We timed it for 12:30, right after his final Mass for the day, and caught him as he headed home for lunch.

Eyes shifting anxiously in the direction of the kitchen and a steak growing cold, he swore to be ready and waiting for us if we came back at 2:00 P.M. When we did come back at two, he was clearly surprised to see us but yielded to the reminder of our appointment. "I'll call him the morning of the ceremony," Claudine whispered as we followed him to the church. The priest had changed from the morning's green cassock to a black suit with the classic priest collar, and he led the way with a long, lopsided stride—not limping, exactly, but more as if he was more aggressive with one leg than the other. "And if he doesn't answer, I know where he lives now. We'll get him there."

Eighty-two, I thought, smiling. I wondered if he kept Irish wolfhounds and would tell me my mother was a saint, an absolute saint, if I went to Confession. Inside the church, the air smelled of stone, thick and cool with a hypnotic ghost of incense. The priest disappeared in the back, searching for papers. Claudine pointed excitedly at the pews. Gorgeous and ancient, they had solid wood doors, worn by so many thousands of hands and so many years the mind boggled. Claudine opened and closed the little doors reverently. "Do you know how old these must be?" she breathed. "I don't think they've made pews with doors on them for centuries. You hardly ever see them in churches anymore."

I sat in one pew and had to brace my feet against the floor to keep from sliding off. Age had given these pews a steep slant. Doze off during a sermon and you would slide right onto the floor.

"Did you ask him about the rehearsal?" I asked her as the priest reappeared. I'd been campaigning for a rehearsal for some time, without much encouragement from any of the French.

She and Sébastien rolled their eyes at each other, but she turned to the priest. "*Ma petite belle fille* wanted to know if it would be possible to do a rehearsal before the wedding."

I had *not* asked if it would be possible. I had asked when we could do one.

The old curé stared at us blankly. "Why does she need a rehearsal?"

Claudine and Sébastien both shrugged. "She's American," Sébastien said apologetically, as if that might explain it.

"To know what we're doing, so as to avoid making idiots of ourselves in front of one hundred and fifty people," I explained. "Basically."

The curé fastened bright blue eyes on me in awe. "She speaks French?"

"Laura, in France we don't go in for that kind of stuff," Sébastien told me, not for the first time. "It's a wedding, not a show."

"One hundred and thirty of whom I've never met and who are already probably thinking that the bride is a barbaric, clumsy American who can't do anything right," I précised.

"French." The curé watched my lips move as though I was a ventriloquist's puppet. "Amazing."

"And you think you can change their minds by doing the wedding right?" Sébastien grinned.

I massaged my neck and glared at him. "Can we at least go over the ceremony and the vows?"

"Vows?" said the curé. "What vows?"

My massaging hand paused. "For the wedding at the ceremony you agreed to officiate at the weekend after next."

"But you're already married."

"Didn't the bishop explain all this?"

"I thought we'd just do a Mass and pass out the collection plate," the curé told Claudine. He seemed a bit put out when Claudine didn't turn and translate that into English for me, as if she was taking the ventriloquist act too far.

I squeezed my neck like a stress ball. "I would rather not have a collection plate, please; we'll be happy to make a donation to the church."

"Of course you will," said the curé. "I already told your mother-in-law how much it would cost."

My jaw dropped, but I supposed an eighty-two-year-old priest was entitled to be direct. "And no Mass, please; we would prefer just the wedding service. Not everyone attending is Catholic."

Sébastien ground his foot into my toe.

"*She's* Catholic, isn't she?" the priest asked Claudine suspiciously.

"Yes," I answered.

He started as if I had never spoken before. "She seems to understand me. Astonishing." He cleared his throat. "Baptized?"

"Yes," I said. Claudine repeated my words in the same language, just to reassure him.

"Communion? Confirmed?"

"Yes." Before they met, my father had wanted to be a monk and my mother a nun, fantasies they sometimes mentioned when their seven kids were squabbling across twenty acres. My mom read Canon Law for pleasure. I'm not kidding.

The curé nodded and turned as an afterthought to the man by my side, French and therefore trustworthy. I don't know why he felt this way. The French had deserted religion in droves over the past half century, and church attendance here was down to about 10 percent. "And you, young man?"

Sébastien the atheist smiled blandly at him. "Of course."

I took a step back because in the Bible Belt where I grew up, you got struck by lightning for lying to religious representatives, but nothing happened. French atheists had it easy.

"Baptized, at least," he corrected himself to be safe. His parents could have baptized him as a baby and never taken him to church again, a fairly common occurrence, so he wasn't actually claiming to have any knowledge of Catholic ritual that way. "Never practicing."

"You should practice," the curé said severely.

"I know," Sébastien said angelically. "Maybe my wife will lead me down the right path. . . ."

I returned to the primary subject before this perjury could go farther. "What we'd like is just a short ceremony, no Mass. We want to do it as a reaffirmation of our vows, with the actual vows, please. Would you mind if we went over the ceremony?"

"Oh, it will be just like any normal ceremony." The curé waved his hand. "You know, you walk in, I talk, everyone sings, you all say your vows."

That certainly summed it up, but I felt I could use more details. "If we could just go over it briefly together, I would find that very reassuring."

Claudine intervened. *"Ma pauvre petite belle fille,"* she said. "She's so nervous. You can understand that, I'm sure. Maybe you could just tell her how things will go and show her the vows they'll have to speak?"

"Well, fine, the vows, I guess." He disappeared into the depths of the sacristy and came back with a ratty old book he must have received sixty years ago in the seminary. "In fact, she should make a copy of this so she can read from it during the ceremony."

I looked up. "Read our vows? Don't you normally say them, and then we repeat them?" Thus avoiding the tacky spectacle of the bride and groom bent over a photocopy instead of holding hands and staring into each other's eyes. I was not confident of my ability to memorize vows in French ahead of time and say them correctly under pressure.

"No, no, you read it," he assured me firmly.

I looked at Sébastien and Claudine. Neither seemed inclined to help me on this point. "But in the U.S. ceremony the deacon read it, and then we repeated it. It worked so prettily, you don't think . . . ?"

He shook his head adamantly. "It will work much better this way; you'll see." He turned to Claudine. "Explain to her that she should read it."

"Maybe we could look at the churches now," she suggested, hoping to stop me massaging my neck that way.

Besides the disdained church on our invitations, we had our choice of three others, all ancient, weathered, and crumbling, all beautiful. At my questions, the curé finally suspended his disbelief in my French-speaking ability long enough to recount their history.

The oldest had been built in the eleventh century. The curé showed me the distinctive zigzag pattern of the stone masonry and how the entrance had been butchered in renovations some centuries ago. Outside it, the stone buildings and red tiled roofs of the town fell away in folds below us into a green valley that stretched out into golden farmland. Inside, it was dark and narrow.

"It's *classée*," the priest sighed, meaning classified as a historical monument and thus protected by the government. "If you take

315

my advice, you'll never get a church *classée*. Afterward, you can't do anything. And you have to get a special architect, who costs four times as much. He tells you what to do, which is pretty much nothing, and that nothing costs, naturally, four times as much. The mayor wanted to lay stones here." He gestured to the gravelly bit between the church and the roadway. "Eh, ben, the architect wouldn't let her because he said we had to spend our money on more important things first. And you saw those pews in there?"

Those wonderful pews, that Claudine coveted. "Oh, yes," she said, her eyes wide with awe.

"Well, the government won't let us replace them. It says this is one of the very few churches still to have them."

"They *are* very rare," Claudine couldn't help saying. I could see the hair standing up on her arms at the thought of their destruction.

"That may be," the curé grumbled. "But they're very uncomfortable. Never get a church *classée*."

Neither of the other two churches were *classées*, the curé having learned his lesson, but each had its own beauty. The second one, thirteenth century, was approached through two matching rows of cypress. The last, St. Remiel, was the youngest of the three at a sprightly fourteenth century. We entered St. Remiel through a great vault of a door; inside it, pale off-white stone soared upward, lending a magical luminosity to the church that none of the others had. Joyful gold filigree etched the dark wood altar. A general air of dilapidation and lack of restoration funds only added to the magic of the place. I could see our wedding here. I had grown up in redneck Georgia and would be confirming my marriage to Sébastien in a church three times the age of my country. Everyone else concurred. This was the spot.

We had such a quaint, kindly, old priest, too. "Why did you tell him you were baptized?" I asked Sébastien indignantly as soon as we were in the car again. "You lied to a priest when I was standing right next to you! Lightning travels, you know."

"So that he would perform the ceremony," Sébastien said, in a tone that suggested I was remarkably dense.

"He would perform the ceremony anyway! The Catholic Church allows mixed marriages now."

Sébastien and Claudine exchanged glances. "The American Catholic Church must have different rules from the French one," Claudine said, puzzled. "You can't do that kind of thing here."

"No, it doesn't have different rules!" I said indignantly. "You're thinking of the way the church was when you were little."

"No," Claudine said. "I'm thinking of it as it is right now."

"You don't know what these village priests are like here, Laura," Sébastien said. "He's eighty-two."

"We're already married by the Catholic Church. What would he try to do, invalidate the sacrament?"

"Probably," Claudine said. "Let's just go with the baptized story, all right?"

The meeting with the baker was more straightforward. It took us three tries to track her down, but once we did, we had no trouble choosing our *pièce montée*. Out of the pages and pages of cream puffs she showed us—stuck together in conical towers, Eiffel towers, castles, fishing boats, churches, bells—one design stood out: an old 1920s convertible car. "Jean-Charles," Sébastien and I said simultaneously. We couldn't wait to see his face.

Last on the list of meetings was the organist. I had tried my best to get a specific address out of her when we had caught her for a split-second between baptisms. "Oh, it's easy to find," she said. "St.-Jude-Vieille-Maison, right by the church."

"Could you give me the street name and number just in case?"

A slender, tense woman somewhere in her late thirties, she looked at me as if I had posed an indiscreet question. "It's right by the church. St.-Jude-Vieille-Maison."

"Did she tell you where she lives?" our curé double-checked when he spoke with us.

"Oh, do you know?" I asked, relieved. "Where?"

"It's easy. The house right by the church, in St.-Jude-Vieille-Maison."

St.-Jude-Vieille-Maison did not appear in our big yellow book of road maps, but the book did show a St. Jude and a Vieilles Maisons (plural), although not exactly side by side. Still, the priest and the organist had considered their directions obvious enough. Optimistically, we set off.

The narrow *départemental* roads twisted and wound through fields and forests, never wider than a single car. Fortunately, population was sparse enough that this narrowness didn't present a problem as often as it could have; I had only seen the aftermaths of two head-on collisions in our errands so far. While Sébastien drove, I took to peering far ahead over the fields for any advance warning of a car heading our direction.

I also tried to keep an eye out for all villages on the horizon that could possibly be the organist's. When we were lucky, the intersection of one road with another would be marked with a white arrow and the name of the next village in each direction. We therefore hoped that if we managed to get within a couple of kilometers of St.-Jude-Vieille-Maison, an arrow would point us the rest of the way. *If* a village happened to number its population in the three figures, we sometimes got lucky enough to see its name appear on the white arrow signs a little early in the game, perhaps two or three intersections in advance. St.-Jude-Vieille-Maison wasn't such a village.

"Sébastien, *look!*" I said triumphantly, after we'd been wandering around in what our map suggested might be the right area for an hour. "That sign actually shows the name of the *road* we're on."

"Rue St. Gabriel" it read, like a miracle. We slowed down excitedly, and I ran my finger over our Michelin map. However, the map, I discovered, didn't actually name any roads, or at least not with names that corresponded to the signs. It only numbered them. "Hmm. Do you think rue St. Gabriel is the same as D30 or as D40? Because if, by any chance, it's D40, then St. Jude and Vieilles Maisons should be that way. But if it's not, then it might be the opposite direction."

We passed the village called Vieilles Maisons, and under the name, a sign, clearly marked "Commune de Saint Jude Vieille Maison." That seemed promising, except that there were no hyphens, which could make all the difference in French village names. There was also one problem, no church. We gazed around a bit, hoping the organist had been mistaken about a church being right by her house, but finally had to give up and head on.

A sign pointed to St.-Jude-en-Laye. That might be promising, too, but then again it might not. France was fond of naming places nearly the same thing, even if they were twenty miles apart—Neuilly-sur-Seine and Neuilly-sur-Marne were on opposite sides of Paris, and Sancy-les-Provins was twenty minutes of country roads from Provins. Sébastien stopped beside an unshaven man walking along the road with a chain saw, always *my* first choice for directions when lost in the middle of nowhere, and asked him about St.-Jude-Vieille-Maison.

"It's back there." The man waved his chain saw in the direction of a series of forks in the road, down all of which we had just hunted for St.-Jude-Vieille-Maison without success.

"We should keep to the right where it says St.-Jude-en-Laye?" Sébastien guessed.

"Well, you can," the man allowed, pushing back his floppy dark hair. "Or you could go the other direction, really. I mean, there are two villages."

"Two villages called St.-Jude-Vieille-Maison?"

"No, two villages that are *part* of St.-Jude-Vieille-Maison. It's a commune, not a village."

I was going to strangle our organist.

"Where would the church be?" Sébastien asked, inspired.

"Ah, the church! Back there." He waved again in the direction of the series of forks. "It's in St. Jude-en-Laye."

"Which would be part of the *commune* of St.-Jude-Vieille-Maison, but not the actual name of the village," Sébastien said. "See how much clearer French road signs are than American ones, Laura? I told you our system worked better." He really did say this. I don't make these things up.

Nowhere on the sign for St.-Jude-en-Laye did it suggest that the village might be called St.-Jude-Vieille-Maison, but it did have a church. By that point, I wasn't surprised to see houses spread out from the church in a veritable star formation, so that you could consider pretty nearly the whole village "right next to the church." We knocked on doors until a thin, nervous, auburn-haired woman we recognized answered one of them. The pale organist let us in, her manner so high-strung I felt I was pushing myself too close to a wild bird.

She showed us to a small salon, a dim room in tones of aged green that seemed to have been decorated in the fifties and never changed, just worn out. Minuscule flowers dotted green across the beige wallpaper, against which were hung framed prints of black-and-white drawings of herbs. I probably would have paid good money for some of those prints in another setting, but here in the dim light, they just looked tired. It smelled musty, but that was no comment on her housekeeping; all of these old village houses seemed to smell musty. She did not invite us to sit in the uncomfortable-looking green armchairs, one of which was stacked with music partitions. She hovered near the black upright piano as if she desperately hoped it would protect her from us.

"Thank you so much for having us over," I said in my most reassuring manner. "We just wanted to talk a little bit about the music."

"Yes, yes, I'll be happy to play anything you want." She didn't look happy. She looked as though she had just managed to get the blood washed off her hands before we walked in and was hoping we wouldn't wander into the kitchen and see the body.

"I really love Handel's 'Largo' from *Xerxes*," I began, this being a beautiful, classic wedding piece. I didn't want to ask her to prepare anything complicated or exotic only two weeks before the wedding.

She hesitated and shuffled music quickly, her hands trembling a tiny bit. "Well, I would . . . that *is* a beautiful piece, of course, but it just doesn't sound right on an organ."

My sister, a pianist who played organ in churches when she needed extra money, had recommended the Handel piece. The last thing I wanted, though, was an organist uncomfortable with the material. I changed to more religious music, figuring that would be safer. "The Bach-Gounod *Ave Maria* is beautiful."

She shuffled more music, the trembling in her hands growing marked. I glanced at Sébastien, but with his typical social poise, he acted as though he had noticed nothing wrong at all. "I don't believe I have the sheet music for that."

Maybe she had had way too much coffee that morning, I thought. Or she wasn't used to strangers. Or she had a phobia about Americans and other savage animals. "I could get it for you, if you want," I offered, thinking that might help.

A sheet of music fell from her hands to the tiled floor, and she bent to pick it up. "Oh, no, that is, no, I don't . . . Let me go get some of my books, and I'll show you what I have."

Sébastien sidled over to whisper to me while she was out of the room. "Do you think she's having a nervous breakdown?"

"What are we going to do if our organist has a nervous breakdown? The priest said we couldn't use anyone else. And how are we supposed to get an organ in there?" There was no piano or organ in the churches themselves. The organist had the only instrument available, an organ that she carried around with her in the back of a special van for four Masses every Sunday.

The organist came back in the room with a giant book of hymns, none of which I recognized. "This one's really beautiful," she said, starting to play and producing a cacophony. My lips parted. I looked at Sébastien, still attentively calm, although his gaze lingered on her hands. Within two chords, her hands were shaking so badly that she couldn't get them on the right keys. Maybe she was under the close supervision of a psychologist and had gotten off her meds?

"What about Schubert's *Ave*?" A Catholic Church organist had to be able to play at least one famous *Ave*.

She trembled more paper together, dug under her piano bench, brought out a few sheets, and played two or three chords. Her hands were jittering so badly now that at least one finger hit the wrong key for each chord. I couldn't tear my eyes away from them, my suppositions growing increasingly wild. Maybe, after an accident, she had been grafted with the hands of a murderer. Maybe those hands were shaking so badly because they wanted to lunge for our throats and strangle the life out of us. Maybe the bridal couple's bodies would be found only years later, when a tough, female detective finally traced the start of a serial killing spree back to this spot. Sure, the organist looked so frail we might assume we could fight her off, but pianists have really strong hands.

She stopped. "An organ just couldn't do it justice."

"Mendelssohn," I suggested in desperation. Surely anyone who played for all the weddings in the area could manage his Wedding March.

Although she made no effort to play this song, her hands bounced on the keys of the organ so hard that traces of notes vibrated forth. She stared down at her fingers as if they were totally out of her control.

"You know what," said Sébastien, unable to wrench his eyes from her hands. "I'm sure you've performed at millions of weddings. Just play whatever you want."

I waited until we were out in the car to hyperventilate. Titi had loaned his tiny twenty-year-old red Ford Fiesta to us for two weeks of wedding errands. "Did you hear what she was playing? And you told her to play whatever she wanted? What is our wedding going to sound like?"

"She looked so stressed. Do you want her nervous breakdown on our conscience? What if she ran amok in the church because of the pressure of playing 'The Wedding March'?"

"I thought of that. But then I realized she'd never get her hands on a good assault rifle in this country, so we would probably survive. If I have a nervous breakdown, however, things could get ugly." I was trying and failing to imagine the sounds that would accompany me down the aisle.

"Oh, you'll do fine, *crevette*." He squeezed my hand. "I mean, we've already gotten married twice in the past few months. How hard could another two times be?"

Thirty-four

Morning," Titi said, setting his tray of breakfast things on the teak table. Five days before the wedding, the sun was shining, and we were still breakfasting calmly in the garden. We were also still eating lunch calmly in the garden and lingering over dinner calmly in the garden, with a total time spent on meals per day of around ten hours. At this pace, getting married two more times in a half-foreign country might not be that hard after all. Somehow, undoubtedly a continued lack of understanding of my culture-in-law, I had imagined us so busy by this point that we wouldn't be taking time to eat.

"Morning," I said from under the *mirabellier*. The *mirabelles* had started coming in a few days before, like condensed sunshine. Tiny little jewels, dark gold flecked with red when ripe, they burst into my mouth in two delicious bites of sweetness, and I considered them an excellent breakfast.

"You're going to make yourself sick," Colette said, coming out with a basket over one arm and heading toward the vegetable garden. It's amazing how many times in my life people have told me that in connection with food. It's almost as if they think I have no self-control or something.

"Desserts today, Justine?" I asked.

She nodded immediately. "You're going to show me how to make the chocolate thing, right? The *fug*."

"Will the fugs keep?" Titi and Colette asked at the same time, startled. "They're chocolate."

"Fudge and cheesecakes are great make-aheads. The cheesecakes will have to be refrigerated, but they'll keep fine."

Two pairs of brows knit. However, earlier that morning at 2:00 A.M. under the stars, I had claimed the French had a critical spirit and never saw anything done that they couldn't do better. Colette and Titi had denied this and so had to take a deep breath and keep their mouths shut, in order to prove me wrong.

Justine and I set to work in the dim, old kitchen full of dark beams, while Colette loaded the dishwasher and Mamie re-washed all the supper dishes that had just come out of it.

"Mom, isn't the dishwasher working properly?" Titi asked.

"I thought I saw a speck on one of the plates," Mamie said. "You never know with dishwashers."

Titi rolled his eyes and went to put in a load of laundry, in the little alcove between the kitchen and the downstairs bathroom. From the mild cursing sounds that followed, we guessed that someone had dumped the clean laundry into the mop bucket again.

In the kitchen, only one tiny window over an old sink let in light, helped by two feeble lightbulbs and the huge door onto the garden. The door partially blocked mobility around the kitchen when open, but we left it that way in good weather, both for the light and because people liked to sit on the three steps that descended there from the garden. I hated cooking in this kitchen by myself; it was too dark, too cramped, too poorly equipped. I knew I hated it when by myself because a few days ago I had spent at least five minutes alone slicing up things for dinner before three people wandered in to help and a couple more sat down on the steps to smoke and watch and keep talking. Once the family was there, cooking in this kitchen became the best job in the world.

Justine and I were making American desserts at popular request. Fortunately, I had made great strides in my France packing method. Where I had once stuffed dental floss, antiperspirant, and black clothes into my suitcases, now I had, well, still black clothes—let's not get carried away—but also a wedding dress, habaneros for Jean-Charles, maple syrup and buttermilk pancake mix for Martine, Oreo cookies for everybody, chocolate chips, evaporated milk, mini-marshmallows, and a thermal bag of cream cheese. We dumped the dessert material on the tiny table in the kitchen and set to work.

A gas stove from the fifties fit into one corner. Beside it stood an old wood stove, but I opted to use the fifties gas oven. On the giant beam over the stoves, amid a clutter of other collectibles, such as ceramic pots and candlesticks, Titi and Bruno had placed a collection of old irons, from the time when they were really iron and had to be heated on a stove. Bruno's mother's toy kitchen set hung on nails along the length of the same beam. I saw none of the American cookie pans and cookie cutters that my childhood set had contained, but among the little tin pots and pans of every shape and size were two little milk pails, a miniature potato purée presser, a colander, a coffee grinder, tarte pans, and skillets.

Here I am, I thought, when I looked at that set. I, who two years ago had inflicted pain on my hostesses by trying to help

325

them cut strawberries, was standing in the heart of a kitchen this imbued with family and history; and I was doing the cooking. In fact, I was lead chef. Granted, my only following chef was a teenager; still, it was progress.

Several rows of shelves lined the top of the opposite wall. One was crowded with different pickled things from the garden—tomatoes, little onions, cucumbers. Titi came back in while Justine and I were stirring two different batches of fudge, took a beer out of the refrigerator, and started stuffing the small peppers we had picked the day before into a jar. "I don't want to lose them," he said.

"Aren't pickles time-consuming to make?" I asked, remembering my mother with a pressure cooker when I was little. "I think the fudge is about done, Justine."

"No! Not at all. It's very simple. Look." He poured vinegar into the pepper-packed jar and screwed the cap back on. "There you are. I just have to let it sit for a couple of years, and we'll have ourselves some pickles. Here, try one from last year." He pulled down a jar of cherry tomatoes.

Strange that my mother's recipes had taken hours, if pickles were so easy. I accepted a cherry tomato warily, rather in the same spirit I'd once accepted Jean-Charles's snails only with more pronounced fears of botulism. The pickled tomato was like eating condensed vinegar, straight. Tears started from my eyes. I tried to speak, and my voice came out as only a roughened squeak.

"Hmm," said Titi. "Do I need to let that last jar sit for another year, or is this because you're an American?"

"You shouldn't be feeding her *that*," Jean-Charles told him, coming in with grout-spattered hands and heading straight for the beers in the fridge. He and Bruno were laying the tile in the upstairs common room. "You might kill an American with that kind of thing. What she needs to try"—he reached up for another jar on the same shelf and brought it down with a thump to the table—"are my cherries."

He fished a couple out by their stems, proffered one to me, and ate the other with relish. I popped mine into my mouth and collapsed at the table in a fit of coughing. "What proof alcohol did you use on these?" I asked, my eyes streaming. "Is that even legal?"

"Nice and strong, aren't they? I'm going to make another couple of jars with some of the *mirabelles,* too," he bragged. "Here, go ahead; have another one."

I grinned at him. The need to impress my in-laws was fading somewhat with familiarity. As we worked together on the wedding preparations, they were feeling more and more like . . . well, like my family. And you don't have to impress your real family, do you? "I don't know. Did you ever eat a second one of those habanero peppers I brought back for you?"

"I'm getting around to it," Jean-Charles said defensively. "I just haven't figured out what wine to serve with them."

Mamie set the last of the dishes aside and picked up the zucchini from the garden, giving the dirt on it a distressed look before she plunged it into the water. "That smells delicious," she mentioned, glancing at the fudge shyly as Justine and I poured our batches into separate pans.

I looked up from scraping the pot and surprised a gleam in her eye. "You like chocolate?" Well, almost everyone liked chocolate; my concern was that no one here seemed *addicted* to it, like me. My French in-laws continued to embarrass me with their restraint toward sweet things.

"Oh-ho!" Titi laughed. "Does she like chocolate? You don't know what you're asking."

A blush climbed up Mamie's round face. She fidgeted with her eyeglasses.

"You can lick the pot and spoon," I promised.

Her eyes met mine, I grinned, and she grinned back like a little girl. She was French, and I was American; she was over sixty and I was under thirty; like her son, she probably thought vinegar was edible in undiluted form; and we definitely didn't understand each other on how many times a dish had to be washed. Nevertheless, chocolate could bridge all gaps, cultural or otherwise. I didn't scrape the pot quite as clean as I could have before I handed it and the spoon across to her.

"Oh, I shouldn't," she said.

"Chocolate is good for your health," I answered. "Tons of studies say so." The sugar in it wasn't, but why quibble over details? Mamie delved in happily.

Sébastien, Justine, and I were outside setting up the oil-drum grills when the barking dogs alerted us to another of Sébastien's cousins stopping by. Sébastien's cousins had lost their novelty. It seemed like every single day another one popped up, black-haired and brown-eyed, and all of them looked horrified when they heard who our priest was. Even Sébastien was surprised to discover how many of his father's side of the family lived in this barely populated ten square miles and how many of them had gotten in car accidents with the curé. Either everyone on Sébastien's father's side drove like a bat out of hell or the eighty-two-year-old priest did.

"So who are you getting to do the ceremony?" this cousin asked, sending his son off to play with the dogs while he watched us work. "Not that old grouch, Monsieur T."

"Is he grouchy?" Sébastien heaved a concrete block out of the wheelbarrow and positioned it to form part of the base for a grill. There was no way around it, Sébastien had some fantastic muscles, I thought, watching them flex. "I thought he was just a bad driver."

"You're thinking of Mom's car," his cousin said wisely.

"Hers, too?"

"He ran straight through a stop sign at 140 kilometers an hour! She'd just bought the car two weeks before, and he totaled it. But that's not the half of it, with that priest."

"He seemed all right when we met him. For a priest," Sébastien added with deep reserve.

His cousin shook his head in slow, elaborate appreciation as if we'd just told him we'd bought oceanfront property in Switzerland. "You know he's the one who baptized my son. It was . . . I thought my dad was going to kill him."

I had seen Sébastien's father once and his uncles not at all; but I had gathered they were all giants, had all played rugby most of their lives, and apparently were all barbaric. Except for the darker hair and brown eyes, they sounded like my brothers. Still, murdering a priest was going a little far, I thought. "What did he *do*?"

"He refused to accept the godparents at the last minute just because they were atheists." Sébastien and his cousin exchanged looks of disgust for such an intolerant old man.

I paused. "From a priest's point of view, atheistic godparents would be a bit of a contradiction in terms," I pointed out delicately. They gazed at me in blank indignation. "You see, traditionally, a child is given a *god*parent so that someone will look out for his religious development and make sure his parents don't let him go to hell."

Now they were both beginning to look disgusted with *me*. I tried again. "You do see how an atheist might be considered unsuitable for the role."

Sébastien grabbed another concrete block out of the wheelbarrow in one surge of outrage. "You mean, according to your rules, I'll never get to be anyone's *godfather*? How unfair!" He tossed the concrete block to the ground sulkily. "This is what I hate about religion!"

I gave up after that and dismissed the cousin's warning as unfounded.

Thirty-five

Three days before the wedding.

"I wonder where Sue and Dwayne are," I said, slicing peppers. We had spent the day before in Paris with our American guests and driven back late at night, after a skating trip on the Seine. Sue and Dwayne had planned to follow today, leaving Paris early that morning to make the ninety-minute trip.

"I wonder if the person who owns that property is going to pick those *mirabelles*," Colette said, her comic, freckled face crunched up as she gazed out the window. "It sure doesn't look like it."

"They're announcing rain for your wedding day," Mamie said.

"Did we get more beer?" Bruno came in, in a blue workman's outfit dusted with plaster. "There are only a few left in the fridge. Where did you girls put it, down in the cellar?"

"Try one of my cherries." Jean-Charles, covered in grease from the cars, hauled down the jar. "That'll wake you up."

"But they would call surely, if they got lost," I said. "Bruno, you left your cell phone on, didn't you?"

"Because the wind's picking up," Colette said. "I'd hate to see those *mirabelles* lost in a storm."

"Rain and hail," Mamie said. "For your wedding day."

"Well, who needs beer when it's about time for aperitifs, anyway?" Bruno said. "Lunch is almost ready."

Titi stepped in and helped himself to one of Jean-Charles's cherries. "First we'd better get that dance floor covered. It's going to rain." He, Sébastien, Bruno, and Jean-Charles grabbed the last four refrigerated beers and hurried out.

330

"And gale-force winds," Mamie said. "All day." She whisked a pepper out of my hand, picked up the other four I had lined up to cut, and carried them over to the sink, where she started washing them again. I put my knife back down on the cutting board and got up to gaze over Colette's shoulder at the approaching storm. The absentee landowner's dozen *mirabelliers* lined the opposite side of the fence, branches draping to the ground under the weight of tiny, golden, perfect fruit. We all looked at the clouds whipping in.

"I think we should pick them," I told Colette. "What a criminal waste."

She, Justine, and I looked at all the things lined up on the table to be sliced, diced, minced, and otherwise chopped, in any interval we could find between when Mamie finished washing them and when she started washing them again. "Let's go," Colette said.

The three of us grabbed huge plastic containers. Winds gusted against us as we ran down to the road and around to the other side of the fence, then back to spread out along the trees. I started to pick them, but Colette shook her head. "Just strip them off," she yelled. She demonstrated, grabbing a branch as high as she could, kicking her big plastic basin under it, and scraping her hands down the length of it, knocking all the plums off and into her basin as she did so. As we imitated her, *mirabelles* bursting with ripeness, more orange than gold, cascaded down around us into the buckets. Our only pauses were to pop fruit flecked with raindrops into our mouths.

The wind began to whip the branches back and forth, so that we had to snag them as they flew and hold them tight to keep picking. Lightning flared at the far end of the fading stubs of the wheat field. We glanced at each other and laughed, deeply enjoying our own craziness. It made an excellent break from wedding preparations and was a moment of perfect union across three generations and two continents. No tie of blood bound any of us, yet we were united in a wild sisterhood.

Damp but not yet soaked, we made it back to the house under the weight of some seventy pounds of *mirabelles* that we had picked in under half an hour. Titi arrived from the yard to discover us sitting in a row on the top step outside the kitchen, staring at the harvest we held with stunned pride, like pirates looking at chests of Spanish doubloons wrested from the teeth of the Spanish Armada. He grinned and took a picture. "You know what I'm going to make for your wedding, Laura? *Tarte aux mirabelles.*"

We made a dozen *tartes* that day, the dark kitchen cheered by all the people that crowded in as the rain fell outside, everyone cutting *mirabelles* in half and placing them on the pie crusts Titi prepared, then sprinkling them with a bit of sugar, and sliding them into the oven. I was always amazed at how simple the preparation of so much delicious French cuisine was. "Which is why the materials," said Sébastien, still not recovered from what Americans considered tomatoes, "have to be good. Are we about done here? I've got to go pick up my old sound system from my cousin Jérôme; you haven't met him and his family yet, *crevette.*"

Jérôme, with his slick black hair and pointy face, was from Sébastien's father's side. He raised prize Dobermans, which pressed against my knees with slimy balls in their mouths and clearly expected me to keep throwing these balls for the whole evening. Normally I would have stopped after a few times, but Dobermans exercise great moral persuasion. Jérôme also mastered the incredible feat of smoking three cigarettes at the same time, one in his mouth and two always burning on the edge of the ashtray. I was going to die of lung cancer from this country; I knew I was. "So who did you get to do the service?" he asked, after describing his Dobermans' last competition for two hours. "Not that old curé, what's his name, Monsieur T."

"That's the one," Sébastien said resignedly. "Why? Did he wreck your car?"

Jérôme pursed his lips together, halfway between sympathy for our upcoming trials and enjoyable anticipation of violence. "I thought your father was going to kill him at our last little cousin's Baptism. We had to grab him and take him out of the church."

And Sébastien thought my family was difficult because they all carried three or four guns in their trucks. Nobody in my family had *ever* tried to murder a priest.

"That sounds like Dad." Sébastien grinned. "What did he do?"

"Well, you know, your dad's not practicing himself, but naturally he wanted to come to his niece's Baptism. So he and your brothers were sitting quietly in a pew toward the back, just watching and not joining in the hymns or anything. And the old curé, when he walked by their pew, stopped and said—*out loud*—'Do you want to join us, or are you just here for the buffet?'" Jérôme pursed his lips in a soft, in-drawn whistle, placed his third burning cigarette in the ashtray, and lit a fourth, remembering the scene. "Fortunately, we managed to get him out of the church in time. I was supposed to be the godfather at another Baptism. Did you hear about that one?"

We got back to the farmhouse in time to help fix dinner and partake of the day's second round of cocktails. Plaster, grease, and all other forms of dirt rinsed off, everyone sank into the red plushness of the parlor. Black-and-white photos of Bruno's and Titi's ancestors surrounded us, framed in gold: Bruno's mother on her belly as a laughing, naked baby, teenage René in his military uniform, and dozens of images far older.

"We watched the weather report while you were out," Mamie said. "Still gales."

Some topics of conversation should really be banned from cocktail hour. "No word from Sue and Dwayne?" I asked. Night had fallen outside. They had planned to leave Paris ten hours ago and had still not called or shown up.

"Maybe they got started late?" Bruno suggested. "The road signs are so clear in France, it would be hard for them to get lost."

"Not like Atlanta," Jean-Charles said. "What a city. All right, have you got my shopping list ready?"

Jean-Charles and Claudine planned to get up at 4:00 A.M., in order to go to a major Parisian wholesale market open only to smaller street-market stall operators and restaurant owners. Fortunately, everyone in France knew at least one person who knew one of those, and Claudine had obtained the necessary member's card from one of her friends.

"So, I've been giving this kebab idea some thought," I said. Titi nodded in the background as if he had thought somebody eventually would. "And I'm just wondering: how many kebabs do you think one hundred and fifty guests staying for several meals will eat?"

"We'll have other food, but six or seven each, at least," Jean-Charles said.

I did some math. "Meaning that we have essentially one day to prepare one thousand kebabs."

"And finish the decorations," Claudine said. "You and I have to do that at the church Friday."

"And make all the other food," Titi said.

"And put up the tents and the lights around the dance floor," Bruno said. "If it ever stops raining."

Traitor. As the weather reports remained ominous, more and more family members were wavering over to Mamie's pessimism. We had the village's party hall reserved just in case, but Sébastien and I adamantly refused to use it. We wanted this party in the garden where we had imagined it that day at the village festival.

"That's about a hundred kebabs to make per person," I said. Éric and two friends of Claudine and Jean-Charles would be adding their helping hands starting the next morning. "Two hundred, assuming that half the people will be working on other things."

Titi nodded strongly. He seemed to have done these calculations before we had. But then, Titi had made most of the food at the famous two-day PACS event, two years before.

"Doesn't six seem a little high?" I said. "I myself wouldn't eat more than three." $3 \times 150 = 450$ kebabs. "Maybe two."

Jean-Charles was appalled. "You can't possibly offer them fewer than five."

"We could make cold cuts," Titi bargained, so promptly you could tell he'd been waiting for us to show sense for some time now. "Pork and beef roasts, sliced on platters, chicken pieces we cook tomorrow and serve cold, *merguez.*" He named the classic North African sausage French people use when Americans would use hot dogs. "And don't forget all the salads we planned to make."

We eventually reached a compromise. Among all the other things we still had to do, we would make six hundred kebabs, twelve enormous bowls of six different salads, half a dozen different roasts, and hundreds of interesting tidbits as appetizers. Fortunately, half the desserts were ready, and the other half were being brought by the baker. It took another two hours into the night to calculate the exact quantities needed of beef, lamb, chicken, pork, turkey, haddock, tomatoes, lettuce, onions, mushrooms, carrots, cabbages, prunes, zucchini, pineapple, melons, grapefruit, celery, radishes, broccoli, cauliflower, and wheels of cheese. At which point Sue and Dwayne had still not shown up.

"I think Claudine and I will head back to Paris tonight and go to the market from there," Jean-Charles said.

"If you see a car broken down on the side of any road on your way in, stop and check, okay?" I said.

They didn't see one, but about half an hour after they left and everyone trooped, in various stages of sobriety, up to bed, a car crept down the circular gravel drive and stopped before the green gate with its cardboard sign, "Laura and Sébastien Are Here. Push Hard to Enter."

It was 2:00 A.M. The house was pitch-black. Everyone was asleep up narrow, worn, wooden stairs that could be reached only through a door some distance from the main one.

"We came in," Sue said, when I found them asleep in their car at seven the next morning. "But we didn't know how to find anyone, and we were afraid it might not even be the right house, so we went back and slept in the car." Her bright red Annie curls were as crushed as it was possible for them to be, and freckles stood out on her pale face. The inside of their car still smelled new, fresh from the rental, but it had been entirely littered with chocolate wrappers.

"What happened?"

"It took us five hours to get out of Paris, although we rented the car at the Orly airport so that we wouldn't ever have to drive near Paris. I don't know how it happened. We hauled all our luggage from the hotel to the Métro, down to Orly, and through Orly to the car rental place, just to avoid Paris traffic; and we must have driven past our hotel twenty times."

"I think Sue started crying about the tenth time," Dwayne, the driver, said reflectively. His wavy brown hair had held up overnight in the car, but his freckles looked as prominent as Sue's against his pallor, and his eyes had deep circles under them.

"And we ran out of the chocolate from that *A la petite fabrique* shop you showed us the fifteenth time. But we didn't want to stop for more just when we might be making progress."

"I have serious logical issues with French road signs," Dwayne said. "Serious ones."

"You should have called," I said weakly.

"Well, we felt we should manage to get out of Paris ourselves. Then, once we did, we couldn't find a pay phone. Also, we didn't know where we were, so we couldn't have asked you for help from there to here anyway."

"I hate French roads," Sue said. "Profoundly."

Keeping in mind my father's homily on strawberries to mend all ills, I offered them *mirabelles* and installed them in one of our freshly vacated beds. Jean-Charles and Claudine arrived as I came back downstairs, produce and meat crammed into every possible corner of Jean-Charles's hatchback. He must have peered between a pineapple and a giant wheel of Brie de Meaux to see out, because food filled every space. "And this is just the first trip," Jean-Charles said. "I have to go back for the rest."

Fitting the meat alone into the refrigerators defied us for some time. No fewer than four different people approached me as we were unloading to make sure that cheesecakes absolutely had to be kept refrigerated. "Yes," I said adamantly. "But I keep telling you to take out the fudge."

They looked dubious. "Fug is chocolate. We don't want it to spoil."

We stacked the fruit and vegetables in the barn, behind the two classic cars that still needed to be polished for the wedding. At the temperatures we'd been experiencing since the *mirabelle* storm, highs in the fifties, the barn was staying quite cool, but we worried about mice. Every time I glanced at the aged rafters around me, I wrapped another layer of aluminum foil around the Brie.

The barn smelled of age, dirt, grease from the old cars, and now, pungently, of cheese. Clouds shifted on this halfway clear day, and sunlight pierced chinks in the tiles for a moment, gleaming on the dust motes we had stirred up with our unpacking. I stood a moment and looked to the right at three stacks of flats that all came up to my waist, then to the left at the fifty-year-old, rusty, white barn refrigerator, which now had to have a heavy weight leaned against its door to keep it closed. Mentally, I added to this quantity all the other things stacked in the kitchen, in the cool cellar below the house, and in the village's party hall refrigerator, waiting to be sliced, diced, mixed, or in the case of the kebabs, stuck together. We were never going to get everything done in time, I thought. Everyone was working as hard as possible with all the goodwill in the world, but to pull off two major wedding feasts on opposite continents in a month just wasn't humanly possible. And if we failed, what would happen? Something had changed these past two weeks as we worked together in such harmony. It's not that Sébastien's family hadn't welcomed me into their lives long before this; they had welcomed me from the very first. I, though, with my usual trusting emotions, had been hovering by the threshold, still feeling outside, an in-law, not family. Something about that position was changing. I didn't feel French, exactly. I still knew I was American, and they still knew it, too, as we gazed at each other sometimes in mutual bafflement. But I didn't feel like an outsider; I felt as if, differences and all, I was right there in the heart of the family with everybody else.

And I didn't want to screw it up by cracking under the stress of transforming a barn, a cellar, and a house full of raw materials into wedding feast food over the next two days. The past two weeks, working along with everyone, surrounded by all that energy and laughter, had been fun. Lots of my experiences in this intercultural relationship had been more than fun; they had been extraordinary, marvelous, fantastic. I had loved so much of it. But in the past two years, I had sacrificed my Ph.D. program at a prestigious university and pretended not to care. I had moved to a country whose government didn't want me and spent months hunting for jobs and visas and being cheated and humiliated by employers. I had given up, to my great shame, and gone back home—and thus forced Sébastien to go through the same thing, to give up his much-loved job and city, to spend months fighting with my government and eating pasteurized cheese. We had spent the past year in wedding preparations for *four weddings* and the past two months in non-stop contact with a crowd of family, both mine and his. I had never been known for emotional stability in the first place, a fact I had been trying to hide from

Sébastien's family for some time; there was no way my French in-laws could still want me in the heart of their family after seeing what I was like when I got hysterical. I could feel the buildup, the long accumulation of stress. If one thing, just one little thing, went wrong before the end of the wedding feast, I might go right over the edge.

I had gotten married a couple of times already this year and had sufficient experience to know one certainty about weddings: *something* was bound to go wrong.

Thirty-six

The day before the wedding. Gray and cold and gusty, but only occasional raindrops.

The first person Claudine saw when she came downstairs was Titi. All by himself in the kitchen, back to her, hands spread out as if to hold down roiling dogs, he was shaking his head very slowly. "*Calme-toi, Titi,*" he was saying, over and over, "*calme-toi.*"

I came in with a tray full of wine bottles left on the table when people went to bed a few hours earlier that morning. I found Claudine bent double with laughter, only her hand against a beam holding her up. "Calm yourself, Titi," she kept repeating. "Calm yourself."

The drain from the upstairs shower passed through that of the downstairs shower, and someone had left a bucket over the downstairs drain. The resulting pond reached into the kitchen. Titi had followed wet dog prints to it.

"But it's okay," said Titi, with a mop. "It's okay."

"*Calme-toi,*" Claudine sniggered, pressing her hand against her stomach to dispel hysterics.

"And I thought you said you would clean up this time?" Titi challenged Bruno, who had come out in a silk bathrobe and ancient cotton boxers to find out what was going on.

"We did . . . oh," Bruno said, catching sight of me and my laden tray. "Well, we thought we did. It seemed like cleaning up at the time."

"Humph," Titi said and thrust the mop into his hands. Bruno gazed at it blearily. The day had begun.

"I wonder where Anna and Ken are," I said, slicing tomatoes across from Justine. Released, the fresh, keen scent of tomatoes briefly took ascendancy over the sweet scent of carrots, the pungency of onions, and the green crispness of the broccoli all waiting to be cut. The tiny brown table was laden with vegetables of all colors, all piled together at the center to make room for our mishmash of warped cutting boards and random knives. "Of course, they didn't say when they were leaving Paris, so they might not get here until later."

"I think I saw a raindrop," Mamie said from the sink. "You know, they're announcing gales and hail for tomorrow."

"Laura, let me know when you're ready to go to the church," Claudine said. "We need to get it decorated today. Mom, why are you washing those onions again?"

Mamie pressed her lips together stubbornly.

"You don't think you're cutting the tomatoes too small?" Justine asked suddenly.

"What?"

"Your tomato slices are a lot smaller than mine."

I never would have noticed on my own, but mine, sliced in eighths, were indeed smaller than Justine's. "So they are. Is that bad?"

"Don't you think they should be the same size?"

"They're kebabs," I said. "What does it matter?"

She looked taken aback. "It will affect how they cook and how pretty they look."

"Did I ever mention to you that your culture is excessively perfectionistic?" I started slicing my tomatoes in quarters with my minuscule knife. Justine had ended up with a giant cleaver. Neither were appropriate to the task, but there were only so many knives to go around.

"Have you seen the melons?" Titi came in. "I thought we had two flats."

"They're out in the barn, behind one of the cars."

"Great. I'll just take these beers with me on my way out there, free up some refrigerator room." He glanced back over his shoulder. "Don't you think you're cutting those tomatoes too big?"

I gave Justine a triumphant look and went back to cutting them in eighths. A peasant wandered in and sat down at a non-spare corner of the table.

This stymied me for a second, both because it blocked access to half of the room at crunch kitchen-use time and because it was a little surprising to have a peasant just wander in off the street like that. Big, dark-haired, and unshaven, he tilted his chair back to watch us, consuming a good fourth of the space. "This is Monsieur B.," Titi said, coming back through. "He's the one who gave us the bales of hay we're using as extra seats."

I wasn't sure the gift of hay excused him for having cramped maneuvering room for knife-wielding women the day before a wedding, but I smiled at him graciously. I liked the idea of associating with peasants. It made me feel as if I was about to lose my head, rather than that I had already lost it.

A few days ago, the first time Titi had mentioned Monsieur B., a local peasant, as a possible source of bales of hay, I had said, "A local what?"

"Paysan," he said. I laughed incredulously. "What, you don't have any peasants in America?"

341

"You still get to call people peasants?"

"Well, sure. That's what he is. You know, he works the land."

I gathered the word meant a career we would call "farmer," but it was still the same word aristocrats had used for peasants for centuries until the latter started cutting the former's heads off, which would tend to straighten out most people's vocabulary. "And they don't mind being called that? Peasants, I mean."

"Laura, how can people mind being called what they are?"

Well, you know, we were busy, and with an attitude like that, I didn't think I'd succeed in explaining America and political correctness to him. Besides, if Monsieur B. was a peasant, didn't that make me a princess? The peasant smiled and asked me how the bales of hay were.

"Fantastic," I said, hoping we weren't going to get into the nitty-gritty detail of their quality. "Nice and, uh, square. Thank you."

Out of the corner of my eye, I saw Mamie free a leaf of lettuce from the pile of heads beside the sink and delicately scrub that one leaf under running water. After a couple minutes of attention, she set it in a bowl on one side and peeled off another leaf, glancing over her shoulder at our work as she did so. "The tomatoes look too small to me."

I sighed and switched to quarters again. A bit of tomato squirted forth and caught me directly in the chin.

"You need to be cutting them in sixths, I think," Justine said.

"They're not too prickly?" the peasant asked. I could call him a peasant in my head and still hold up the American dream, I swear.

"No, no, not prickly a bit," I said. "In sixths. You don't think that's unnecessarily complicating the production of six hundred kebabs, by any chance? We can't stick with simple cutting techniques?"

"But it's not hard! Look." She positioned another of her tomatoes on the cutting board and neatly sliced it in sixths. It certainly didn't look hard when she did it. Darn French teenagers. I was considered a good cook where I came from.

"We have six hundred kebabs to make! Size doesn't matter enough to cut things in sixths!"

"They've got to be a bit prickly," the peasant said, surprised. "They're bales of hay."

Damn, but I wished I had some cake to offer him. What an opportunity to miss.

"Okay, okay," Justine said. "It's your wedding." She gave my tomatoes a grave look, as if they might besmirch her family's reputation, and went back to cutting.

Sébastien came in from setting up the tents outside and ran a finger between my eyebrows. He gazed at the droplet of tomato seeds he'd collected on his fingertip a second but did not comment. "You haven't heard from your sister yet?"

"Those bales of hay working out for you?" the peasant asked, recognizing him. "Comfortable enough?"

"No, but she probably won't get here until late."

"Perfect," Sébastien told the peasant. "Nice and square." He looked from my tomatoes to Justine's. "Maybe I should cut the tomatoes for you."

"You know what?" I said. "I'm going to go make the coleslaw."

I took a position out on the dining-room table with Claudine and Colette, who were attacking some of the other salads. The dining-room table could sit fourteen without crowding. Behind it, the fireplace could easily be renovated to form an extra guest bedroom. Collectibles from Jean-Pierre and Bruno's flea market scavenging surrounded us: a Grecian head, silver candelabra, a fifteenth-century-style tapestry, bits of embroidered hieroglyphics framed like rescued fabric in a museum, even a piano with a sound that had deeply suffered from the damp of the old stone house, but which Justine insisted on playing anyway every time she got a break. The coleslaw was another recipe demanded by my new in-laws after their visit to the U.S. By the time I finished stuffing twelve heads of cabbage through the food processor, I had shreds of purple and green dangling from my hair and everywhere else.

Trailing cabbage like confetti, I carried an enormous purple bowl to the refrigerator and encountered a problem. It wouldn't fit.

"Put it in the parlor," Titi suggested. "That's where we're starting to store the big items."

"But . . . it's got mayonnaise in it."

He nodded and took it from me. "Good, that should keep."

The wedding feast wouldn't start for another twenty-eight hours.

"There are two bowls of it," I mentioned weakly as if that might make some difference.

"Um-hmm," Titi said absently and disappeared into the parlor.

"We can take the fudge out to make room!" I called after him. "I swear! It will be fine! Lasts forever, fudge!"

He peered back out at me, frowning. "I'm surprised at the way you, of all people, are trying to treat chocolate, Laura. I really am."

I went to find my husband, the person who was supposed to negotiate with his family when their persistent Frenchness started to menace my health. "Sébastien," I murmured in his ear. "Your uncle put the coleslaw in the parlor."

"Um-hmm," he said, making short work of his six-part tomatoes. He didn't have any tomato seeds clinging to him, I noticed. Not even on his hands—he just held the tomato firmly with the tips of his fingers and sliced away, neat as could be.

"You know, I can get more bales if you need them," the peasant said. I was starting to see why pre-guillotine aristocrats liked to be able to just shoo peasants away with a flick of the hand.

"It's got mayonnaise in it."

Sébastien cut his eyes to me. "You're not going to start going on about that salmonella thing, are you?"

"It's a genuine illness!"

"Not in France, it isn't."

"I know three people who caught salmonella in France."

He nodded thoughtfully. "Do you know any French people who caught salmonella in France? Or were these all Americans?"

"No!" I said, stung. "Only one of them. The others were, um, Canadians."

"You know, maybe you guys should quit washing your hands after going to the bathroom. Might toughen you up a bit."

He dumped the tomatoes into a bowl and went into the dining room to pick up a butcher knife and start hacking up meat for the kebabs. Standing as he was before that enormous fireplace, it made for a primordial scene. And I was pleased to see that even he got his hands a little squishy when cutting up huge masses of meat.

Mamie carried something through the room to the parlor and stopped by her daughter on the way back to the kitchen. "Do you really think you should put the pepper next to the chicken on the kebabs, Claudine? I would put the onion first."

I fled to the kitchen in search of tuna for a *salade niçoise* and discovered Titi covering with aluminum foil a pan full of dozens of chicken thighs he had finished cooking earlier. "Maybe we should pack them into something smaller," I said. "I don't see how we'll fit that into any of the refrigerators."

"Laura," he tsked. "They're cooked. Why put them into the refrigerator? They'll be fine."

"But . . ."

"I wouldn't leave them out forever, but they'll be fine for twenty-four hours."

"Maybe I should leave this *salade niçoise* for the last minute," I said, gazing at the can of tuna.

"If you want." Titi shrugged. "There are plenty of other things to be done."

Without explanation, the peasant got up and wandered back out of the house, wishing us joy in our marriage as he went. I felt bereft. My fifteen minutes as a princess were over, and I had a pile of onions to cut.

"Justine!" Claudine said. "Where are the extra kebab sticks your dad got?"

"How should I know?" Justine retorted. "Why do you always ask me? I can't keep track of everything!"

There was a rapid explosion of fire between the two, kind of what you could expect from a mother and teenage daughter under a lot of stress. Eyes streaming from the first onion, I turned back to find the others had disappeared.

"I saw a speck of dirt," Mamie said from the sink.

I turned to the rice I'd been boiling, only to find *it* had disappeared. Mamie couldn't possibly be washing it. "Where's the rice I made for the *salade niçoise?*"

"Oh, I finished that salad up for you," Titi said. "It only needed the tuna and mayonnaise added. I put it in the parlor."

I decided to concentrate on the tabouleh, which contained no animal products, only peppers, tomato, parsley, olive oil, lemon juice, couscous, and raisins. Knowing this salad might be the only one not lethal, I made three gigantic bowls of it. "Laura! You shouldn't have made that so early," Claudine said, horrified. "Or that much. Where will we find space in the refrigerator?"

I paused in wiping couscous grains off my hand. "We'll leave it out," I said blankly. "Like the rest of the salads, you know, the ones filled with mayonnaise and tuna."

"*Mais non, non, non, non, non!*" Claudine grabbed a bowl of tabouleh protectively. "With lemon juice and olive oil in it? You're not thinking, Laura; if we leave it unrefrigerated, it might taste funny."

I opened my mouth and closed it, feeling very foreign. Well, actually, being that I was an American and ethnocentric and all, feeling that everyone else around me was very foreign, and even, perhaps, stark raving mad. "I wonder when my sister will get here?" I said out loud. I didn't normally consider my siblings sane, but it was the contrast.

"Who cut these tomatoes?" Colette said from the dining room. "I can't find two the same size to fit onto a kebab."

We made kebabs until we were ready to commit hari-kari on the damn sticks. We grabbed squishy meat. We stabbed. We grabbed squishy meat. We stabbed. Someone wandered through and said maybe the pepper should go on the other side of the meat, just to be more decorative. We grabbed that person. We stabbed. Okay, that last was just one of my personal fantasies. Only half a dozen of us focused on the kebabs, but everyone else was working just as frantically hard outside. I wished *I* could be outside, instead of stuck here stabbing meat. I knew we were in trouble when we didn't stop for lunch or even cocktail hour. The men drank their sustenance standing, and I depleted Titi and Bruno's candy stock. Putting store purchases away, I'd discovered a surprising amount of chocolate they'd hidden in the back of cupboards just prior to my arrival. And I had always thought them so hospitable.

I was pleased to note that nobody else cared what the hell the tomatoes looked like by the end of the day, either. I did try to sneak the kebabs into the refrigerator but couldn't figure out how to fit them in. Six hundred kebabs take up a lot of space.

"Oh, don't worry," Claudine said. "They'll be cooked before anyone eats them; they'll be fine."

I made one last-ditch effort to save the bowl of mayonnaise that Jean-Charles made as a dip to accompany the vegetable basket. Whipped together with raw eggs and a slow, steady stream of olive oil, the rich golden concoction would fit perfectly into the last spare corner of the kitchen refrigerator.

"Are you *crazy?*" Colette threw herself between it and the icebox as if saving the mayonnaise from a bullet. "If you put it into the refrigerator, the change in temperature will affect the flavor!"

At some point, we got the church decorated, and Sébastien left for Paris to pick up his teenage brother Grégory, who was coming in on the train from a summer internship in Ireland. Sébastien called us three hours later, just about the time we were starting to prepare dinner. In America, we would have called Domino's at this point, but here we were about two hours away from the nearest pizza place. Besides, my French in-laws thought that people who had worked so hard all day deserved to enjoy a good meal, even if that meant preparing it. Over the cell phone, Sébastien sounded tired and annoyed. "Grégory missed his train and will be here in another three hours."

Sue and Dwayne came back from a visit to Vaux-le-Vicomte in time to join us for dinner around 10:00 P.M., but there was still no word from my sister. Outside, lightning flared wildly, and hail scattered shot through the rain. I was now a besieged island in my determination to continue plans to use the garden the next day. Everyone else wanted us to run up to the village's *salle des fêtes* and try to get it into shape to host a party in twelve hours. Given the weather, Sébastien's and my conviction that we would be able to hold the wedding in the garden the next day seemed optimistic at best. It was surprising that I, usually the most pessimistic of souls, persisted in it. Come to think of it, persisting in things I felt sure couldn't work seemed to be a character trait of mine; and at least in the case of my relationship with Sébastien, I had no regrets so far. A strong desire for sleep and a conviction I was about to fall to pieces and bring this whole beautiful house of cards tumbling down around me, but no actual regrets.

"We're having it in the garden," I said faintly, but definitely.

Unfortunately, Sébastien wasn't there to support his fading bride. Three hours after the first call, he called again. He sounded as if he was speaking through his teeth. "Wrong train station. He told me the wrong train station. What? In the garden, of course!"

"We're having it in the garden," I repeated feebly but stubbornly, after hanging up.

An hour later, he called back. "A flat tire." He seemed to have sunk into a place of eery, incredulous calm. "We just had a flat tire."

Only Sue was left to support my side, and she could do it only in English, patting my head. "It will be sunny; I know it will," she said. "Where's your sister, anyway? Not coming from Paris, I hope? If you're within a hundred kilometers of Paris, it *sucks* you in."

I responded something unintelligible, my lips too tired to move. My kebab-stabbing hands could barely hold a fork. Sébastien's family, just warming up, looked at me with some concern as they poured another round of wine, toasted, and complained laughingly about how tired they were. "Maybe you should go to bed," Claudine and Colette said.

It was quite lowering, really. How could they maintain their energy and gaiety while I could barely keep from pitching face forward into my plate and blubbering uncontrollably? They seemed to be getting by on love and laughter, which was an interesting lesson. I obviously still needed to develop a higher level of both, and it's discouraging to realize your skills in love and farce need yet more work just before you get married the fourth time in eight months to the same man.

"Maybe I should," I said, not wanting to start the blubbering bit and ruin my relationship with the family. Just one more day to get through without succumbing to fatigue and stress; surely I could manage that and not pitch a fit, or burst into tears, or in some other way ruin my new French family's opinion of me?

Bruno's cell phone rang as I was getting up. "It's your sister."

I grabbed it. A din of loud music blared through the receiver into my ear. "Anna? Where *are* you? Don't tell me you and Ken got lost, too."

"No, no, we're not lost," she said, far too cheerfully for this to be a good sign. I strained to hear her through a medley of voices and clinking glass.

"Oh—well, good. Did you decide to stop at a hotel?"

"No."

Oh, dear. "You're, ah, calling from a restaurant where you've just had a wonderful meal."

"No." A couple of beeps sounded, the kind a phone makes when the person on the other end of it accidentally presses a button.

"Anna? Are you still there?"

"We ran"—another beep—"out of gas."

"What?"

"We're in a bar with a huge Caribbean woman who is supposed to be able to communicate with English speakers. She does this by repeating herself over and over again in French very slowly and very loudly. She and a very drunk Frenchman have been trying to dial for us for the past half hour, and they're still doing so *even though we're already talking on the phone.* A whole crowd of very drunk people are arguing with them about how to do this, and we don't have any gas."

"How did you . . . how did you manage to run out of gas?" I just might have sounded a tad hysterical at that point.

"Maybe you should talk to Ken."

Ken came on. "Laura," he said, his voice tight-edged, "you didn't think to mention to me that all the gas stations closed at seven o'clock."

It was true that I had known this; it had just not occurred to me that other people didn't know it, just as it had not occurred to me to mention the No Beer Sunday. I realized, alarmed, that I had become as responsible for interpreting French society to my American relatives as I was for interpreting American society to the French. Not only that, but apparently I was as incapable of doing so, since I was beginning to take most things for granted. How had that happened? I still believed in salmonella.

"No," I admitted, head hanging. "I didn't."

"We kept driving and driving, thinking we would run into a place that was open twenty-four hours or at least until ten, but no. Then we kind of hoped that maybe we'd find your damn farmhouse before we ran out of gas. But no. Fortunately—or maybe unfortunately, it's still too early to tell—we ran out near a bar, and now we have a lot of very drunk people around us trying to help us dial."

I stared down the table, seeing not a single person I could ask to go in my stead, after they had all already worked so hard for me. And I couldn't drive a stick shift without stalling. It was going to be a long trip over there in the middle of the night, with me stalling at every stop sign.

Sue reached over and stroked my hair. "We'll go get them," she said.

"Sue, if I had only one bar of chocolate left from *A la petite fabrique,* I would give it to you. Unfortunately, Mamie and I ate it for lunch. But you are a true friend."

I turned back to the phone to give Anna and Ken the promise of rescue. "By the way," Anna said, "we called Sébastien's phone first. I'm pretty sure I heard him say, '*Merde,* my turn!' before somebody named Grégory came on the line and gave us Bruno's number. Sébastien wasn't in Paris when I called him, was he? If he missed a turn in that city, it will be *hours* before he gets out of it."

By the time I went to bed, Sébastien and his brother Grégory still had not arrived. I lay awake listening to Bruno and the rest singing below and imagined wind whipping away the tents, hail pounding down on the guests, and an entire hospital ward full of my *belle famille,* all on IVs and cursing the American bride for food poisoning them.

Thirty-seven

Sébastien and Grégory finally reached the farmhouse at 2:00 A.M. I learned of their arrival not when two weary men climbed up the stairs to bed but when two fine tenors joined in the dirty ditties down below. Sébastien and his family didn't go to bed until 3:00 A.M.

The first alarm went off at 5:30 only a few feet from my ear. "Oh, my God," I said. "What's that?"

The second alarm sounded from the other side of the room, Grégory's watch. As if the insanity were contagious, a third alarm bleeped from over by Colette's mattress.

"It can't possibly be time to get up yet," I said, about ready to cry. I hadn't even dreamed of hundreds of guests vomiting in the grass, because I hadn't fallen into a deep enough sleep.

Claudine sat up *laughing*. Somebody had forgotten to tell her that it was 5:30 in the morning after a day in which she had made six hundred kebabs and gone to bed far later than I had. "Oh, we wanted to make sure to get an early start. All right, everybody, up and at 'em. Let's go, let's go!"

When I got downstairs at 5:45, the first thing I noticed was the gray day and the flecks of rain that caught me on the face as I crossed the gravel to the dining room. The second was Claudine, Titi, and the tall, lanky, dark-haired Grégory laying out an elaborate breakfast, complete with full place settings and everything.

"What?" I stumbled to a halt.

"This day, of all days, we had to make sure everyone got off to a proper start." Claudine beamed at me. "What would you like to drink?"

"Arsenic," I said. "No, no, don't get up. I'll get it."

By 5:50, everyone was gathered around the breakfast table for a leisurely breakfast of coffee, juice, bread, and jam, to start the day off right.

"This might be it," I muttered to Sébastien. "This might be the breaking point. I might really not be able to take your culture."

"Okay, so it's not bacon, eggs, and biscuits," he said, offended. "But people have been working really hard, Laura; they don't have time to prepare an American-style breakfast."

I looked at him. I looked at my watch: 5:55. "You know, we can speak each other's languages all we want, but we'll never understand each other."

The leisurely breakfast lasted until 6:30, an hour's sleep for which I would gladly have made do with a candy bar. Properly reinvigorated, we launched anew into the wedding preparations, meaning all those things that couldn't be done until the last minute and all those things that could have but had been forgotten.

"The wedding's at eleven," I said to everyone, multiple times. "All I ask is that I get the bathroom at nine and have the next hour to get ready."

The fourteenth time I said this, my teenage brother-in-law handed me a worry-stone he had brought back from Ireland, a small piece of marble with an indentation where centuries of thumbs were supposed to have rubbed away cares. "No, no, keep it," Grégory said. "I want you to rub it a lot."

At nine, I climbed the narrow, worn wooden stairs to the common room and its newly installed bathroom. The door was closed, and the shower was running.

I dove my hand in my pocket for the worry-stone, smooth and cold against my hand. "Who," I said to Justine, who had taken her shower at 8:30, "is in the shower? And how long has he been in there?"

"Titi." Darn. He was one of the owners of the new bathroom, so I couldn't kick him out and make him use the twenty-year-old, perfectly functioning, but less attractive bathroom downstairs. Unfortunately for me, the minuscule bathroom downstairs was cluttered with mop buckets and other things that didn't fit anywhere else; there was no way I could get into a wedding dress in it and still have that wedding dress be presentable. "But he should be out in five minutes," Justine added anxiously, at my expression.

Bruno pounded up the stairs. "I get the bathroom next; I've got to take a shower!"

"But I've got to get ready," I said, feeling on weak ground arguing with our host about whether or not he could use his own bathroom.

"I'll be quick," he said and disappeared downstairs again. I rubbed my thumb hard against the worry-stone.

At 9:05, Titi appeared, flushed from the bathroom humidity. "Oh, were you waiting for me? It's all yours!"

"Well, no, it's Bruno's, apparently," I said, but Bruno didn't appear. I called several times from the top of the stairs, waited five minutes, and finally, at 9:10, decided to go ahead.

I was just stepping naked under the shower when I heard him knock on the bathroom door. "She went ahead and took a shower?" he exclaimed to Justine, indignant. "I said I needed to go next!"

I wavered between embarrassment at my own self-absorption and the frantic conviction that I needed to have first dibs on at least one bathroom and mirror this morning. Caught under this pressure, I took the fastest shower of my life and burst out with knotted hair and soap still streaming off one shoulder.

"Finally," Bruno said, jumping up from the couch where he had been waiting for me. "It's getting late, I've got to hurry."

"But—" The door closed and locked behind him, leaving my toiletries and the worry-stone on the wrong side of it, on the edge of the sink.

I looked down at my towel-wrapped, streaming self and at Justine, who, having hit the shower before any of us, was calmly painting her toenails. "Don't forget to do yours," she said. "Mom said not to let you reach the altar without fingernail and toenail polish."

"Umm . . . can I borrow a comb?"

I had pulled on jeans again and was wondering if I dared do my hair without a mirror when Bruno got out of the shower. At the same time, Mamie climbed up the stairs to help me. "You haven't done your hair yet, Laura?" she said. "It's 9:30."

"I know," I said, grabbing someone's towel and scrubbing the fog off the bathroom mirror. "I'm working on it." I toweled all the moisture I could out of my hair and was starting to put mousse in it when Claudine burst up the stairs.

"I've got to get a shower, or I'll never be ready in time!" she said. "Laura, you aren't ready yet? It's getting late!"

"But, I"—I thought of the downstairs bathroom and bit my mouth shut. She was the mother of the groom, and her role in this French wedding had been much closer to that of the mother of the bride's, so she was probably stressed, too. Anyway, what was I supposed to do, tell all these people who had worked so hard for our wedding that I should have priority on the nice bathroom just because it had the only decently lit mirror in the house?

They would think I was being selfish. I desperately missed my sisters, who already knew I was selfish. They also knew how loud I could yell, so I would have been able to do so without ruining our relationship. But my only American relative here this time around was at her hotel, as was Sue; and they probably wouldn't even find the church, the way things were going. Come to think of it, I *hoped* they were at the hotel; I actually had no idea what had happened after Sue and Dwayne left to find Anna and Ken.

The men boomed up the stairs: Jean-Charles, Éric, and Sébastien all at once. "Tell me you've taken a shower," I said.

"Not me," Sébastien said. "But I've just been cutting wood, so I definitely need to. Can you believe we forgot the wood for the grills? I'll hurry."

I stared at him, tears of panic fighting behind my eyes. Clearly the groom did have to take a shower. Clearly he should have priority on the nice bathroom, too. But the other bathroom had only this tiny, foggy mirror and no lighting. I was going to get married in front of 130 people I hadn't met and twenty I had without any makeup on.

"We're fine," Éric said of himself and Jean-Charles. "We just have to change."

"Up here?" I said, my voice shooting up an octave.

Nobody even noticed.

"It's 10:05," Mamie said.

She's a sweet old lady, I said to myself, a sweet old lady; don't say anything. Claudine came out in a lace bra and a towel knotted at her waist, solving the question of how the men and women were going to change in the same room. Well, maybe not solving it, from my point of view, but certainly putting it in a French perspective.

"Leave the door open while you shower," I told Sébastien. "I've got to get at that mirror."

He must have detected something in my voice because he patted me on the nearest available body part, my elbow, as he stripped off his clothes.

"And take your time," I added as he closed the shower curtain. "As long as you're in there, nobody else can force me out of this bathroom."

"I can't do that," Sébastien said from under pounding water. "Other people need to use this shower."

Don't panic, I told myself, hyperventilating in short moist puffs against the mirror. Don't panic. If you're ten minutes late, that's normal. This is France; if you're on time, nobody will be there. I looked around for the worry-stone, but it had disappeared. That couldn't be a good sign.

356

"Did you ever talk to Bruno about doing the first reading, Sébastien?" I checked.

Dead silence from under the shower. Sébastien poked his soap-sudsed head between the curtain and the shower wall and stared at me. "No."

Bruno was going to kill us. "Go find him as soon as you get out of the shower, and tell him to start practicing. Apologize *profusely*."

"It's 10:10," Mamie said.

"I—know." I paused between words to school any shortness out of my voice and reminded myself that she had spent a couple of hours yesterday evening making a beautiful bouquet as a surprise for me. And telling me that they predicted hail all day today, but still. I tried not to look out the window at the gray skies.

"I'm out," Sébastien said. "Can I have the mirror to shave, Laura?"

I had everything on but my lipstick and didn't want to do it in front of the dark, tarnished mirror because it was permanent and I had lost the oil that took it off. I was now breathing in short, tiny bursts, but no one noticed, of course. Twelve people all trying to get ready, who had time to notice? Éric, who had gotten ready in five minutes and was now sitting on the couch watching the rest of us, raised his eyebrow at me. "Laura, don't you think you should put on your dress? We have to leave."

I stared at him, and at Jean-Charles, who was busy knotting his tie, and at Claudine, still in a bra and towel, doing *her* makeup in a tiny hand mirror she had cleverly thought to bring with her. I was getting married, for God's sake, even if it was for the third and fourth time. Were my father-in-law and the groom's best friend just going to watch me change into my wedding dress and the special corset-style bra that had to be worn with it?

"It's 10:25," Mamie said.

I burst into tears, picked up my wedding dress, and threw it across the room, and in front of everyone, began stripping off my clothes. "Everybody keeps telling me what time it is, and no one will let me get dressed! No one will help me!" I bawled.

This temper tantrum removed two problems instantly. Jean-Charles and Éric got out of the room so fast they left a wind in their wake.

"What is the matter with her?" Claudine demanded of her son, her voice rising. "She's been up here since nine o'clock! How much time does one person need to get ready?"

It was the moment I had been afraid of all this time. I had cracked under pressure; Sébastien's family was seeing the real me for the first time, and I was about to lose all the support that was the only thing that made this intercultural marriage possible. But I couldn't make myself stop. I could barely speak I was crying so hard. "Up here since nine o'clock? Nobody will—can't you use *the other shower?*"

"Laura, don't you even start this." Sébastien, stressed himself, was tight-mouthed with rare anger. "You are *not* going to pitch a fit with my family. Everyone's been working so hard for us."

"Fine, fine, fine!" I opened the window and tried to throw my wedding dress out of it. Down on the gravel below, Éric and Jean-Charles craned their heads back, transfixed. "I'll just go as I am, shall I?"

"Don't you two fight," Claudine said sharply to her son. "Sébastien, go away. You two are not going to fight on your third wedding day. Justine, run get a glass of water." She snatched the wedding dress back from the window and then took my shoulders. "Laura, stop. I want you to be happy; that's all any of us want is for both of you to be very, very happy. We just wanted to give you a French wedding, you know; we just wanted you both to have this."

"You wanted *me* to have this?" I stared at her, so startled there was a second I might almost have stopped crying. "I'm doing this for *you.*"

"Right, of course you are," Claudine said soothingly, not about to argue with someone in that stage of self-absorption. "Now, you have to stop crying, whatever you think is so upsetting doesn't matter. What's the matter?"

"Nobody will *help* me," I sobbed. "And I can't get ready."

"We'll help you. You look beautiful. What do you mean you can't get ready? You look beautiful."

"I–don't–have–any–lipstick–on—" I sobbed in short bursts. Not to mention I was in a bra and old jeans, but I had forgotten that part.

"That can be solved, but you have to *stop crying*. Here." She took off her sapphire necklace. "I want you to wear this for me. Didn't you say in America you had to wear something old, borrowed, and blue? Although it's not very old," she added doubtfully. "Only a couple of centuries."

I laughed in a hiccuping, hysterical way. "That's what I'm *talking* about. It will never work. Our cultures are too different. And I'm so tired. We keep going back and forth between both cultures trying to pull both sides together; it's an *impossible* thing to make work."

"It will work," Claudine said. "We ate grits, didn't we? It will work fine. Now don't get sidetracked on other issues. You said your problem was the lipstick; let's stick with that, why don't we?"

By the time we got to the church, I had calmed down enough to feel deeply ashamed of myself, but my stomach was still roiling. Sébastien's probably was, too, but I couldn't know for sure. Bruno was driving the groom's car, decked out in a twenties gangster tuxedo, and they had left the house first, without a cell phone. From far back on the country road behind them, in the bridal car, Jean-Charles, Justine, Mamie, and I had watched helpless as they took the wrong turn. I hoped it was a wrong turn, and Sébastien hadn't decided to flee his third marriage to me. He'd been pretty annoyed when I started yelling and throwing my wedding dress around; he might finally have seen the light and realized he deserved a lot better. We circled around the little stone village a few times to wait. Jean-Charles wanted us to arrive last, as was only proper for a bride and her 1931 Citroen C4, which had to be seen in all its glory.

At a top speed of thirty miles per hour, Bruno couldn't really speed to make up for lost time, but the groom's party finally found a way out of their shortcut. Jean-Charles circled one more time while Sébastien and his mother and attendants disembarked. We were fifteen minutes late.

In French tradition, guests wait outside the church to see the bridal party arrive, even on freezing gray days like this fine August morning; but as I descended from the car I spotted Claudine frantically trying to force the crowd of guests into the church while Sébastien stood tight-lipped in front of the priest, staring off at some fixed point in the distance. Sébastien's oversized father and uncles were eyeing the priest in a way that couldn't be good.

"What's wrong?" I muttered to Sue and Anna as they joined us. Sue was wearing a sexy strapless black dress with a flirty skirt and looking half frozen. Anna, in the long midnight-blue bridesmaid gown that had worked so well in a Georgia summer, didn't look much warmer. Goose bumps had sprung up on all our arms. At least they had made it out of last night's bar alive and found the church, though, which was more than I had been expecting at this point.

"I don't know, can't understand a word anybody's saying," they said.

"I thought the priest said something about cold steak, but I must have misunderstood," said Dwayne, baffled at how useless those college French classes had proven.

"Oh, my God," I said. "We can't possibly make him late for his lunch. It's 11:15, and there's no Mass. The wedding should last only half an hour."

Sébastien's brother Grégory, who had attended ceremonies by this curé before, gave me an odd, startled look, but didn't have time to say anything. The organist had begun to pound out . . . something. My sister, the professional pianist, sent me a look even more startled than Grégory's, but said nothing.

Voices rang out, joining the organ. Everyone jumped a foot. I peered around all the people lined up to go into the church before I did. Up in front stood three ladies singing. I dimly remembered the curé's complaining no one properly joined in the songs these days in church and saying he would try to find some nice young ladies to lead the singing. Apparently, he had done so. Young was clearly as relative as the word "singing," though. All three were around the curé's age, and while they might have been beautiful singers at one point, their voices and their ear for harmony had aged. I reminded myself how kind of these three villagers it was to volunteer their time and their voices to make two young strangers' wedding beautiful. Éric, due to be one of the first of the bridal party to walk in, coughed quickly into his hand, lifted his chin, squared his shoulders and the corners of his mouth, and started down the aisle.

"Where are we supposed to sit?" my sister asked me suddenly.

"Well, you see where the, er, choir has placed those three hideous green plastic chairs?" I answered conversationally. "Those are blocking the gorgeous antique wood seats where the groomsmen were supposed to sit. You were supposed to sit opposite them; but rehearsals are a pompous American tradition, so we'll just have to see how it goes. Good luck!" I pushed her in the back to get her going.

As she walked to the altar, I had just time to notice that the decorations Claudine and I had put up the day before looked surprisingly charming, the bouquets of wheat, bright yellow, and blue bringing humanity and life into that soaring, spiritual church. The organist charged into another song, the ladies arching into the high end of my hearing range, as Jean-Charles proffered me his elbow. Jean-Charles had tamed his hair today and traded his normal paint-stained T-shirts for an elegant golden suit; he looked so serious I knew he must be nearly as nervous as I was. He had been first stunned and then, I think, pleased, when I asked him to stand in for my father here.

We walked down the aisle at a timely moment. All faces turned toward us, and only he and I could see the game of musical chairs going on up front. During the time we walked down the aisle, the priest directed the bridesmaids to the wrong side of the church; Claudine got up to move them back to the right side; the groomsmen sat in the front bench reserved for the parents and Mamie; the groomsmen exchanged whispers, got up quickly, and approached the choir for a whispered conversation that managed to get the three ladies to advance their plastic chairs a foot; and I made subtle hand gestures trying to direct things. Everyone noticed the hand gestures, but they assumed I had developed a nervous twitch.

Halfway up the aisle, I realized the words and rhythm of the music bore a strong resemblance to a funeral march. I met Sébastien's eyes as I reached the altar, and we immediately looked in opposite directions, biting our lips. Behind the ladies, I saw Éric valiantly trying to harmonize their voices with his fine tenor. He met my eyes and ducked his head away quickly, so that the audience couldn't see his face convulse. After the hysterics this morning, I was pretty sure if I started laughing now, somebody would stick a needle in my arm. I added Éric to my list of people to avoid looking at. Sébastien stared straight ahead, trying to keep a straight face.

Bruno came up to give the first reading, St. Paul's famous passage on love, which he did quite well, I thought. Grégory got up to follow him. "Well," said the curé, out loud, standing right by the microphone, "I hope you'll do a better job than that first guy."

Sébastien and I closed our eyes briefly, not daring to peek back at Bruno's face. Eighty-two, I reminded myself. Eighty-two-year-old priests who kindly agreed to carry on pastoral duties for four villages long after retirement age were entitled to a few eccentricities.

"Speak clearly, now," the curé told Grégory, placing a fatherly hand on Grégory's—was he touching Grégory's tush? Nineteen-year-old Grégory kept a rigidly straight face and stepped up to the microphone. The curé, in a white cassock, stayed supportively by his side, patting his waist from time to time.

Grégory read very clearly and escaped back to his seat. The organist and accompanying choir plunged into another dirge. I tried to sink through the floor, but the boned bodice of my wedding gown wouldn't let me.

The song finally ended, and the curé launched into his sermon. "Marriage," he said, "should be for love and not just because you're looking for a retirement pension." I pressed my lips together hard, feeling bubbles of hilarity start to well up my throat like hiccups. "That first person read so poorly you might not have understood him, but he said that love is not jealous. What this means is that no matter how much the man has his soccer matches, his bars, and his nights out with his friends, the woman should not tell herself that he has his life easy. And no matter how many electrical appliances the woman has in the kitchen, the man should not tell himself that she has her life easy."

I was trying to kind of flatten out the bubbles of hilarity between my tongue and palate as they came up. This led to an odd twitching of my lips that was making my non-French-speaking sister look at me with great concern. Justine was staring at her toes.

" 'Love bears all things, believes all things, hopes all things, endures all things.' What beautiful words of St. Paul, that love endures all things. What this means is that just because a woman is getting married isn't an excuse for her to stop trying to look like Claudia Schiffer. This is something she must strive for all her life, for love of her husband."

I bit severely into the side of my cheek. I don't like to put myself down, but holding Claudia Schiffer up as my personal standard in appearance might prove demoralizing. The curé looked up from the yellowed, tightly typed, mimeographed pages he held in his hands, and I tried to guess how many of those pages there were. It looked ominously like at least twenty.

"'Love is patient,' St. Paul tells us. 'Love is kind.' So no matter how much your wife deserves a beating from time to time, young Sébastien, you should try to be generous and restrain yourself."

Several people choked, and a murmur broke out in the audience behind us. Turning my head slightly, I could see people nudging each other, wondering if they could possibly have heard correctly.

Into his stride now, the priest kept on in this vein for forty-five minutes. Next, despite our having paid him generously for his services, he sent my pretty bridesmaids to take up a collection. He seemed a bit surprised when the baskets came back with some buttons in them. "It was the way he yelled at us when you guys were late," one of the button-giving guests later explained. "It wasn't *our* fault you couldn't get there on time." Others were more generous and gave large bills. "It was the most hilarious sermon I've heard in my life," they explained.

But the large bills didn't seem to make up for the buttons. The curé gave an openly disgusted look into the baskets as he took them from the bridesmaids. "Well, now we need to get the vow part out of the way," he announced over the microphone. Out of the way. "Sébastien, Laura."

We positioned our lame photocopied pieces of paper on the kneelers where we could peer at them. Sébastien took my hands and decided to ignore the priest. "Laura Marie, *veux-tu être ma femme?*"

"What's that?" the curé barked. "No one can hear you. Speak up!"

Sébastien took a hard breath, kept smiling at me, and repeated himself as loud as anyone possibly could, "Laura Marie, *veux-tu être ma femme?*"

"They can't hear you!" the curé called over his microphone.

"*Oui,*" I said loudly, ignoring him.

"*Je te reçois comme épouse, et je me donne à toi,*" Sébastien continued determinedly, gazing into my eyes.

"He just said," the priest interrupted, " 'Laura Marie, will you be my wife?' and . . . oh, and she said, 'Yes.' And then he said, 'I take you as my wife, and I give myself to you.' "

Sébastien and I were still gazing into each other's eyes, but Sébastien's nostrils were flaring just a tad.

"Now you try, young lady. Speak up."

I flicked a quick glance sideways at my photocopied sheet. "Sébastien Michel René, *veux-tu être mon mari?*"

"*Oui.*"

"She just said," the priest interrupted, " 'Sébastien Michel René, will you be my husband?' And he said, 'Yes.' "

"*Je te reçois comme époux,*" I shouted as loud as I could.

The priest heaved a loud sigh over the microphone. "I'll tell you what. I'll read it, and then you repeat it. That way people will have an idea of what you're saying."

If I crumpled both of our stupid photocopied pieces of paper into a very tight ball, I fantasized I might be able to get him between the eyes. I clasped Sébastien's hands more tightly to avoid temptation and dutifully repeated my vows after the priest. "*Je te reçois comme époux, et je me donne à toi.*" ("I take you as my husband, and I give myself to you.")

And together: "*Pour nous aimer fidèlement dans le bonheur ou dans les épreuves, et nous soutenir l'un l'autre, tout au long de notre vie.*" ("To love each other faithfully in happiness and trials, and to support each other all the days of our lives.")

Despite everything, the moment was deeply romantic. For the first time, I truly felt how important it was to have done this wedding in French, in the language and country home to Sébastien, as well as in English, in the language and country home to me. I had known it was important, but I had not really felt that importance until now. I smiled at him as he gave an extra squeeze to my hands and our eyes held. He had deep circles of fatigue under his, I saw, but the warmth and sweetness that had first attracted me to him were still there.

"She can actually speak French," the curé said out loud over the microphone. "Isn't that amazing? Well, we got that over with. Now I think it would be nice if the couple led us all in the Lord's Prayer."

The romantic moment broke. I stared at the priest, and Sébastien gazed at the stained glass behind the altar. Fortunately, he hadn't taken to rugby the way his father and uncles had.

"I can only recite it in English," I said. I would have thought the curé would have guessed that himself, since he still started every time I spoke French. "I never memorized it in French."

And Sébastien, as we had told him, was not a practicing Catholic; he was even an adamant atheist, something the priest may have begun to suspect. I *knew* God would eventually make us pay for that Baptism lie.

"You'll do fine," the curé said. "Recite the Lord's Prayer."

"I can't in French," I said.

"Recite the Lord's Prayer."

I threw up my hands. "I can't in French," I said very loudly. Cameras flashed all over the place. I supposed it was a bit unusual to see a bride argue with the priest in the middle of her wedding.

"Go ahead," the priest insisted.

I gave up and shrugged. Sébastien calmly closed his mouth, locked eyes with the priest, and said nothing at all. Several minutes of dead silence followed.

The old curé finally recited the first two lines. I had been to enough Masses in French that I could nearly follow along, like a half-memorized song, if I could hear someone else saying it, so I joined in quietly.

The curé stopped.

Again, silence. Several guests had started to join in; but without his lead, their voices gradually trickled off. Behind the choir ladies, I noticed Grégory trying to mouth the correct words to me. Éric, who was as unbaptized and atheistic as Sébastien but who had somehow learned the "Our Father" in his childhood education, tried to mouth the words to Sébastien. The problem was the two couldn't make eye contact and keep a straight face. If anyone knew how much Éric hated religion, it was Sébastien. Sobriety was additionally hindered by another friend of theirs who was filming the whole thing. We couldn't see him; but every time Éric looked past us his face spasmed, causing Sébastien to stare at the stained glass as diligently as he could, the corners of his mouth trembling.

The curé said two more lines. Behind him, Éric and Grégory tried desperately to feed them to us, but to no avail. Sébastien was pretty much not going to say an "Our Father" for anything short of being saved from the stake. Anyway, every time we tried to lip-read off them, suppressed laughter distorted their mouths.

The curé waited, said a few more words, then waited again. Éric stopped trying and stared resolutely at his feet, his lips twitching wildly. Not a sound came from the rest of the audience, and its members simply sat and stared at the priest. In this manner, with frequent pauses to emphasize our silence, the curé reached the end of the prayer.

"Amen," he snapped. "I think young Sébastien needs to learn his 'Our Father.' "

He slapped his hand down on his twenty pages of sermon. "And I think we've wasted more than enough time on this little repeat ceremony of theirs. So let's go." He strode out from behind the podium and grabbed us by the elbows. The organist tried valiantly to turn this into a recessional, but her hands had started shaking again under the pressure.

Sébastien and I removed our elbows from the curé's hands, and I took Sébastien's elbow instead. In France, the guests are supposed to leave the church first and bombard the couple with rice or flower petals as they come out, so there was a mad scramble for the door. Only a few of the kids managed to get out first, but the priest cut their petal-throwing short. "None of that here," he said. "It might stain the stones."

After seven hundred years of fervent faith, church attendance, and wars, we were about to ruin those stones with our rose petals? The remaining guests flooded out, ignoring the priest, and a storm of hugging and kissing began. But the curé had a final word to say. He strolled up to Claudine, the mother of the groom, as she was being embraced on all sides. "For what I made in the collection, it was hardly worth all this fuss," he told her.

And with that, he turned and strode back into the church, leaving us to stare after him with open mouths.

"Well, think about it this way," said one of the guests, coming up to kiss Sébastien and me as we stood on the church steps. "Only one more wedding to go."

I'm sure he meant it as positive reinforcement.

Thirty-eight

I had been raised to consider the Catholic Church a fairly benign institution, on the side of Good and therefore, of course, myself. No foreigner had ever been able to claim the French government was benign, so the reminder of our fourth wedding petrified me. What did the civil ceremony hold in store?

Clouds still covered the sky, but they were lighter now, more white than gray. The two classic Citroens waited proudly in front of the steps. Sue and Claudine and I had donned socks a few days before and polished the cars until they *would* shine, if only the sun would come out, and then decorated them with lace and bows.

Bruno redonned his 1920s hat and held open the door of the red and blue car for Anna and Ken, delighted to share the classic car experience with them. Sébastien and I climbed into the back of the beige, with Jean-Charles at the wheel and Mamie beside him. Jean-Charles honked the horn loudly, a growling *woo* echoed from Bruno's car, and off we set. Headed by our two classic Citroens, a long cortège of honking cars wound down country roads and through a couple of hamlets back to Titi and Bruno's little village. People came out of their houses and waved as we passed.

Imposing and formal in a navy-blue skirt and blazer, the mayor awaited us with the blue, white, and red sash of her office draped from right shoulder to hip, evoking the power of France. She led us into her office and stood before her desk with us in front of her, as the whole crowd flowed in behind us and packed the room full.

In a ringing voice, she declaimed: "We welcome today the tenth of August 2002, to the House of the People, Monsieur Sébastien Florand and Madame born Laura H———, who come before Us to make known to those bound to them by both blood and friendship—and perhaps, a little, to make it known to themselves as well—that the magic word of three letters they pronounced a little over seven months ago, the twenty-sixth of December, 2001, in C———, the State of Georgia, before the Judge Madame———was a big YES." She grinned at us. "We are now going to employ ourselves in the verification that this YES was indeed a DEFINITE YES."

A murmur of chuckles ran around the room.

"Monsieur Sébastien Florand, do you consent to recognize that you were right to take Madame Laura H———, here present, as your wife?"

Sébastien grinned, looked at me, and nodded. "Yes."

"Madame Laura H———, do you consent to recognize that you were right to take Monsieur Sébastien Florand, here present, as your husband?"

Going with the flow, I studied him, put a finger to my lips, and mulled it over. "Umm . . ."

The crowd burst out laughing. All the tension left over from the curé seemed to flow away.

"Yes!" I said.

The mayor tried to stop laughing. "Then in the name of conjugal harmony and in virtue of the powers conferred upon me in my function as mayor, we declare you apt . . . to continue to be united in marriage."

More laughter.

"We present you our best wishes for your happiness and for your future life as a couple. And we wish you good luck for your Cotton Anniversary in a little over four months."

Applause erupted all around us. This was more like it, the perfect final touch. The town's official representative of the French people had gone out of her way to confirm our union with wit and warmth. Now we were married in both cultures, on both continents, for both families, in all manners possible—the cheap and quiet, the solemn and ceremonial, the hilariously bad, and the hilariously good.

When we came out onto the steps, the old cars gleamed in the sun. Half the sky showed blue, the clouds dispersing with a vengeance. Petals showered around us. Claudine had somehow managed to sneak the baskets of unthrown flowers to the children who now darted with them among the guests. Petals caught in our hair, my lace, the mayor's sash. Bombarded, cameras flashing, we ducked into the rear of the beige Citroen and headed off in a blaze of giddy glory.

People ran after us screaming. I waved and kissed. "No, I think they're really screaming," Sébastien said. "They want us to stop."

Jean-Charles braked to a halt and climbed out. At the sight of his face, Sébastien and I followed him. The left rear tire had blown up to the size of a crane wheel, swollen and deformed, surface shiny and taut as a balloon. Jean-Charles glared at it, humiliated at this abrupt ending to his cars' grand finale. We had to leave it there and make the last hundred yards to the stone farmhouse in the Al Capone red and blue car.

Above the teak arbor that led to the garden, a sign had been nailed: "Laura & Sébastien," it said, in curling French blue, with sheaves of wheat framing it on either side. "Éric painted it yesterday in the barn," Sébastien whispered in my ear. "And my mother decorated it this morning."

Long white pavilions, oil-drum grills, and bales of hay filled the yard. Multicolored lights strung from tree to tree and around the dance floor set up in the center. Valérie had come to dance at our wedding, although Giulia was pregnant and too close to her due date, and Adela was in Spain. We circulated, people took pictures, and I complimented Sébastien's father and uncles for not killing the priest. "Congratulations to you, too," they said, looking down at me from a bulky height. I came up to their navels. "We heard about the wedding dress through the window episode, so we were afraid we might have to pull you off him. But except for the little argument over the 'Our Father,' you were impressively self-disciplined."

"This is beautiful," my sister Anna said as family all around carried out food and got the grills going. "What a fantastic end to all these weddings. You are done with the weddings, right? I can throw out this dress now? By the way, did I tell you I had to change into it in the confessional in the church, and I accidentally flashed the priest? . . . Laura? Are you okay?" She slapped my back vigorously until I stopped choking.

As the guests lined up for food, I sidled up to Sue, a microbiologist. "What are your feelings toward chicken that's been left at room temperature for over twenty-four hours?"

"Gratitude that I'm a vegetarian. Well, except when meat looks too tempting, like these kebabs here."

"And homemade mayonnaise with raw eggs in it?"

"Are you telling me there's nothing here we can eat?"

"No, no, no. There's always cheese. I'm just curious; I'm not saying any of these things necessarily happened."

She pursed her lips. "It's been so cold these past few days that probably everything will be okay. Would you say it ever got above fifteen degrees Celsius?"

"In a farmhouse with stone walls two feet thick? No."

"Then I *think* it will probably be fine." I sighed, my shoulders collapsing in relief. A Ph.D. in microbiology was so reassuring about this kind of thing. "Of course, I specialized in plant spores," she added, collecting a plate full of kebabs and heading over to a grill.

My sister waved me to a stop. "Laura, what's wrong with the water? Didn't you tell us we didn't need to pack iodine tablets if we were coming to France? Your friend Éric keeps telling us not to drink it, or we'll get sick."

"What? It's fine. You're either getting the spring water we bought or the bottles of tap water we froze for ice. But I'll go check."

I went to where Éric was working the card-table bar, beside a brown plastic garbage can filled with drinks. "Why do you keep scaring my sister about the water? It's fine!"

Éric, who had seconded his compatriots in refusing the refrigeration of mayonnaise, tuna, and both raw and cooked chicken, stared at me. "Are you crazy? That water's been frozen, thawed, refrozen, and thawed again! She could catch all kinds of diseases from it!"

I sighed and stood shaking my head, realizing more clearly than ever what a miracle it was when a Frenchman and an American got together and lived to tell the tale. All this time I had been selfishly afraid Sébastien would give me salmonella when at any minute I could have eliminated him with a careless ice cube.

The next few hours were a blur of party hosting and juggling multiple requests for copies of the video from our church wedding. "Why?" I asked. "What are you going to do with it?"

"Um, nothing," the guests said, not meeting my eyes. "Don't you ever have a clip of something you just take out and look at whenever you're depressed?"

"Or show at parties and in funniest home video contests?"

"Hey, we got back at your priest for you," said a couple. "Remember how he was yelling at all the guests that you were going to make him late for his steak?"

"No," I said. "I missed that part because I was the one late. But I've heard reports."

"Well, we pulled in front of him when he was leaving the church. We stopped at the stop sign and turned to each other so he could see us and just kept up the liveliest conversation for the longest time. You should have heard the way he laid on that horn. It made us a little late for the mayor's ceremony, but it was worth it. By the way, have you started auctioning off the video yet? We definitely deserve a free copy."

Late in the afternoon, Dwayne, Ken, Grégory, and Sébastien—two men from each country—carried the *pièce montée* out on a huge foil-covered board. A peanut brittle license plate on the front of the classic car gave the dates, and a big sign on the back said, *"Vive les Mariés."* Jean-Charles grinned when he saw it.

As night fell and temperatures plummeted, we danced the "Macarena," the dance where all the men had to take off their shirts, a French version of the hokeypokey, and this absolutely beautiful number where we had to act like S&M chickens. I think. Maybe I just have a kinky imagination, but since we had to flap our arms and legs and pretend to whip someone, that's what I got out of it. Children pelted us with ripped-up grass, leaves, and anything else they could pretend was a flower petal for hours.

To think this day was a gift I had almost refused, from pure fear of love, more work, more people, more cultural expectations. I looked around me again, at all these people I hadn't even known two years ago, so many French I would have assumed I didn't like and wouldn't like me. Under the multicolored lights, Anna, Ken, Sue, and Dwayne danced among the French, having crossed an ocean for the first time in their lives as something more than just tourists. I had never even seen Ken and Dwayne dance before, not even at our second wedding; they usually sat music out on the sidelines.

I spotted Mamie sitting by herself at one of the deserted tables, watching everything, and walked over to her. "Are you all right?"

She nodded. "Just a little tired." She squeezed my arm. "It was just nerves this morning, just a little crisis, yes?"

I nodded. "Thank you for the bouquet you made for me. It's beautiful."

She nodded, and we sat there together watching the festivities for a few minutes. People kept adding clothes until all the elegant dresses and suits had disappeared under sweats and wool sweaters. To keep warm, everyone danced or gathered around the grills. Dwayne brought out Frisbees around 2:00 A.M., and a handful of guests, many of whom had never played this American game before, spread around the yard.

374

Bruno sat with the other wedding organizers by a grill and, without moving, dominated conversations all around the yard, roaring names across the garden in a growly enormous shout as though trying to gargle his throat out of his mouth: "Grégory! GRRREEE-GOOO-RRRRY!"

A Frisbee flew out of an inexperienced hand and landed on his head.

"So tell me, Sébastien," I said as we crossed paths trying to catch the same Frisbee. "Is that man who just grabbed two handfuls of my ass from your father's side?"

Sébastien looked past me. "No, no, he's my sister's godfather. Damn it, Jean-Charles promised to keep him under control."

"That explains a lot about your attitude toward godfathers. By the way, your dad just gave me some very explicit advice about our wedding night."

Sébastien groaned.

"I guess that's the rugby player in him, hmm?"

Exhausted guests crawled into tents, the backs of their cars, or any spare mattress or layer of blankets in the house; but most were still going strong around 3:30 in the morning. I took a break by a grill to hold my hands over the fire. Jean-Charles looked fuzzily concerned. "Are you cold? I'll warm you up!" He picked up a bale of hay and threw it on the fire.

"Good God!" Everyone jumped back, but the bale of hay didn't explode in flames. It had covered the entire grill and blocked all the oxygen, so now there was no heat, only sullen smoke seeping out from under the hay.

Jean-Charles frowned, indignant. "Oh, stubborn, are you? Don't worry, we'll get you warmed up!" He picked up a can of lighter fluid and started splashing it all over the hay.

I backed up. "Sébastien, maybe it's time for us to head for our hotel."

"So soon?" he said, aggrieved. It was now almost 4:00 A.M.

"Not," Bruno said, appalled, "before you eat your *soupe à l'oignon.*"

"Oh, no, no onion soup, thank you," I said. "I'm full. Also exhausted, but I'm feeling kind of guilty about that, since no one else seems to be."

"Onion soup is a tradition," Bruno said. "You wait." He dashed off for the kitchen.

"And the *pot de chambre!*" Titi jumped up and raced after him.

People had been making taunting references to this *pot de chambre* for weeks now. I could imagine a lot of wedding traditions that might be called a chamber pot, none of which promised to be good things for the bridal couple.

"Really," I said to Sébastien. "I'm about ready to go. We can come back tomorrow morning and do the *pot de chambre* thing at breakfast."

Sébastien, who knew what a *pot de chambre* was but had joined his family in refusing to tell me, looked horrified. "That's the old-fashioned way, but no one in my family is that cruel."

"No, really," Claudine said. "The morning after, a *pot de chambre* would make you vomit. It's better to get it over with."

I redoubled my efforts to get through the guests, while Sébastien dragged his feet. "The *pot de chambre,* Laura. We can't miss that."

Behind us, the bale of hay on the grill finally burst into flames, and I batted sparks out of my hair. "Yes, we can. I feel no qualms about it at all."

Unfortunately, we had to pass through the kitchen to get our packs for the hotel. Bruno spun away from the counter and presented us with a cup. Titi frowned down at the pot he was stirring over the stove. "The onion soup's not really done."

"The *pot de chambre* is," Bruno said. "Have a taste."

I looked down at the mess in the cup, which stank with an ungodly odor and in which I could clearly distinguish a thick streak of ketchup and a tuft of toilet paper. I knew for a fact that we had run out of toilet paper some time ago.

"No," I said.

"It's tradition. You both have to eat it until you figure out every ingredient that's in it!"

"Americans have lousy palates," I said. "Sébastien, this sounds like a job for a Frenchman. But I'll give you a head start—ketchup and toilet paper."

In what seemed to me extraordinary fidelity to tradition, he accepted a spoon, dipped it in, and tasted. His face screwed up. "Vinegar and coffee," he said. "And chocolate, of course. Chocolate is always the primary ingredient."

"It *is*? That's barbarous."

He handed the cup back. "I think the parents of the groom should have to figure out the rest." He grabbed my hand again, and we ducked past Bruno.

"I hope it wasn't *good* chocolate," I was still muttering as we grabbed our packs and ran for the car.

Thirty-nine

Panic seized me the next day when I saw only a few dozen people under the breakfast pavilion and a dozen more prone on the grass. Were the other hundred in the hospital, or did even my in-laws slowly fade after so much partying and start to head home? As I approached Jean-Charles, stretched facedown in the grass, he put a finger to his lips. Gray hair sticking out around his head like a wild man, he dragged himself forward on his elbows combat-style toward an innocently sleeping Bruno. Claudine patted the empty chair beside her. "Come sit by me, *ma petite Laura*. I want to talk to you about that chamber pot."

"Uh-oh," I said, backing up. "You didn't save it for us, did you?"

"No, no. Its makers insisted it be eaten right away."

"Good." I met her eyes. "I mean . . . oh, dear."

"And do you know who had to eat it for the cowardly bride and groom? Their parents, of course. Every last bite of it!"

I grinned. I'd kind of liked the way she said "their" and also that the awful conglomeration was all gone.

"You have a sick sense of humor," Claudine said, misunderstanding.

"Hey, I didn't come up with that tradition." I sat down beside her and picked up the marmalade as Sébastien came up.

"Sébastien, come sit by me, *mon petit chou*."

"Dad just told me." he grinned. "It's just wonderful the things a mother will do for her children."

"Nobody got sick in the night and had to go to the hospital?" I checked.

"No, why?" Claudine asked, puzzled.

It was nice to know my salmonella lecture had had an impact. "You know, if we could unlock the secrets of French genes, we could revolutionize medicine."

After the past week's hectic pace, we practiced lazy bliss. As the sun crawled across the sky, we ate stray cream puffs, leftover tabouleh, plums, and *merguez* cooked over our grills. I finally got to throw out the salad of smoked haddock and melons, now on its third day of open-air exposure. Sébastien's family had done the dishes as a group before we even got there. "Have I mentioned that I love your family?" I murmured to Sébastien. He smiled a tired, happy smile. The rest of the cleaning we accomplished in unhurried bits and pieces. There was a lot to do, but somehow, without anyone feeling he was working hard, it got done.

Bruno and Claudine appeared in the afternoon, advancing solemnly out from the back of the house. Bruno carried a gentlemanly walking stick and wore his gangster's tux from the day before. Claudine had a florist's moss wreath on her head, stuck with plastic flowers and dangling a long piece of tulle. She was laughing so hard she walked literally doubled over, as they attempted to imitate a bridal couple. That skit finished, Jean-Charles claimed Bruno's place and nearly burst the gangster tux jacket as he tried to squeeze his broad shoulders into it, his efforts making people laugh so hard they collapsed on the ground. As one by one other couples tried the roles on for size, or even switched them, the men donning the veil and marrying their tuxedo-clad wives, somebody just had to open more champagne to celebrate all these weddings. Bruno, I believe, started the champagne battle, spewing Jean-Charles "completely by accident."

I shielded my face and watched them, laughing. "Seriously, you don't want to move back here?" I asked Sébastien. I had renewed my contract at my North Carolina university for another year so we could afford the weddings, but Sébastien and I had trouble deciding which country we wanted to live in after that.

Sébastien looked sulky. "Can't we stay in the U.S. at least a couple more years? I'm having an adventure! Plus, it ups my reputation no end when dealing with French clients. 'You live in the U.S.? *Putain*, you must be *mad*! So is it really like *Friends?*' "

"But if we lived here"— I ducked a geyser of champagne and caught it in my ponytail instead—"we could spend more weekends with your family! And going to *fêtes villageoises* and eating chocolate." Champagne trickled down the nape of my neck, and I shuddered involuntarily.

"Yes, but we'd never see your family! And your brothers are crazy." He said that with great pleasure just before spewing champagne hit him right between the eyes. He ducked, grabbed my hand, and ran. We crouched behind a table, his eyes streaming.

"And your family's sane?" I checked.

"I think I got some up my nose," he said. "Either wait here or go for the bottle Titi's got." He leapt up and headed at a run for Bruno.

"It is true we'd get to eat better in France, though," he said later, when things had calmed down again. "Unless we go to Annette's every weekend. It's too bad it's such a long drive."

Guests wandered, picking champagne-spewed plums and eating them off the trees. The wheat sheaves now dangled in places, and the latticework arbor had a man's tie looped through it. A swing drooped askew to the ground, one side broken.

"Bruno, Jean-Charles, and Titi all climbed into it together around five in the morning," Claudine explained.

"Ah." I glanced at the scorched earth that ringed a couple of the grills and at the greatly reduced number of bales of hay. "Well, all's well that ends well."

"Well. Begins well, really." She sat down on the grass beside me. "Isn't it wonderful the way you two got us, and even Mamie, traveling on the other side of the world, and your family over here, and all of us together?"

I smiled. "We might have started it, but we could never have predicted how far our families would take it." I had, in fact, predicted exactly the opposite reception from both sides: not an enthusiastic embrace of the other but arms folded in cold aloofness.

"I saved some wedding favors for your mother because I know she hated to miss the wedding here. You have to tell her all about it."

I handed her the sapphire necklace she had lent me, instead of ejecting me from the family, during my fit of hysterics the day before. I was still surprised they were speaking to me after the way I had behaved. But Sébastien's family seemed to have accepted me so wholeheartedly that the ties they had formed with me wouldn't be easy ones to break. Kind of like real family. "Thank you. Really. Thank you."

I sat down on the edge of the algae-covered pond, feeling fuzzy. If I had just finished a marathon, I would have aching muscles. Since the marathon hadn't been so much physical as mental and emotional, I didn't have sore muscles but the spiritual equivalent. I kind of liked the feeling. I felt as if I'd been stretched so much bigger, I could barely recognize myself, let alone my weird, wonderful, so much richer life.

I had done the right thing in jumping off that cliff two years ago, in letting go of the bushes I caught on the way down. Sébastien had been right; when you block out a relationship out of fear, you block out life. He had put his money where his mouth was by jumping off that cliff right after me.

I shook my head. "It's a miracle we ever got through this."

"A *miracle*?" said the husband with whom I shared so much in common. "Now you're getting into that religious fanaticism again. I call it our families." Our families, our friends, a bus driver, a restaurant owner . . . and ourselves, too, right? We had to give ourselves *some* credit. Even if one of us had tried to throw her wedding dress out the window.

"They are pretty special, aren't they?" I agreed, just as Titi, Bruno, and Jean-Charles came out of the house, looking resigned.

"It's the septic tank, it's got to be," Titi said. Sébastien froze. "People started flushing paper towels down it when we ran out of toilet paper."

Claudine jerked her head up. "Speaking of which, where did that toilet paper in the *pot de chambre* come from?"

"We'll have to dig the septic tank up tomorrow after the guests leave," Jean-Charles said. "Good thing you and your friend Éric are still here to help us out, Sébastien."

"But I helped dig up a septic tank on my *first* wedding!" Sébastien groaned.

Eleven o'clock on a Monday morning two days after our last wedding. A bucolic farmhouse in the French countryside. Sébastien balanced over a pit full of sewage, hoping desperately not to have to touch any of it as he helped clean the thing out. The men had decided the septic tank had been overwhelmed and they needed to empty it. Bruno had manfully volunteered to descend into the thick brown soup and bail it out. He now wore galoshes, some kind of yellow plastic pantsuit/raincoat, and dishwashing gloves, and he had duct-taped every possible opening until he looked like an alien in a B-grade film. Sitting at the edge of the fishpond with Colette and Justine, watching the action, I had once again a sense of spiraling back around over a starting point. I wondered why in all the love stories I had read and seen on film, excrement never seemed to have a starring role.

"Is it just me?" I asked. "Do I have some kind of gift?"

Colette shrugged. "*C'est la vie.* Life is fun, but it's real."

Right, I thought. We had had fun, tears, stress, and lots of love and surprises, all of these real. Despite all the problems, everything had worked out all right, too.

I stretched my arms up high and rolled my shoulders, looked around at the garden and the family and smiled. I was getting the hang of this, I decided. I don't know if Sébastien felt like he was getting the hang of it, over there digging up a septic tank for the second time in four weddings, but as long as I held my nose, I was doing just fine. I had gotten this down: two cultures, two countries, two families, the whole love thing. And besides, the hardest part was over. This must be the way Sisyphus felt when he finally got that rock up the mountain. It was downhill from here.

"At least after this, diaper-changing will seem easy," Claudine said, sitting down beside me. "Speaking of which, where are you two planning to live? I think it would be *much* better for you to have your first baby in France, don't you?"

ACKNOWLEDGMENTS

I am not good at showing people how much I value them, so I wrote this book instead. I hope that my sense of humor doesn't disguise my very sincere thanks to all the people involved in this story. This whole book can only give the smallest inkling of all the love and support and enthusiasm our two families offered us. Grandparents, parents, aunts, uncles, siblings, cousins, friends adopted into the family, nieces, one nephew (we only have one!) . . . thank you, thank you, thank you.

Just as we would never have made it without our families, we also would never have made it without our friends. A big, huge thank-you to all of you who people these pages!

I have to name the "church ladies," who get only a glancing reference in the story. These real-life people volunteered to cook and cater the wedding of a girl they had not seen since she was a teenager; out of friendship for her parents, friendship for each other, and kindness and generosity to me. And they were not just ladies, husbands got involved, too. So sincere thanks to Betty and Frank Miller, Dan and Vicki Jones, Bernice Bishop, and Lee Strazay—truly astonishing, wonderful people.

In the writing of the book; thank you to my best readers and editors: Dai, Anna, and Grace McNamara. A group of writers led by Charisse Coleman also gave me invaluable advice on some of the chapters. Thank you, also, to Ted Weinstein, for pulling my book out of his slush pile and making me rewrite, rewrite, rewrite; to my agent Kimberley Cameron, for taking on the book and my writing career with such enthusiasm; and to Natalia Aponte and all the editors at Forge who worked on it. But this book would have been impossible without MY PARENTS, who have supported my writing in every way possible ever since I was nine years old and started filling notebooks.

And, of course, I want to thank Sébastien. It is the wonder of my life that I should have met him.

CPSIA information can be obtained at www.ICGtesting.com
Printed in the USA
LVOW08s1100261113

362894LV00001B/19/P

"Now," Jean-Charles announced, once all the live snails had been triaged into the new crate, "we've got to make them drool."

"I beg your pardon?"

"Drool," he said. "*Baver*. You know, vomit their insides out."

"Oh, *do* we?"

Jean-Charles tsked and shook his head. "Don't want to eat that slime."

To accomplish the vomiting part, he propped the crate at an angle against the cherry tree and sprinkled a healthy handful or two of *gros sel* or rock salt over the snails, then splashed them again with a little water. Pretty soon, foam emerged from the shells, followed by the snails themselves, and last their drool. When Jean-Charles lifted the crate fifteen minutes later, snail drool dangled through its holes like multitudinous strings of pizza cheese, although oddly enough, less appetizing—at least to me. Sébastien would later have some things to say about American pizza commercials that would make me realize all was relative.

I was actually getting into this endeavor by now, but here I ran into a problem in my exploration of the snail-cooking art. Fifteen minutes before my encounter with Jean-Charles, I had promised to go shopping with the others. No one seemed very understanding of the fact that I didn't want to go anymore because I wanted to stay in the garden and watch snails vomit.

"It'll take a while," Jean-Charles said. "I have to keep splashing them with salt and water every half hour or so, for a couple of hours. You go on."

Naturally we got stuck in Paris traffic, and by the time we returned, the snails had finished vomiting and sat cold and dead, a sickly gray-brown, in the refrigerator. Jean-Charles had washed them off without me and boiled them for half an hour. He gave me well-relished descriptions of the white and yellowish mess that had covered them and that he had washed off under repeated doses of running water. Living in Paris I must have devel-

up and make sure they're all still alive and worth eating." He dipped the empty bucket into one of the rain barrels and dumped water over the plastic crate full of snails. "The water gets them to stick their heads out."

They didn't have to stick their heads out far for Jean-Charles to spot a live one. In fact, they barely had to start looking moist. Staring down at a slit of flesh starting to open, I had a brief, flashing image of the female sexual organs but decided I really didn't want to go there.

Jean-Charles gave the snails about ten minutes, then dug his hands in. I was impressed. I mean, I, personally, would have used gloves.

He paused, his hands full of snails, one of which curled immediately around his index finger. "You are going to help, aren't you?"

A pair of gloves didn't seem to go with that question. "Er . . . um . . . yes. I was just trying to get a good idea of how it was done first, that's all. Wouldn't want to accidentally mix up a live snail with a dead one."

I had a strong suspicion Jean-Charles was giving me a gift. But it was a challenging gift. Could I take his culture straight, undiluted for foreigners? And if I could, here was a shot of it in all its fascinating richness.

I inspected the snails carefully and then selected the biggest, brownest one, with the cleanest shell, and delicately closed my fingertips around it. I flinched. My choice had gotten slimed on the far side by a fellow escargot. I placed it as quickly as possible into a second crate, where the live ones went; but having lost my snail-slime virginity, I felt I might as well keep trying to impress my future in-laws and so continued picking out snails.

Sébastien, whose fault this was because he had been worth changing my life, wandered into the backyard at that moment and spotted what was happening. He grinned and sat down on the bench to watch, a safe distance from the proceedings. I glared at him. He stretched out his legs and blew me a kiss.